The Hall Chair

To order additional copies, please contact us.
BookSurge, LLC
www.booksurge.com
1-866-308-6235
orders@booksurge.com

The Hall Chair

A Satirical Novel on the Medical Malpractice Crisis in America

Christopher Smythies

2006

The Hall Chair

Veritatis Defensor

ACKNOWLEDGMENTS

A handful of people (and one bear) gave me assistance with the writing and production of this novel. I would like to take this opportunity to mention their names and thank them for their efforts.

Rick Rapport and Jim Bean are fellow neurosurgeons who read early versions of the manuscript and offered valuable input at a critical time. Sandra Browne and Mary Lynn Wimpsett work in my office and have been forced to watch the creative process for more than four years. Hats off to them for surviving the ordeal. Doug Hofmann, an outstanding lawyer at the Seattle branch of Williams, Kastner & Gibbs answered my questions related to legal issues in a way that even I could understand. Koa Metter used his artistic skills to do a nice job with the cover design. Steve Babitsky deserves accolades for organizing an excellent SEAK seminar, Medical Fiction Writing for Physicians, which I attended two years in a row on Cape Cod. Diego Piacentini introduced me to Booksurge.com which, in my own humble opinion, is the best thing to happen to publishing since William Caxton, giving unknown wannabes like myself a fighting chance to be heard. Grazie, amico mio. I also thank Bill Mullen, Professor of English at Purdue University and an editor for Booksurge, for critiquing my manuscript six months ago and giving me encouragement when it was needed the most. Giulia, my eldest daughter, kept me on track with her masterful editing of the final version. My other children, Stephanie, Francesca, Michael and Chiara, all supported me with their love.

Last of all, and by no means least, I would like to thank Edward for agreeing to pose in his pajamas for the front cover—not an easy thing to do for a bear so distinguished as himself.

CS
Medina, Washington
June 1st, 2006

To Elisabetta

PROLOGUE

7:45 p.m., Thursday, November 4th, 1965

From the beginning, Hugh Montrose was destined to be a neurosurgeon.

When the boy was only eight, he had already left his home in Edinburgh for a rugged boarding school in northern Scotland. At this latitude, the land was bleak and forlorn. Moors lay windswept by moaning gales and ribbons of gnarled trees clung for survival along bubbling streams the color of whisky. Helmsdale Manor stood rooted in time at the bottom of a glen, a jarring illusion in the desolate landscape. Its grey stone walls were crowned with a maze of steep slate roofs, parapets, and square towers that reached towards the leaden sky. Hugh and sixty-two other young boys had been sent by their parents to be educated there and for eight months of the year they lived within the lichen-encrusted walls of the estate, studying in classrooms that hadn't evolved in centuries. Wooden desks with inkwells were arranged in neat rows, each one heavily inscribed with initials that immortalized prior generations of students. Hunched over their desks, the boys were fed a steady diet of Latin, French, arithmetic, history, geography, scripture, and English. In the afternoon, they were sent out to the playing fields to chase some ball or another in the mud. Afterwards, they undressed in cramped and grimy changing rooms and bathed in tubs of tepid water. They ate in the dining hall together, prayed together, and at night, they lay in cold, drafty dormitories, hugging their teddy bears and thinking of home.

"Lights are going out now," said the Master in a gravelly voice as he withdrew from the austere room where Hugh and six other boys huddled in their beds. His hawkish face with its bushy white eyebrows receded into the darkness beyond the door. "Go to sleep, and *no* talking."

The door closed. A naked light bulb hanging from the ceiling blinked out and the dormitory was plunged into blackness. The sound of creaking—was it floorboards or the Master himself?—grew fainter, then . . . silence.

Hugh burrowed deep into his bed, leaving only a narrow shaft through the blankets for air. In his hand he held a small torch, its bulb glowing orange from low batteries. In the dim light he studied Edward, a teddy bear whose well-worn appearance was ample evidence of the love that had been bestowed upon him over the years. A woolen green cap with holes for his ears covered his bald head, lilac booties warmed his feet, and he wore rumpled white pajamas with blue stripes. His clothes had been knitted and stitched together by a great-grandmother who knew how to reach down three generations and make a little boy smile. On this night, however, Hugh set aside all sentimental thoughts; he couldn't afford to have them. He was a world-famous neurosurgeon whose little furry patient had brain cancer. It was up to him to saw a hole in the bear's skull, reach into his stuffing with his fingers, and save his life.

Whispers permeated through the blankets from outside.

Hugh pressed the button on his torch and the light died. He poked his head into the cool air of the dormitory, but the blackness was absolute and he saw nothing.

"Don't make any noise!" he quietly implored his friends.

"You'll get caught and the Master will send you to the Hall Chair."

"Shut up, Montrose," somebody shot back. "We can do whatever we want. *We're* not afraid."

Hugh sighed, burrowed back into his make-believe operating room, and turned his torch back on. He returned his attention to Edward's head, gathered his thoughts, and tried to imagine where the first cut should go.

Hugh's neurosurgical craze began during the summer holidays when his father had taken him to the faculty club at the university, not far from the Grass Market behind Edinburgh castle. While the elder Montrose was playing a game of squash, Hugh had sat alone in a lounge, sipping canned orange juice and playing with some bottle tops he had found on the floor. Presently, an elderly gentleman wearing corduroys and a tweed jacket with elbow patches settled nearby. He placed a gripsack on the floor, sipped dark, frothy beer from a glass, and rustled open a newspaper. At first, Hugh had paid no attention to him, thinking he must have been just another of the many professors that he often saw in this place. Then, as his gaze wandered idly about, he looked through the gripsack's partially opened zipper and drew in a sharp breath. Inside, padded and protected by a towel, was a human skull.

Hugh had immediately forgotten about his bottle tops and studied his neighbor with renewed interest. Could he be a bloodthirsty murderer? Certainly, he did not look like one, having intelligent eyes and a patrician poise as he quietly read the paper before him. His hands were small and delicate, turning the pages with precise and measured movements. However, Hugh would not allow himself to be fooled by appearances. After much internal debate, he concluded that the skull belonged to the man's wife; he had been nagged once too often and had stabbed her through the heart that morning. Then he had chopped off her head and boiled it in acid to dissolve the flesh. Now he was proudly carrying around the skull as a trophy. The story was as reasonable as any other he could think of.

The man grew aware of Hugh's stare, then broke into a pleasant smile as he understood the object of the boy's interest. "Would you like me to show it to you?" he asked, gesturing towards the skull.

Hugh edged away into the shadows.

"It's perfectly all right," said the man, as if reading Hugh's thoughts. "I'm a neurosurgeon. I use the skull to teach medical students."

"What's a neurosurgeon?" asked Hugh suspiciously.

"A doctor who operates on peoples' brains."

"Really?" Hugh's gory murder theory was instantly debunked and he moved closer once again to get a better view. "Yes, I would love to look at it!"

The neurosurgeon reached into his gripsack and gently lifted out the skull. With a reassuring nod of his head, he handed it to the boy.

Hugh turned the skull over in his hands, gazing at it in awe. He found it hard to believe that this had once been a living, breathing human being with its own face, thoughts, and feelings. He touched one empty eye socket and then the other, gingerly feeling the delicate bones that formed their walls and trying hard to imagine what those eyes must have once looked like.

"Who is . . . *was* this?" he asked.

The neurosurgeon's eyes grew distant. "Her name was Matilda," he said. "She was about twenty-five years old when she died. It happened a few months ago. Very sad, really. She was so pretty."

Hugh's eyes grew larger and he looked at the skull with

heightened interest. This wasn't some old relic that had been sitting in a dusty display cabinet in a museum for centuries. In his hands was all that remained of a beautiful girl whom he imagined had long blonde hair, blue eyes, and an enchanting smile. She had been living until recent times, sharing the same world and seeing the same sights as him. Now she was only a bunch of bones in a bag.

"Why did she die?"

"She had a cancer in her brain."

"Did you operate on her?"

"Yes."

"How did you reach the cancer when it was inside the skull?"

The neurosurgeon abruptly lifted his glass to his mouth and drank some more beer. "I made a hole in the bone with a drill and a saw," he explained, pointing to a hole about the size of a large coin on the side of the skull. Then, noticing the captivation in Hugh's eyes, he explained further: "It's not so difficult, really. First, I shaved her hair off. Then, I made a cut in her scalp with a very sharp knife, drilled four holes in the bone, and connected them with a saw. Next, I lifted out the piece of bone and work through the opening. When I was finished removing the cancer, I put back the piece of bone and stitched up the skin with some thread."

"Wow!"

"She did well for a while and had a few good years with her family before the cancer came back."

A burning question occurred to Hugh. "How did you get her skull?" he asked.

"She gave it to me."

"Huh?"

The man must have realized an explanation was needed, for

he smiled patiently and said, "Matilda was a very unfortunate young lady. She was born into a poor family and throughout her life she depended on others to feed, clothe, and shelter her. Yes, she was unfortunate, and yet, at the same time, quite extraordinary. When she found out that she had cancer, she signed papers giving her body to science after she was dead."

"Why?"

"After depending on charity for so many years, she had a strong desire to make herself useful. Maybe she wanted to be remembered for something after she was gone—to give her life some meaning. Having no money or education, there wasn't much she could do. So she gave what little she had: her own body. She was particularly insistent that I should receive her skull, telling me that I could use it for teaching students. I think she was hoping that, one day, somebody might come along and . . ." His voice trailed away and he regarded Hugh pensively.

"Yes?" said Hugh, eagerly listening. "And do what?"

"Become inspired to learn all about the brain and help people with cancer—maybe somebody such as yourself, for example. Do you think you might like neurosurgery?"

"Oh, yes! I'd love it!"

The neurosurgeon's eyes lingered over Hugh's shining, up-turned face, then he suddenly drained his drink. "Well, I must be going now," he said, reaching for the towel. He carefully wrapped the skull and placed it back into the gripsack. "You've been a most attentive student. What's your name?"

"Hugh. Hugh Montrose."

"My name is John Worthington. You can call me Sir John."

"Sir John? Are you a knight?"

"Yes, I am."

"Double wow!"

"Well, Hugh," said Sir John, leaning closer and lowering his voice as if he was sharing a secret, "remember this: everybody has a dream—the greatest amongst us as well as the lowliest . . . the good people and the bad. You ought to have one too. Maybe one day, if you work hard, you can be a neurosurgeon and help people like Matilda too." Then, he stood up, collected his newspaper, and walked to the lounge's entrance. He gave his youngest student a wave of the hand, smiled kindly, then left.

Hugh was lost in a jumble of thoughts, chief among them being a burning desire to save the lives of beautiful girls—to stop them from becoming old bones like the ones he had just held in his hands. Now he had a dream of his own: to become a neurosurgeon just like Sir John—a knight in shining white armor.

The whispering in the dormitory grew louder.

"Hey, Mackenzie, have you been drinking a lot of water?"

"Yes, I have. What about you, Sutherland?"

"Buckets. I'm bursting to pee. Who else is ready?"

Four other boys said they were.

"Good. Let's go!"

Hugh was wrenched back to the present. Not this again! Almost every night now, Mackenzie, Sutherland, and a few other trouble-makers would gulp down as much water as possible just before Lights Out. When all was quiet, they would spring from their beds and encircle the pot that stood on the wooden floor in the center of the room. Small torches would be switched on, illuminating the target below. They would pull out their willies and pee into the pot until it was filled to the brim. Then, they would leave it there, a hazard to everything that passed nearby. Sometimes, it was accidentally bumped, resulting in a puddle named Loch Pee. At other times, it was kicked hard across the dormitory, a seismological event that would lead to the creation

of the Yellow Sea. Whichever body of water was formed, however, the penalty was the same: whoever was responsible had to
mop up the mess with his own towel. Even if there wasn't any
spill during the night, the boys derived pleasure from imagining
the fat, clumsy cleaning ladies trying to empty it the following
morning.

"You're making too much noise," Hugh hissed, pulling
down his blankets with a hand. "You're going to get caught."

"Oh, shut up, Montrose! You're such a goody-goody."

"You don't want to go to the Hall Chair."

The boys ignored his pleas and soon the pot was so full,
a meniscus bulged at the top. It was well primed; the slightest disturbance would result in a spill. Giggling gleefully, they
scampered back to bed. "What shall we play?"

"Let's see if we can go around the dormitory without touching the floor."

"Easy-peasy! I'll beat you for sure."

Holding their torches in their hands, they pranced from
one bed to another, all circling in the same direction, with the
pot and its contents standing at the center like a sacred offering
to the gods.

Hugh abandoned his operation and watched with dismay.
"Oh, come on!" he implored. "Let's go to sleep!"

"I bet you can't catch me!" cried Mackenzie, bouncing past
him. Bedsprings creaked loudly under his bare feet as he danced.
On his next circuit, Mackenzie swung at Hugh with a pillow and
managed to catch him square on the side of the head. It was a
jarring blow and Edward tumbled away. Hugh quickly retrieved
him and gripped him more firmly than before. But Mackenzie
now had an idea. The next time he passed by he grabbed the bear
and pulled hard. Hugh resisted and Edward's head ripped apart.

Hugh was left holding one of his ears and part of his forehead, while Mackenzie escaped with the rest of him.

"Give me back my bear!"

"Come and get him!"

Enraged, Hugh flung back his sheets and leapt from his bed. He ran over to Mackenzie, narrowly missing a collision with the pot. Just as he arrived, he caught a glimpse of Edward flying through the air to the opposite corner of the dormitory. Sutherland caught the bear and waved him around.

"Here he is!" he taunted.

Hugh turned and ran back. This time, his bare foot gave the pot a glancing blow. Some urine slopped out and splattered across the floor. The sound was unmistakable and the boys cried out in feigned revulsion.

"Montrose has spilled the pot!"

"Loch Pee! Loch Pee!"

"Get your towel and mop it up, Montrose!"

Hugh felt something warm and wet dripping down his ankle. He knew he had no choice but to clean up the spill, but first he was determined to retrieve Edward. With a howl of anger, he lunged at Sutherland. Once again, the bear was launched into the air.

This time, Edward fell short of his intended target. There was a loud splash as he landed head-first into the pot, followed by horrified silence. Torches were switched on and their beams of light gathered onto the ditched bear.

"Look what you've done!" Hugh said as tears welled in his eyes.

"Sorry, Montrose," replied Sutherland. "I didn't mean to." He and the other boys were standing motionless on their beds, as it became clear that things had gone too far. Hugh gingerly stepped through the newly created Yellow Sea and reached down to rescue Edward.

Suddenly, blinding light flooded the dormitory. All the boys dropped under their bedcovers as though gravity had been suddenly switched on. Hugh was caught in the open, unable to save himself.

The Master stepped the room. Above his head, the light bulb had been struck by the flying bear and was swinging at the end of its wire, casting deep shadows that danced wildly across the floor.

"Who's talking?" he demanded.

Silence.

"What are you doing out of bed, Montrose?"

Hugh cowered. "I was going to the pot, sir."

The Master looked at the floor below him. "What's that *bear* doing in the pot?"

"I dropped him, sir."

The Master grunted his disbelief. Then he pronounced sentence, slowly and with deliberation: "Go to the Hall Chair, Montrose."

Hugh was stunned. This was just what he feared most.

The Hall Chair stood outside the school's study and was made of wood, with a straight backrest and a thin leather pad on the seat. It was very old, some said as old as the school itself. Every male in the Montrose family had attended the school since 1740 and all of them must have been familiar with this notorious piece of furniture. Certainly, Hugh's father and grandfather had mentioned it, but they had refused to say anything more when a six-year-old Hugh had started to ask questions. His curiosity aroused, he had questioned his older brother, James, who was a Helmsdale New Boy at the time. At first, James wouldn't tell him anything either, fearing that Hugh was too young and sen-

sitive to know the truth. That changed one Sunday when Hugh
and his parents were on a family visit to the school. After Even-
song, a number of adults were gathered in the Hall, exchanging
some last words with the masters before they left for the long
journey home. James waited politely and quietly, dressed in his
kilt. Hugh, however, didn't share the same patience. Soon, his
legs grew weary, and he looked around for a place to rest. He
saw the Hall Chair nearby, so he sidled up to it and sat down.
He may as well have turned into a headless ghost playing the
bagpipes, for the effect on his brother would have been the same.
All semblance of calm composure melted. He blanched at the
sight of his brother and hurried over to him.

"Don't sit there!" he hissed.

"Why not?"

"Get off that chair!"

"No. I want to sit here."

"You can't!" James nervously looked at the adults who
hadn't yet noticed what was going on, then grabbed his younger
brother's hand. "All right, I'll tell why you can't, but not here.
Come with me."

"You can tell me now."

"It's a secret."

"Then whisper."

Realizing he wasn't going to budge Hugh without attract-
ing attention, James had knelt beside him and cupped his hand
around his brother's ear. "*Nobody* is allowed to sit on this chair!"
he whispered. A trace of uncertainty seeped into Hugh's stubborn expression and James capitalized on the moment. "If you
are found here by any of the masters, they'll take you into the
study and spank your bottom with a gym shoe!" Uncertainty
changed into fear and Hugh sprung to his feet as if he had sat
on a cactus.

No, the Hall Chair was no ordinary piece of furniture. It was the means whereby a handful of masters maintained control over sixty-three boys. If an infraction of the rules occurred, sentencing was simple: the guilty one was told to sit on the Hall Chair. There were never any arguments or discussion; he would always go without question. Some of the younger boys might burst into tears while others remain stoically silent, but they all went there and stayed until they were found, beaten . . .

. . . and taught the meaning of fear.

When Hugh reached the dark entrance hall, he saw a chink of light underneath the door of the study. He lowered himself gingerly onto the Hall Chair, feeling its icy coldness through his thin pajamas. This was his first time here. Sure, it was bound to happen . . .

But not *now*. Not *this* way.

His knuckles turned white from the injustice of it all. It just wasn't right! He had done absolutely *nothing* to deserve this, lying quietly in his bed and pretending to be a neurosurgeon. It was those other creeps' fault; they always liked to make trouble, so events had spun out of control. *They* were the guilty ones. And where were they now? Burrowed underneath their blankets upstairs, trembling with relief that they had escaped punishment. Meanwhile, Hugh was the one sitting on this wretched chair, his neurosurgical dreams shattered and lying in a smoldering heap at the back of his mind.

Nothing this ignominious would ever have happened to Sir John Worthington.

After ten agonizing minutes, the door to the study creaked open and the Master's long shadow was cast across the floor, framed by a carpet of gold. "You may come in now," he said.

The study served as a common room for the masters and it was the only place in the noisy school where those grey men could withdraw for some peace. Entry was strictly forbidden to any boys unless, of course, they were being taken inside to get beaten. Hugh had never been there and, as he trailed meekly in the Master's wake, he felt he was entering the unfamiliar and frightening world of adults. In the middle of the room, there was an expansive double-sided partner's desk; on its dark leather surface were scattered some essays handwritten with blue ink. Hugh recognized the homework that his form had labored to produce earlier that day. Countless lines of neat italic script were being marked with a red ballpoint pen; the pen itself was on the floor, presumably flung there when the interruption from the dormitory upstairs had occurred. A set of golf clubs and a shooting stick were leaning against a corner. Books were crammed haphazardly into towering bookcases along the walls, and some of them on the higher shelves were as old and musty as the masters themselves. The stained carpet and drab curtains were luxuries in this barren school and they, together with a pervasive smell of pipe tobacco, exuded an atmosphere of privilege.

This was no place for young boys.

Then, Hugh saw the gym shoe lying on its side on a table, a large, worn-out hole in the middle of its sole.

The Master reached for it and turned to him. "Take off your dressing gown and bend over," he ordered, gesturing towards a flowery armchair with his weapon.

With his face reddening with shame and terror, Hugh did as he was told. He leaned against the closer of the two arms of the chair and noticed how much more worn the material was on this side from years of use. He presented his bottom as a target, screwed his eyes tight, and gritted his teeth.

A tremendous whack echoed through the empty wooden hallways and classrooms of the school, followed quickly by another. The searing pain exploded through Hugh's body and he felt driven against the arm of the chair. There was no such thing as being struck only once; the minimum sentence for the gym shoe was two. After the second one, his mind was screaming:

Oh, my God! No more! No more! Please!

Another whack . . . and another. Some papers fell off the edge of the desk and fluttered to the floor. Now, Hugh gasped for air and tears sprung from his eyes.

That's enough! That's enough!

He rose from the armchair, but a heavy hand shoved him down again. *Whack! Whack!* Six of the Best! The maximum sentence. Now, surely, it was over. He straightened and, with shaking hands, closed his dressing gown.

"Don't let me ever catch you misbehaving after Lights Out again," growled the Master.

"Yes, sir." Hugh's voice was a pitiful whimper, his face crimson.

"Go back to bed."

"Yes, sir."

Hugh fled from the study, his bottom sizzling with pain. He ran upstairs and at the first landing he ducked into the washroom. In the near darkness, he hurriedly plugged a sink, spun the taps, and heard the whoosh of water. Then he dropped his pajamas, turned around, lifted himself backwards, and slowly eased himself in. The water was freezing cold, but it gave him relief he was seeking and he let out a long, shuddering sigh.

Nothing as horrible as this had ever happened to him before. Of course, he had heard all the legends about boys being sent to the Hall Chair in the past. Once, a master had missed his target and had accidentally let go of the gym shoe. It had rocketed across the study and had smashed a window. On another occasion, the shoe had disintegrated upon contact, and the boy had had to wait, trembling with terror, until another could be found. He had laughed at these stories along with everybody else, never taking any of them seriously. Now, for the first time, he was actually experiencing the pain himself and it was worse than he could have ever imagined.

He wiped some tears away and noticed a dark shape lying in the sink next to him. He climbed out of his sink, dried himself off with a handy towel, pulled up his pajamas, and reached for it. Whatever it was, it turned out to be submerged in water; he felt his fingers dip underneath the frigid surface. They curled around something soft and furry.

"Oh, Edward!" he cried, pulling out his bear. The torn fabric where his forehead and ear had been ripped off looked terrible. Edward didn't seem to be bothered by it though, his beady brown eyes staring back with their usual enigmatic expression. Nevertheless, Hugh felt a tremendous ache in his heart and hugged his bear, paying no attention to the mixture of water and urine that he squeezed out of him and over his own pajamas. He had always loved his bear. Now that he was seriously damaged, he loved him immeasurably more. Edward needed mending with a needle and thread; his missing piece had to be found and sewn back on. Only a short time ago, Hugh, the world-famous neurosurgeon, might have taken on the task with unabashed enthusiasm. However, the Hall Chair had sucked everything out of him and he felt incapable and uninspired.

Hugh gripped Edward's paw and shuffled back to his cold, dark dormitory. The other boys were hiding under their covers, hardly breathing. He climbed into bed, buried himself deep under the blankets, and pulled his soggy, stinking bear close. Sleep evaded him. Instead, he listened to the wind moaning over the moors and, in the valley far beyond, the haunting cries of trains hurtling through the night.

CHAPTER I

Maxine Doggett, J.D., R.N., was blissfully unaware that she had a time bomb inside her brain and that it was about to explode.

The bomb was a cerebral aneurysm, perhaps the most feared creature in the realm of neurosurgery. In the beginning, it was born as a tiny weakness in the wall of a dividing artery where the turbulence of the passing blood was at its maximum. Over time, the relentless buffeting enlarged this defect and the layers of elastic tissue began to stretch. A small blister appeared and the damage worsened. Like a cobra uncoiling itself from a snake-charmer's basket, the blister slowly reared into an aneurysm with a neck and a dome. Some of the blood flowing down the parent artery was diverted from its normal course and passed into the growing aneurysm. Once inside, it swirled around with the ferocity of a tiny tornado, further expanding and thinning the dome like a balloon. The aneurysm had been enlarging for years and now the cells that made up its wall had reached their breaking point.

All it would take was a cough, a sneeze, a strain on the toilet or raw, unadulterated sex—the variety that sends blood pounding down arteries with the force of a jackhammer.

A sleek, black limousine silently glided along the rainy streets of downtown Portland, Oregon. Inside, Maxine was being conveyed to the banquet that officially opened the 1998 meeting of the Congressional Association of Neurological Surgeons (CANS), an event that would draw more than a thousand

neurosurgeons from all over the world to the downtown Sheraton hotel. *More than a thousand of them!* The thought of so many
potential defendants in one place had been making her giddy
for weeks now and she had feared that she might make a mistake when time came to execute her plan. Now that her wheels
were literally in motion, however, the old confidence that had
uplifted her so many times in the courtroom gathered muster
and gave her strength. She felt like a predator outside a chicken
coop. From her vantage point, she could spy on all those fat
birds smugly strutting around, cackling amongst themselves and
feeling secure inside the fence. She knew of a break in the wire
and could snatch as many as she wanted, but on this particular
occasion she was only after one of them, Dr. Frank Dickey from
St. Vincent's Hospital in Astoria.

"Ms. Doggett?"

Maxine imagined a flurry of squawks and feathers, then
the tanned, leathery face of her security chief, Carl Zeiger, coalesced in the gloom in front of her. He was perched on his edge
of his seat, his elbows resting on his knees. His blue eyes were
upturned towards her, his forehead deeply furrowed.

"Ms. Doggett, are you listening to me?"

Maxine focused on her companion. "Of course I am."

Carl grunted, then handed her a white card. "Here's your
entrance ticket," he said. "I obtained it from the usual source.
Don't lose it or they won't let you in."

Maxine nodded. The 'usual source' was Dr. Manfred Horman, active member of CANS, professional testifier, and somebody who was willing to say *anything* under oath for a price. She
turned the ticket towards the overhead light so she could see
better. "'Jessica Dunlap, R.N. Nurse member. CANS'," she read
aloud. "So I'm to be Jessica tonight?"

"You can't exactly introduce yourself as Maxine Doggett. Defendant Dickey will recognize the name of the lawyer who's suing him."

Maxine smiled. "I almost wish he would!" she said. "I'd love to watch him squirm."

"So watch him squirm in court," said Carl, "and not at the Sheraton tonight. And just in case he's seen your face before somewhere, I brought you a disguise." He reached into a paper bag and handed Maxine a dark brown wig that contrasted strongly with the mass of red, curly hair that sprung dramatically from her head and cascaded around her shoulders. "Wear this. Make sure it fits tightly. I don't want it coming off in the middle of *things*."

Maxine glanced at Carl, checking for any hint of impertinence. However, the roof light cast deep shadows across his face and he appeared every bit as serious as his credentials suggested: ex-Navy Seals, Vietnam veteran, mid-level CIA officer, and eventually a consultant in a D.C. security firm that protected many of the nation's most powerful citizens. Maxine had met him years ago on a lobbying trip to the nation's capital on behalf of the Confederation of American Trial Lawyers (CATL). She was attending one fund-raiser after another for U.S. senators and was shoveling out enough lawyer-dollars to make the Saudi petro- variety look like pocket change. She needed somebody discrete and efficient to manage the shadier areas of her practice, so she took Carl out to dinner and offered to double his salary if he worked for her. He accepted and had served her faithfully and flawlessly ever since.

Maxine slipped the wig over her head while Carl looked on approvingly. When she had finished tucking her own curls out of sight, she inspected herself in a compact mirror which she had retrieved from her purse. Through some unkind twist of nature, she fell well short of beauty. She had a slender face, thin lips, and penciled eyebrows that arched into her forehead and gave her a haughty look. However, it was her chin that really spoiled things; it was disproportionately large, giving her left cheek a permanent sneer and her face an overall harshness that would freeze the passions of the average man.

"My God, I don't even recognize myself," said Maxine.

"Then Defendant Dickey won't either, especially if he's drunk. Now give me your jewelry."

"My jewelry?" Maxine uncurled her fingers and admired her flashy collection of diamonds and emeralds.

"You're supposed to be an underpaid, overworked nurse. If he sees this treasure trove he'll get suspicious. Take them off and give them to me. I'll return them later."

Maxine grudgingly slipped the rings off her fingers one by one and dropped them into the palm of Carl's outstretched hand.

"Your necklace too."

Maxine sighed. She reached behind her neck, unclasped a heavy gold chain and handed it over.

Carl dropped the jewelry into a small leather pouch, then tied its neck closed with a string. "Remember," he said, slipping the pouch into his inside jacket pocket, "the banquet will be held in the Cascade Banquet Hall which is in the basement. There'll be a lot of people there, doctors and their wives, so it might take time to locate Defendant Dickey. Once you've found him—"

"I know. I know. We've been over this countless times."

"Escort him to your room. Did you remember the key?"

"It's in my purse."

"The video camera I planted will already be running by the time you get there. It's miniaturized and well hidden, so there's no chance he'll spot it. I'll be in the next room watching on my monitor. If anything goes wrong, call for me and I can be there in seconds."

"Nothing will go wrong," said Maxine, returning her critical gaze to her mirror.

"I wish I could share your confidence," said Carl. "Listen— are you sure you don't want to hire a whore to do this job? It's not too late, you know."

Maxine shook her head. "I'm the only person I can trust to get things right. If anybody found out the truth, I could be disbarred, or worse. I can't afford any mistakes. I know it's risky, but there's no other way."

Carl hesitated and cleared his throat. "If I may be permitted to speak freely . . ."

Maxine snapped shut her compact and turned to face her security chief. "We've known each other long enough," she said. "What's on your mind?"

"This mission tonight . . . how can winning be so desperately important? Your client, Pedro Gonzalez, is a penniless illegal."

"I know," said Maxine. "Ever since his brain surgery, he spends most of the day smiling vacantly at the ceiling of his nursing home. But his neurosurgeon, Defendant Dickey, is who really counts. Now *there's* a doctor with a big, fat insurance policy and plenty of personal assets."

"So, is it all about the money?"

Maxine looked distantly out of the window, focusing on nothing in particular. "No—not really."

Maxine quietly admitted to herself that there was a time when her remarkable drive had *everything* to do with money. She remembered growing up in a rusting single-room shack at the edge of a Louisiana swamp. Her father was a drunk who died in a car accident shortly after she was born. Her mother succumbed to tuberculosis four years later. Thereafter, she was raised by a distant aunt who was as warm and loving as an icicle and resented having to take care of the little girl. Maxine received few presents, rarely played with other children, and was always hungry. At her loneliest moments, she vowed that one day she would be rich enough to keep her stomach filled and never worry whether or not she could buy something nice for herself. After all these years, she *was* rich and owned everything a human being could possibly want, and yet it still wasn't enough . . .

"If it's not money, then what could it be?"

Maxine turned to look at Carl with penetrating eyes. "Dreams are very powerful," she said. "They can govern peoples' lives more than anything I know. Everybody has them. Why should I be any different? Did I ever tell you about mine?"

"No."

"I want to give my life meaning and direction before I die, Carl—to be remembered for *something*. More than ever, I want to be . . ." Maxine's voice trailed away.

"Yes?"

"I want to be a *superstar*."

"You already are one, Ms. Doggett."

"Thank you, Carl," said Maxine with a fleeting smile. "Maybe you see me that way, but I can assure you that my fellow trial lawyers, CATL, and the rest of the world don't."

"*Everybody* knows you've reached the peak of your profession," he persisted. "You have more expertise and experience in medical malpractice cases than anybody else in the entire country. Your success record is unparalleled, winning the last ten lawsuits that went to trial and having settlement rate of nearly ninety percent. You provide an invaluable service to your clients, achieving results when nobody else thinks there's a chance."

"All true," said Maxine, "but none of that makes me a superstar."

"What would, then?"

"I'll tell you . . ." Maxine leaned forward and tapped Carl on the chest with a long spidery finger. "A case unlike any other in history—one that will capture the imagination of every person in this country and prove beyond any shadow of doubt who's the leader of the pack. I'm talking about the *ultimate* case."

"And you think this thing against Defendant Dickey is the ultimate case you're waiting for?" said Carl, his voice filled with skepticism.

Maxine shrugged. "You never know."

"A gawked-out illegal alien who's suing a neurosurgeon from Astoria?"

"Whether it is, or not," said Maxine brusquely, "I must be always prepared. Winning is still what counts here: winning against a prestigious and resourceful neurosurgeon. *That's* what the world might remember. And I'll do whatever it takes . . ."

Maxine looked distantly out of the window once again and sighed. A faint wisp of condensation flickered across the cold glass in front of her face. One fact was persistently nagging at her: despite the huge sympathy factor that Pedro was likely to elicit from a jury, the case against Defendant Dickey was showing some serious cracks and she was being haunted by premonitions of defeat. "I've *got* to force that man to agree to a settlement," she murmured. "Once he sees himself on the video we're going to make tonight, he'll do what I tell him."

"But surely there are limits—" began Carl.

"I don't know any limits," Maxine interrupted with barely a whisper. "That's my biggest weakness."

The limousine pulled up in front of the convention center.

The chauffeur jumped out smartly and opened the rear door. Without a word, Maxine gripped her purse and reached for the opening.

"Ms. Doggett . . ." Carl called after her and hesitated when she turned to look at him.

"Yes?"

"*Please* be careful. It could be dangerous and I won't be able to watch you every second you're with that man."

Maxine smiled, but there was no warmth behind her eyes. Only ice. "Don't worry about me," she said. "I'll look after myself." Then she stepped into the wet, blustery street. Carl watched her as she receded into the gloom—a lonely, determined figure bent against the driving rain.

As she prowled through the shadows of the banquet hall, Maxine was shrouded in darkness, yet her eyes were luminous and filled with purpose. She searched the festive throng around her, ignoring the heavy drinkers, loud talkers, or the occasional lecher whose eyes lingered over her skin. She compared the faces she saw with the one she remembered from the photographs. Her prey was supposed to be a handsome man in his fifties with sweeping blond hair, intelligent blue eyes, and an air about him that spoke of self-confidence and pride in his professional accomplishments. Inside, she had learned that he was very different, and very vulnerable. While she slowly circulated, waiting patiently for the right moment like a spider at the edge of its web, she tempered her appetite with some food and wine.

Maxine did not have to search for long. She spotted Dickey standing not far from one of the many bars around the room. He was shorter than she had expected and was fingering a glass of white wine in his hand. She felt the filaments of the web she had spun tremble ever so slightly. She unloaded her own drink onto a tray that drifted by and edged closer to him with a smile.

"Excuse me. Are you a neurosurgeon?" she asked.

Dickey turned to see who had spoken. Maxine saw that he was as handsome as he had appeared through Carl's telephoto lens. Looks meant nothing to her, however. She had learned over the years to trust only the eyes, and his were glazed with alcohol.

"Yes," he replied. "Are you?"

"Oh, heavens no. I'm just a nurse." An incomplete résumé, to be sure, but one that would do for now. "The name is Jessica. Jessica Dunlap." She thrust out her hand.

First, Dickey focused unabashedly on her body: modest breasts, a slender waist, and plump buttocks . . . His eyes slithered over them all. When he eventually turned his attention to her face to assess her looks, Maxine worried for a moment that he might have second thoughts and lose all interest. To her relief, he was more inebriated than she had supposed. His lips melted into an approving smile and he took the hand that was offered.

Maxine glimpsed a glint of gold on one of his fingers.

"A nurse?" he said. "Fascinating! My name is Frank Dickey."

"I hope I'm not bothering you," said Maxine. "You see, I've never met a neurosurgeon socially before."

"Of course you're not bothering me."

"It's just that . . . I think neurosurgeons are really amazing. I mean, just imagine operating on peoples' brains! I don't know how you do it. What's it feel like?"

"Nothing special," said Dickey, glowing in the flattery. "It's just a job. After a while you get quite used to it."

"You're just being modest. I bet it's fascinating, saving lives every day and being respected for what you do."

"It has some good moments, I have to admit."

"And the money!"

"I make a decent living."

"You *are* modest, aren't you? I love modesty in a man. Would you like to offer me a drink?"

"Sure, Erica."

"Jessica."

"Jessica. What'll you have?"

"A Screwdriver."

Maxine watched him navigate unsteadily towards the bar and silently mocked him for being such a blind fool. This was no chance meeting, as he no doubt believed, but the culmination of weeks of careful research. By now, she felt she knew Dickey better than his closest friends. They, for instance, might have been naïve enough to believe his twenty year-old marriage to an interior designer was a happy one.

Maxine knew better.

Some weeks ago, she had learned Dickey had been having an affair with a nursing student at the hospital, a tart with big breasts. Unfortunately, he was clever enough not to leave behind any paw prints. As hard as she'd tried, Maxine was unable to dig up any hard evidence of his infidelity. Within a short time, the affair was over and her opportunity to gather some dirt on him was lost.

Or was it?

Maybe she couldn't use the nursing student against him any longer, but what if she led him astray herself? He was weak and vulnerable to entrapment. It was just a question of catching him at the right moment and using the right kind of lure. Of course, Mrs. Dickey might have already discovered her husband's dalliance and was keeping a tight leash on him. This possibility had been bothering Maxine for some time now. When he returned with her drink in his hand, she noticed that he'd slipped his wedding ring from his finger and her fears subsided.

This was going to be too easy.

"So, where are you from, Jessica?" asked Dickey, handing over her drink and drawing close.

"Louisiana."

"New Orleans?"

"No—a small place near Lafayette. Just a swamp, really."

"So, what made you decide to go into nursing?"

Maxine smiled at Dickey, not because he was so dashing, as he undoubtedly believed, but because he had asked a question for which she was well prepared. "I started off in high school as a hospital volunteer."

"You? A candy-striper?"

"That was when I discovered what nurses were all about. They were my heroes, dedicating themselves to the care of sick people all hours of the day and night, giving them comfort, alleviating their pain, all for pittances. So I decided to be one too. I won a scholarship to nursing school and the rest is history."

Maxine imagined how a lie detector might react to her answers. Doubtlessly the needle would be having seizures by now, furiously scratching a deep trench in the paper and sending ink splattering far and wide. When she was in high school, she didn't pass her free time as a candy-striper but as the pampered mistress of a local divorce attorney, Hezekiah L. Potts. In the quiet time-outs between bedroom frolics she read some of his books on law and developed enough of an interest to start asking questions. The notion that his red-haired filly possessed a brain never occurred to Potts and his answers were always short and uninformative, bracketed with phrases such as 'Don't trouble your pretty little head with that, my dear,' or 'A young woman like you would never understand.' On one occasion, however, he opened up during pillow talk and shared some thoughts that launched Maxine's career. 'Med-mal—medical malpractice law . . . *that's* where the money is!' he declared with a voice that was uncharacteristically filled with passion. 'But the lawyers who are really good at it are the ones who get a degree in nursing first. With an RN under their belts, they're unbeatable.'

Potts kept a parrot in his bedroom, and every once in a while after that, sometimes during the most awkward moments, the bird would suddenly start squawking *'Med-mal! Med-mal!'* Ever since she could remember, Maxine had always believed that her feathered friends had a supernatural ability to shape her life. The trick: knowing how to interpret the signs. The auspices played an important role in the ancient Roman Empire and Maxine saw no reason why she couldn't apply its principles to the development of her own. After hearing the same message erupting from the parrot a few dozen times, she was sure the bird was telling her to go to nursing school, then law school, and ultimately to become a medical malpractice lawyer.

She had discovered her calling in life.

In nursing school, she quickly learned that she hated taking care of sick people. They were always filling their sheets with stool and never failed to complain when she left them to lie in it. However, after four years, she learned just enough about medicine to be especially dangerous in her subsequent legal career. Law school went more smoothly as she already possessed many of the qualities that serve lawyers well: confrontational, argumentative, a thick skin, and flexible morals. When she obtained her J.D. and became a fully-qualified medical malpractice attorney-nurse, she felt primed and ready to take on the world.

"So, how come you're attending this conference?" asked Dickey, spearing a nearby olive with a toothpick and popping it into his mouth. "Do you work for a neurosurgeon, or something?"

"Oh, no. Nothing like that. I wish I did, though; it would be so interesting! But those jobs are impossible to find. So I've had to settle for working on the neurosurgery floor at my hospital."

Dickey spat the olive pit out and it flew into a nearby garbage container. "Your hospital in Louisiana?"

Maxine felt mildly alarmed. Dickey was asking far too many questions and it was time she drew attention away from herself before she made a mistake. "That's right," she said, "but let's talk more about you. You're much more interesting than I am."

Dickey didn't deny it. "What do you want to know?"

"For instance, what do you like to do when you're not saving lives?"

Dickey launched into a lengthy monologue about his large waterfront home, two boats, and a float plane. When he'd run out of things to say about them, he rambled on about his wine cellar, his Porsche 911, his condominium in Maui, and the land he recently bought in Alaska. Maxine smiled and cooed as if she was impressed, but none of this stuff was news to her. The charts and graphs on the walls of her office told her exactly what he owned and how much he was worth. She derived great pleasure in knowing that his wealth paled in comparison to her own.

While Dickey prattled on, he never mentioned his wife.

Perfect.

Satisfied that she wasn't wasting her time, Maxine moved to the next step in her plan. She started to deliberately touch him, just a little: a gentle brush here, a nonchalant pat there. Nothing too obvious. She confessed she was bored and was looking for some fun. She had hoped she would find it here, at the meeting. Her luring eyes said the rest. And while Dickey was being reeled in, he was oblivious to the gathering danger.

"Shall we go somewhere a little quieter?" she murmured, "and a little more private?"

"Where did you have in mind?"

"My room is on the twelfth floor."

Dickey's forehead broke out in a sweat, his eyes started to swim, and his mouth twisted into a stupid grin. Maxine took these signs to mean that her invitation had been accepted, so she quietly set aside her drink, collected his hand into her own, and led him out of the banquet hall. An elevator whisked them to the twelfth floor. Once the door to her room clicked shut behind them, she dropped her purse on the ground and coiled herself around him like a serpent. Her tongue flicked into his mouth and it was a while before he could surface for air.

"My God," he gasped breathlessly, "you don't waste time, do you?"

"I've always wanted to make love to a neurosurgeon," she moaned, kissing his neck while her hands slipped off his jacket. She served up her breasts and his hands kneaded them like dough, groping and squeezing, triggering a cascade of bodily reactions. Adrenalin was secreted from her internal glands as though it was being wrung from a sponge. A tidal wave of chemicals and hormones surged through her cardiovascular system, electrifying her body and stimulating her heart. As the thudding in her chest grew stronger, her blood pressure rose and quickly reached dangerous levels. The aneurysm in her brain bore the brunt of this assault and swelled a few microns larger. Maxine did not sense the impending disaster. She wriggled out of her tight dress and unhooked her bra. Then she kicked away her shoes and lowered her panties. The curls between her legs were flaming red, yet those on her head were dark brown. Dickey was already hopelessly entangled in her trap and was in no state of mind to notice the incongruity.

"This isn't fair!" she breathed heavily over his face. "I'm naked and you're not."

Before Dickey could say a word, Maxine's fingers reached for his shirt and swiftly unfastened the buttons. She unbuckled his belt and his pants dropped around his ankles. Then she dropped his underwear, reclined onto the bed, and guided him towards her.

The aneurysm was stressed as never before. By now, its wall consisted of only two or three layers of highly stretched cells. No further expansion was possible. Under this final assault, the basement membrane between the cells was becoming unglued; the final disintegration was only seconds away.

The rhythm of the sex quickened and her breathless cries became indiscreet. The headboard banged against the wall. Somebody might have been trying to sleep in the next room, but she was beyond caring.

All that mattered was making this look good for the camera.

So she squealed as though exquisite sensations were being generated between her legs and were flooding throughout her body. She dug her long fingernails into his shoulders, thrashed her head from side-to-side, and gulped down air, pretending to be drowning in pleasure. With each thrust, she put even more of her heart and soul into her acting until she felt as though she was going to burst.

At the moment of climax, the pounding inside Maxine's head suddenly stopped and there was a strange stillness as if the aneurysm had taken a deep breath . . .

. . . followed by a violent explosion inside her brain.

Not an orgasm, but the most agonizing headache that she had ever experienced in her life. What had been cries of phony ecstasy suddenly became a genuine bloodcurdling scream as the pain split her skull apart like a rotten melon.

Dickey scrambled away from her. "For God's sake, what's the matter?"

"My head! My head! I can't stand the pain!"

"Not so loud! Somebody will hear you!" He grabbed her shoulders with his hands and shook her, but Maxine was beyond his reach. Nausea mushroomed within her abdomen like a rising atomic cloud. Her stomach contracted and shot a stream of partially digested hors d'oeuvres out of her mouth as though somebody had turned on a powerful spigot. It was projectile vomiting at its worst and the food splattered messily across Dickey's chest.

"Oh, shit!" he hissed. He snatched her dress from the floor and wiped away the steaming chicken, cheese and crackers, and carrot soup that dripped down his front.

Maxine's screaming tapered into a low moan. "Carl . . . Carl . . . Help me, Carl!" Then she slumped against the pillows behind her and spoke no more. Her head tilted forward, slightly cocked, and her chin rested on her chest. Vomit intermittently erupted out of her mouth amongst a background of gurgling and belching. It dribbled between her breasts, over her belly, and pooled in her lap.

Maxine's lips were turning blue.

"*Carl?*" said Dickey, glancing wildly around himself. "Who's Carl?"

It didn't take him long to find out. A moment later, the door flew open and a tall man with silver hair rushed in. He went straight for Maxine, paying no attention to the naked neurosurgeon poised over her.

"I'm here! I'm here!" he cried.

"Who *the hell* are you?" demanded Dickey.

"You—shut your face!" Carl shoved the neurosurgeon hard with his hand, sending him flying into a corner. He snatched Maxine's clothes from the floor and effortlessly scooped her unconscious body into his arms. Dickey staggered to his feet and took some steps towards the intruder in a pointless attempt to block his escape. Without letting go of Maxine, Carl kicked him hard in the crotch. Dickey screamed in pain, doubled over, and sagged to his knees.

"Hey—asshole," said Carl as Dickey finally collapsed onto the floor. "Not so loud! Somebody will hear you!"

Then he left the room with Maxine cradled in his arms.

CHAPTER 2

Hugh Montrose looked down at Maxine Doggett as she lay on the gurney, uncertain whether he should feel revulsion, fear, or kindness. The woman had arrived by ambulance, accompanied by a tall, muscular man named Carl who claimed to be her security chief—whatever that meant. According to him, she was quietly minding her own business, watching television in her hotel room, when she suddenly suffered the sudden onset of a blinding headache—the worst one of her life. A CT scan revealed a hemorrhage and an angiogram confirmed that the source of the bleed was an aneurysm. Hugh was the neurosurgeon covering the Emergency Room at Columbia Medical Center that night and had been catching up with some old friends at the CANS banquet downtown when he'd received the call. He'd hardly arrived at the hospital before the ER physician, Dave Holz, had hurriedly drawn him aside and whispered in his ear that the woman was none other than an attorney-nurse who specialized in medical malpractice.

"Look," he had continued, "this bitch is nothing but trouble. Take my advice: ship her to some poor sucker at the university. They would never turn away a patient, not even this one."

"Maybe you're right," Hugh had said, "but I've always treated patients the way I would want to be treated myself. If I were this woman, I wouldn't want to be transferred to the other side of town."

"You're forgetting who she is!"

"Sorry I disappoint you, Dave, but in my practice everybody gets treated the same, even if they're a medical malpractice trial lawyer. Whether I like it or not, she came to my Emergency Room and I'll do my level best to help her."

"Sounds like you've never been sued before."

"No, I haven't."

"Well, *that* explains everything. I've been sued . . . a number of times, and there's nothing quite like a lawsuit to change your tune. You'll find out for yourself when it happens to you . . . and it will, sooner or later."

"I'll never change, Dave."

"All right, my friend," Holz had said, placing a conciliatory hand on Hugh's shoulder. "Believe whatever you wish, but don't say I didn't warn you."

As Hugh examined his latest patient, he saw a woman with so much make-up slapped onto her skin that she looked as if she might have been wearing a mask. Now the creams, powders, mascara, eye shadow, and blush were streaked with tears and her natural blemishes underneath blossomed in the glare of the overhead lights. Flecks of vomit glistened in her hair and the stench of gastric juices hung heavily in the air.

"Maxine?"

Her eyelids fluttered open. Even with enough sedatives on board to drop a charging rhino, her grey eyes were still intense and accusing. Hugh had the creepy feeling that he was guilty of something before he'd had the chance to utter a word.

"Maxine, my name is Dr. Montrose and I'm a neurosurgeon. The ER doctor asked me to see you because you've had a hemorrhage from a brain aneurysm. How are you feeling?"

For a few moments, her eyes moved up and down and she appeared to be coldly assessing him from head to foot. Eventually, she said, "You're afraid, aren't you?"

"No, of course not. I've operated on lots of aneurysms before."

"Not of the aneurysm. Of *me*."

Hugh felt a surge of adrenalin. "Why should I be afraid of you?" he asked as if he had no idea what she was talking about.

"Because I'm a medical malpractice attorney."

"It doesn't matter to me what you are," said Hugh, maintaining his cool. "I'm a neurosurgeon and you've got an aneurysm. You need me to operate on you so you can get well again."

"*Operate?*"

"Your aneurysm has leaked some blood through its wall. If we don't do anything, sooner or later you'll have another bleed and you might not be so lucky the second time. In this situation, the best approach would be to perform a craniotomy, make an opening in your skull, and put a small clip across the neck of the aneurysm. Do you understand?"

"Yes, I understand," she replied. Then she added with an air of superiority: "I *am* a fully qualified registered nurse too, you know. I'm familiar with craniotomies."

"Then you'll also understand there are risks—"

"I already know all about the risks," she snapped.

"Nevertheless, let me go over them with you," Hugh persisted. "The aneurysm could rupture before I can reach it and bleed out of control. Of course I would start a transfusion, but we may not be able to replace the blood fast enough. If something bad like that happened, you . . . might not do very well."

"Are you trying to tell me I could . . . *die?*"

Hugh weighed his answer carefully. The cerebral arteriogram had revealed a relatively large aneurysm arising from the one of the more difficult arteries to access; a cluster of tortuous blood vessels snaked around its dome like the tentacles of an octopus. Each one of them was vitally important and any inadvertent damage could be fatal. On the other hand, he did not want to alarm this patient, at least not as long as her life was hanging by a thin layer of cells.

"I'm sure you'll do just fine," he said eventually.

Maxine's gaze switched to the ceiling. "It'll take more than a silly aneurysm to stop me," she muttered.

Hugh wasn't sure this woman had yet understood the seriousness of her problem, so he resumed his discourse on the risks of surgery. When he finished a long laundry list of potential complications, Maxine propped herself up on her elbows and tugged at his sleeve.

"Don't feel you have to be afraid of me!" she insisted.

"I'm not—"

"Why else would you spend so much time going over the risks?"

"I cover everything carefully with all my patients. Now lay back down and rest."

"All doctors are afraid of me," said Maxine. "There's no reason why you should be any different. But I don't want *you* to feel that way. I promise I won't sue you if something bad happens."

"I'm relieved to hear that."

"I know what I'll do." Maxine looked around herself to make sure there were no unwelcome eavesdroppers within range, then whispered, "I'll put you on my 'Do Not Sue' list. That way, you won't be distracted when you're operating on me. Not many doctors can say they have that privilege, you know." She smiled as if she had just bestowed the greatest honor in the world upon him.

Hugh didn't feel any stirring pride. Instead, he imagined that somewhere under this woman's powdered, painted skin there had to be a small frightened child. It was to this part of her that he spoke. "You've got nothing to be afraid of," he said. "I'm going to take good care of you."

Maxine must have understood for she sighed with relief and settled into her pillow.

Hugh was beginning to have serious misgivings about his charitable attitude towards this charming little package and wondered whether it was not too late to follow Holz's advice and ship her to the neurosurgeons at the university. Just as the temptation to do so was about to eclipse any concern for the consequences, a long crooked finger reached out and tapped him on the chest.

"I'm counting on *you* to get me through this," said Maxine, as if she had an uncanny ability to read his thoughts.

"Me?"

"*You*. Nobody else."

Anger flashed through Hugh—anger at the way this woman was talking to him and at his rotten luck for being the one on call tonight. He was hopelessly locked in, with nowhere to go with her but the operating room.

"I'll do the best I can," was all he could think to say before leaving to get some fresh air.

In the OR, Hugh morphed into an alien from another galaxy. He was completely covered with cap, mask, and gown; 2.5X magnifying loupes were perched on his nose and headgear was wrapped around his skull. Two fiber-optic cables that glowed neon blue swept over the top of his head, merged in front of his forehead, and ended in a lens that cast a dazzling beam of light in whichever direction he was looking. The identity of the patient under the drapes was long forgotten, her poisons irrelevant to the task at hand. There were two others present aside from himself: the scrub tech standing next to him whose job it was to hand him instruments, and the circulating nurse, or circulator, who bustled around, doing whatever needed to be done to keep things moving.

Hugh wiggled a wedge-shaped instrument through a hole he'd just drilled into her skull and asked for silence in the room. When all was quiet, he gave his lever an abrupt jerk downwards. A trapdoor of bone—the bone flap—popped up with a loud crack—a jarring noise that somehow pleased him and heralded the intracranial part of the operation. Underneath, a thick fibrous membrane was exposed: the dura mater ('tough mother' in Latin), or more simply known as the dura. This membrane contained the brain, spinal cord, and clear, colorless cerebral spinal fluid (CSF). Despite what the Romans may have thought of its toughness, a number fifteen scalpel blade made short work of it. Within minutes, Hugh was admiring the pulsating brain underneath while the beam from his headlight danced over its moist surface. Normally, the brain was a cream color with myriad blood vessels that branched in random directions, grew smaller, and dove out of sight into the substance of the brain. This one was marred by an angry purple bruise: blood that had leaked from the aneurysm.

In more formative years, Hugh might have felt dryness in his mouth and an acceleration of his heart rate at this point in the operation. Adrenalin would stimulate his kidneys and a nagging pressure would grow deep in his abdomen. However, after hundreds of similar cases, the hormones of fright and flight had lost their potency and he entered aneurysm country with silent confidence.

Hugh grew aware of a presence behind him. He glanced around and saw Richard Forrester, the youngest of his three neurosurgical partners. He had just finished washing his arms at the scrub sink and was holding them hoisted in the air while water and brown soap bubbles dripped from his elbows.

In the outside world, Richard was bearded, handsome, and his lusty brown hair fell halfway down his back. Inside the OR, however, his head was covered with a cap and mask. Only his eyes were visible; dark, intense, and showing the powerful energy that burned within. He had the body of a body builder and was enamored with his own physique, often pausing in front of reflective surfaces—mirrors, windows, glass cabinets to strike a pose. Not long ago he had been a resident at the university and rotated through Columbia. Like everybody else, he worked hard, routinely putting in as many as a hundred and twenty hours each week, and his vast experience prepared him for just about any situation that he might face in the future. *Unlike* everybody else, however, he never complained, and even seemed to relish the frenzied pace when things careened out of control. He was the epitome of the neurosurgery resident: so much in love with operating on the brain that he was willing to risk self-destruction in the process of learning how. When exhaustion and depression threatened to overwhelm him, he would tuck in his chin, take a deep breath, and plough ahead with the momentum of an icebreaker. Hugh observed that Richard had the rare qualities to be an excellent neurosurgeon and offered him a position as soon as he finished his training.

"I heard you were operating on a medical malpractice attorney," said Richard, taking a drying towel from the scrub tech and wiping off his arms. "Personally, I think you're nuts. Your kindness can really get in the way of sound judgment sometimes."

"She's only human, just like the rest of us."

"You should have shipped her to the university and let somebody else take care of her," said Richard reproachfully.

"But, as long as you insisted on going ahead with it, I thought you might as well have some company."

"Very considerate of you," said Hugh with a smile that was hidden under his mask. This was vintage Richard Forrester, offering to lend a hand even if it meant exposing himself to peril.

"Believe me—I'm only being selfish and thinking of myself. If I passed up this opportunity to rearrange the brains of a medical malpractice lawyer, I'll be kicking myself for the rest of my life."

Richard tossed aside his towel and casually admired himself in the dark reflective glass of the wall cabinets. He performed a subtle flexing routine with his chest and upper arms, checking angles and posture. When he was satisfied, he put on his gloves and gown.

"My God! She actually has a brain!" he cried, drawing closer to the patient and peering with feigned shock at the operative field. "Does that mean she's got *feelings*?"

Hugh's weapons for this hunt were the surgical instruments; each of them was finely crafted, very expensive, and exquisitely designed. Fragile blue veins that bridged the gap between the surface of the brain and the base of the skull were positioned between the tips of a bipolar coagulator. When a tiny current was switched on, the veins crackled and popped, then blackened and shriveled. Hugh searched for and soon found the olfactory nerve; it hugged the undersurface of the brain and was responsible for transmitting the sensation of smell back from the nose. For Hugh, it served as an important landmark, guiding him forward to the optic nerve, a thicker nerve which carried visual signals from the eyes to the brain. Right behind that, he found the internal carotid artery and the third cranial nerve. He dissected them into the open, taking care not to inflict any damage. The third nerve was particularly sensitive. If he merely touched it, the patient could wake up with a permanently drooped eyelid and double vision—impairments that could be very debilitating.

So many tiny details of anatomy and each one so important . . .

Hugh's headlight and loupes were removed by the circulating nurse and a $200,000 operating microscope, its precise features obscured by a sterile plastic drape, was swung into position. The two neurosurgeons nestled up to it and adjusted their seats until they were comfortable. The view that greeted them through the eyepieces was spectacular. All the intricate structures that they had seen earlier blossomed into a vivid display of anatomy that was sharply focused and infinitely detailed. Tiny arteries and veins played together in little tangles on the surface of the brain before dividing over and over like the branches of a tree, carrying nutrients into a strange world of cells, molecules, and atoms. Delicate membranes hung as misty veils and gently swayed in crystal clear cerebral spinal fluid that milled up from deep cisterns, sparkling like diamonds as it flowed. They saw the shimmering iridescence of individual nerve bundles coursing within the optic nerve, where billions of tiny impulses worked together to convey images of the outside world. The splashes of color were visually striking—a performance only ever seen in nature itself. Hugh's micro-dissectors probed around, searching for an elusive enemy. The internal carotid artery divided into smaller arteries, and as the tissues fell away, even smaller branches came into view. Hugh followed one of them, sucked away a small, expendable portion of the brain, and carefully approached the lair of the brooding aneurysm.

Then, with silent fury, it erupted.

The worth of neurosurgeons can be gauged not by how they swagger and posture around the hospital, but by how they behave in the operating room under extreme pressure. Those without breeding or self-control spend more time making an exhibition of themselves than they do taking care of the task at hand. The amount of noisy profanity generated is often inversely proportional to their technical skills. Others, however, react by ascending into a higher plane of concentration while the world around them retreats like an ebbing tide. Hugh pressed his eyes more closely to the microscope and steadied his breathing as he drew strength from deep within himself. A jet of crimson was spraying out of the aneurysm under high pressure and quickly obscured everything in sight. Blood rose up towards him in a turbulent, swirling flood, overflowing the scalp edges. Somebody closely watching him would never have guessed that he was in the midst of a calamity, for his eyes were alive with excitement, as though he had tracked down and cornered a wounded beast.

"The aneurysm has ruptured," he announced calmly as he reached for a larger sucker with his left hand and positioned its end near the source of the bleeding. The clear plastic tubes that snaked around their feet like water hoses at a fire scene suddenly turned red with blood, adding dramatic flare to what was already an electrifying statement.

"Start transfusing and stay ahead two units. Give me a temporary clip, please."

There was a flurry of activity in the operating room as the anesthesiologist and the circulator followed their instructions. Aneurysm clips have the appearance of a pair of miniature scissors with blunt blades. Gold ones are intended only for temporary use when the blood-flow to some crisis downstream had to be stopped, not unlike shutting off the water main to a house in order to fix a leaking pipe. The scrub tech fixed one to the end of an applier and passed it to the surgeon's outstretched hand. It glinted in the brilliant glare of the microscope light as it passed into the craniotomy opening, and once again as it was quickly withdrawn.

"No good. It's bleeding too fast. Give me a cottonoid."

A tiny white pad appeared. He gripped it with forceps and nudged it through the turbulent blood. Then, using his sucker with the other hand, he worked to stem the flow.

"How much blood has she lost?" he asked.

"About five hundred cc's."

About a pint, in only two or three minutes, thought Hugh. *At this rate, she's going to die.*

Using a combination of suction and pressure, Hugh gained some measure of control and the flow of blood eased, just enough for him to glimpse the main feeder. This time the little gold clip found its target. Its jaws gently gripped the vessel and occluded it. The blood loss slowed, but did not stop. Although back-bleeding was still a problem, the suction caught up and some of the anatomical landmarks re-emerged. The patient was no longer in any imminent danger of bleeding to death, but critical areas of the brain were now being deprived of oxygen.

The race against time was still on.

With precise movements, Hugh's hands moved quickly, making good use of the micro-instruments at his disposal. With Richard assisting him, he cleared away debris, and one by one, more arteries came into view—arteries that were essential to identify and preserve.

"There's A1," Hugh said quietly, using a language spoken only by neurosurgeons. "It's leading to A2. See them?"

Richard grunted in the affirmative.

"Huebner branches off just proximal to the anterior communicator," continued Hugh as he worked. "And there are A1 and A2 on the opposite side coming into view. Both look atrophic, just as the angio predicted. If I could only peel that perforator away, I think I'll see the neck. Yes, there it is! Easy now. . . . Don't tear it."

The aneurysm emerged into view and resembled a small berry as it nestled in a tangle of pulsating tendrils. The wall was so thin as to be almost transparent and a tornado of blood could be seen swirling angrily inside. A fine jet of blood was spraying from a tiny hole in its dome. Hugh placed some synthetic collagen and a small cotton pad against it and maintained light pressure. Then, ever so gently, he removed the temporary clip.

Hugh held his breath, then relaxed when he knew that the plug was holding.

"Blood loss?"

"Two thousand cc's."

Now it was time to strangle the bastard.

Hugh focused on its neck. This was the vulnerable part where the dome was connected to the parent vessel. Choke it with a permanent clip, and the operation was over. Tear it instead, and it was the patient's life that was over. He studied it intently, quietly calculating angles and distances like a pro golfer on a putting green. When he was finally certain of his intentions, he held out a hand.

"Give me a permanent straight Yasargil, please."

The scrub tech passed him a clip applier with a silver clip fixed to its end. He took it with his right hand and, with great care, slid it towards the target. Something wasn't quite right and he veered off.

"I'll have to use my left hand," he said, passing the applier to his non-dominant side. Once again he lowered the clip towards the aneurysm, only this time his control wasn't so precise. Despite the challenge, he was still able to find the neck. Once he was sure it was trapped, he released the spring and the clip closed. Immediately, the aneurysm blanched and withered, and as he prodded and probed its dead carcass with his dissector, he afforded himself the briefest moment of triumph.

"It's clipped now," he announced, relaxing his shoulders and pushing away the microscope. "Everything looks good; she'll do fine. Bring her blood pressure back up. Let's close. Richard, go home. I can close by myself. Thanks for your help."

Richard stepped back from the operative field. He took a deep breath, expanded his chest to maximum girth, and ripped away his paper gown with a satisfied grunt.

"Congratulations, Hugh," he said, checking his appearance one last time in the wall cabinets. "You just saved the life of a medical malpractice lawyer. I hope you realize that none of your colleagues will ever speak to you again."

"How could I refuse her?" said Hugh, his eyes twinkling with mirth. "She promised to put me on her 'Do Not Sue' list."

Richard tore his eyes away from his reflection and looked at Hugh with incredulity. "She has a goddamned '*Do Not Sue*' list?"

"That's what she told me."

There was a pause. Then, Richard asked hopefully, "Do you suppose she'll add my name to that list too?"

"I'll ask her."

"Thanks," said Richard. "If she does, then we'll be two sons-of-bitches she won't sue in the future." Then he left the room, gently shaking his head.

CHAPTER 3

"I've killed him! I've killed him! I *know* I've killed him!"

Dr. Dan Silver, third year neurosurgery resident rotating through Columbia Medical Center, threw up his arms and backed away from the operative field, stamping his feet and shaking his head. A sucker dangled at the end of its plastic tubing where he had dropped it and was now low enough to be considered contaminated. However, Dan paid no attention to his clumsiness. He could only stare in horror at the unfolding disaster before him and mutter muffled obscenities under his mask.

The anesthesiologist, Tom Harrison, was a round little man who wore wire-rimmed glasses with thick lenses that made him look like an owl. Normally, he would keep out of sight behind light blue paper drapes, read newspapers, and pass gas for hours without saying a word. However, when the trouble had started, his magnified, unblinking eyes had popped into view above the drapes and were monitoring the situation with heightened concern.

"Bonnie, I need a new sucker," said Denise, the young scrub tech, her forehead moist with perspiration.

Bonnie Davidson, the circulating nurse, was a middle-aged woman with soft green eyes. She bustled over to one end of the room and rummaged around in a cupboard.

"Where the *hell* is Dr. Forrester?" demanded Dan.

"I already told you, sir," said Bonnie, selecting the peel-pack that contained new suction tubing. "He's on his way in."

"I wish to God he'd hurry up!"

The patient lying on the operating table, Mr. Brown, was riddled with lung cancer. His family physician had made the diagnosis a year earlier when Mr. Brown had started spitting up blood and losing weight. The tumor was bombarded with radiation and chemotherapy, but in the end it kept growing and spreading. When he developed morning headaches and a flat affect, his wife took him back to the family doctor. Several CT's and MRI's later, they were informed that his cancer had spread to his brain. Dr. Richard Forrester saw him in consultation and made arrangements for surgery, but the tumor had an agenda of its own. The night before his scheduled operation, Mr. Brown was gripped by a terrifying seizure and his condition plummeted. He was rushed to the hospital and Dan had been called to see him in the ER.

"Go ahead and operate," Richard had told his resident over the telephone. "Expose the brain and find the tumor. Don't start taking it out until I get there. Are you comfortable with that?"

"Yes, sir!"

Dan hadn't slept at all the night before and was exhausted. In spite this, the case started well. He sawed a square opening into the skull with an air drill, gently rocking the hand piece back and forth as he had been taught. When he removed the bone flap, he gripped it firmly between his fingers, taking special care not to drop it. He opened the underlying membrane with a fine pair of scissors. When the pulsating brain appeared underneath, his ego soared like a bird, only to suddenly plunge back to earth and crash into the ground with a resounding *splat*, leaving an ugly smear of feathers.

He couldn't find the damn tumor.

At first, Dan sank a metal probe into the brain and watched the centimeter markings on its side being swallowed one by one. However, his fingertips didn't encounter the tell-tale resistance of a tumor, no matter how many times he tried or how deep he went. With each failed attempt, his hands trembled more and his voice climbed higher. He finally cast aside the probe and grasped the bipolar coagulator and sucker instead, a much cruder way to find an elusive tumor, but one that covered more ground in less time. Bits and pieces of cerebral tissue were then excavated and removed, yet the target still could not be located.

Now the brain looked as if he had slipped on an over-ripe banana.

Dan's self-confidence was shattered and he was harshly reminded, yet again, that neurosurgical operations were much more difficult than they looked. When his professors breezed through challenging cases, it was not because they had absorbed their skills from reading books or listening to lectures, but because they had spent years on the front lines, day and night, learning from the thousands of operations that they had performed. Experience counted for a lot in neurosurgery and every time he felt he was making modest progress in his training, a catastrophe like this had to happen.

"I just don't understand," said Dan, close to tears. "I *really* don't."

"What don't you understand?" asked Bonnie who was now fiddling with the suction canisters.

"It's a whopper sitting in the middle of the frontal lobe. Right *there*." Dan prodded the brain with his finger and it wobbled like jelly. "But I've looked everywhere. It's simply not where it's supposed to be. How's the suction coming along?"

"Try it now."

Dan returned to his operative field, snatched the new sucker from Denise, and poked around with it. The brain shuddered and shook, then a large chunk of it suddenly disappeared up the tubing with a loud slurp as if a fat kid was using a straw to inhale the last dregs of an ice cream sundae.

"Whoa! Turn it down! *Turn it down!*"

"Okay, okay," said Bonnie, twisting knobs on a nearby wall. "I hear you."

Tom Harrison's eyes blinked.

Dan resumed his search. "It's at times like this I wish I never had gone into neurosurgery," he muttered into his mask. "Nobody ever warned me it was going to be like this, spending my whole life behind these walls, working my ass off the whole goddamned time and never seeing my family. And for what? So I can spend all night digging around in other peoples' brains looking for tumors that aren't there? It isn't worth it! I should have been a dermatologist."

"So why don't you quit then?" asked Denise.

"I've tried many times," said Dan, "but the chairman always convinces me to hang on a little longer. He lounges comfortably behind his desk and tells me that one day things will get better—that some day in the future it'll all seem worthwhile. That's easy for him to say; he goes home at the end of the day and forgets about this shit. Well, I'm the one who has to spend my life like a slave and I can't stand it any more! No human should have to put up with this. He can't convince me to stay any longer. Tomorrow I'm going to quit for sure! You'll see!"

The door suddenly opened. Richard Forrester swept in with the confidence of a concert pianist making his way to center stage. The sense of relief that filled the room was like a gust of fresh air.

Tom Harrison's eyes sank from view.

"My God, what have you done to his brain?" said Richard, peering at Dan's work. "Looks like you've turned it into a goddamned pizza."

"I've been searching for the tumor, but it's not there. And I've looked *everywhere*."

"That, I can tell. Explain to me how this guy is oriented."

"His nose is here and his ear is there," replied Dan, pointing with his finger at certain landmarks in the midst of the operative field.

"I see." Richard brushed past Bonnie, approached the MRI scans hanging on the view box and studied them carefully. Then he made an exasperated sound that unnerved Dan even more than the display of tomato sauce and mozzarella cheese in front of him did and beckoned towards his resident. "Take a look at these films," he said when Dan joined him. "See anything wrong with them?"

"No . . ."

"Are you sure you don't?"

"I think so."

"*I* see something wrong with them: they've been hung *backwards*."

Silence.

Only the beeping and whooshing of the anesthesia machine were heard as its bellows blew air into Mr. Brown's lungs. As seconds ticked by, the silence grew deeper and more resonant. Dan's soul screamed in agony as it plunged into hell.

"Oh, my God . . . *I opened up the wrong side of his head!*"

"Yup! Looks like you got confused between left and right. My nephew had the same problem . . . *when he was about five years old*."

"Oh, no!" cried Dan. Once again, he dropped his sucker and it dangled close to the floor.

"Fix that mess and zip him back up," said Richard. "You'll have better luck finding the tumor if you operate on the opposite side." Then, as if he had suddenly lost interest in the operation, he turned his attention from the X-rays and checked his reflection in the wall cabinets with a critical eye.

"I can't believe this!" moaned Dan. "What have I done?"

"You've just taught yourself an important lesson," said Richard, gently flexing his biceps. With an air of dissatisfaction as if something he saw in the glass disagreed with him, he turned and headed towards the door.

"Where are you going?" cried Dan.

"To the hospital gym."

"You can't leave me here . . . alone!"

"Sure I can. Listen, Dan—you got yourself into this mess, now you're going to get yourself out of it. I'm not always going to be around to hold your hand when you get into trouble. This is the time to learn how to deal with complications, not when you're alone in practice."

"But what do you want me to do?"

"I already told you: close him up, reposition his head, and start again on the correct side. Let me know when you've found the tumor."

Apparently more preoccupied with the condition of his muscles than Mr. Brown's brain, Richard left the operating room and the door swung closed behind him.

For a few moments, Dan was silent, horrified by his blunder. Then he softly moaned, "This is the end of everything: this patient *and* my career." He shot an angry glance at Denise. "Why the hell didn't you tell me I was operating on the wrong side?"

"How was I supposed to know?" demanded Denise huffily. "I'm just the scrub tech. My job is to hand you instruments."

"You could have said *something*. And what about you, Bonnie? You're supposed to be the circulator."

Bonnie's face reddened.

"Oh, hell—it doesn't matter any more." moaned Dan.

"This is going to be the last case of my short and brilliant career anyway. Give me some 4-0 silk. Let's close."

Three hours later, Richard and Dan left the operating room together. Mr. Brown and his tumor had been successfully separated. The tumor was suspended in a jar of formalin in Pathology, waiting to be sectioned, stained, and put under a microscope, while Mr. Brown was in the ICU. He had already emerged from anesthesia and had already asked for a drink of water. As proof of the extraordinary resilience of the human brain under direct assault by a neurosurgery resident, the operation hadn't paralyzed, blinded, or muted him, and his powers of higher reasoning were wholly intact. The only hint that not *everything* had gone to plan was the pair of mirror-image incisions on opposite sides of his shaven head.

Dan felt himself sucked along behind his teacher as they walked down a long hallway.

"I don't think you should feel so bad about this," said Richard, speaking over his shoulder.

"I feel terrible. Nothing like this has ever happened before."

"Plenty of people make mistakes. It's only human. In neurosurgery, the important thing is to recognize the ones you make, correct them as quickly as possible, and learn from the experience."

"But operating on the wrong side of the head? That's unforgivable."

"You would be surprised how many neurosurgeons have done it, myself included."

"I know you're trying to make me feel better," said Dan, "but it won't work. I've had enough. Tomorrow, I'm handing in my resignation."

"I'll make a deal with you," said Richard, stopping and facing Dan with serious eyes. "Go home, make love to your poor, lonely wife, then get some sleep. I'll take call for the rest of the night. If you still feel in the same way in the morning, I won't stop you from quitting."

"*You'll* take call for me tonight?"

"Sure," said Richard, puffing out his chest and snorting like a race horse. "I haven't forgotten how, you know. Believe me—you'll feel better when you've had some sleep."

Dan solemnly nodded his agreement.

Later, as they approached the surgery waiting room, Dan grew more restless and drew closer to Richard as if he was looking for protection. "What about the family?" he asked. "What do you tell *them*?"

"The family? No problem. Just watch me."

Mr. Brown's wife was a small, grey-haired granny who was knitting a green scarf as she waited. When she saw the surgeons approach, she struggled to her feet, her eyes filled with anxiety.

"The operation is over," announced Richard with a big, reassuring smile. "We've got great news for you. Surgery went *really* well."

"Oh, thank you, Doctor!" she cried, breaking into a toothless grin. "I was praying so hard."

"We were able to remove the whole tumor—"

"All of it?"

"Every bit of it. And now he's waking up normally. So far, there don't appear to be any complications. The breathing tube is out and he's moving everything just fine."

"Yippee!" squeaked Mrs. Brown, clenching her fists and shaking them in the air. "Thank you so much, Doctor! I can't tell you how relieved I am!"

"There's more good news," continued Richard.

"Yes, Doctor?"

"We wanted to be sure there weren't any other tumors hiding somewhere else, so we made an opening on the other side of his head and looked around. We're delighted to tell you we didn't find a single one."

Mrs. Brown could hardly handle so much good news at one time. She hugged Richard first, then Dan, as tears of gratitude sprung from her eyes.

CHAPTER 4

At five in the morning, Thursday, June 28th, 2001, Julie Winter's alarm clock erupted into life. All the rattling and clanging was for nothing though. She had already been awake for most of the night, staring at the ceiling above and dreading the day ahead. The long wait was finally over. At last, the day had arrived when she was supposed to surrender to her pain and have surgery on her back.

She reached over to the bed table to switch the alarm off and was greeted by the first spasm of the day. The muscles in her back knotted until they were as hard as steel, stirring up pain that crackled through her like a fork of lightning. She gasped for breath and her arm flailed wildly, sweeping the clock and a collection of open medicine bottles off the bed table. Her Oxycontin, Percocet, muscle relaxants, anti-inflammatories, and stool softeners scattered across the hardwood floor. She gritted her teeth until the spasm loosened its grip.

"G-Gary . . ."

Gary Winter slept in a separate bedroom across the hallway from his wife. At the sound of his name, he cracked open an eye, focused on his own alarm clock, and groaned. A few months ago, he had been driven from the bed he had shared with Julie by her incessant tossing and turning. He had soon discovered that his new sleeping arrangement wasn't much better; he was often awakened at all hours of the night by her cries.

"Gary!"

"I'm coming, I'm coming." Gary yawned, forced his legs out of bed, and struggled to his feet. He rubbed his bleary eyes and ran his fingers over the stubble on his chin. Then he shuffled out of his room, squinted as he passed under the light in the hallway, and entered Julie's room. He snatched the alarm clock off the floor and silenced it with the flick of a finger. The dozens of colorful capsules around his feet caught his attention. "Spilled your pills again?"

Julie nodded.

"No problem," he said. "I'll get them for you."

"No, just leave them there."

"And let the dog find them?" Gary bent down and started to pick up the pills one at a time between his thumb and forefinger, popping them back into their bottles. "If that wretched animal ate just one of these, he wouldn't live five minutes."

"Leave them there. Please!"

Gary looked up from the floor, one eyebrow raised. "What's the matter?"

"I've been thinking—"

"Thinking?"

"Thinking about changing my mind."

Gary set aside the bottles. "What do you mean?"

"I'm not sure I want to go through with this operation after all."

"Why not?"

"I'm afraid, Gary. *Really* afraid. Everything seems so rushed."

Gary arose from the floor and sat on Julie's bed gently so as not to jolt her. He slipped his arms around her shoulders and nestled close.

"Did you have another of those nasty spasms?" he asked.

Julie nodded.

"Has it passed yet?"

"I—I think so."

"Give it a couple of more minutes just to be sure."

While she recovered in Gary's gentle embrace, Julie's mind wandered back to the time before she had chronic back pain. She hadn't appreciated how good things had been when she'd had excellent health and a perfect body. Before she'd met Gary, she had been an elementary school teacher and loved being around children. After she had a couple of her own, she left her job in order to raise them. She soon discovered that being a mother was even more time-consuming than her teaching position ever was. She would run around all day, delivering them to their extracurricular activities, and barely had time left for her own personal favorite: volunteering at the Humane Society.

Of all the things the family did together, the Winters loved traveling the most. They scrupulously saved the money Gary earned as an auto parts store manager and had bought a previously-owned camper, proudly christening it Harvey the RV. Sometimes they would take off for a weekend and camp in one of the local state parks, cooking marshmallows over a fire and singing songs late into the evening. Three times each year, they would go away for longer, exploring the Great Northwest and absorbing its beauty. In the spring of 1998, they made ambitious plans to spend the entire summer holidays on an expedition to the east coast. It promised to be the experience of a lifetime and they pored over maps for weeks, plotting their route so they could hit as many of the national parks as possible. Sadly, it never happened. Just days before it was supposed to start, Julie's back problems began and everything had to be cancelled.

Julie still possessed a beautiful body, but beneath her curves everything changed. Constant aching pain seethed in her low back as if somebody was sticking a knife into her and twisting it around. She was forced to give up her work at the Humane Society and hired a teenager to taxi around her children. The family's camping trips became more infrequent until even the short ones became a thing of the past. Now, Harvey sat abandoned and forgotten in the front yard, slowly rusting amongst the brambles.

Julie could understand that pain was one of Nature's most necessary creations—a warning when something goes wrong within the body. It could mean an ulcer burning its way through the wall of a stomach, an inflamed appendix, a festering wound infection, or any number of other afflictions. The misery it caused often saved lives and when its usefulness was over, it subsided with healing.

But what in God's name was the purpose of her own chronic pain? Was it there just to make her life a living hell?

Two weeks ago, Gary had decided that something had to be done and made Julie an appointment to see their family doctor, Dr. Taylor. The kindly old man said that she had a difficult problem and admitted that there wasn't anything he could offer. She needed a specialist and so he referred her to Dr. Bruno Clegg, an orthopedic surgeon who worked at Columbia Medical Center. At first sight, Julie was discouraged; Dr. Clegg had a big, bald head and the brutish features of a Neanderthal. He smiled little and grunted words more than he spoke them. Despite his unfortunate appearance, the doctor seemed intent upon making a good impression and offered to expedite her treatment. The first step, he explained, was to find out what was going on. He ordered a lumbar myelogram: a test which involved sticking a long needle into her back, injecting contrast dye, and taking X-rays. At her follow-up appointment a few days later, Dr. Clegg had appeared preoccupied as he studied the medical record and quickly excused himself from the examination room. He returned after thirty minutes, looking more relaxed as if whatever issue was bothering him earlier had been resolved. He had declared that one of Julie's discs was worn out and that the two vertebrae on either side of it were rubbing against each other. She also had stenosis—a narrowing of the spinal canal. As if to emphasize his point, he threw one of the X-rays up on a viewing screen and jabbed a banana-like forefinger at the image. An operation to fuse the bones together was a definitely an option, and the sooner the better.

"When?" Julie asked.

"We have an opening on June 28," Clegg said casually as he stuffed the films back into their jacket.

"But . . . that's only two days from now!" Gary spluttered.

"I'm booked up for July and August. It's either now or you'll have to wait until September."

The idea of waiting more than two more months to get any relief from the pain was abhorrent to Julie and she had quickly agreed to the early date.

Gary gently wiped a tear from Julie's cheek with his thumb as they sat together on her bed. He stroked her long, dark hair and looked into her eyes. "It's perfectly normal to be afraid," he said. "But you must remember that the operation will be over quickly and you'll be on the road to recovery before you know it."

"I'm not afraid of the cutting."

"What is it then?"

"Oh, it's just that . . . Well, this is all so sudden. I'm afraid something will go wrong."

"Nothing will go wrong. Dr. Clegg is an *excellent* surgeon."

"I know, I know . . . But my pain may not necessarily get better. It could worsen, or I could have a hemorrhage and suffer nerve damage. Dr. Clegg said so himself."

"There are always risks," said Gary, now cradling his wife's chin in his fingers, "but the chances of something bad happening are very small. You have to put your trust in Dr. Clegg."

"Of course I trust him," said Julie, taking Gary's fingers in her own. "But maybe there's some other way aside from surgery."

"You saw the films."

"But I didn't really understand them. Did you?"

Gary shrugged his shoulders.

"Maybe we should get another opinion," said Julie. As soon as she finished speaking, a great wave of pain arose in her back again. This time, it flowed down her right leg and frothed amongst her toes. She gripped her husband until the spasm passed, then said, "Or maybe a second opinion would be a waste of time."

There was a knock on the bedroom door.

"Come in," said Gary.

Two children entered, dressed in their pajamas. Jennifer, sixteen, led her eleven year old brother, Patrick, to the foot of the bed. Both of them bore a strong resemblance to their mother, having dark hair and brown, almond eyes.

"We brought you some things to take with you to the hospital," she said, "so when you're there, you'll never forget we love you." She prodded Patrick.

"Look what I've got you," he said, pushing his way forward. He proudly held up a bear that was outfitted like a surgeon, complete with cap, mask, and green gown. "He's for good luck. Take him with you."

"Oh, Patrick . . ." A rare smile flickered across Julie's face. "What's his name?"

"Just call him Surgeon-Bear."

64

"I'll keep him with me always," she said, taking the bear from her son. "Thank you."

"And I've got you this," said Jennifer, handing her mother a small wooden box. Julie opened the lid. Inside was a collection of small hearts cut out of colored paper. Each one was marked with one word: KISS.

"What's this?"

"They're kisses for when you're in the hospital," Jennifer explained, peering into the box with her mother. "I made a hundred. I hope that'll be enough. If we're not around to give you a real kiss, just open this box and put one of these against your cheek."

Tears welled in Julie's eyes. "That's a wonderful idea," she said. "Your presents are beautiful." She set them aside on her bed table.

"How long will you be gone?" asked Patrick.

Julie paused. She noticed that Gary was watching her closely.

"I'm not sure . . . I'm not *quite* sure I'm still going to the hospital."

"What do you mean?" asked Jennifer, frowning.

"I'm having second thoughts about having surgery today. Maybe we should think about it more—"

"*Mom!*"

"What, honey?"

"Of *course* you must have it!" cried Jennifer, drawing closer. "You *can't* keep going like this. Anybody can see *that*."

"You've *got* to have surgery," protested Patrick. "I miss Harvey!"

"But something could go wrong," said Julie. "Mommy might feel worse. Then think how it'll be for you."

"That doesn't matter," said Jennifer. "I'll always take care of you, no matter what happens."

"Me too," said Patrick.

Gary agreed with the children. "All those in favor of Mom going to the hospital and getting fixed, say 'aye'."

"Aye!" they cried in unison.

"It's unanimous, Julie. You're going. We'll be there for you, whatever happens."

The Winter family fell into a group hug, each one hanging onto the other, not a dry eye amongst them. The operation offered a glimmer of hope for an end to Julie's suffering—hope for the chance to flush all those pills down the toilet and to lead a normal life once again.

And nothing would be as bad, Julie supposed, as having no hope at all.

CHAPTER 5

Number 50! thought Bruno Clegg triumphantly as he sank his scalpel into Julie Winter's back. *I did it, Olufsen, you big galumphing oaf!*

The blade sawed through the skin with wild, jerky movements. It was a sloppy incision, befitting a surgeon who was celebrated amongst his colleagues as Bonehead Bruno, or simply Bonehead. It was generally assumed that his brain, if, indeed, he possessed one at all, was very small and that his head was almost entirely solid bone.

Clegg liked to make bets with Bent Olufsen, a rival orthopedic surgeon who reminded him of a Viking warrior with his chiseled face, blond hair, bulging muscles, and rakish tattoos. Long ago, they had attended the same college together and started their betting careers by putting money on the football games they watched on television in the dorm. Later, they diversified into other sporting events. Over time, however, they searched for something more exciting and began to focus on patients in the hospital. At first, they weren't involved in anything more harmful than test results and X-ray reports. As they became more engrossed in their odious pastime, almost everything was put on the table: how long an operation might last, where the next complication was going to occur, who would live, who would die, and so on. Things evolved to the point where it didn't matter who actually won or lost. Even the amount of money wasn't important; the usual prize became a half-pound double cheeseburger, super sized French fries, and a large root beer from Frank's, the local diner. Rather, the challenge was finding the crudest, most tasteless issue on which to complete a wager.

The bet that had been consuming most of Clegg's attention over the last four weeks was a particularly outrageous one. At the end of a busy day, he had bragged that he could perform fifty lumbar spine operations in a single month. Olufsen had scoffed at the idea, saying that there wasn't enough back pain in Portland for any surgeon to make such a claim. Some bravado was exchanged and the bet was made. Once again, a greasy cheeseburger, a surgeon's ego, and the opportunity to set a new record in tastelessness were on the line. Clegg had instructed his office to schedule as many cases as possible during June and launched himself into the month with a steely determination to win.

Clegg worked day and night like never before, railroading his patients into the operating room as if the month after June—July—had been cancelled. By Tuesday, June 26, he had sliced and diced forty-nine of them. He picked through his final clinic of the month, searching for the last case and worrying he might fail . . .

. . . until Julie Winter had returned for a follow-up appointment, carrying her precious myelogram films and accompanied by her husband.

What a stupid, ignorant, naïve couple they had been! They had sat in his office, gaping at him as if he was a god who was about to perform a miracle. When he didn't bother examining Mrs. Winter, he didn't arouse any suspicion. When he showed them an X-ray, they hardly looked at it. When he told them that Julie had to have an operation, they didn't ask about alternatives. When he told them that his schedule was full for July and August, their faces fell. When he told them that he had an opening in only two days' time, they eagerly took the bait. They had asked only a handful of questions and weren't interested in getting a second opinion. They had simply wanted a fix and were willing to sign the consent without delay.

It was all too good to be true.

Then, Clegg had stumbled across a problem.

When she'd had her lumbar myelogram, CSF had been drawn off and sent to the lab for analysis. A lab slip told him that the level of protein was 140, almost three times the upper limit of normal. Clegg had wondered what this meant. A quick literature search while his patient was waiting in the examination room came up with an answer: she could have a tumor somewhere in her brain or her spinal cord. The woman had no other symptoms aside from her low back pain, and, from Clegg's point of view, an exam wasn't likely to show anything either. More importantly, an investigation would involve ordering MRI's, something that which would take time and push her case into July.

Clegg crumpled up the lab slip and threw it into the wastepaper basket; he wanted to complete the bet with Olufsen, not waste time chasing something as trivial as an elevated CSF protein level. As far as Clegg was concerned, a neurologist could safely do that afterwards and take as long as he wanted.

But nobody could have a single day in June.

Clegg laid aside the scalpel and took up the monopolar coagulator, a device made out of blue plastic and held in the hand like a pen. When electric current ran through its metallic tip, a small orange flame danced around and charred adjacent tissues, allowing a good clean cut with minimal blood loss. He watched the yellow fat melt and boil with a sizzling hiss, sniffed at the plume of acrid smoke that swirled out of the wound, and thought of the big, juicy cheeseburger that would soon be his prize.

His stomach growled.

Clegg exposed the lumbar spine, grabbed an instrument that resembled the jaws of a dinosaur, and attacked the bone, ripping pieces out and throwing them aside. Once inside the spinal canal, he found himself working close to dura with delicate nerves inside, yet he showed no caution and his progress did not slow. He had trained primarily on bones—simple things that he could understand and required nothing more than the same basic tools as he might find in his garage. Nerves, on the other hand, were beyond his understanding and he often wondered about those ballsy neurosurgeons whose job it was to operate on them.

The principle of the surgery was quite simple: Rotor-Rooter the spinal canal, then lay down rebar and pour in concrete, only the rebar happened to be titanium cages, screws, and plates, and the concrete was bone chips harvested from the hip. While the metal served to immobilize the bones so a fusion could take place, it was the bone graft packed around and inside the metal that provided any real and lasting strength. Over time, two vertebrae would be transformed into one.

After five hours of hammering, scraping, grinding, and screwing, Mrs. Winter's back had all the ingredients in place for a successful fusion. The operation appeared to have passed without complication; the dura hadn't been accidentally ripped open for a change, nobody had seen any amputated nerve roots waving around at them, and blood loss was acceptable.

Yes, everything *looked* good.

On this day, however, looks were deceptive. Unbeknown to anybody, Julie's operation had caused a tiny, yet momentous, change in the internal dynamics of her spinal canal. The volume within the dura increased as it filled out, and consequently the pressure of the spinal fluid was lowered. In a normal spinal canal, this wouldn't have any significance; a gentle current would be generated between one place and another and equilibrium would be reestablished. Julie's was far from normal. For years, attention had been focused on her lower lumbar area for this was where her pain was located. But as the CSF protein had suggested, there was a far greater danger higher up—a danger that hitherto made its presence known in subtle ways that had escaped attention. Disaster was now imminent and there was no longer anything Clegg, Julie, or anybody else could do to stop it.

Clegg grunted his pleasure; after a month of hard work, he had proved to that clonk, Bent Olufsen, that he could, indeed, operate on fifty backs in a single month.

How would the two of them ever dream up a wager more tasteless than that?

It seemed impossible to beat.

After he took off his gown and gloves, Clegg stood at the scrub sink and washed the bone dust, blood, and sweat from his face. When he was clean and refreshed, he reached for a wall phone and called Olufsen to break the news.

CHAPTER 6

When Julie regained awareness, she saw her husband sitting by her bed and reached for him.

"How did the surgery go?" she asked in a hoarse whisper.

Gary threw away the magazine he was reading and took her hand in his own. "Dr. Clegg says everything went perfectly," he told her. "No complications. How are you feeling?"

Julie focused her attention on her back. To be sure, there was plenty of pain, but it was the kind that came from her surgical incision and not the kind that had been tormenting her for the past few years. If there was any such thing, it was a *good* pain—the kind that responded to the morphine pump hanging by her bed. She only had to press a black button, the little friendly machine whirred, and a few minutes later, she would feel better.

She afforded herself a tiny smile. "I have to admit that I already feel different, like a great load has been taken off."

"See?" said Gary, squeezing her hand. "You were afraid for no reason. Things are going exactly as we'd hoped. We have a lot to be grateful for."

"I'm sorry I was so nervous early this morning," said Julie. "I shouldn't have been."

"That's okay," said Gary. "I love you anyway."

Julie turned her head and winced.

"What's the matter?"

"It's my neck," she said, frowning and rubbing it gently.

"Your neck?"

"Yes. Strange, isn't it? Nothing too bad; just a little pain. I'm sure it's nothing serious."

A nurse named Brenda offered some reassurance when it was time to take vital signs. "After all," she explained as she pumped up a blood pressure cuff and listened to the artery in Julie's arm with a stethoscope, "you had surgery on your lower back, not your neck. It's probably the way you were positioned on the operating table." She studied the pulsing needle on the dial, then released and removed the cuff. "One-forty over ninety," she said, straightening up. "A little high, but it's probably the pain doing that. I'll get you a nice hot towel and some extra morphine. Okay?"

"Yes, thank you," said Julie. "You're already making me feel better."

Later in the evening, the children visited their mother, bringing get-well cards and flowers with them. They sat on either side of her bed, played with Surgeon-Bear and the box of kisses, and talked about the future.

"When can we go camping again?" asked Patrick.

"Soon," said Julie.

"How soon?"

"Maybe later this summer—"

"When?"

"Don't be pushy," admonished Jennifer, nudging her brother. "We'll go when Mom has gotten over her surgery."

"I can't wait!"

"Me neither," admitted Gary, eagerly rubbing his hands together. "I'm going to take Harvey to the garage next week. It's time we fixed him up and got him ready; we'll make him look as good as new again. Maybe we can go on a weekend trip by the end of the summer. We'll have to ask Dr. Clegg if it's okay. We'll do whatever he says, of course."

"Yay!" cried Patrick.

"That's not a promise!" said Gary quickly. "It's a *maybe*."

"That's good enough for me," said Jennifer. "Oh, won't it be great for all of us to be doing something together again?"

As the evening passed, Julie's episodes of neck pain became more frequent and intense like the flickers of lightning from an approaching storm. If it were as a result of her positioning on the operating table, why was it getting worse and not better? Why was her heart beating so much faster than before? And what was this strange sense of unease she had, as if something bad was about to happen? The next time Brenda took her vital signs, Julie's blood pressure had risen ten points. She reached for Gary. Any kind of movement was now uncomfortable for her neck, but touching her husband with her hand helped to calm her worries.

Eventually, Julie was sufficiently drugged from the morphine to be having difficulty opening her heavy eyes. "It's late and you've got work tomorrow," she murmured to Gary. "It's okay for you and the children to go home now."

"Aw, Mom!" protested Patrick. "Do we *have* to go?"

"You heard her," said Gary to his son. "Mommy's getting tired and needs her sleep. It's time for us to head home." Then, to Julie, he said, "Are you quite sure you can manage on your own?"

"Yes. Brenda is here in case I need anything. I'll be okay."

Gary remembered the nurse's kindness and was reassured. "Call me first thing in the morning and let me know how you're doing."

"Of course."

"Promise?"

"Yes, yes."

Julie gave her husband and the two children each a tender

kiss on their cheeks. "Thank you for being such a good family," she said. "I would never have made it without you."

"We love you," said Gary.

"I love you too."

Soon after her family had left, Julie fell asleep, bringing closure to a long and difficult day. Her dreams were vivid; a frenzy of jumbled images rushed through her mind as if she was flipping rapidly through the pages of a black-and-white comic book. She saw herself playing games as a child, running to school with her books, struggling to undo the knots in her shoelaces. She was slipping a wedding ring onto her husband's hand and discovering the delicious intimacy of his body on her honeymoon. She was chasing her giggling children around the house and driving them to school. She was clasping her hands together at the dinner table, asking God to bless the meal and protect her family's health.

Shortly before midnight, Julie woke up with a start as if the approaching storm was now upon her and a lightning bolt had struck her bed. The morphine had drained from her system and now her mind was electrified. She reached for the call button, but her fingers refused to move. She wanted to call out, but was afraid of causing a disturbance. Instead, she anxiously waited until Brenda came to take her twelve o'clock vital signs.

At one-thirty, an hour and a half late, the door flew open and a chunky nurse with a stern face that could have been carved by Stalin's favorite sculptor entered the room. She busied herself with the morphine pump next to Julie's bed, muttering quietly to herself.

"Excuse me," said Julie in a tiny voice.

The nurse continued to fiddle with the machine.

"*Excuse me*," persisted Julie.

The nurse pulled a plastic thermometer out of her pocket and, without a word, thrust it into Julie's mouth.

Julie mumbled a feeble protest.

"Please, no talking," ordered the nurse in a thick Russian accent, then returned her attention to the pump. After a minute, the thermometer beeped. She withdrew it from Julie's mouth, squinted at the read-out, and scribbled numbers onto a piece of paper.

"Where is my regular nurse?" asked Julie meekly.

"Brenda went home. I'm the night shift. My name is Bogdana." She flashed an impressive collection of gold teeth at Julie. "What do you want?"

Julie hadn't considered the possibility that Brenda would eventually have to go home and felt a strong sense of unease. She remembered reading a story in a ladies' magazine about night shift nurses—how they were overworked, underpaid, and often trained abroad. Suppressing her natural tendency to imagine the worst, she said, "My neck is killing me."

Bogdana shrugged and Julie was reminded of the time when she took her television to a Russian repairman. After listening to a description of the malfunction, he had shrugged in the same disinterested way and had told her in a similarly heavy accent, 'That is *your* problem, not *my* problem.'

Was the neck pain Julie's problem and nobody else's?

Bogdana gripped Julie's wrist in a bear-like grip and solemnly watched a clock on the wall.

"If I had surgery on my back, why does my neck—?"

"Shhh! I'm counting."

Again, Julie waited. When her pulse had been taken, she tried again. "Do you know why my neck would hurt?" she asked.

Bogdana turned the corners of her mouth downwards and shrugged again as if she had been asked the price of tea in China, then clamped her stethoscope to her ears so she could take a blood pressure.

"Everything below my neck feels numb," said Julie. "My fingers too. And I can't seem to be able to move my legs, and my arms are weak. My fingers don't want to do anything either . . ."

Bogdana wasn't listening to her, only to the sound of pounding blood in her ears. When she had finished taking a reading, she put away the stethoscope and said, "It's from the way you slept. Happens all the time. Why don't you press the button and give yourself some more morphine? That'll make your neck feel better."

"Hadn't you better call Dr. Clegg? Maybe something is wrong."

"And wake him up in the middle of the night? Nyet! He'll be very angry with me."

"Please . . ."

"*Nyet!* All you need is some more morphine." Without waiting for permission, Bogdana reached for the pump's black button with a big, pudgy hand and squeezed it.

Julie eyed a small bubble of air as it crept along the IV tubing towards her arm. After progressing a few inches, it suddenly stopped.

"Have some extra, just to make sure" said Bogdana. "I have a lot of patients tonight." She pressed the button a second time and the bubble moved forward again. She left before Julie could say another word.

Now Julie was alone and scared. In the dim light, she saw Surgeon-Bear lying by her side. At that moment, the fuzzy stuffed animal seemed to represent everything warm and loving in her life and she instinctively reached for him. When her fingers refused to grip him she grew frustrated. She had plucked up enough courage to call back the nurse when her mind became numb as though it was being smothered by a heavy blanket. She fought back, but her will withered under the assault of the powerful pain-killer and she was soon asleep again.

At 4:00 a.m., Julie woke up and found Bogdana bustling around in her room. She moved her head from side to side to check the pain she had been experiencing and said, "My neck doesn't hurt any longer. I still can't move anything, though. While you're here, can you help turn me, please?"

"You need *help*?"

"Please . . ."

"If you want," said Bogdana with obvious irritation as if helping somebody was the last thing she imagined she would ever have to do as a nurse. "First, I'll pull you up in bed." She stood beside Julie's bed and gripped her firmly under the armpits. "I can't do this by myself. You must push with your legs. Ready? One . . . two . . . three . . . Push!"

Julie's legs didn't move.

"I told you to help."

"I'm trying."

"Try harder. One . . . two . . . three . . . *Push!*"

Again, Julie wouldn't budge. Bogdana was already out of breath. She straightened up and looked at her patient, pink-faced and puzzled. "Move your legs," she commanded.

Nothing.

"And your fingers?"

Still nothing.

Bogdana scratched her head as if she had no idea what was happening. "I must speak with Betty, the charge nurse," she said finally. "I will be back. Okay?"

"What's the matter?"

Bogdana mumbled something in Russian, then ambled to the nurse's station outside where she conferred with an older woman, also quite large. Soon both of the nurses were bending over Julie, testing her muscle strength and scratching pins along her skin.

"Can't you feel anything?" asked Betty.

"No."

She slowly dragged the pin up Julie's torso towards her head. "Tell me when you feel something. Okay?"

At first, there was nothing. When the pin was at the level of her chest, she suddenly cried out.

Betty shook her head and her double chin wagged from side to side.

"What's the matter with me?" Julie whimpered.

"Don't worry about a thing," said Betty. "It looks like I'll have to wake up your doctor. Okay? I'm sure he'll have a very simple explanation and everything will be perfectly all right. Okay?"

Julie noticed that the nurses were saying 'okay' quite often now, which probably meant things *weren't* okay. "Something's happened, hasn't it?" she dared to suggest. Without waiting for an answer, she reached for the telephone. She had poor control over her arm, however, and knocked it off the bedside table. It landed on the floor with a loud crash. "I want to call my husband!" she cried.

"I'll call him for you from the nurse's station, after I've notified Dr. Clegg. Okay?"

"I want to talk to him now!"

"In a few minutes—"

"*Please!*"

Betty scurried from the room followed by the much slower-moving Bogdana, and, once again, Julie was alone. She reached for Surgeon-Bear, but only swept him off the table too. He rolled into a dark corner of the room. The box of kisses was next to go. As it fell, the lid flew open and a hundred miniature paper hearts scattered across the floor.

Thirty minutes later, Clegg arrived. He was unshaven and his shadowy eyes stared stonily at the floor as he walked through the ward to Julie's room. He approached the bed cautiously, as though he was afraid of what he might find there. Then, uttering short, precise instructions, he briefly examined his patient, making a note of the strength of each major muscle group, the extent of the numbness, and the presence or absence of any reflexes. When he was finished, he slowly backed away from the bed.

"What's happened to me?" she asked, her voice trembling. "Tell me, please! I would like to know!"

Clegg's face was pale and haggard. He mumbled a few incomprehensible words.

Julie persisted. "Am I . . . paralyzed? Tell me!" she demanded.

No answer.

"Gary! *Gary!*"

The orthopedic surgeon retreated from the room and sank his hulking frame into a chair at the nurse's station. For a few moments, he remained motionless, staring at a telephone as if wondering what it was used for. Then, he picked up the receiver and punched numbers on the keyboard with his forefinger.

He cupped his hand over the receiver so nobody would hear him. "Is this Grand National Insurance's 24 hour hotline?" he asked in a husky voice. "Yes? Good. I'm really sorry about the early hour, but I need to talk with one of your claims people immediately. Yes, of course it's important—*very* important. I'm afraid there's been an incident at Columbia Medical Center."

Cautiously, he lifted his weary eyes and looked into his

patient's room. She hadn't moved since he had examined her: paralyzed, scared, alone, and pining for her husband over and over again.

"A *very serious* incident."

CHAPTER 7

Clinic, in Hugh's opinion, was the most challenging part of his practice. In the operating room, he was often overworked, sleep-deprived, and up to his ankles in blood, but he loved the fast pace. Once he had found the proper rhythm, the days flew past until they merged into one exhilarating blur. Clinics, on the other hand, invariably brought him harshly back to earth. The vast majority of patients presented with non-surgical problems, and although he tried to help them too, he was often frustrated by how little he could do.

Hair-trigger referrals for pain management were becoming commonplace. The typical patients were those who had recently hurt their backs. Family doctors who were afraid of missing an important diagnosis ordered expensive MRI's as the first step. After the scans were done, the radiologists omitted nothing from their reports lest they be accused of neglecting some tiny, but significant, detail. When they read through the radiologists' reports, the family doctors would get hopelessly lost separating the wheat from the chaff and would resort to a consultation with a specialist. By the time they arrived at Hugh's office, the patients were convinced that something ghastly was wrong with them and that it would take nothing less than a hog-killer operation to fix it. Hugh would quietly assure them that they needed nothing of the sort, suggesting a few days of bed rest instead. Then it was back to the family doctor once again. All the health care professionals were afraid of getting sued and a culture of fear drove the whole process forward. The net result was a colossal waste of money and time and a terrifying roller-coaster ride for the patients.

Hugh hated being a cog in this machinery, but he knew there was nothing he could do about it. Each time he blamed a family doctor for being overly cautious, somebody would show up in his own clinic complaining of some seemingly minor ailment and demanding to be scanned from head to foot. If he refused to be cooperative, the patient would often swell toad-like with indignation, sputter that they didn't pay sky-high health insurance premiums for nothing, and insist on getting every bit of their money's worth. Hugh tried to resist, but it was ever more risky to do so. Once in a blue moon, one of those scans would pick up something significant. Certainly it was rare, but occurred often enough to make him think twice whenever he balked.

Clinic was approaching its usual three o'clock rush when Trish, Hugh's young, attractive secretary, chased down her boss.

"Dr. Clegg is on line 1," she said. "He's got an urgent consultation for you."

Hugh groaned. "Oh, no . . . not another one."

"I'm afraid so."

Bonehead had adopted Hugh as his favorite neurosurgeon lately, a dubious distinction at best. Whenever he messed up one of his spine cases—not an infrequent occurrence—he would ask his neurosurgical colleague to bail him out of trouble. Currently, he was running a special on CSF leaks. Bonehead never completely understood the delicate nature of nerves or the fragile dura that surrounded them and often tore into one or the other, or both. Watery spinal fluid would gush from the resulting hole. Either he noticed the problem during the operation, or later on when the patients would spring a leak at home and call to complain. That's when he would ask Hugh for an urgent consultation and would invite him to repair the damage since he knew he didn't have the dexterity to do it himself.

Hugh retreated to his small office and settled behind his desk. On one wall, he kept a collection of his diplomas, so many of them that he had been unable to find enough space for them all. On the others, he had hung photos of himself standing with former colleagues, a few pictures that he had taken while on a recent vacation to Scotland, and a large portrait of Harvey Cushing, neurosurgery's Founding Father. A set of tall shelves stood within arm's reach of his seat and was crammed with textbooks and journals. One shelf at eye level, however, was set aside for framed pictures of his wife, Michelle, and their five children. The next shelf higher up was occupied by another family of sorts: his collection of skulls. There were six of them in all, mostly adults originally from India and Mexico, although one had belonged to a newborn baby and another to a small child.

Hugh picked up his phone. In his mind, he visualized Bonehead's own amazing skull. He had often caught himself studying its shape with a professional eye, hoping that the next-of-kin would give it to him in the event of some unfortunate accident so he could add it to his collection. "Hello, Bruno. How are you?"

"Not so good, I'm afraid," the orthopod grunted hoarsely. "I'm in trouble. You've got to help me."

"What can I do for you?"

"Yesterday, I did a lumbar fusion on a woman called Julie Winter. The case went well. No complications. She was doing fine until the middle of the night when she suddenly became quadriplegic."

"*Quadri*plegic? Or do you mean *para*plegic?"

"Definitely *quadri*plegic."

Hugh knew that any complication at the site of the low back surgery, such as a postoperative clot, might result in paralysis, but only of the legs. If the arms were also involved, it could only mean that something had gone wrong in her neck. "Why quadriplegia?" he asked.

"We did a cervical MRI scan. Stan Reeder, the neuroradiologist, just called me to tell me she's got a big goober in her cervical spinal cord."

"A tumor?"

"Yes!"

"That would explain things."

"How was *I* supposed to know about it? She had no symptoms aside from her back pain."

Hugh sighed. Aside from his big head and his incompetence in the operating room, Clegg was also known for his paranoid attitude towards lawyers. He had been sued half a dozen times in the past and had settled the cases before going to trial. The experiences had stoked his fear of lawyers, and now he saw them hiding in bushes and hanging from trees wherever he went.

"The tumor must be growing slowly," said Hugh in an effort to reassure his colleague. "Otherwise, it wouldn't have reached such a size without coming to light somehow."

"Nobody can blame me for missing it," said Clegg. "Other doctors would have done the same."

"Don't feel bad," said Hugh. "It sounds like she was very unlucky."

"*She* was unlucky? What about *me*? I do a simple elective back operation on somebody and the next thing you know, she's a damned quad. How often does that happen? Now she'll get some damned lawyer to say I was responsible"

Hugh sighed again. Classic Clegg.

"Listen," continued the orthopod, "I'm really busy in my

office right now; there are a lot of patients waiting to see me and one of my secretaries called in sick. Besides, spinal cord tumors are out of my league. Do you mind taking over primary responsibility for her care?"

"If that's what you want," said Hugh, less than thrilled about being handed somebody else's disastrous complication.

"If you decide to take that *thing* out of there, be my guest."

"Sure."

"Good!" said Clegg, sounding immeasurably relieved. "Thanks for doing this for me, Hugh. I knew I could depend on you. I make it up to you one day."

"Sure."

Stan Reeder, a short man with a comb-over, was seated in front of a bank of viewing screens in the MRI center. Large, square spectacles reflected the dozens of small square scans he was studying. The spinal cord in the middle of the woman's neck was grotesquely abnormal. Ordinary nervous tissue had been replaced by a mass that completely filled the spinal canal, obliterating everything. Instead of a normal smooth grey color, the cord was mottled with magnetic signals of varying density ranging from pure white to the darkest black, suggesting that something evil and dangerous was growing there.

"Big, isn't it?" he said, completely absorbed by the images in front of him as if he was viewing the Grand Canyon for the first time.

Hugh was standing next to the radiologist, also studying the pictures. He silently nodded his agreement.

"Must be a record," Stan added. "At least, I've never seen anything quite like this before."

"How old is she?"

"Forty-three. The mother of two."

Hugh thought about his own children. How would they all feel if their mother was suddenly paralyzed? He shook the unwelcome thought quickly from his mind, returned his attention to the rows of images, and asked, "What do you think it is?"

Stan pulled out a magnifying glass, leaned forward in his chair, and studied the films closely. From Hugh's angle, the lens had the effect of bending bones, fat, muscles and discs into surreal rubbery shapes. "My guess: either an ependymoma or a low grade astrocytoma, both benign. See the small cysts that seem to define its upper and lower limits? They suggest an ependymoma. On the other hand, there are parts that look infiltrative, like an astrocytoma. I don't suppose it makes much difference which it is. Either way, she's still quadriplegic. One thing that has me *really* worried though . . ."

"Yes?"

Stan tapped lightly on the films with the point of a pencil. "See all this light grey stuff streaking through the spinal cord above and below the tumor?" he asked.

"Yes?"

"Cord swelling. One hell of a lot of it too, extending as far north as the brainstem."

"I see what you mean," muttered Hugh. "The whole of this woman's spinal cord is really sick, not just the parts close to the tumor. If I'm not careful, this thing could kill her."

Stan tossed his pencil away, leaned back into his seat, and looked directly at Hugh for the first time. "I heard a rumor that Bonehead missed the diagnosis," he said. "Is that true?"

"Probably," said Hugh. "I haven't had a chance to look over the chart yet."

"I wouldn't be surprised," said Stan. "That numbskull wouldn't recognize a cervical spinal cord tumor if it wrapped itself around his neck and throttled him. So what are you going to do?"

Hugh thought carefully. "It's too late to reverse her paralysis," he said. "Her cervical cord died hours ago. As I see it now, my job now is to keep her from getting any worse."

"Well, good luck, whatever you end up deciding to do," said Stan, reaching forward and pulling the MRI films off the viewing board.

"Thanks. I'll need it."

When Hugh arrived on the surgical ward, he plucked Julie Winter's chart out of the rack and skimmed through its pages. He soon learned that she had been suffering from low back pain for years, yet she had never tried any conservative form of treatment such as physical therapy or steroid injections. Instead, Bonehead had immediately ordered a lumbar myelogram, an old-fashioned test rarely performed anymore, then had scheduled major surgery.

The first and second mistakes: an aggressive approach when a much simpler one might have worked equally well, and a myelogram instead of an ordinary MRI scan.

So, Mrs. Winter had had a lumbar fusion which had lasted about five hours and, initially, there hadn't been any problems. Early the following morning, however, the nurses noticed that the patient was not moving her arms very well, and her legs not at all. Bonehead had been notified by telephone. To his credit, he had responded promptly and saw her at 5:45 a.m. After examining her, he'd scribbled a note into the chart, indicating his patient was quadriplegic.

Okay, so far.

What did he do then?

Evidently, he didn't realize that the neurological exam was pointing directly to the neck as the source of the problem like a huge, blinking neon arrow, for he ordered another myelogram, again of the lumbar region. His notes indicated that a postoperative clot might be compressing her nerves at her surgical site. His miniscule brain could think of no other explanation for her quadriplegia.

Hugh shook his head and felt anger rising inside. *No, no, no.* Wrong test. Wrong part of the body. What was with Bonehead and *myelograms?* Hadn't he ever heard of MRI's? The third and fourth mistakes.

Not surprisingly, the myelogram was negative. Bonehead was out of his depth and oblivious to what was really going on. Obviously he knew he was lost for his next move was to ask for a neurology consult. Nice try, but another mistake all the same.

Mistake number five.

A catastrophic paralysis like this was the domain of a neurosurgeon, not a neurologist, at least while an emergency operation was still a possibility. More time was wasted while a neurologist had poked and prodded the patient, using all the diagnostic aids in the little black bag he always carried around with him. At least *he* arrived at the correct conclusion, writing in the chart that the patient probably had a hitherto unknown tumor in her cervical spinal cord. She needed an immediate MRI to prove it, followed by an urgent neurosurgical consultation.

It was already nine in the morning and nothing meaningful had been accomplished.

Bonehead's flailing didn't end there. Clearly, an emergency situation existed, yet three hours passed before the patient was eventually transported to the MRI scanner and *another* three hours before Hugh received the telephone call in his office. Where was the orthopod all this time? Clearing a path through the usual hospital inefficiencies and entanglements so Julie would get prompt attention? Not likely. Hugh lay on odds that the he had spent the entire day hiding in his clinic like a coward, seeing patients and trying to put this mess out of his mind.

The sixth mistake, one only a man like Bonehead would make.

To be sure, there had been plenty of mistakes after the operation, but if one wanted to be charitable, one could say that, in the end, they made no difference to the eventual outcome. Given the appearance of the MRI scans, the patient's fate was sealed as early as the day before, when her back had been opened up. The surgery had lowered the CSF pressure within the lower portion of the spinal canal. Since the tumor had been so big and was effectively blocking the normal compensatory flow of CSF around it, the net result was the tumor had shifted downwards ever so slightly, slowly jamming it even tighter within the canal. What was left of the cervical spinal cord was severely compromised, and in the early hours of the morning, the patient's paralysis had started. The postoperative myelogram the next morning had drained CSF from the space below the tumor, further lowering the pressure and worsening the situation even more. Any chance for recovery of neurological function, however remote at that point, was surely extinguished by the worthless test.

Hugh, however, was in no mood to be charitable. Knowing Bonehead, there must have been plenty of errors before the surgery too—errors Hugh might never uncover since he did not have access to this patient's clinic file. He assumed the worst, however, and stifled his rising indignation at the orthopod's incompetence.

Hugh gently knocked on the door to the patient's room and pushed it open. Julie Winter was buried in her hospital bed—a haggard, pale face peering out from a jumble of sheets and blankets. Knotted, sweaty hair tumbled down around her head. Her brown eyes were large and unblinking like those of a terminal cancer patient, searching for some small measure of understanding of what was happening to her. Her husband was at her side, holding her hand. When he saw a doctor enter, he leapt out of his seat.

"I'm Gary Winter," he said, shaking his visitor's hand. "You must be the neurosurgeon."

"Yes. My name is Dr. Montrose. Dr. Clegg asked me to come and see your wife."

"Thank you *so* much for coming. This is Julie."

A wispy greeting flickered across her face.

"Can you do anything for her?" asked Gary anxiously.

"That depends. May I sit down?"

"Of course."

Hugh settled on a corner of the bed. "How are you feeling, Julie?"

She shrank from him.

"Listen, I know you're scared. But I'm here to help you. Can you tell me what happened?"

Her eyes flitted to her husband.

Gary smiled at her reassuringly. "Go ahead: tell him what he needs to know."

"I can't move anymore," she said in a tiny voice. "I don't know what happened."

"When did you first notice you couldn't move your arms and legs properly?"

"In the middle of the night. It was so sudden."

"And now I've got a really important question," said Hugh, leaning forward as if to emphasize his point. "Since you first noticed your weakness, have you stayed the same or have you continued to get worse?"

"The same."

"Are you sure?"

"Yes."

Hugh stood up from the bed. "Let me take a closer look at you," he said.

Again, Julie seemed to suck herself deeper under her bedcovers like a tortoise withdrawing into its shell. After some gentle coaxing, however, she reemerged and allowed Hugh to examine her. He proceeded with care, testing the motor and sensory functions in her arms and legs, and also her reflexes. His findings confirmed those of the two physicians that had previously examined her: she was a C 6 quad. Her biceps strength was normal, but everything below was gone.

Hugh lowered the blanket and raised Julie's gown so that he had good view of her chest and abdomen. "Can you take a deep breath for me?"

She obediently did as she was asked. Hugh watched her body and saw that as she drew in air, her chest was not expanding. Instead, her belly bulged, as her entire inspiratory effort was now being provided by her diaphragm. Not only was this further evidence that her quadriplegia was complete, but it also served as a grave warning that her breathing was compromised. Any further injury might lead to respiratory arrest.

Hugh covered Julie up again and thought carefully.

Gary spoke up, his voice edged with desperation. "Tell me there's something you can do to make her better."

"What has Dr. Clegg already told you?"

"Nothing much. He called to say that he had found some kind of tumor in Julie's neck and that you would be coming to see her. I had plenty of questions, but he said you would answer them."

"And so I shall. There's a tumor inside the upper part of the spinal cord. It's a very large one and probably been there a long time, slowly growing. Last night, something happened and a lot of damage was done. That's why Julie is having difficulty moving her arms and legs—"

"You can take it out?" interrupted Gary, wringing his hands together.

"Technically, it's possible," said Hugh thoughtfully. "However, in my opinion, it wouldn't be safe right now. The MRI shows that there's a lot of swelling in the spinal cord. There's a substantial risk that surgery could make her worse."

"Worse? Worse than *this*?"

"Yes, I'm afraid so," sighed Hugh. "She could lose the ability to breathe on her own and have to be put on a ventilator. Or she could also lose *all* function in her arms. No, we ought to wait and let things settle down. We'll give her steroids to help reduce the swelling. In a couple of days, when it's safer, we can remove the tumor."

Gary now clasped his hands together to control their shaking. "But if we delay surgery, won't that take away any chance she has of ever moving her arms and legs again?"

"The spinal cord tissue around this tumor has already been seriously damaged, I'm afraid. An operation now has absolutely no chance of reversing her paralysis."

"Oh, my God," moaned Gary. "I can't believe this is happening to us!"

Julie asked, "Are you saying I'll never walk or move my hands again?"

Yes, that's exactly what I'm saying, thought Hugh, but he knew he could not be so blunt. Sometimes delivering all the bad news at once was more than a person could take, so instead he said, "I think the chances of that happening are not very good, but I would never give up hope for the future."

There was a brief silence as his answer sunk in.

Suddenly, Julie filled the room with a howl of anguish, then dissolved into heart-rending sobs. Her husband leapt from his seat and hugged her, but his consoling words had no effect.

She continued to wail until only the weakness of her breathing forced her into a long spells of moaning interrupted by short, sharp gasps for air.

"I think she understands you, Doctor," said Gary, as he held his wife. "Please . . . *please* do whatever you can for us."

"I will," Hugh promised, then quietly withdrew. Outside the room, he clenched his fists until his knuckles turned white.

Congratulations, Bonehead, he simmered. *You've really done it this time!*

Two days later, Julie was taken back to surgery.

The Mayfield clamp looked like an instrument of torture that had been handed down from medieval times for the benefit of modern neurosurgeons: a modified vise, with three sharp spikes—two on one arm and one on the other. Once Julie was asleep, Hugh gripped it tightly with his hands and carefully positioned it around her head. When he was ready, he squeezed together the arms as hard as he could. The spikes dug deep into her scalp, firmly fixating her skull between them.

Julie's heartbeat accelerated and her blood pressure rose. She was deep under anesthesia and was not aware of any pain, but her physiological system was nonetheless responding to the powerful stimulation.

"I always hate this part," said Dan Silver, who had kept his position in the neurosurgery training program at the university despite sawing two holes in Mr. Brown's head when one would have been sufficient. "It's so brutal."

When her blood pressure stabilized, Julie was rolled over onto the operating room table and her head, face down, was attached to it with a system of adjustable arms. The smooth skin at the back of her neck was now exposed. Hugh shaved the peach fuzz off with a razor, put on his headlight and loupes, and went

CHRISTOPHER SMYTHIES

outside to wash his hands. Soon after, he was peering into a deep hole. The bright beam from his headlight danced across glistening bones, muscles, and ligaments.

"So how many laminae are you going to take out?" asked Dan, referring to the bone that had to be removed in order to gain access to the spinal canal.

"Whatever's needed," replied Hugh. "To start with, I'll take off two of them: C5 and C6. Anything less won't give us enough exposure. Then we'll see where that leads us. Give me a wide Leksell."

The scrub tech handed him the instrument he wanted and he used it to gnaw off chunks of bone. Then, with another instrument, he removed smaller pieces while controlling blood loss from the marrow using wax. Gradually, the arches of the two laminae disappeared and the dura inside the spinal canal was exposed. The anatomy appeared far from normal. Instead of its usual healthy bluish color, the dura was sallow, bulging, and non-pulsatile. He squirted some saline solution onto it and the membrane magically became transparent. The spinal cord inside appeared grossly pregnant. Meandering arteries and veins along its surface were pressed close to the inside of the dura. It was easy to see how irreversible damage might have occurred. Very little blood, if any, could be passing through those vessels.

"Microscope, please."

The circulator pushed the microscope into position. Hugh grasped the controls and adjusted them until the operative field was in focus.

"Number fifteen blade."

The scrub tech handed Hugh a small scalpel which he used to nick the dura. Normally this move would be followed by a torrential flood of CSF escaping from inside, but the tumor had expanded to fill the spinal canal and nothing drained out.

With a few quick, measured movements, he split open the dura vertically for about four centimeters of its length. The edges separated and the cord underneath bulged through the gap.

"My God, just look at that," whispered Hugh, backing off and taking a moment to stare at the angriest, sickest cord he had ever seen. Some areas were mottled by inflammation, appearing red under the harsh lights of the microscope, while others were lumpy and brown where tumor was breaking through the surface. Hugh found it hard to imagine anything so large not giving some sign, not even a hint, of its presence when Bonehead had first seen Julie in his office two weeks ago, *before* she became quadriplegic. Perhaps some weakness, or numbness, or unusual reflexes. . . . Something.

Anything.

Like a good resident, Dan started to ask all the right questions. "How long do you think this thing has been here?"

"Years," replied Hugh without taking his eyes from the microscope eyepieces.

"Why wasn't it found before now?"

Because Bonehead is a bungling idiot, thought Hugh. "It grew so slowly, it might not have given any signs it was there," he said instead.

"But it would have paralyzed her eventually . . . right?"

"If nothing was done, yes."

"If it had been found in time, you would have operated on something this big?"

"Of course. It would have been risky, but the alternative would have been much worse."

"And she wouldn't be paralyzed now?"

"Most likely not. It was the back operation the other day that tipped her over the edge."

Hugh asked for the scalpel once again, reached in, and cut. The knife blade separated the thin layer of cells that encapsulated the cord and the giant tumor was exposed. First, he used an ultrasonic aspirator to gut it. Then, with utmost care, he dissected around its margins, gently separating it from the insides of the spinal cord. It gradually loosened and filled the field of view of the microscope. Thirty minutes later, when it eventually came free, he dumped it unceremoniously into a specimen container.

"Send the damn thing to pathology."

The cord was now much smaller, pulsating, and CSF was flowing back into the operative site. There wasn't any bleeding to control; the nerve tissues were quite dead.

"Now let's close."

As expected, Julie did not win back any neurological function over and above her baseline quadriplegia. She spent the night after surgery in the Intensive Care Unit for close observation, fragile human debris amongst a forest of wires, tubes, and monitors. However, the swelling in her spinal cord remained stable and she did not require a ventilator. In the morning, she was transferred to the surgical ward.

Over the next few days, she convalesced uneventfully, mired in severe depression. She was attended by an army of hospital personnel—nurses, physical therapists, occupational therapists, rehabilitation specialists, all of whom pushed and pulled on her limbs, trying to wring out of them every ounce of neurological function. Her medical care, however, was suspended whenever her husband brought the children for a visit. Everybody stayed at a polite distance and there were no dry eyes as they watched Jennifer and Patrick sit with their mother, their young minds trying in vain to make sense of what had happened to her.

Hugh saw Julie only one more time after she left the hospital. She had just finished her course of rehabilitation and was returning to the office for a follow-up visit. Sullen and bloated above her level of paralysis, wiry and wasted below, she steered her elaborate wheelchair by nudging a joystick with her balled-up right hand. She came with postoperative MRI films to evaluate for any residual tumor. When Hugh saw them, he was struck by the transformation that had taken place. The large tumor was gone. A withered string of tissue was all that remained of the spinal cord.

No doubt about it: Julie was going to be quadriplegic for the rest of her life.

CHAPTER 8

Richard Forrester's first and only medical malpractice lawsuit came from a most unexpected quarter. For six months following his brain cancer operation, Mr. Brown returned for follow-up appointments with his neurosurgeon every few weeks. Each time he came, he would report that he never felt better and repeatedly thanked him for the wonderful job removing 'that nasty thing in there'. He usually brought a small, inexpensive gift with him: chamois leather for washing his car, a penknife, a packet of cookies.

On the eighth month, however, he didn't show up for his appointment.

On the tenth month, Richard Forrester found out why when he was served with *Brown vs. Forrester.*

In the Complaint, Mr. Brown claimed that he had never been the same after his surgery, suffering from depression, delusions, and dizziness. Supposedly, his personality had changed irrevocably and he had been emotionally traumatized by the experience. The cause, he said, was obvious: he'd had an unnecessary operation on the wrong side of his head. The fact that it was the resident that had made the mistake was irrelevant; since Dr. Forrester was the attending, *he* was responsible. Even worse, he had made a deliberate attempt to hide the truth from Mr. Brown and his family afterwards.

Negligence was bad enough. A cover-up made matters much worse.

Richard often racked his brains over how the Browns knew the truth in such vivid detail when not even a single medical professional in the hospital had asked any awkward questions. The two wounds were plainly visible for everybody to see, yet the family doctor, oncologist, therapeutic radiologist, rehabilitation specialist, physical and occupational therapists, and all the nurses assumed that that was exactly the way it was supposed to be. And why did the Browns change their tune so suddenly? One moment, they were heaping praise on Dr. Forrester and bringing him gifts out of gratitude . . . the next, they were slapping him with a ten million dollar lawsuit.

None of it made any sense.

So what if Mr. Brown had mirror scars on his head? After only ten months, the man had lived way beyond his life expectancy and was enjoying quality time with his family. Didn't that count for something?

Then Richard read the lawyer's signature at the bottom of the Summons:

Maxine Doggett.

That infernal woman again! He had always assumed that he was on her 'Do Not Sue' list ever since he had assisted on her aneurysm surgery some years ago. However, any notion of granting him immunity must never have occurred to her, for later on, during the discovery phase of the lawsuit, she went after him with unabashed enthusiasm. At his sworn deposition, after he had been badly mauled and lay bleeding, he demanded to know why she was doing this to him.

She remained as cool as ice and replied without hesitation, "Because the Browns have been horribly wronged and they deserve compensation."

"But I'm on your 'Do Not Sue' list!"

"Nonsense. I never put you on that list. Only Dr. Montrose."

"But don't I deserve something too?" Richard pleaded. "After all, I was the assistant."

"You have my personal gratitude," replied Maxine with indifference. "Isn't that enough?"

"Frankly, no. Call off this ridiculous lawsuit."

"My client doesn't think it's ridiculous."

"Then why do *you* have to represent him? Why not get somebody else to do it?"

"Because I'm the best there is," Maxine answered bluntly, as if she was stating the obvious.

The trial started almost exactly two years after Richard was originally served. For three weeks, he was trapped in the Multnomah County Courthouse in downtown Portland, feeling like a fish snared from the sea and thrashing around helplessly on the deck of a fishing boat. His glassy eyes stared in mute terror while creatures from a different world fought over his flesh with their knives and hooks, inflicting pain with each of their jabs.

When the jury finished its deliberations, they returned to the courtroom to deliver its verdict. All that was left to do, Richard felt, was for them to heave his stinking, steaming guts overboard and move on.

As he sat awaiting to hear his fate, Richard knew that the key to his unending questions about the origins of this lawsuit lay somewhere behind those cold, grey eyes that were drilling right through him from the other side of the room. Each and every minute he was the target of Maxine's attention was a minute of psychological torture which had, at times, come close to driving him mad. By now, he was desperate to escape this chamber of horrors, return to his normal life, and salvage what was left of his practice.

Maybe he would go for a Hawaiian vacation . . .

Waving palm trees, gentle waves caressing the golden sand, a deep blue sea underneath fluffy white clouds, girls in bikinis, fawning over his bronzed body . . .

Or perhaps Bora-Bora in French Polynesia . . .

Yes, Bora-Bora would be better, for it was further away. Right now, he wanted to put as much distance as possible between himself and *that woman.*

Richard's defense attorney was John Denmark—a tall, lean man with sandy hair and engaging blue eyes. Throughout the trial, Richard had positioned himself leeward to him, using his lawyer's body as a shield to protect himself from the poisons that wafted from the direction of the plaintiffs' table. Even Denmark himself was not impervious to them. Early in the discovery phase of the trial, in a rare moment of exasperation, he had confessed to his client that he had opposed Maxine in court on several occasions before and that she was the nastiest, most dishonest, double-crossing attorney he had ever known. So far, he had failed to find the right formula for beating her and had, most unfortunately, lost each of the previous confrontations. He assured Richard, somewhat optimistically, that his luck was long overdue for a change. As *Brown vs. Forrester* progressed, however, Maxine scored point after point through deceit and connivance and it looked as though history was bound to repeat itself. Denmark handled his stress by deriding the way she looked and dressed: her wicked stepmother face with its ugly chin, her expensive designer clothes, a different outfit for every day of the trial, and her dazzling jewels. Both sides had finished presenting their case now and the jury had been deliberating for five days, never a good sign for the defense. As a loss was looking even more likely, Denmark's jokes and insults yielded to silent, vitriolic hatred.

"Please stand for the jury," said the bailiff as she held open the door to the courtroom.

Everybody rose to their feet: the judge, the clerk, Maxine and her clients, Mr. and Mrs. Brown. Denmark also stood up, buttoning his jacket as he did so. He put a reassuring arm under Richard's elbow and helped him to his feet. Once he was standing, Richard towered above everybody else. His long hair was gathered neatly into a ponytail, and he clasped his hands together in front of himself, imagining he had already been clapped in handcuffs. Nobody resumed their seat until the jury was settled.

The judge, a balding man with a pinched face and a thick moustache, was the first to speak. "I understand you have reached a verdict," he said, addressing the jury.

"Yes, we have, Your Honor," replied the spokesman, an elderly man with a long white beard.

The verdict form was passed from spokesman to bailiff, to clerk, to judge, then back again to the clerk. The small woman started reading from it. "'We, the jury, make the following answers to the questions submitted by the Court: Question #1—Was the defendant negligent? Answer yes or no. Answer . . .'"

There was a pause. The attorneys on both sides edged forward in their seats.

". . . yes."

There was an audible gasp from the defense table. Richard buckled at the knees. Denmark was grim-faced.

"Question #2—Was such negligence a proximate cause of injury to the plaintiff? Answer yes or no. Answer . . . yes."

Denmark laid a consoling hand on his client's shoulder.

"Question #3—What do you find to be the plaintiff's amount of damages? Answer . . . ten million dollars."

This final figure struck Richard like a bolt of lightning. He folded up and buried his face in his hands. *Ten million!* It was exactly what the plaintiffs were demanding and nine million dollars more than his policy limit. All he had ever wanted to do with his life was take care of patients. Now one of them had ruined him.

How did they find out? And why did they turn on him like this?

It no longer mattered.

The judge began to speak, but Richard was lost in his own crushing thoughts and didn't listen. The jury filed out of the room, followed by the triumphant Brown family, dollar signs written all over their faces. Soon the courtroom was quiet. As he sat with his mind reeling from the verdict, Richard could only hear the hypnotic sound of his lawyer's voice in his ear, repeating over and over again: "We'll appeal . . . we'll appeal . . ." like the clickety-clack, clickety-clack of train wheels running along a track.

Richard heard Maxine's voice, a sound more grating than if those wheels had suddenly locked and were screeching along amid a flurry of sparks. "Counselor, I'm sorry things didn't turn out better for your client."

Richard looked up with bleary eyes. Maxine had left her table and was approaching Denmark with a smug swagger. Today, she had picked an outrageously loud orange outfit from her wardrobe. A golden hummingbird bejeweled with multi-colored gemstones was pinned to the left side of her chest.

"For an ordinary defense lawyer, I thought you made quite a good effort," she continued, choosing this moment to conduct a quick inspection of her long, red fingernails. "I was actually worried you might win for a change. How many times have I beaten you now?"

"I would have won if you hadn't cheated and lied," snapped Denmark.

Maxine glanced at her adversary and her eyes flared like embers in a stoked fire. "I offer you compliments and you respond with insults?"

"It wasn't fair! Some of the things you did—"

"You don't think it was fair?" Maxine shrugged, taking one last look at her nails before curling them back into the palm of her hand. "I don't believe the judge would agree with you."

"Perhaps he might not, but I can guarantee that the Court of Appeals will."

Maxine's voice rippled with shallow laughter. "Talk about a sore loser!" she cried. "You know that judges don't like to overturn jury verdicts; ninety percent of appeals are unsuccessful. You wouldn't have a chance. As for your client . . ." Maxine cocked her head back and looked down her long nose at Richard. Her skin smelled of expensive perfumes and the golden hummingbird leered from her chest. "I want your client to know that it was . . . *nothing personal.*"

Richard started to rise in anger, but a firm hand landed on his broad shoulder and thrust him back into his seat.

"We'll meet again, Counselor . . ." said Denmark, his voice shaking.

"I'm sure we will," sneered Maxine. "You're the sort of stubborn fool who'll never give up trying to win a case against me."

". . . and when we do, I swear to God I'm going to destroy you."

Maxine grinned with bemused contempt. "An *amateur* like you? Not in a million years." Then she tossed her red curls and strutted away.

CHAPTER 9

As she drove home in her black Bentley Arnage, Maxine savored her victory. There was nothing in this world quite like the thrill of a favorable verdict—gaining control over clueless jurors, molding them into die-hard supporters of her cause, and watching the delight on the faces of her clients when they hit the jackpot. Best of all, it was gratifying to once again confirm that among all the medical malpractice attorneys in the country, she was clearly the best.

The cell phone rang.

"Hello?"

A voice crackled on the other end of the line. "Ms. Doggett?"

"Yes?"

"My name is Billy Funk. I'm a lawyer in town."

"I don't recognize your name."

"That's because I just graduated from law school a few weeks ago. We've never met, but I feel like I already know you quite well."

"Oh? How so?"

"I've been a fan of yours for some time now."

"A fan? Really?" The sound of screeching tires flew past Maxine's right ear as she careened through a stop sign.

"Sure. I've studied all of your cases and I'm familiar with most of the articles you've written. My favorite is the one that came out in Good Housekeeping ten years ago: Ethical Dilemmas in the Practice of Medical Malpractice Law. A classic . . . a *real* classic."

Maxine remembered it well. Her theories were so outrageous, the outcry against her had spread far and wide and she came close to getting disbarred. "Those were the days . . ." she murmured.

"Times have changed, Ms. Doggett," said Billy. "Your ideas of pushing ethical issues to their limits were revolutionary in those days. Now they're accepted as the norm."

"Nonsense—"

"I'm deadly serious. When I was in law school, I spent hours discussing your work with my classmates. I have a lot of friends who feel the same way as I do. If only they could see me now, talking with you, they'd be green with jealousy!"

"Oh, come now . . ."

"One day, I would like to be a medical malpractice lawyer, just like you."

Maxine gasped. No lawyer had ever told her that they wanted to follow in her footsteps; she found the comment uncommonly flattering. "It's a long, hard road," was all her befuddled mind could think of saying. "There's much to learn."

"I'm willing and able. Can we meet? I have a message to deliver to you from my employer, The Grand National Insurance Company."

"All right," said Maxine, feeling a cooperative spirit sweep through her. "Make an appointment with my office."

"Can we meet now?"

"Now?"

"It's important."

Maxine hesitated. Was something fishy going on here? The man on the phone was a stranger and, given her line of work, it wasn't inconceivable that he was really some disgruntled doctor with a gun who wanted to avenge something she'd done. Then she remembered that her security chief, Carl, was working in his basement office at her house tonight and knew she would be safe. Besides, Grand National was an insurance company with some of the deepest pockets in the country; anything they had to say was probably worth hearing. "Okay, come to my private residence," she said. "That's where I'm heading now. I'll give you the address—"

"I don't need the address. I know where you live."

"You do?" Maxine felt a twinge of alarm. She had picked a piece of property far out of town on which to build. Its remoteness was deliberate; she wanted to get away from annoying interruptions when she wasn't at the office.

"I know the area. Every year I go hunting in the nearby woods. I can be there in thirty minutes."

"I . . . suppose so. What do you hunt? Elk? Bear? Cougar?"

"Oh, no—nothing like that. I hunt quail with my shotgun."

"*Little birds?*" cried Maxine. She stomped on her brakes and her car screeched to a halt in the middle of the road amongst clouds of vaporized rubber.

"Is there something wrong?"

"Don't tell me you go around murdering little birds!"

"Well—"

"I absolutely *refuse* to meet with anybody who—"

Billy realized he must have said something terribly wrong for he quickly confessed that he was a lousy shot and that the little buggers always got away.

"You're just saying that," said Maxine, ignoring a blaring horn behind her.

"No, it's true! I promise!"

"I happen to love birds. They're always trying to help us with our lives and never expect anything in return."

"I understand, Ms. Doggett," said Billy. The tone in his voice, however, suggested that he had absolutely no clue what she was talking about.

"All right, then," said Maxine, flipping her middle finger at the car behind her, then driving on. "Since you know where my house is, I'll see you in a few minutes."

"Great! I can't wait to meet you."

When she arrived home, Maxine pulled up in front of a pair of heavy iron gates with vertical bars that had been salvaged from a medieval Swiss dungeon. Two ravens were sculpted onto the locking mechanism in the center and appeared as if they were mating when the gates were closed. Maxine pressed a button on the dash of her car. The ravens separated with a click and the gates swung open. She passed through, leaving them open behind her for her visitor.

Maxine's house was a Victorian mansion that stood on top of a promontory on the west shore of a lake. She had overseen its design and construction, and had become embroiled in innumerable arguments with the people who were supposed to be in charge of the project. After three years, four contractors, two engineers, five architects, and twelve lawsuits, she finally moved in. In the end, she felt that the hassle had been worth it. The house accurately reflected her personality and was the place where she felt most at ease.

Maxine steered the Bentley up the long curving driveway and into a loop lined with tinkling fountains. She parked in front of the house, skipped up the steps to the heavy oak front door, and let herself in.

The main hall had a high ceiling, a couple of imposing windows, and a curving stone staircase that led to the upper floors . . . and nothing else. The area was completely devoid of any furnishings or decoration: no tables or chairs, no pictures on the walls, carpets on the floor, or draperies around the windows. It was as if the house had just been built and its owner had not yet moved in. The light was grey and the air was cold. Maxine shivered, decided to keep her coat on, and walked through a wide doorway into the living area. Here, too, the room was also huge and sparsely furnished. A couch sat in front of a large stone fireplace and was flanked by a couple of armchairs. A huge portrait of Maxine reclining naked on a leopard print couch hung over the fireplace, spotlighted by recessed lamps in the ceiling. Tall windows afforded a view of a lake about a mile across, rimmed by evergreens. Rising above this landscape, Mount Hood brooded in the distance. The sun was low in the west, a few degrees above the horizon. Its harsh light swept across the land and washed against the volcano, bathing it in gold and casting its eastern glaciers into deep shadows.

Maxine greeted a handsome macaw that was perched on a wooden stand.

"Toby!" she said, scratching the colorful bird under his beak and kissing him on the top of his head. "How is my sweet darling?"

The macaw squawked, cocked his head, and shifted his weight impatiently from one foot to another. When Maxine offered him a finger, Toby hopped onto it and peered at his owner with a beady orange eye.

"Are you hungry, my dear?" asked Maxine.

"Awk! Toby wants a cracker!" said the macaw, bobbing his head up and down. "Toby wants a cracker!"

"You poor thing. I know how you hate going hungry. Mommy will feed you right away." Maxine walked over to a switch on a wall and flipped it. Cold, blue flames leaped from gas burners in the fireplace and licked the underbellies of artificial logs. Then she went into the kitchen, extracted a packet of fortified crackers from a cupboard, and gave a couple to her bird. "Here you are, my precious little friend." said Maxine.

"Maxine is a peach! Awk! Maxine is a peach!"

Maxine was titillated by the thoughtful compliment.

Soon afterwards, the doorbell rang. Maxine returned Toby to his perch and answered the front door. As he stood outside, Billy Funk looked young enough to have recently graduated from college, not law school. His face was fresh and smooth, and a shock of wavy brown hair angulated into the air above him. He was wearing a suit that was too big and he held a briefcase awkwardly under one arm. Maxine had difficulty imagining him as a hunter, even if it was only a small bird he was after. She didn't feel threatened in the least and decided not to alert Carl in the basement.

"You've no idea how much of an honor this is, ma'am," said Billy, vigorously shaking Maxine's hand.

Maxine returned a brief smile. "So, you're a fan of mine?"

"Absolutely," replied Billy, stepping inside the hall. "My God—what a big place you have!"

"It *is* rather roomy, isn't it?" said Maxine, casually glancing around herself.

"Do you live in this place all by yourself?"

"Yes. I like it that way."

Billy was shown into the living room. He rambled on about Maxine's great accomplishments, but lost his train of thought as he became overwhelmed by the sheer size of the house's interior. Evidently, he had never seen such dimensions before; he gaped around himself like a schoolboy in a museum and said, "Medical malpractice must be a *very* lucrative business."

"Yes, it is," said Maxine, her high heels clicking emptily across the wooden floor. She didn't have the heart to tell him that the money for this mansion had come from the winnings of a single favorable judgment. "Why don't you have a seat and explain to me why you're here?"

"Of course." Billy set his briefcase onto the floor and sat on the couch in front of the fireplace while Maxine fell into an armchair opposite. "I think I have a case for you—one that might especially interest you. As you know, Grand National provides medical liability insurance for thousands of physicians and hundreds of hospitals across the whole country. One of the physicians is a local orthopedic surgeon named Bruno Clegg. Have you heard of him?"

"No," said Maxine, flicking a speck of lint from her sleeve, "but I'm sure to have a complete dossier on him at the office."

"And one of the hospitals they cover is Columbia Medical Center. About a year ago, Clegg suffered a nasty complication after an operation at Columbia—a lumbar fusion on some woman with back pain. During the night following the surgery, she suddenly went quadriplegic. Turns out she had a tumor in her spinal cord that he should have known about, but didn't."

"*Quadriplegic?*"

"Complete C6."

Maxine felt a surge of excitement. Quadriplegic patients were the most pitiful victims imaginable—sawn off from the neck down and unable to do anything for themselves. They were rare, but when they showed up, they invariably won the maximum compensation for their condition. They required years and years of expensive care and it wasn't hard to bring a jury to tears over their plight, especially if you propped them up in their elaborate wheelchairs and planted them in the courtroom like the scarecrows they were. If all the possible medical malpractice cases in America were a pack of cards, then a retained foreign body was the Two of Clubs, an amputation of the wrong limb (or 'a limb-off') was the Jack of Diamonds, accidental death was the Queen of Hearts, and a fresh quad was the Ace of Spades.

"Clegg missed the diagnosis?" asked Maxine.

"Yes. Grand National analyzed the medical record in detail and found the results of some obscure lab test that was done shortly before the patient's surgery. The original report was missing, but there was a copy of it buried in a section where it wasn't supposed to be. The numbers indicated a very high level of protein in her CSF. Apparently, it was a tip-off that she had a tumor."

"And Clegg didn't investigate it further?"

"No."

"Why not?"

"Nobody knows. Maybe he never saw it."

"My God, what a colossal screw-up!" exclaimed Maxine. "He could have referred the patient to a neurosurgeon instead of operating on her back. If the tumor had been removed right away, she might not be quadriplegic now."

"There was more than one mistake," said Billy. "The nurses didn't immediately recognize what was going on and delayed calling Dr. Clegg."

"So the hospital is liable too."

"Yes."

"Excellent! *Excellent!*" cried Maxine, pleased as Punch. Then her expression suddenly changed and she looked at Billy with suspicion. "But why are you telling me these things? Don't you realize that I can make millions off this information—your employer's money?"

"Grand National would like to make a deal with you."

"What kind of deal?"

"They'll tell you the name, address, and phone number of the quad, on condition you agree to leave their clients, Clegg and Columbia Medical Center, alone."

Now Maxine was puzzled. "What kind of feather-brained deal is that?"

"A good one. You see, there's another doctor involved—a neurosurgeon. You can take the information we give you and file a lawsuit against him instead."

"So Grand National is trying to protect its clients?"

"And especially itself. This other guy is insured by Surgeon's Protective Insurance, SPI, one of the competitors. Grand National wouldn't mind at all if SPI took it on the chin for this one."

"Who's the other guy?"

"Some poor sucker by the name of Hugh Montrose."

"*Montrose!*" Maxine's hand flew up to her left temple and the tips of her fingers lightly touched her skin. Carefully hidden by her hair, the neurosurgeon's simple, curved signature served as the only reminder of her aneurysm surgery more than three years ago.

"You know him?"

"*No!* I mean . . . yes." As if guided by an unseen hand, Maxine slowly rose from her armchair and walked over to a window. The lake below her was as still as glass before the approaching night and distant house lights were winking from the far shore. High above, the golden light had been snuffed from the summit of Mount Hood and its glaciers were fading to a soft indigo. Suddenly a bald eagle appeared from the south, gently flapping its wings and making lazy circles over the water, its white head and tail feathers flickering against the backdrop of darkening trees. Then, without warning, it swooped low over the water and its talons struck below the surface. A moment later, it was climbing into the air again, slowly and majestically, a large salmon thrashing in its grip. Maxine was mesmerized by the auspicious moment. The sign was unmistakable, as if an oracle had whispered clearly into her ear. She and the eagle were one. The dying salmon in her claws was Montrose.

This must be it! she thought. *This must be the ultimate case I've always been waiting for!*

"I've never seen an eagle dive for a fish before," said Billy.

Maxine glanced sideways and saw her visitor standing behind her, gazing out of the window. "That's not just *any* eagle," she explained. "His name is Augustus. We've been close friends for years."

"Friends?"

"Sure."

"For years?"

"Ever since I first visited this lake about four years ago," said Maxine. "I was scouting for a suitable land to build my house when he flew out of nowhere and made circles in the sky above this precise location."

"You believe he was telling you something?"

Now Maxine faced Billy squarely. "Of course. Isn't it obvious? Birds are always trying to tell us things. Unfortunately, most people are retarded and don't pay them much attention. I do, though. Over the years, I've learned how to listen to what different species are telling us—parrots, ravens, sparrows, seagulls . . . even quail. Eagles are by far the best, though—especially Augustus. He looks after me and helps me make many of the major decisions in my life. He always knows what's best for me even when I have no clue myself."

"An eagle can't do that!"

"Augustus is different. He *knows*, and I love him for it."

"Does he return your love?" asked Billy, obviously trying to make sensible conversation under difficult circumstances.

"You know, I've never asked myself that question," said Maxine thoughtfully. "I suppose he does. . . . I would assume that all birds love people who love them. Wouldn't you?"

Billy shrugged, not having a clue how to answer.

Maxine stepped closer to Billy. "Tell me how Montrose is involved with this case," she asked, her voice laced with excitement now.

"Hugh Montrose was consulted to deal with the tumor," said Billy, appearing relieved that the subject of conversation had moved to firmer ground. "For some reason, he decided not to do an immediate operation. Instead, he procrastinated for a couple of days and eventually took it out when it suited him."

"So how does the quad feel now?"

"She's still paralyzed."

"I know *that*," said Maxine, rolling her eyes. "Once a quad, always a quad. I'm a fully qualified registered nurse too, you know. I understand these things. What I meant was: is she willing to sue?"

"She has been approached by a number of lawyers, but has rebuffed them all. I suppose it's possible she might actually *like* her doctors."

"Most people do," said Maxine, looking sad all of a sudden. "But money speaks louder than any feelings of gratitude or loyalty, especially if you need it badly enough. Quadriplegia is expensive; it takes the kind of money that most people don't have."

"Aren't you afraid she might rebuff you too?"

"Piffle!" exclaimed Maxine. "Nobody has ever turned me away. I doubt this quad will be any different. I have certain tricks up my sleeve that never fail. I'm far more concerned what she might think if Clegg isn't named in the lawsuit. Won't she wonder why I'm letting the guiltiest party off the hook?"

"She doesn't know about the high CSF protein."

"She's bound to find out about it eventually."

"Not if we don't tell her."

Maxine grimaced. Most medical malpractice lawyers generally observed the most fundamental rule—to serve their clients to the best of their ability. In this case, not only would she be obliged to share the information about the CSF protein with the quad, but she would also be remiss if she didn't include in the lawsuit Clegg, the hospital, and every health care provider who came in contact with the patient. If she had understood him correctly, Billy had no such ethical constraints and was evidently willing to ignore the rules to suit his own needs before those of the quad.

"You're suggesting keeping it secret?" she asked, frowning.

"Why not? And if it does come out during discovery, we'll simply deny we ever knew about it, just like Clegg does. Who would be any wiser?"

"I don't like it," said Maxine, shaking her head. "There could be serious repercussions. Potentially, the quad could sue me for legal malpractice."

"It's possible, but not likely," said Billy. "Look—all you have to do is impress her. Make a demand of some extraordinary amount of money from Montrose. Once she sees how much she's going to win, her eyes will flash dollar signs and she won't bother asking any awkward questions. So, what do you say?"

Maxine considered carefully. It was certainly an ingenious little scheme, obviously concocted by some faceless insurance executive with more imagination than money and sense combined. Technically, making a case against Montrose would be easy; he was screwed the minute he picked up the phone and spoke to Clegg. No matter what he had decided to do with the patient, he could be targeted with a lawsuit. If he had chosen immediate emergency surgery, then he could be tagged for recklessly endangering the life of the patient. On the other hand, if he had delayed surgery, as apparently he had done, then it would be easy to make him look negligent and uncaring. It didn't matter which approach was taken. Malpractice cases involving quadriplegics were remarkably malleable. The patients themselves and their shocking condition were what generated sympathy and carried the day. It didn't matter how they got there.

But could she really sue the man who had clipped her aneurysm and had literally saved her life?

Maxine's fingers returned to the scar on her left temple. Her surgery had been several years ago, yet she remembered everything as if it had happened yesterday: the frightful pain in her head, the terror of being inside an ER and at the mercy of her natural enemies, waking up in the Intensive Care Unit afterwards feeling overwhelmed with relief that she wasn't paralyzed, mute or blind. One little detail, however, stood out more than the rest: Montrose's confidence, self-assurance, and his refusal to show fear when faced with having to operate on a medical malpractice attorney. It was an attitude that had bedeviled Maxine for years and had forced her to face the inadequacies in her own life. Montrose had obviously attained *his* dreams years ago, while *she* was still struggling to realize her own. Even though the unfairness of it all had grated against her nerves and made her feel powerless and cheap, she still felt a small wisp of gratitude for what he had done for her and had promised never to sue him, putting his name on her highly coveted 'Do Not Sue' list.

On the other hand, Augustus himself had given her an unmistakable sign. This *had* to be the ultimate case she had been waiting for, the lawsuit that was going to make her a superstar and force the world to recognize her talents. What could earn her more notoriety than suing a neurosurgeon who had once saved her life? How could she more clearly demonstrate her grit and resolve? What could better demonstrate the sacrifices she was capable of making on behalf of a plaintiff? Besides, the lure of a real live quad was overpowering, striking a resonating chord in every legal fiber that coursed through her body. She knew she was too weak to pass up a chance to play the Ace of Spades, no matter what the risks.

"So what do you say, Ms. Doggett?" said Billy. "What do you want me to tell Grand National? Will you take this case?"

Maxine sat deep in thought. Given the circumstances, the decision amounted to a choice between Montrose's survival and her own. There was no middle ground on this particular battlefield. When put into such stark terms, the choice didn't really seem so difficult after all. Montrose would understand; he was a grown man and was surely mature enough to know that it would be nothing personal. She smiled and the natural sneer on the left side of her face deepened.

"Tell your friends at Grand National I'll take the case," she said to Billy.

Toby chose this moment to start squawking again. "Awk! Maxine is a peach!" he said. "Maxine is a peach!"

Billy laughed. "Great! They *will* be pleased. Even your parakeet likes the idea."

"Macaw," corrected Maxine coldly. As if to compensate Toby for her visitor's faux pas, she walked over to him, gave him another cracker, and kissed him on the top of his head.

"There's one other matter . . ." Billy started to fidget nervously.

"Yes?"

"I would like to ask you . . . Oh, this is embarrassing . . ." Billy thrust his hands into his pockets, crossed his legs at the ankles, and looked down at his feet.

"What?"

"May I serve as your . . . co-counsel against Montrose."

"You? *Co-counsel?*"

Billy looked up with hope in his eyes. "Yes—officially your co-counsel; your right-hand man. In reality I would be nothing more than your assistant, of course. You'd be the lead attorney; the one giving the orders."

"I don't know about—"

"This would be a dream come true!" interrupted Billy. "I would learn so much about medical malpractice law, seeing somebody of your reputation in action. I promise I won't make a nuisance of myself. What do you say?"

Maxine digested this request with profound distaste. As co-counsel, Billy would gain certain rights. For one thing, she didn't like the idea of having another attorney sitting *beside* her in the courtroom and not *behind* her like the usual arrangement. He might get in the way, make her waste valuable time teaching or, worst of all, give the jury an unfavorable impression of himself, which, considering Billy's youth and inexperience, was not unlikely. No, Billy was definitely *not* her idea of the perfect co-counsel. On the other hand, he was a *fan* of hers. When was the last time she had one of those? He might pamper her, flatter her, and say all manner of nice things about her just when she needed it the most. He would be a morale-booster and somebody to carry her through the darkest days of the trial ahead. Most of all, he would offer her some respect—and respect was what she coveted the most.

"*I'm* in charge. There's no question about that?"

"You're in charge, Ms. Doggett," said Billy. "I'll do everything you tell me."

"And we split the winnings ninety-ten. I take ninety percent. You can have what's left."

"Whatever you say, Ms. Doggett."

"And there's one more condition . . ."

"Yes?"

Maxine stroked Toby's beautiful red, green, and yellow plumage, and looked lovingly into his orange eye. "Never hunt quail again, or any other bird, for that matter."

"Never hunt—?"

"If you won't agree, the deal's off!" she snarled, suddenly turning her head and confronting Billy.

"Okay, okay. I won't shoot at any more birds. I promise."

"Then you've got yourself an agreement," said Maxine, all liquid honey again. "We'll work together on this one."

"Yes!" cried Billy, punching the air with his fist.

"Maxine is a peach!" squawked Toby again, reaching for his mistress with an outstretched claw. "Maxine is a peach!"

"But before you let your youthful enthusiasm get out of control," added Maxine, "I still don't know if the quad is willing to sue."

"Let's call and ask her right now."

"No—not yet," said Maxine, and her eyes narrowed . . . calculating. "I'll have to make an appointment to visit her home. If she needs a little persuading, I'll want to give it . . . the *personal* touch."

When it was time for Billy to leave, he bowed and scraped all the way to his car, promising Maxine that this was undoubtedly the beginning of a long and prosperous relationship between her and Grand National. If they were lucky, there would be plenty more medical mistakes in the future and a steady supply of plaintiffs. They shook hands and Maxine watched his taillights disappear down her driveway.

Once he was gone, Maxine retrieved Toby from his perch and returned with him to her armchair in front of the fireplace. What a memorable day it had been! First, the *Brown vs. Forrester* triumph, and now this! After years of patiently waiting, the ultimate lawsuit was within sight. Maxine would try her best to persuade the quad to cooperate and was sure of success. That would make Montrose a defendant . . .

Defendant Montrose!

The title in front of that doctor's name certainly had an appealing ring to it. Maxine laughed gleefully and stroked Toby gently on the top of his head. He looked back at her with one of his orange eyes.

"Tell me, Toby," said Maxine. "Do you love me?"

"Awk! Maxine is a peach!" he screeched.

"Of course you love me. Now, can you learn to say: Maxine is a *superstar*?"

"Peach! Peach!"

"No, Toby," said Maxine patiently. "Superstar. Maxine—is—a—superstar . . . su—per—star."

Toby bobbed his head again, then, with a flourish of his wings, said, almost perfectly, "Maxine is a superstar!"

Maxine kicked her head back and cackled wildly.

CHAPTER 10

When the doorbell rang, Gary Winter was on his knees with his index finger inside his wife's rectum. A large, hard stool had become lodged, and even though her anus was flaccid, he was having difficulty reaching around it and pulling it out. As he kept trying, gushes of gas erupted through the loose sphincter, not with the loud, rasping sound of healthy flatus, but with the smooth *pssssss* of air escaping a flat tire. The odor in the bathroom was stultifying, and as accustomed as he was to bad smells in his own house, Gary was starting to gag.

"Damn! The lawyers are early," he said, shifting his weight back onto his heels and straightening his stiff back. A glob of lubricating jelly dripped off his rubber glove and splattered on the floor.

Julie was hunched in her specially adapted chair, naked except for a bra. Her body was pale and bloated, and ugly, raw sores had opened up at various pressure points around her hips. Her wasted legs stuck out from her pelvis like a couple of bent sticks and her hands lay uselessly on a round belly that ballooned as she drew in breaths.

She picked up her sagging head and looked at her husband. "Did you say *lawyers*?" she asked in a hoarse whisper. Her impaired breathing muscles meant she could only speak slowly and with difficulty. Listening to the faltering rhythm of her words required considerable patience.

"Yes, that's right."

"You didn't tell me anything about lawyers."

"Didn't I? Maybe I forgot—"

"I've seen enough lawyers."

"But we've got to do *something*, Julie," said Gary, looking at his wife with pleading eyes. "We can't keep on going like this. Our savings are all gone and the bills keep coming in. At this rate we're soon going to lose our home. Jennifer and Patrick will have to kiss college goodbye."

"How are more lawyers going to help?"

"Maybe these ones can get us some money so we can survive."

"We've been through this before, Gary . . . countless times," said Julie. "Each time the lawyers start poking around, they tell us the same thing: nobody made a mistake. Dr. Clegg had no reason to know that I had a tumor in my spinal cord and Montrose removed it without causing more damage. A lawsuit would be a waste of time and energy. To tell you the truth, I don't have much of either these days, not after three hours of getting ready every morning."

"But one of these lawyers is the best," said Gary. "At least, she claims she is. Her name is Maxine Doggett. She told me that if there's a way of helping us, she would find it."

Julie was unimpressed. "That's what they all say."

"This time it's different. I promise."

"Frankly, Gary, I'm afraid."

"How could you possibly be afraid of a couple more lawyers?"

Julie shook her head. "It's not about the lawyers," she said. "I'm afraid of a big legal battle. I'm afraid of losing and the whole thing being a waste of time. I'm afraid of finding out things about my tumor that are best left alone."

"Finding out things?"

Julie gave a long, trembling sigh. "My worst nightmare is to discover my paralysis was a result of a medical mistake," she said. "I just don't want to know; I couldn't bear it. I can't help having the same bad feeling about this as I had when I first saw Dr. Clegg. Seemed harmless to try an operation on my back, but look what happened. Starting a lawsuit could end the same way."

The doorbell rang again.

"Well, they're here now," said Gary, popping off his soiled glove and tossing it into the waste. "We can't keep them waiting. I'll let them in, then come back and get you cleaned up and dressed. Okay?"

"It doesn't look as though I have much choice. Just like my back surgery."

Julie watched her husband leave and allowed her head to sag forward once again. She'd been suffering now for about a year, totally dependant on her family and whatever meager nursing care they could squeeze out of their skinflint insurance company. In the morning, she was hoisted out of bed with a lift that resembled a crane and was strapped into her potty chair. On some days, she was rolled into a shower and her unfeeling skin washed as she sat under the water. On others, Gary lay under her as if he was working on a car and emptied her rectum. At first she had felt embarrassed and humiliated, but by now she had become so used to it she no longer cared. Dressing took half an hour or more, a laborious process since she could be no more cooperative than an infant. It began with putting her into support hose to prevent her female organs from turning inside out and dropping from her pelvis. A plastic bag was then strapped to her leg to collect the urine that flowed down her in-dwelling catheter. Finally, various layers of clothes were pulled on, the trousers being the most difficult of all. Her teeth had to be brushed, her hair combed, and her face washed. After she was finished, she rarely went outside the house, spending what was left of the day parked in front of the television in the den.

In the beginning, the rehabilitation specialists had told her how lucky she was to have some function left in her arms. At least she could feed herself using special implements that were strapped to her hands—slowly, and not without spilling most of her food onto the floor. But she *could* do it. She was also able to nudge a joystick on her wheelchair with balled fists and have some control over the direction in which it moved. She had scorned those experts and their contrived opinions and invited them to trade places with her.

"What good are arms without hands?" she would ask them. "What good is life without a body?"

Julie wanted to cry, but her tears had run dry long ago. She wanted to scream, but her lungs were too weak and she could only muster a hoarse whisper. Most of all, she wanted to shake her fists at God, but her hands were no more functional than those of a mannequin. There was a time when she believed that He might exist, living inside her, loving her, and always looking after her family. Now she saw things much differently: if He existed at all, He was cruel and distant, enjoying the misery He inflicted on the world while He sat comfortably in heaven. He was the worst kind of sadist, and Julie no longer wanted to have anything to do with Him.

***

Shock and awe was a tactic Maxine often used to recruit her most reluctant clients. On the day she first visited the Winters' home, she used it without restraint, wearing a stunning yellow designer outfit and enough gold and jewels to make her look like a Fabergé egg. As she waited on the front porch with Billy, she looked around with undisguised disapproval. The house was seriously neglected; paint was peeling from the wood siding, a few windows were broken, and weeds were sprouting from the roof. The garden might have once looked pretty, with a gently sloping lawn down to the road and a small vegetable patch to one side. However, brambles had broken loose and were running amok. Their thick, prickly stems ran across the uncut grass in long, spidery fingers. Some of them had found an old abandoned camper parked on the driveway and had grown up its sides. Tender green shoots curled and twisted along its rusty windows as if they were trying to pry their way inside.

"I hate it when people leave junk littered around their front yards," Maxine declared, nodding in the direction of the camper. "It's such an eyesore. They should have it hauled away."

The front door opened and a man with a thin face, deeply furrowed skin, and stubbly jaw appeared. When he saw the glitzy spectacle standing on his doorstep, he was startled. "Hello?"

"Mr. Winter? I am Maxine Doggett and this is Billy Funk. We're the lawyers you've been expecting."

Gary broke into a smile. "Oh, good, good!" he said, looking from one face to the other. "Please come in." He led Maxine and Billy through a hallway and into a living room. After a few pleasantries about the weather, he explained that he was still busy getting his wife ready for the day and politely excused himself.

Maxine and Billy looked about themselves. Outside, it was warm and sunny, yet the curtains were drawn, allowing only dim light to filter in. The room was a study in monochrome: cheap, faded paintings hung on the walls, a few pieces of grey furniture were scattered about, and a well-worn carpet lay beneath their feet. Abundant scuff marks and dents were clustered low around the doorways, evidence that somebody in this house was using a wheelchair and was none too adept at steering it. A television stood in a corner. There was no armchair or couch in front of it, just open space. No plants, flowers, or color. Instead, the smell of antiseptics hung heavily in the air, reminding Maxine of the miserable time when she worked in a hospital.

Maxine ran the tip of her index finger over the surface of a side table, then held it up, inspecting it for dust. She frowned, rubbed it quickly against her thumb to clean it, and said to Billy in a hushed voice, "Now remember—they haven't agreed to file a lawsuit yet, so we can't afford to make any mistakes. Do you understand?"

Billy stood rigidly at attention, his eyes nervously darting about and his hands thrust into his pockets. He nodded without saying a word.

"I'll do all the talking. You keep your mouth shut and your eyes open. Watch and learn. Okay?"

Billy glanced back towards the hallway and looked as if he was planning his escape route.

"What's the *matter* with you?" demanded Maxine.

"This place gives me the creeps."

"You haven't spent much time with the handicapped before, have you?"

"No, I haven't. It's so depressing."

Maxine snorted her disapproval. In the few days since Billy's appearance on her doorstep, he had already proved that he knew nothing about medical matters and she'd had to waste valuable time explaining to him the basic anatomy of the spine, among many other things. Hezekiah L. Potts, the divorce lawyer whose mistress she'd once been, was absolutely right about one thing: in order to be successful in medical malpractice law, one had to spend time working within the medical system, learning how it worked, breathing its culture, and exploiting its weak-nesses. Thank goodness she had followed his advice! She had invested four years of her life in nursing and, as he'd predicted, every moment had proved invaluable in her subsequent legal career. Billy was acting as if he'd never even studied high school biology and she felt sure his future in medical malpractice law was going to be a short one. Fan or not, there were already times when Maxine wished he would go back to Grand National and leave her alone.

After a while, a door opened and a woman guided her mechanized wheelchair into the room, followed by her husband.

"Here we are," announced Gary with a flourish. "I'm sorry we kept you waiting."

"Mrs. Winter? I'm Maxine Doggett. This is Billy Funk."

Billy thrust out his right hand. When Julie didn't do the same, he realized his blunder and his face turned a deep shade of red. "I'm—I'm sorry," he stammered.

"Don't be embarrassed," said Julie with resignation. "People do it all the time."

Maxine glared angrily at Billy, then turned towards Gary and Julie, her face easily liquefying into an expansive smile. "Thank you very much for inviting me into your home today," she said. "I know how difficult it is for you to have visitors. I just want to let you know how much I appreciate your hospitality."

Gary smiled back. "It's really nothing," he said, gesturing towards a lumpy-looking couch. "Won't you make yourselves comfortable? Can I offer you something to drink?"

Billy was about to accept the offer of refreshments when Maxine cut him off. "No, thank you," she said. "I won't be very long." She sat down on the couch, positioning herself exactly halfway between two large stains. Coffee? Urine? Something even worse?

Billy sat in a nearby armchair.

"I know my visit must be quite stressful for you, so I'll come straight to the point," said Maxine, "I am an attorney who specializes in medical malpractice. Mr. Funk is my assistant who'll be—"

"Co-counsel," corrected Billy barely under his breath, his eyes averted.

"Of course. How silly of me. Co-counsel. He'll be assisting me. I've had a great deal of experience in matters like this and have brought untold relief to countless struggling families. I heard about the unfortunate . . . *thing* that happened to you a couple of years ago and know how much of a financial strain it must be. Quadriplegia is a terribly expensive condition, with all the special equipment that's needed, and so on. Every victim is forced to file a lawsuit these days just to stay ahead of the rabble at the collection agencies. I was wondering why you haven't already done so yourselves. You *haven't*, have you?"

"No, we haven't," replied Julie.

"May I enquire why not?"

"I'll tell you what all the lawyers say: Clegg did his job, and did it well. My quadriplegia wasn't his fault, or anybody else's. So what's the point in suing him?"

"I certainly agree with them," said Maxine. "It sounds to me like Dr. Clegg is totally innocent. In fact, we could use more fine doctors like him in this world. But have you thought about suing anybody else . . . perhaps?"

"Who? There wasn't anybody else."

"Let's see . . ." Maxine looked up at the ceiling and rubbed her big chin. "What about what's-his-name, the neurosurgeon? What *is* his name? Mon . . . Mon . . ."

"Dr. Montrose?"

"That's right!" cried Maxine, clapping her hands together. "I *knew* you'd remember his name!"

"But he didn't do anything wrong either."

"Mr. and Mrs. Winter . . ." said Maxine, sounding serious now. "May I call you Gary and Julie?"

"Please do."

"Thank you. To be perfectly honest with you, Gary and Julie, medical malpractice lawsuits have nothing to do with right and wrong. They're all about *money*. And *only* money. And it seems to me," she added, looking around herself with disdain, "that you can use a little more of it."

Gary vigorously nodded his agreement.

"Let me explain to you something," Maxine continued. "Most lawsuits to go in one of two directions: either a settlement or a trial. Trials are extremely expensive, so most of the time the defendant will settle just to make the problem disappear. The parties simply come to an agreement over the numbers. In a serious case like yours the amount is usually the limit of the doctor's insurance policy—say, one or two million dollars."

"I've heard similar figures before," said Gary, nodding again.

"So, you see," said Maxine, "the doctors themselves aren't actually paying any money. They don't see lawsuits as anything personal. In fact, they *expect* to be sued. If they weren't sued, they might think something was seriously wrong with their practices, like they're not busy enough, or something. It's all just part of business."

"As you can see," said Gary, "my wife is severely handicapped. She spent three hours this morning just to get ready to see you. Filing a lawsuit would be emotionally exhausting for her, even if it resulted in a quick settlement. God forbid a trial. Something like that would be very difficult."

"I would do everything to protect her from any undue stress," said Maxine reassuringly. Even in the low light, her rings flashed as she casually dismissed the problem with a wave of her hand. "During the discovery phase, she would only have to show up for a deposition. I could even spread it over a few days to make it easier on her. If we went as far as a trial, I would only ask her to appear on two or three days—Opening Statements, Closing Arguments, and the day when she takes the stand herself. Maybe an extra day here and there. The judge will be very understanding."

"But you can't have lawsuits without plaintiffs," said Gary. "Maybe we're a little old-fashioned, but we actually appreciate what Dr. Montrose did for us. I told him so on more than one occasion."

Maxine looked horrified as if appreciating a doctor was the worst sin in the world. "A jury may not be so quick to judge him innocent," she said coldly.

Julie's head had been drifting lower, as it so often did when she was getting tired. However, Maxine's last words made her snap back to attention, her eyes wide and increasingly fearful. "What do you mean by that?" she demanded.

"Julie, I've told you that I'm medical malpractice lawyer," said Maxine, leaning forward in her chair, placing her elbows on her knees, and batting her eyelashes to show that she was now locked into her highest level of engagement. "But that's not all I am. I'm also a fully qualified registered nurse and have spent long years of my life working in hospitals. In that regard, I stand out in the crowd of regular riff-raff lawyers who have already spoken to you. You see, I have a *medical* background and understand these things better than most. When I reviewed the facts of your case, some interesting questions immediately came to my mind."

"Like what?"

"Like—why did Dr. Montrose take so long to see you on the afternoon of June 29th, 2001? After all, the MRI was done around noon. Isn't that right?"

"Yes . . ."

"Yet, he didn't write his consultation note in the chart until four in the afternoon. A jury will interpret that as an unnecessary delay. And why did he wait for a couple of days before he performed surgery? Was that another delay? A jury might be persuaded that by *not* operating right away, he took away any chance you had for regaining any function—"

Julie's growing fear now exploded into horror. "*Gary!*"

Her husband leapt from his chair and rushed to Julie's side. "I'm here, dear! I'm here!"

"I told you something like this would happen! She's telling me a mistake was made! She's telling me I didn't have to be like this! Get her out of here! I don't want to see her again!"

Maxine was momentarily thrown off balance by Julie's outburst. She quickly regained her footing and lost no time repairing the damage. "Julie!" she barked. "I'm not saying that! I don't believe for a second that you could have avoided your paralysis! Not at all! It's what the *jury* can be led to believe. And believe me—they'll swallow *anything* you spoon-feed them. The truth can be manipulated and twisted in all kinds of ways to suit *your* interests. And right now, your interests are to get some financial assistance so you and your family can lead as normal lives as possible!"

Julie heard none of this. Instead, she burst into tears. Her sobs sounded like gigantic hiccups as her diaphragm struggled to move air. "These damn lawyers!" she cried to her husband. "They're all the same. Digging up things best left alone. Tell her to go away!" A powerful odor of stool emanated from her and quickly filled the room. "Oh, God! *Not now!*" she sobbed.

Maxine's olfactory system reeled under the assault and she fought to keep a straight face. "If you send me away," she cried, "you won't have another chance to get any compensation. There's a statute of limitations, you know. In this state it's two years. I have to file a lawsuit soon, if nothing else just to keep the door of opportunity open. If you decide later you're not up for it, I can always drop the suit."

"Ms. Doggett . . ." began Billy, rising from his chair.

"Not now, Billy," growled Maxine from the corner of her mouth.

"Ms. Doggett, I *have* to go . . ."

Maxine stole a glance at Billy and saw that he had turned a light shade of green. "Okay—go, if you have to!"

With an ugly gagging noise arising from his throat, Billy stepped quickly towards the front door, pulled it open, and ran out.

Gary snatched a tissue from a pocket in his wife's wheelchair and wiped the tears away. "That okay, Julie," he said. "Accidents happen. We'll just have to clean—"

"I've had enough of getting cleaned up!" wailed Julie, clumsily beating her arm against her husband out of frustration. "It takes so much time. I'm so helpless. You're such an angel, Gary, but every person has his limits. Why don't you just stick me in some nursing home and be done with me? Or better still, just shoot me and put me out of my misery!"

Gary turned to Maxine with tormented eyes. "I'm really sorry about this," he said. "I understand that there's not much time, but it looks to me as though a lawsuit is not such a good idea after all. Look how much it upsets her just talking about it. Imagine what it would be like going through a trial. Perhaps you'd better leave now, Ms. Doggett. Thank you for coming. I need to take care of things here."

Maxine stared at Julie in disbelief. She knew that if she left right now, her attempt to enlist these people as her clients would end in failure and there would be no lawsuit against Montrose. She felt like a climber who'd lost their foothold and was beginning to fall; her arms were flailing wildly around, looking for something to grab onto.

Then, an idea struck her.

"Let me help!" she said, rocketing from the couch before she had a chance to reconsider.

"Help? What do you mean?" asked Gary.

"Let me help you clean up your wife."

"You?"

"Of course. I told you I'm a nurse as well as a lawyer. I have a lot of experience caring for the disabled. If I help you, you'll get done much faster and it won't seem nearly so bad. You'll see! How about it?"

"What do you think, Julie?"

After a few moments silence, interrupted only by the distant sound of retching in the garden, Julie said in a small voice: "A lawyer? Cleaning me? If she doesn't mind . . ."

"Of course I don't mind," said Maxine.

"Then follow me," said Gary. He took the handles to his wife's wheelchair and pushed her towards the bathroom.

Thirty minutes later, Maxine found Billy waiting in her Bentley. She yanked the driver's door open and collapsed into the seat. Her face was as white as a ghost and her hair a tangle of knots.

"The things I'll do to get a case," she fumed, her chest heaving up and down as she stared through the windshield. "I swear I've have never done anything so *disgusting* in my life! *Never!*"

"What did you do?"

"I dug a bucket-load of shit out of that woman. I've never seen anybody so impacted, not even in nursing school. The stink was *awful!* These clothes will have to be burned." Maxine suddenly turned to look at Billy directly in the eye, her teeth bared like a jackal. "And where the hell were you?" she demanded.

"I—I didn't feel well."

"So while you were relaxing comfortably in here, surrounded by hand-stitched leather and burr walnut, I was up to my elbows in crap trying to save the day?"

"I'm sorry. My stomach couldn't take it. I'm not used to this sort of thing."

"And you think I am?" Maxine exhaled a lungful of air, blowing aside some hair that had fallen over her face. For a minute, she didn't say a word as she fought to regain control of herself. Then the corners of her mouth slowly widened and she broke into a cunning grin. "My effort was worth it though," she said with eyes that were now suddenly shining. "Congratulate me, Counselor! I've got myself a couple of clients!"

Billy whooped loudly and slapped his knee with the palm of his hand. "*Really*? They agreed to sue Montrose?"

"Yes, they did!"

"I can't believe it! Tell me what happened!"

"My idea worked. They said that if I was kind-hearted enough to help them clean up the accident, then I was certainly qualified to represent them in a lawsuit. So they agreed to sign a contract."

Billy laughed and clapped his hands together. "That was brilliant!" he cried. "Absolutely brilliant! Come on, Ms. Doggett! You've snared us a real live quad! Let's go out and celebrate!"

"It's too early to be celebrating," said Maxine, laying a calming hand on Billy's shoulder. "There's a lot of hard work ahead."

"What's the next step?"

"First, I have to file the lawsuit before the statute of limitations expires. Then I'll gather together all the medical records and make copies of them. It'll take a few acres of bird habitat to do the job, but that can't be helped. Then I'll have to go through them in minute detail, analyzing every little morsel of information to see what helps our case, and what doesn't."

"I could assist you."

"I suppose you could," said Maxine with little enthusiasm, "but unless you have some sort of medical background like me, you'll soon get lost. The way those health care people scribble indecipherable notes into the record is absolutely atrocious! Even I'll have to hire an expert witness to help me. In this case, I'll need a neurosurgeon."

"Do you have anybody in mind?"

"Yes, I do," said Maxine. "I certainly do."

"Who?"

Maxine snapped her seatbelt on and inserted a key into the ignition. The engine started.

"Come on," insisted Billy. "Tell me his name."

"His name is . . . Manfred Horman."

"You think this guy . . . Horman . . . will do the job for us?"

"Horman will do whatever I tell him," said Maxine with a crafty smile. Then, she trod on the accelerator. Tires squealed and the Bentley fish-tailed into the street.

CHAPTER 11

Hugh Montrose began his long, slippery slide into hell on Sunday, June 22nd, 2003, when he and his family had returned home from church and were in the front garden playing French cricket. He stood on the lush, green grass of his lawn, his feet firmly planted together, holding a cricket bat in front of his legs. His back was hunched so the bottom of the bat was hanging between his toes and an expression of feigned concentration was etched into his face. He was surrounded by his three daughters, Marie, Renee, and Anna, who were bubbling with laughter and tossing a tennis ball between themselves. Once in a while, one of them would throw the ball at her father's legs in an attempt to strike them, and he, in turn, defended himself with the bat. By the rules, he was not allowed to shift his feet and so at times he became twisted and unbalanced, making it difficult to hit the ball away. His son, Jack, was sitting nearby with Michelle, occasionally sniffing away a tear. He had been the last batsman and at four years old, he hadn't lasted long under his sisters' withering attacks. When the tennis ball had hit his shins, he had flung away his bat with a howl of frustration and had sought consolation from his mother, whose belly was large with her fifth pregnancy.

French cricket was popular amongst English children who couldn't gather enough players for regular cricket. Hugh remembered playing it as a schoolboy at Helmsdale Manor and now he was passing along the tradition to his own children.

Marie, Hugh's eldest daughter, was thirteen. She knelt on

the grass and faked a couple of throws at her father's legs, trying to trick him into swinging. When she saw her opportunity, she let go of the ball, but he was too fast for her. He hit it away and sent it soaring through the air. Ten-year-old Renee leapt for it unsuccessfully with an outstretched arm. Angus, the Golden Labrador, had been keeping a wary eye on the outfield from his position under a shady tree and ran after the ball as it disappeared under some rhododendrons. After snorting and sniffing around for a minute, he emerged with his trophy in his mouth.

"Angus!" cried Marie. "Bring the ball back here! *Angus!*"

Angus had other plans. He was far more interested in chewing the ball to pieces in some quiet corner of the garden and quickly disappeared from sight.

"What are we going to do now?" moaned Renee, throwing up her arms in exasperation.

"We can either stop playing," said Hugh, "or find another ball. Anna, why don't you have a look in the garage for one?"

Anna, the youngest, pouted with her hands on her hips and dragged her feet. However, when she saw Jack leap up and run towards the garage, she rushed after him, shouting, "Daddy told *me* to go!"

Hugh tossed the bat aside and lowered himself onto the lawn next to Michelle. He closed his eyes, felt the warmth of the sun against his face, and cast his mind back to the first time he had met her. He was a medical student at the time in Jackson, Mississippi, and was spending some downtime traveling through Europe. He had seen her in a café in her hometown of Aix-en-Provence and had started talking. Hugh had found her beautiful, exotic, and irresistible, and he quickly dumped his plans to see the rest of Europe in order to linger in Aix for three extra weeks. The language barrier did not stop love from taking root, and when the painful moment arrived for Hugh to tear himself away and return home, they tearfully promised to keep in touch with each other and not allow something as trivial as two continents and the North Atlantic Ocean to come between them.

They didn't. For two years, long letters were exchanged, phone calls were made, and their love only grew. Hugh learned some French, and Michelle improved her rudimentary English. Knowing she would never be happy unless she shared her life with Hugh, Michelle chose to leave her family and friends behind and immigrate to America. Although the decision to move was an easy one, the actual assimilation once she arrived was far more difficult. The culture was very foreign and, early on, she was far from proficient with the language and made few friends of her own. Worst of all, her husband soon graduated from medical school and started to work as a general surgery intern at a local hospital. The work was much harder now and involved spending long hours away from home. Things got twice as rough when the neurosurgery training started a year later and Michelle found herself spending even more time alone. No matter how difficult things were, however, she never regretted the path she had chosen for herself. Indeed, she and her husband viewed the durability of their relationship under these unique circumstances as living proof, if they ever needed such a thing, of their steadfast love for each other.

Michelle was now thirty-eight. As the years passed by, her beauty only grew. Subtle lines in her face reflected her age, but they also underscored her elegance. Her large brown eyes remained as soft and luminous as the day he first saw them, and ever since she had become pregnant with her latest child, they positively glowed. Hugh propped his head on an arm and gazed at her, never regretting a moment in their eighteen-year marriage.

"Michelle?"

"Oui, mon cher?"

"It's really beautiful here, isn't it?"

Michelle looked around. Their home was large, painted white, and had a cluster of gables that pointed towards the limpid sky. A pathway lined by tall lavender led up to the front door. The entrance was constructed of brick and a collection of terracotta pots were arranged on the steps, welcoming visitors with their colorful displays of geraniums, daisies, and forget-me-nots. The rest of the house was covered with climbers and creepers of every description, their green leaves and tendrils twisting and turning through a network of wooden trellises. Roses and clematis predominated, and dense clusters of buds promised a spectacular splash of purple later in the summer.

"I love it," said Michelle with a French accent as she gazed into the park that lay beyond a white picket fence.

At that moment, Angus bounded from the rhododendrons that bordered the lawn and erupted into a violent outburst of barking, his teeth bared and his eyes fierce. A rusty old car was rumbling down the driveway. The driver, a young, scruffy man with long greasy hair, pulled up and cracked open his window.

"Can I help you?" asked Hugh, approaching the car. Michelle grabbed Angus' collar, dragged him away, and put him inside the house.

"You sure can," said the man with a toothless grin. "Are you Dr. Hugh Montrose?"

"Yes, I am."

"And is that your wife, Michelle?"

"Yes."

"I'm Jake, the delivery man, and do I have something special for you! Let me see if I can find it." He turned his ignition key. The engine coughed and sputtered to a stop. Then he twisted around and rummaged through a pile of papers scattered across the back seat. While he was searching, Michelle cautiously drew nearer while Marie and Renee followed closely behind her. Anna and Jack had abandoned their search for another tennis ball and watched from a safe distance.

"What does he want?" Michelle asked Hugh.

"I don't know. Something about a special delivery."

"Here it is," cried Jake. "There are always so many of them, they're hard to keep organized." He extracted some papers out of the pile and rolled down his window further. The smell of cigarette smoke and sweat was powerful and Hugh backed away. "I've got a Summons and Complaint to give you. You're being sued, my friend."

"*Sued?*"

"Yup. You're a physician, aren't you?"

"Yes."

"Looks like you must have screwed up, because there's a Gary and Julie Winter who've filed a lawsuit against you. It says it all right here in the complaint: *professional negligence, failure to obtain informed consent, personal injuries and damages.* I've looked through this one myself. Makes quite interesting reading. I thought about going to law school myself once—"

"Let me see that!" Hugh snapped, holding out his hand.

"Sure, man."

Jake passed the papers through the car window and Hugh quickly scanned the first few lines:

SUMMONS
IN THE SUPERIOR COURT OF OREGON FOR
THE COUNTY OF MULTNOMAH
JULIE WINTER AND GARY WINTER, wife and
husband, plaintiffs v. HUGH MONTROSE,
 individually and on behalf of the marital community
composed of

HUGH MONTROSE and MICHELLE MON-
TROSE, defendants.
TO THE DEFENDANT (S):
A lawsuit has been started against you in the above-
entitled Court by
JULIE WINTER AND GARY WINTER, plain-
tiffs . . .

Julie and Gary Winter? *Julie* Winter? Hugh cast his mind
back through a couple of years of neurosurgical practice and
thousands of patients, locking onto the gaunt face of a woman
with long, dark hair. As the pixels of his memory coalesced,
other features came into focus. She was paralyzed. Her hands
and legs were useless. Her scans had shown—

That's it! She was the one with the huge spinal cord tumor!

"Michelle," said Hugh, keeping a low, calm voice. "Take
the children inside, please."

"Hugh—"

"Please, let's not discuss it. Just do as I ask."

Michelle took note of her husband's urgent tone and quickly herded the four children into the house. Angus was still barking from inside, making it clear he wished to substitute Jake for
his chewed-up tennis ball.

"You've got some kind of nerve driving in here on my Sunday off and serving me in front of my family!" Hugh said to
Jake, his voice shaking with anger.

"Don't get pissed off with me, man. I'm paid to deliver these
papers. I had nothing to do with writing them."

"You could have taken them to my office."

"Your office is closed today, and besides . . . you're here, not
there."

"Why didn't you bring them to me tomorrow?"

"I only work weekends. Now, I'd better go. I've got all these other lawsuits to deliver before five o'clock. If I spend too much time talking to you, I'll never get it all done. Have a great time in court."

Jake backed his car out of the driveway and rattled off, leaving behind a trail of blue smoke.

When the unwelcome visitor was gone, Hugh looked at the documents in his hands.

On or about June 29th, 2001, and thereafter, Julie Winter came under the care and treatment of defendant Hugh Montrose. As a direct result of defendants' negligence . . .

Negligence?

. . . plaintiff Julie Winter was permanently and severely injured and disabled, and has sustained both general and special damages, in amounts to be proven at trial . . .

Trial?

. . . Defendants failed to inform plaintiff Julie Winter of the risk of permanent injury and disability due to delay in diagnosis, medical treatment and care . . . Defendants failed to inform plaintiff Julie Winter of alternative methods of diagnosis, medical treatment and care . . .

Hugh felt a cloud of butterflies swirl in his stomach and his knees weaken.

As a direct and proximate result of defendants' failure to obtain informed consent, plaintiff Julie Winter was permanently and severely injured and disabled.

Hugh sank into a garden chair, aghast at the accusations against him.

In order to defend against this lawsuit, you must respond to the complaint by stating your defense in writing . . . within twenty (20) days . . . or a default judgment may be entered against you without notice . . . If you wish to seek the advice of an attorney in this matter, you should do so promptly . . . Dated this 21st day of June, 2003 By
Maxine Doggett (signed)

Maxine Doggett!
The name explained everything.
Michelle appeared at his side. She rested a gentle hand on his arm. "What is this all about, Hugh?"
"I'm being sued," answered Hugh flatly.
"Mais non! By whom?"
"By somebody I cared for about two years ago—a woman, about your age."
"What happened to her?"
"Bonehead operated on her back."
"Bonehead?"
"Bruno Clegg, the big, ugly orthopod at Columbia. You know—the guy with the skull I'm always talking about. There was a bad complication—"
"Yes?"

Hugh swallowed a lump that was rising in his throat and said, "After her operation, she suddenly became paralyzed from a tumor in her spinal cord. Nobody knew it was there until it was too late. By the time I was called to see her, there was nothing I could do."

"So why are *you* being sued?"

Hugh sighed deeply, held out the papers for Michelle to see, and pointed towards a signature at the bottom of the last page.

"Maxine Doggett?" Michelle read. "Do you know her?"

"Unfortunately, yes. She's a well-known medical malpractice attorney in Portland. I saved her life once. Looks like I might have made a big mistake."

"You saved her life?"

"She was brought to the ER at Columbia with a brain hemorrhage from an aneurysm. I happened to be on call that night, so I operated on her. She did very well and promised she would never sue me."

Michelle looked up. "You saved her life and *this* is how she repays you?" she asked, brandishing the papers in her hand.

"I'm telling you, Michelle: this woman is really lethal," said Hugh, taking them from her. "She has a degree in nursing, so she automatically thinks she knows everything there is to know about neurosurgery. She's successful too. Wins or settles almost all of her cases. Everybody in town is afraid of her. Getting sued by her is like catching the bubonic plague."

"But you're innocent!"

Hugh sighed again. "I know. But that's not going to stop her from coming after me. She is a *driven* woman who stops at nothing."

"You'll just have to find a defense lawyer who's her equal," declared Michelle with an air of determination.

"There's nobody in the world that fits that description," said Hugh. "Richard thought he had the right man, but in the end the poor guy was completely demolished."

Michelle suddenly paled. "She's the lawyer who sued Richard?"

"She's the one."

"Mon Dieu!"

Michelle suddenly had good reason to be worried. Richard had been a very talented neurosurgeon, if not a little unconventional with his long hair and his love for his own physique. He had seemed happy with life, right up until the day he lost his trial. The Court of Appeals had upheld the jury's verdict and Richard had been ordered to pay the full amount of its award. Since he didn't have the extra nine million dollars it would take to settle the debt, the judge made special payment arrangements that would drag on for twenty years. Richard's life quickly fell apart and his attitude towards neurosurgery plummeted. It was no longer a calling, rather just a job—one with the sole purpose of making the Browns richer by the day. He put on weight, cut his hair short, shaved off his beard, and no longer spent time admiring himself in front of mirrors. He still operated at Columbia Medical Center, but had become ineffective and unhelpful, distrusting his patients and fighting *them* rather than their diseases. He drank too much, passing time in seedy watering holes, and spilled his guts to anybody who would listen. It was clear to Michelle that he was unraveling and that it was only a matter of time before something snapped.

"She destroyed your partner," she cried as the full horror of what the papers meant dawned on her, "and now she's moving on to you. You could end up like him!"

Hugh fell into Michelle's arms and hugged her tightly, feeling her round belly pressing against him. Naturally, he had always known that there was a possibility—no, a *probability* that, one day, he would get tangled in a lawsuit. Ever since he was in medical school, he had heard residents whispering amongst themselves about 'those damned lawyers' and the unspeakable things they did. Sure, it was bound to happen . . .

But not *now*. Not *this* way.

His knuckles turned white from the injustice of it all. It just wasn't right! He had done absolutely *nothing* to deserve any of this. He was sure he had closely followed the standard of care when he had treated Julie. On the other hand, Bonehead had screwed up every step of the way and things had spun out of control. *He* was the guilty one, yet the Summons Hugh had received made no mention of any co-defendants. So, what was that damned orthopod doing now? Probably trembling with relief at the bullet he'd just dodged.

Hugh heard his wife's words echoing within his head.

She destroyed your partner and now she's moving on to you.

Suddenly, other words, more ancient ones, entered his mind as if a seismic quake had occurred deep within his memory—a command that had the power to span forty years.

Go to the Hall Chair, Montrose.

A cloud appeared from nowhere, passed overhead, and cast a giant shadow over the Montrose home. The air became ice cold, and he shivered.

CHAPTER 12

When Hugh stepped into the lobby of Moskowitz, Pursley & Boggs, forty-one floors above street level, he was stunned by its sheer size and opulence. The square footage between the elevator and the receptionist's desk alone was enough to swallow his entire clinic. Rich mahogany paneling covered the walls and antique oil paintings were illuminated by subtle spotlights recessed into the ceiling. Far to his left, a statue of a naked Greek goddess stood in an alcove of its own, her featureless white eyes watching a grand oak staircase that led to the floor below. To the right, plush couches provided a comfortable place where clients could quietly await their appointments.

"May I help you?"

A distant receptionist welcomed him with a big smile. He hiked across an acre of Italian marble and handed her a business card. "I'm Dr. Montrose. I have an appointment with Mr. Denmark . . . for the next *four hours.*"

"Oh, yes," she replied. "He's expecting you. Won't you have a seat?"

Hugh retreated to the waiting area. He gazed absent-mindedly at the priceless Persian rug at his feet. Curling tendrils and multi-colored flowers were woven into a deep burgundy background. The simple truth was that he didn't have four hours. He might not even have four *minutes.* When he had walked out of Columbia Medical Center only a short while ago, he was leaving a potential crisis in the hands of Dan Silver, who by now was the Chief Resident. An accountant had been carried into the ER after falling at work. He had cracked his skull against a concrete floor and lain unconscious for a few minutes. When he had first arrived at the hospital, he was awake, alert, and neurologically intact. A CT scan had shown that a small amount of air had leaked through a fracture in his skull; small bubbles were distributed over the surface of his brain, normally a harmless condition known as pneumocephalus. Over time, the air would normally be absorbed into his system and a full recovery could be expected.

The air in the accountant's head, however, had different plans.

Not long after his return from CT, he slid downhill. Initially, he had become confused and groped the nurses around him, calling them whores and ordering them to take their clothes off. Next, he spewed up his breakfast and his abusive speech became less coherent. By the time the Chief arrived to evaluate him, he was lapsing into unconsciousness.

Dan had called Hugh for advice, catching him as he was leaving the hospital parking lot for his lawyer appointment. "What the hell do I do?" he asked.

"Scan him again," Hugh replied.

"But he just came out of the scanner. Aside from a little air, everything looked okay."

"Something might have changed."

"What? You think he might have a new hemorrhage?"

"More likely a tension pneumocephalus."

"A *what*?"

"Tension pneumocephalus. You know what a tension pneumo*thorax* is, don't you?"

"Of course."

It was an unnecessary question to have asked; every medical student beyond third year knew the answer—air sucks into the chest through some wound that acts as a one-way valve, can't escape again, and the lung collapses under the building pressure.

"The same thing can happen to the head," Hugh explained. "Air accumulating inside the skull can compress the brain and cause the patient to slip into a coma."

Hugh had received confirmation of his suspicions as he was driving through snarled downtown traffic. The Chief called him in a frenzy and reported that the collection of air inside the patient's skull had indeed expanded, putting severe pressure on the brain from all directions and making it look shrunken.

"A walnut brain!" Hugh cried.

"Excuse me?"

"That's what it looks like, doesn't it—a shriveled up walnut inside its shell?"

"Well, I suppose it does . . ."

"Stick a tube into his head and let the air out," Hugh told Dan. "That'll allow his brain to re-expand."

"I've never done anything like that before."

"Nothing to it. Do it the same way you would do a ventriculostomy to drain spinal fluid. You've done millions of those. Aim for the largest collection of air. When you think you're in the right place, listen carefully. You'll hear his brain fart at you."

"His brain's going to *fart* at me?"

"That's right. If you don't listen closely, you might easily miss it. Good luck."

As Hugh recalled the events of the morning, he afforded himself a brief smile. Maybe the situation in the ER really wasn't very funny, but if he didn't have a sense of humor in this business, he would soon go insane.

Hugh looked out of the towering windows. At this time of morning, the sky was crystal clear. The sun was rising above the jagged Cascades in the east, casting long shadows across the foothills that lay outside the city. Mount Hood dwarfed all the other peaks, a beacon of grace whose glacial slopes rose steeply upwards and converged towards a snowy summit. A couple of fluffy contrails were lazily intertwined in the stratosphere above it, the signatures of aircraft carrying travelers to distant cities.

Hugh saw none of this. He fixed his eyes on the complex of beige buildings that made up Columbia Medical Center and imagined his Chief Resident laboring deep within its bowels, trying hard to save his patient's life by making his brain fart.

"Hugh Montrose?"

Hugh turned around and recognized Denmark from the time he had defended Richard more than a year ago. "Yes?"

"Hi. I'm John Denmark. Very pleased to meet you."

They shook hands.

"Come to my office. We can talk there."

Hugh followed the lawyer through a rabbit warren of secretary's desks, bookshelves, conference rooms, and filing cabinets. They entered a spacious corner office with windows along two of the walls, affording spectacular vistas to the west and north. Hugh thought of his own hovel with its beautiful vista of a brick wall across the alley. No matter, he reassured himself; he would rather be a neurosurgeon with a brick wall for a view than a lawyer with downtown Portland and the Columbia River at his feet. In any case, nothing compared with the views he was afforded in the operating room.

"Thank you very much for coming this morning," said Denmark. "We have a lot to talk about. But first, may I offer you a drink? Coffee?"

"No, thank you. I don't drink coffee."

"Tea?"

"I don't drink tea either."

"Orange juice then?"

"Nothing, thank you."

"I'll get something just for myself then. Make yourself at home and I'll be back in a minute."

While Denmark was away, Hugh's attention wandered to the city below. The highways below were filled with cars. There were so *many* of them, probably all filled with ambitious lawyers, jostling with each other in order to get ahead. The sidewalks were busy with the same people hurrying to their offices. He looked through the windows of the surrounding skyscrapers and saw them arriving at their desks, hanging up their coats and turning on their computers . . . faceless, nameless, and depressing in their countless numbers.

Suddenly weary of the view, Hugh nosed around Denmark's office. Several photographs showed him holding up one kind of dead fish or another while he mugged for the camera. A trophy fish stood on top of a bookshelf and a couple of rods were discreetly standing behind the door.

So, his lawyer was a man who liked to fish.

Hugh *hated* fishing.

Then Hugh noticed an unusual piece of furniture sitting in a corner: a podium, only this one had small wheels so it could be pushed around with the minimum of effort. He went over to it and nudged it gently with his fingers. It felt solid and heavy, yet shifted easily.

"It was a gift to me from a professor in law school about twenty-five years ago," said Denmark, returning with a can of orange juice in one hand and an apple in the other. "I never go to trial without it. Call it a good luck charm or a security blanket, or whatever. . . . Its smooth, dark wood has a profound calming effect on me whenever things get tough. My podium and my notes; two things I really depend upon in a courtroom."

"Your notes?"

"It seems like my memory sometimes fails me as I grow older. Concepts are pretty easy for me, but it's the nit-picking details that don't stick too easily. So I take detailed notes with me to court, all the questions I plan to ask, the case history I need to refer to . . . that sort of stuff. As long as I have my podium and my notes, I'll be okay."

Hugh could relate. There were things he depended on in the operating room too: his magnifying loupes, headlight, and an old pair of gym shoes. Without them, he wouldn't feel as secure either.

Denmark sat behind his desk and Hugh made himself comfortable opposite him. "SPI called me recently about representing you in this lawsuit," he said, biting into his apple. "I told them I was far too busy and couldn't possibly take it."

"So, what am I doing here, then?"

"I was just about to hang up when they happened to mention who the plaintiffs' attorney was."

"Maxine Doggett?"

"That's right. Maxine Doggett—*The Dog*." Denmark spat out her name as if his apple was rotten and full of worms.

"Appropriate name for her."

"She's known by many others. If you ask me, she's the most indecent, amoral woman I've ever known, the kind of creepy lawyer who gives us all a bad name; a disgrace to the legal profession. Even her fellow trial lawyers hate her, and for good reason: she believes she's in a special class of her own and is always trying to prove it. Personally, I think she's possessed by demons."

"Aren't you being a little soft on her?" asked Hugh.

Obviously, for Denmark, Maxine Doggett was no joking matter; he didn't even crack a smile. "I've been battling that bitch off and on for twenty years," he continued, looking grim.

"Whenever we have faced off in the courtroom, she always beats me. Every time!"

"Oh, great. That's encouraging."

"The last time I clashed with her, I was defending your partner, Richard Forrester."

"And lost that one too."

Denmark scowled and threw his apple into a waste paper basket. "Quite right," he said. "And we lost the appeal too. You should have seen some of the things she did. Unbelievable! The judge was too blind to notice and she got away with her sordid little tricks every time. I swore on my mother's grave I'd get my revenge, so when SPI told me the other day that she was involved in your case, I had no choice but to accept their offer. I shunted all my other work elsewhere and cleared my desk for you."

"I'm flattered to death."

"Simply winning your case wouldn't be enough to satisfy me," continued Denmark, looking at Hugh with fire in his eyes. "My dream is to beat her so badly, she'll crawl back to her kennel with her tail between her legs and never come out again."

"What makes you think you can win this time," Hugh asked, "when you've always failed in the past?"

"I've got more experience now," replied Denmark, his eyes growing cool and distant as his mind returned to the past. "I know her better than anybody else and can anticipate her every move. A new opponent would get creamed. At least I might have a fighting chance."

Hugh wasn't convinced. He sighed and said, "I'm sure you were able to free up a lot of your own valuable time for my defense, but I'm afraid I'm not afforded the same luxury. You *must* get rid of this lawsuit for me, quickly and quietly. There are far too many sick people who depend on me. Coming here today has caused a great deal of inconvenience at the hospital. As a matter of fact, there's a patient in the ER right now——"

Denmark chuckled.

"What's so funny?"

"It's refreshing to meet somebody so naïve as yourself. I've always believed there's such thing as innocence in this world, and you're *it*."

"I'm not so innocent, you know. I've seen plenty in my time."

"Perhaps in an operating room, but not in a courtroom. You have no idea what kind of trouble you're in."

Hugh felt a tinge of warmth rising in his face. "What do you mean?"

"This isn't some puny wound infection, you know." Denmark leaned forward and stabbed a finger at Hugh. "*You've* been accused of negligence by a quadriplegic."

"So?"

"Quads always win their cases."

"Are you telling me you can't make this case go away?"

"That's exactly what I'm telling you." Denmark eased back into his chair and locked his hands behind his head. "This is big. *Really* big. The Dog's not going to let go of you until she's chewed your bones into little pieces. Over the next couple of years you'll spend a great deal of your time with me."

"I don't have time," Hugh protested. "What do you want me to do? Tell somebody with a brain hemorrhage that I'm meeting with my lawyer and to come back next week, *if* they survive that long?"

Denmark looked unconvinced. "Your colleagues will have to cover you."

"I only have three of them: Richard Forrester, Dr. Morton, and Dr. Lumsden. When Richard was forced to run the gauntlet at the Multnomah County Courthouse, he quit working; he couldn't defend himself in court and expect to care for patients at the same time. It was too stressful. The rest of us picked up the slack. I'll be honest with you: we barely made it. Or, perhaps, it would be more accurate to say the *patients* barely made it. Elective operations had to be put off for a month or two. Some emergency cases were done by the junior residents without supervision. Mistakes were made. Once or twice, I thought somebody was going to die. It got really ugly."

"I'm sorry to hear it."

At this moment, Hugh's pager erupted. He checked the numbers on the LCD, then threw up his arms in exasperation. "This is the perfect example of what I was talking about. There's a crisis going on in the Emergency Room right now and I'm sitting here wasting my time with you instead of being at the hospital where I'm needed!"

"You can use my phone if you have to," said Denmark, nudging it across the desk.

Hugh dialed the ER's number was soon talking once again with Dan.

"I stuck a tube into that guy's head like you told me to," he said, his voice high-pitched and urgent. "I listened closely, like you said, but I didn't hear any goddamn farting. Now he's getting worse."

"What's he doing?"

"He won't wake up any more when I pinch him. He's lapsing into a coma. I don't know what else to do. You've got to come here and show me what to do!"

"Hang on a second." Hugh put his hand over the receiver, then addressing Denmark, he said, "I'm sorry, but we'll have to continue this meeting another time."

"If you must," said Denmark, rolling his eyes.

"I can come back next week."

"Something else will be going on. Something is *always* going on."

"But a man is *dying!*"

"Why don't you try to find somebody else to help your resident?"

Addressing the Chief who was waiting on the line, Hugh asked, "Isn't there some other help around? How about Dr. Forrester?"

"He's upstairs in the OR removing a rear-view mirror from somebody's brain."

"What's Dr. Morton doing?"

"He had to go to court for the day. He's a witness in a trial."

"And Dr. Lumsden?"

"He's also in the OR. He's starting a neck in a few minutes."

Hugh put his hand over the mouthpiece. "There's no other help," he said, addressing Denmark. Then he rose from his chair, still holding the phone in his hand. "I have to go. This is exactly what happened when Richard was on trial. We were scrambling to cover the service every day for three weeks. Why can't lawyers pick on somebody else for a change and leave physicians alone so we can do our jobs?"

"Go, then," said Denmark with an air of resignation. "You'll be paying a heavy price, though."

"Money! It always comes down to money, doesn't it? That's all lawyers can think about. Well, not everybody thinks the same way. I don't give a damn about money." Then, he shouted into the phone: "Hang in there, Dan! I'm on my way over!" He hung up and bolted for the office door. He was just stepping out when he heard Denmark's voice behind him, clear and persistent.

"You don't care about money? Not even . . . fourteen million dollars?"

Hugh froze. *"What* did you say?"

"Is fourteen million dollars unimportant to you? I ask only because that's how much the Winters are demanding from you."

"Fourteen million?"

"That's right. I have the plaintiff's statement of damages right here." Denmark picked up a document from his desk and read from it. "$1.2 million for past economic damages—things like her medical bills, in-home care services, equipment, and so on. $4 million for future economic damages. By the way, that includes $120,000 for a wheelchair-accessible RV."

"A *what?*"

"You heard me correctly. Apparently, the Winters are camping enthusiasts who would like to hit the road again. Non-economic damages add up to $9 million. $7.5 million for Julie's grief, sadness, pain and suffering, anguish, emotional distress, depression, disability, disfigurement, and loss of enjoyment of life. $1.5 million for Gary's own grief, sadness, pain and suffering, anguish, emotional distress, depression, loss of enjoyment of life and loss of spousal consortium due to his wife's quadriplegic condition, blah, blah, blah—"

"Spousal consortium? What's that?"

"The right of a husband to enjoy the conjugal affections of his wife."

"You mean sex?"

"You could put it that way if you wish."

"They've put a dollar value on *sex?*"

"Everything has a dollar value. It's all here on the plaintiff's statement of damages. Take a look for yourself."

Denmark tossed the document onto his desk. This gesture

had the effect of sucking Hugh back into the office. He picked it up, started reading, and soon forgot all about farting brains in the ER.

"I don't *have* fourteen million dollars. My malpractice policy has a maximum of one million dollars per occurrence."

"If the jury ends up agreeing with the plaintiffs, looks like you're going to come up a little short, doesn't it?" said Denmark. "You'll have to pay the rest out of your personal assets. Your home and everything inside it will be sold and your wages will be garnished to force you to make payments to the plaintiffs for the rest of your life, just like Richard. While you and your family are living in some shack down by the railroad tracks, you can think of the Winters touring the country in their brand new wheelchair-accessible RV."

The air in the office suddenly felt stifling. Hugh searched for some sign of amusement in his attorney's face—any hint that this might be a joke, but those eyes across the desk from him remained deadly serious.

"You don't look well," Denmark observed. "Are you sure you wouldn't like some orange juice?"

"Yes . . . Actually, no . . . Yes, I'll have some, please. I'm suddenly very thirsty."

While Denmark made another trip to the corporate refrigerator, Hugh suddenly remembered the patient in the ER and urgently called Surgery at Columbia. Yes, Lumsden's patient had just been taken back to the room. No, she wasn't asleep yet. Yes, we can page him for you. Moments later, Hugh was begging his partner to postpone his case and to help Dan with the pneumocephalus problem.

"But my patient's on the table. They're about to put her to sleep!"

"I'm sorry, but this is very important."

"She's an emotional woman. She'll freak out. I wouldn't blame her either. How would you like it if somebody yanked you off the operating table just as you're about to go under anesthesia?"

"I'll talk to her later and apologize," said Hugh. "I'll try to explain everything so she'll understand."

After some persuasion, Lumsden reluctantly agreed to abort his case.

When Denmark returned, Hugh took a can of orange juice from him, popped open the top, and drank deeply. "I handled the problem at the hospital," he mumbled, wiping his lips with the back of his hand.

"Good," said Denmark, showing his appreciation with a smile. "I was quite certain you'd find a way. Nobody's *that* indispensable—not even you. You might be a big shot at Columbia Medical Center, but in a courtroom you're just another two-bit defendant. It's time to bury your ego and do everything I tell you."

"But why are they suing *me*?" asked Hugh, his voice sounding dangerously close to a whine. "The risks of early surgery easily outweighed the potential benefits. I knew there was no chance I was going to make her any better. I could have made her totally paralyzed and dependent on a ventilator for the rest of her life. It wasn't a hard decision for me to make. Anybody else would have done the same thing."

"Maxine must have gotten her hands on an expert witness who'll testify that your decision was wrong; you were negligent and did exactly the opposite of what you should have done. Had you operated on her right away, she would no longer be paralyzed now."

"That's bullshit!" Hugh exploded. "The tumor had destroyed her spinal cord more than twelve hours earlier. I can't bring the dead back to life. Nobody can!"

Denmark was unperturbed by the outburst. "Maxine's expert will do his best to raise as many questions in the minds of the jurors as possible," he explained calmly. "Maybe it *hadn't* really destroyed her cord, maybe Julie *wasn't* completely quadriplegic, maybe you performed a substandard neurological examination. He'll make it sound as if you weren't even willing to give her a chance. You went home and had a nice evening with your family while your patient's *reversible* paralysis became an *irreversible* one. Then you sat around, delayed for a couple of days, and only operated on her after it was too late."

"This is ludicrous! He would be twisting the truth. It was not that way at all!"

"These days, expert witness testimony has nothing to do with the truth," said Denmark. "Everybody knows that."

Hugh sank into a chair, weary and beaten. For the next four hours, he pored over the case against him with his lawyer, dissecting it as if it was a complex tumor. First, they scoured Julie Winter's medical records from the offices of Clegg, Montrose, and her primary care physician, as well as the ones from Columbia Medical Center. Every line on every page was examined closely. Where the handwriting was illegible, a magnifying glass was used to clarify the scrawl. Even the unwritten words between the lines were sniffed out, their meaning interpreted, noted down, and stored away. Hugh protested when he thought that Denmark was carrying things to an extreme, but was curtly told that any lawyer who didn't know the medical record backwards, forwards, and inside out wasn't doing his job to the best of his ability. Not until he had attained a thorough understanding of the way events had been documented did Denmark gather the two-foot high mountain of papers together and return them to their box.

Next, they covered the anatomy, physiology, and pathology of spinal cord tumors. Denmark had obviously done his homework for he was already familiar with many of the basic scientific facts. With the help of a plastic model of the spine, he broadened his knowledge, inspecting the bones from every angle and asking Hugh to show him all the important structures. He was impressed by how small the cervical spinal canal was—a little more than a centimeter from front to back at its most narrow point—and how easily a spinal cord would be compressed by a growing tumor. He wanted to know everything about the swelling on the MRI—how it got there and the part it played in Hugh's decisions. This was Denmark's first opportunity to ask questions of a neurosurgeon and he had hundreds of them. What kind of spinal cord tumors were there? Were they benign or malignant? Could you tell the difference from looking at the MRI, and, if so, how? What kind of symptoms do they produce? What can one find when one examines patients with these tumors? When do you decide to take them out? How do you take them out? What are the potential complications?

How? What? Why? The questions never ended and Hugh did his best to fill the gaps in his lawyer's knowledge. Using the model, he showed Denmark how the operation was performed, pointing at the bones with a pencil and demonstrating which ones were removed. By noon, Hugh was having difficulty focusing.

"You've had enough for one day, haven't you?" said Denmark.

"I'm exhausted," Hugh admitted.

"Maybe it's time we wrapped this up. Go and see your patient in the Emergency Room."

Hugh smiled, but there was no amusement behind his eyes. "It's a little late for that now. Either Lumsden saved him or he's already dead."

The latter possibility didn't seem to bother Denmark. "I'm sorry I was rough on you earlier," he said, "but I had to make you understand that things are different now. You're no longer in control. There are other forces in your life now—unfamiliar forces, more powerful than you could ever imagine. You can't fight them. You have to learn to bend or you'll break in the middle."

Hugh thought of Richard, lowered his eyes, and nodded his head in submission.

When he was finally dismissed, he headed straight for the elevator. Once he reached his car, he called Trish at his office.

"Cancel my afternoon clinic."

"You—you can't do that!"

"I have to go home."

"But you're fully booked!"

"I know."

"Some of these people have been waiting ages to see you. They've traveled long distances."

"Right now, I want to be with my wife. Reschedule everybody."

"What should I tell them?"

"Tell them I'm sorry for the inconvenience."

"Sorry?"

"*Very* sorry."

"Yes, sir."

Hugh hung up and nursed his wounds. He had never canceled his clinic on such short notice before. It was an unkind thing to do; many of his poor patients were in devilish pain and believed their appointments to be desperately important.

For the first time in his neurosurgical career, Hugh was going to put himself first.

He turned the ignition and headed for home, and Michelle.

CHAPTER 13

Dr. Robert Bull was fifty-seven years old, graying, over-weight, out of shape, yet his neurosurgical practice in the sub-urbs of Portland was widely recognized as one of the most prosperous in the state, having an extensive referral network of primary care physicians, a waiting room that was constantly packed, and a weekly list of cases that was every surgeon's envy. All that changed in the late 1990's when he became the target of two ludicrous lawsuits. Both led to trials that he eventually won, but he was an emotional man who didn't bend very well under the voracities of the American legal system. Instead of picking himself up and dusting himself off as he was supposed to, he started drinking heavily, then separated from his wife, and finally hit rock bottom when he attempted to hang himself from the overhead lights in an operating room. Recognizing that he would never survive if he remained in Oregon, he closed the doors to his practice one sunny morning in 2000 and joined the ranks of tort refugees that roamed the country looking for a friendlier place to work.

Bull was welcomed in Indiana where the citizens had enact-ed liability reform and the lawsuit climate was less tempestuous. He started a hospital-based practice and within three years he had stopped drinking and was once again shoe-horning patients into the surgery schedule. His success could be attributed to the three A's: affability, availability, and ability, all of which he pos-sessed in abundance. Of the three, the first, affability, was by far the most important. In practical terms, it meant foregoing the pressures of medical practice and spending extra time with his patients, giving them reasons to be optimistic and fully answering their questions. The primary care physicians, the source for most of those patients, also had to be coddled. He visited all the clinics within a fifty mile radius of the hospital and met all the doctors he could find, putting faces to names. He explained that it was his job to fulfill their neurosurgical needs whenever they arose and promised to see their patients promptly, sometimes even on the same day if they were in severe pain.

Once they saw how well things were working out, the administrators at his new hospital congratulated themselves for recruiting this man from Oregon. They had looked beyond his alcoholism and paid attention to his attributes as a person and a neurosurgeon. They were sure that incidents in the past would remain in the past, and from their point of view, their gain had been somebody else's loss.

Bull's peaceful way of life was interrupted in late 2003 when he received a phone call from John Denmark. The lawyer introduced himself and explained that an important case had come up: a woman had been paralyzed by a tumor in her spinal cord and a Portland neurosurgeon was being accused of being negligent in her care. Would he mind being the principle expert witness for the defense?

Bull had responded by using some colorful language and almost hanging up on Denmark. No—there was no way he would consider being anybody's neurosurgical expert witness, especially in Portland, even if it *was* on behalf of the defense. The years he lived there had been the worst ones of his entire life. Wild horses couldn't drag him back if he was required to testify in a trial. As he talked, he could feel his blood rising to his face.

Denmark had patiently listened while Bull had vented his feelings, then, after he was completely finished, had quietly told him that the defendant was none other than his old friend, Hugh Montrose.

The tone in Bull's voice had abruptly changed from seething anger to intense concern. "Hugh's in trouble?"

"Yes, he is," replied Denmark simply.

"Tell me how I can help," said Bull without any hesitation. Hugh Montrose had been a thoroughly decent friend and colleague, one of the few people who had stuck by him while the trial lawyers had torn him to shreds.

When the package of medical records had arrived, Bull saw its return address label and shuddered. The familiar red and green logo of the Moscowitz, Pursley & Boggs law firm seared into the emotional centers of his brain like a scalpel, stirring half-forgotten feelings of fear and humiliation. How he had dreaded receiving mail from his attorneys during those years he was defending himself in Portland! Every time he had ripped open an envelope from them, he imagined the worst and his heart had thudded inside his chest.

Bull dumped the package into the furthest corner of his office and promised himself he'd deal with it soon.

Two weeks passed and he did nothing.

He received another phone call from Moscowitz, Pursley & Boggs, this time from a tiresome secretary. Had he reviewed the records yet?

"I'll start on it tomorrow," he replied, then quickly hung up.

Bull kicked the box a little nearer to his desk, but still didn't have the courage to open it. In its new position on the floor, however, he could not ignore it so easily and found himself distracted whenever there was work to be done.

The secretary called again after another couple of weeks.

"Half way through," he told her, then shifted the box even nearer. Now it figured prominently in his field of vision and began to give him headaches.

As the days passed, the secretary bugged him again and again, and the box took more tentative steps across the floor. The closer it came, the more he stared warily at it, until the desire to throw its contents into the shredder was almost over-powering. When his headaches became intolerable and he was beginning to crave a drink, he decided to get the ghastly task over and done with. He opened the box, dipped his trembling hands inside, and lifted out the top folder.

The quad's name was Julie Winter. Aside from prenatal care for her two children, there wasn't much in her primary physician's notes: pelvic exams with Pap smears, a couple of minor cuts that required stitches, and an episode of cystitis. When she started having back pain, she was referred to Bruno Clegg. Bull remembered the orthopod from the days he worked at Columbia and was hardly surprised that he was involved. The man was a clod who cared only about himself. He tossed the top folder aside and went on to the next.

The file from Dr. Clegg's office was much thicker. Bull read through all the clinic dictations, letters between the various doctors, a very long, rambling one from Clegg to the primary care doctor, a wad of lab results and X-ray reports, physical therapy narratives . . .

Then, after an hour of careful perusing, something caught his eye.

It was a small scrap of paper, a copy of a lab slip reporting the chemical analysis of the spinal fluid from her myelogram.

Patient Julie Winter. Cerebral Spinal Fluid Protein: 140

Normal Range: 15 – 45

140! Almost three times the upper limit of normal! Bull wondered what Clegg had thought about that. He carefully searched through the pages, but found no reference to it.

He pushed away the papers and leaned back in his chair.

A CSF protein above one hundred in a healthy patient without symptoms strongly suggested a tumor growing in the spinal cord or the brain. At the very least, a thorough work-up was required, yet there was no evidence Clegg had even seen the result.

Bull picked up a phone and dialed a number that he read on the outside of the box. He was connected to Denmark.

"I found something," he announced.

"What?"

"Something important."

"*What?*"

"Clegg ordered a lumbar myelogram on Mrs. Winter in 2001, just before her operation."

"I already know that," said Denmark, sounding disappointed.

"There's more," said Bull quickly. "Radiologists will often draw off spinal fluid and send it to the lab for routine analysis. That's what they did in her case. The level of protein in the CSF was more than three times the upper limit of normal."

"I didn't know *that*," said Denmark, his interest piqued. "What does it mean?"

"It's strong evidence that she had a tumor in her spinal cord," explained Bull. "Clegg should have known about it before he operated, but I've been through the record several times and there's no evidence he did."

Denmark drew in a sharp breath. "Wow! This is big!"

"Yup—it looks like Clegg missed the diagnosis," continued Bull.

"You mean he screwed up?"

"Big time. A neurosurgeon could have operated on her spinal cord to remove the tumor and maybe she wouldn't be paralyzed now."

"This is really big!"

"Clegg is the one who should be the defendant in this case, not your client."

"This is *really, really* big!"

"Why didn't the plaintiffs' lawyer name him too?"

"I've no idea."

"Maybe she hasn't seen the lab slip," Bull suggested.

"She knows about it, all right," said Denmark. "That woman wouldn't overlook even the smallest detail; she's too good. There must be some other explanation—a secret she's keeping from us." Denmark thanked Bull for his good investigative work and asked him to call back if he found anything else.

After he hung up, Bull gazed at his office ceiling for a few minutes. How wonderful it was to be safe within Indiana's borders! He had never regretted moving from Portland, especially at times like this when he learned what was happening to the poor sods he had left behind, people like Hugh Montrose. Whenever he heard about them, they always sounded so stressed, so unhappy, and, thank God, so far away.

With a sigh of relief at having finished his task, Bull threw all the files back into their box. He'd had enough of *Winter vs. Montrose*. Besides, it was almost three o'clock in the afternoon—time to go home. He carried the box back to the furthest corner of his office where it belonged and dumped it there. Then he left, closing his door firmly behind him.

CHAPTER 14

Hugh stood on Columbia Medical Center's helipad and nervously fingered the certified letter he held in his hand, worrying whether he was breaking the news to Richard in the best way. He had thought a distraction might help; he would tell him all about it when some head trauma patient needed their widely dispersed brain to be put back together again. That way, he might see that things *could* be worse and, *maybe*, he wouldn't get so upset. As if his plan was being approved by some unseen authority, an opportunity presented itself only a few hours after the letter's arrival. A young woman in eastern Oregon failed to completely kill herself when she pointed her boyfriend's gun at her temple and pulled the trigger. Thus reassured, Hugh called Richard and asked him to drop what he was doing and meet the incoming medevac flight with him.

Hugh had labored throughout the night in the operating room, draining rivers of green, foul-smelling pus from the brain of a dying drug addict. When he had been up to his knees in the thick of it, he had dreamed about escaping outside, breathing deeply and drawing fresh, clean air into his lungs. Now that he was standing under a clear morning sky, the case was all but forgotten. He clutched the letter tightly and cared only how he was going to spill the beans.

"So what's all this about?"

Hugh turned and saw Richard approaching. He was wearing scrubs and a white lab coat, and appeared overweight and out of shape. His long hair and beard were gone and his face was round and unfamiliar; he was no longer the robust, muscular *Conan the Barbarian* of the past, but a picture of living, breathing disillusionment and decline.

"A self-inflicted gunshot wound is coming from the other side of the mountains," Hugh explained. "It should be arriving soon."

"Oh, come now, Hugh," said Richard impatiently. "Since when do you pull me out of rounds so I can meet medevac flights with you at the helipad? You've got something else on your mind."

"Well, there *is* something . . ."

"Bad news, I suppose."

"I wanted to talk to you about this," said Hugh, brandishing the envelope in his hand. "It arrived from SPI today. They're . . ." His voice trailed off as his confidence drained away.

"Out with it," said Richard. "Nothing surprises me any longer."

"Well, they're giving us . . . the boot."

Hugh expected Richard to stiffen with shock and indignation. Instead, he simply shrugged as if it was news he had been expecting.

"Did you hear me?" asked Hugh, whipping a sheet of paper from the envelope and unfolding it with trembling fingers. "It's addressed to all four members of our group. Let me read you the important part. . . . *Please accept this letter as notification that, after a careful review of your underwriting file and claims experience, your policy referenced above will not be renewed for another year.*"

Richard cast his eyes down and thrust his hands into the pockets of his lab coat.

"Aren't you going to say anything?" said Hugh, taking a step closer and looking up enquiringly into his friend's face.

"What do you want me to say?"

"You could at least start yelling, cursing, or *something*. Getting dropped by our insurance company is the worst thing that could have happened to us."

"I don't see how it really matters any more."

"What's wrong with you?" demanded Hugh. "This is the sort of thing that would have turned you into a raving maniac in the past. Can't you get up a head of steam any more? Your trial and my lawsuit, the only times our group has ever filed any claims with our insurance company, and *this* is what they do to us!"

"Apparently, they were enough to make us a bad risk."

"But I haven't even been found guilty of anything yet!" cried Hugh.

"Makes no difference whether you're guilty, or not. SPI is only estimating how much we're going to cost them in the future and they obviously don't like the numbers they're seeing. They've made up their minds to get rid of us and nothing is going to change their mind."

"Where *the hell* are we going to find new insurance?" said Hugh, speaking loud enough to draw the attention of some orderlies and nurses who had started to gather nearby. He grinned sheepishly and waved at them to be sure they weren't left with the impression that he and Richard were arguing, then lowered his voice. "Look—Grand National is the only other company in this state that still offers medical malpractice, and *they've* just announced they're not taking any new clients due to so-called 'dire financial conditions'. We'll have to enter the high risk insurance pool, and that'll be extremely expensive."

"Do our other partners know about this yet?" asked Richard.

"Yes. Lumsden went berserk, as I predicted he would. After his nitroglycerine kicked in, he announced his immediate retirement. Morton is abandoning ship too. He found a job in California and will be moving there by the end of the year."

Richard flicked a pebble off the helipad with his foot and sent it flying into some nearby bushes. "Nothing will ever be the same after this," he muttered. "Sooner or later, you'll be the only one left."

"And what about you?" said Hugh, anxiously searching Richard's eyes. "You're not going anywhere, are you? You can't leave me here. I'll never survive on my own."

"I have no immediate plans to go," said Richard. "But it's only a matter of time before something happens."

"Like what?" asked Hugh. "What'll happen?"

"I wish I knew, Hugh. I wish I knew."

The Bell 206-L-I medevac helicopter was heard before it was seen. First, there was a deep *wop-wop-wop* as its rotor blades beat the air at two thousand feet, keeping it aloft and moving forward at a hundred and fifty knots. Over a couple of minutes, the noise became louder and more persistent until Hugh could discern a tiny black dot hanging in the sky to the east. Initially, it didn't appear to be moving at all, but as the roar of the engines continued their crescendo, the distant helicopter grew larger and lost altitude. It changed from black to a familiar red and white, and when it was close enough, bold letters could be deciphered along its side: TRAUMA I. The reception committee of order-lies and nurses now huddled together with their hands over their ears as the noisy machine hovered above, whipping up a vicious windstorm and propelling clouds of dust into the air. It settled onto its skids and the high-pitched scream of the turbojets died away. When the rotor blades had stopped moving, the group approached the helicopter. A side-door opened and a flight nurse clambered out.

A few minutes later, the patient was wheeled past, tightly strapped onto a gurney with only her head poking outside the blankets. Hugh saw swollen, purple eyes that resembled large plums and skin white as chalk. A blood-drenched Ace bandage was tightly wrapped around her head and an endotracheal tube had been inserted into her airway. A bag of blood was hanging from an IV pole. The flight nurse was squeezing a rubber bag in the shape of a football, forcing air into her lungs and making a loud sucking sound every time she released her grip.

"How's she doing?" Hugh asked.

"Not so good, I'm afraid," she shouted over the noise of the helicopter. "Shot herself a couple of hours ago. Entrance wound, right temporal area. Exit wound midline, frontal vertex. The medics who picked her up couldn't stop talking about the dripping mess on the ceiling of her apartment. Her mother is a nurse, which is the only reason why she's still alive. The woman put a pressure dressing on the hole before her daughter bled to death. Be careful when you take it off. It's real bloody underneath. Here are her X-rays. There was enough time to get plain films and a CT scan while they were waiting for us to arrive."

Hugh took the package and tucked it under his arm. "What kind of condition is she in?"

"Surprisingly good, considering. She's making purposeful movements with her arms and legs but she won't follow any commands. Her pupils are difficult to assess. I tried prying open her eyes, but they're too swollen to see anything."

Once inside the Emergency Room, Hugh hung up the films while a swarm of medical personnel buzzed around the patient, extracting blood through some tubes, squeezing it in through others, poking, prodding, and preparing her for surgery. The plain films showed a shattered skull that looked as though an elephant had stepped on an egg shell. Fragments of metal were scattered throughout the frontal areas. The CT scan gave additional information such as the location of brain damage and blood clots. When he put everything together in his mind, Hugh could not muster much optimism.

"I used to really love neurosurgery," said Richard, materializing behind Hugh. He was gazing at the pictures with a distant look in his eyes. "Just look at it: the skull in a million pieces, dead brain everywhere, buckets of blood. . . . I would charge into the middle of it all with nothing more than a sucker and a bipolar and track the bullet into some distant corner of the skull. There's nothing like the sound that lead makes when it's dropped into a metal pan, you know . . . except, maybe, helping a patient claw their way back to life against impossible odds. This is the sort of case that used to make it all worthwhile. Now, I couldn't care less. My trial changed everything. *Everything!*"

"Come on, Richard," said Hugh. "Why don't you try to forget about your trial? Wallowing in your grief won't change things." He left the X-ray viewing area and returned to the patient's side. He bent over and started to examine her.

Richard followed closely. "I *can't* forget it," he said. "Everywhere I go, I'm thinking of the same thing: how everything was perfect and now it's ruined . . . how I was happy and now I'm always depressed. There was a time when I liked my patients. Now, I hate them! I was talking with Trish the other day and called one of them dog shit."

"*Dog shit?*"

"Yeah. Can you believe it? I have a patient who I operated on for a ruptured disc years ago. Now he has chronic back pain. Keeps coming to see me every three months even though there's nothing I can do for him. When he talks to me about his problems, he sounds like a broken record. I sound like one too. We're both saying the same things over and over again to each other, but neither of us is listening. I told Trish it was as though I had stepped in some dog shit and now I can't get it off my shoe."

Hugh slipped on a pair of gloves and slowly, carefully unwrapped the Ace bandages. When he removed the last of them, he saw two wads of gauze dressing pressed against the patient's head, one at the entrance wound on the side and the other at the top where the exit wound was located. He gently exposed the entrance wound first and noticed the powder burns. Liquefied brain matter was oozing out—mushroom soup straight from the can.

"What kind of way is that to talk about another human being?" Richard continued. "I've never called any of my patients dog shit before."

Hugh gently lifted up the other gauze and cautiously peered underneath. He was met by a vigorous flood of dark red blood that ran over the young woman's face and dripped onto the sheets. Hugh hastily replaced the gauze and applied some pressure.

"Listen, Richard," he said, compressing the gauze with his finger. "This kid's in big trouble. The bullet has obviously ripped up her sagittal sinus. Certainly looks like it on the X-rays. Why else would she be bleeding so much? I could use some help in the OR. You're not busy, are you? Besides, it'll help keep your mind off things."

Richard's eyes grew larger and he furtively glanced from side to side. "I don't know about that, Hugh," he said quietly. "I've been trying to avoid that place lately."

"Avoiding the operating room?" said Hugh incredulously. "Why on earth—"

Richard put his fingers to his lips. "Shh! Not so loud!"

Hugh was startled, then decided to humor his friend. "Is this better?" he whispered.

"The OR is no longer our sanctuary," explained Richard. "An alien force has found a way in. Things are going on that we couldn't even imagine—"

"An alien force? What are you talking about?"

"Can't you guess? Something dark and evil."

"Darth Vader?"

"This is no joking matter!" retorted Richard, his face flushing with anger. "Nothing you say or do is private any more. She's watching every move you make."

"*Who's* watching?"

"*She* is!"

Hugh sighed. Richard had seemed as docile as a lamb when he learned of his medical malpractice insurance crisis, yet had become as inflamed as an abscess when talking about something as simple as stepping into an operating room. He wanted to understand him better, but this was neither the time nor the place to get into a discussion who 'she' was, although he could venture a guess. "Are you going to help me or not?" he finally asked.

Richard wrung his hands together. "I guess I'm not likely to get sued for holding a retractor, as long as I keep my mouth shut. I suppose I could do that."

"Good! That's a start." Then, addressing a nearby nurse, Hugh said, "Wrap her head with another Ace bandage. Keep it tight. Then make sure the blood bank knows to stay four units of blood ahead. We're in for a very messy operation. Get her up to the OR as quickly as you can. If you see any family, put them in the Quiet Room and tell them that things look bad. Okay?"

"Okay."

"Good." Then, giving Richard a reassuring smile and a friendly pat on the arm, he said, "Let's go to surgery."

The surgeon's lounge at Columbia Medical Center was identical to thousands of others in hospitals across the country: dictation booths along one wall, dingy couches along another, a television permanently tuned to CNN, and a coffee machine percolating in the corner. A framed copy of *Physician's Weekly* hung on the wall and a computer monitor sitting on a desk displayed labwork, X-rays, and medical records at the touch of a button. It was a place where surgeons put up their feet, exchanged news, and cracked jokes.

Hugh and Richard were silently sitting on a couch and waiting for their case to start, each immersed in his own thoughts. Richard was eating some cold, ketchup-drenched French fries he had found abandoned on the coffee table in front of him while Hugh stared at the front page of a newspaper, unable to read a word. He knew he should have been primarily concerned about the dangerous case ahead, but instead he was still fretting over that damned letter from SPI. He had known colleagues who had been forced into the high-risk insurance pool by frivolous claims and there were few happy endings. Most of them had left the state and had found jobs where they were appreciated more. Others had strong personal reasons for wanting to stay and had limped from one year to the next, trying to make ends meet while their premiums soared. They would hold out hope for an eventual return to the normal insurance market, but they would invariably succumb to the relentless pressures and would wind up penniless and broken.

Maybe the public didn't take much notice what was happening around them, but medical students and younger physicians certainly did. Why bother with a training program that was so long and rigorous when all one had to look forward to was a minefield of litigation, declining reimbursement, and possible bankruptcy? As critical as it was, neurosurgery had become a shrinking profession, with far fewer people entering it than leaving. Ten years before, there were over four thousand neurosurgeons in the country. Now, there were barely three thousand, and the numbers were dropping year after year.

Like the Spotted Owl, the Neurosurgeon had become an endangered species. *Unlike* the bird, though, nobody cared.

When the only other surgeon in the lounge stood up and left, Richard wiped some residual grease and ketchup off his face, leaned close to Hugh, and quietly said, "I swear I'm going to destroy that bitch, if it's the last thing I do!"

Hugh's image of a Spotted Owl poofed into a cloud of feathers and he put down his newspaper. "Are you talking about The Dog?" he asked.

"Shh! Keep your voice down! Things aren't safe here either. The walls have ears!"

Hugh glanced around and confirmed they were alone. "What are you—?"

"She destroyed me," said Richard, yanking foam rubber out of a hole in the couch. "Now, I'm going to do whatever it takes to destroy her."

"And just how are you going to do that?"

"I've been wrestling with that question for months but I can't seem to reach a satisfactory solution. Got any ideas?"

"You could become active in promoting tort reform in this state," said Hugh. "Join the people who are making a big political push to get things changed. A limit on non-economic damages would clip her wings."

"*Phooey!*" retorted Richard, throwing the couch innards into a corner. "They have good intentions but they're going about it in the wrong way. There's no way we're going to have tort reform by playing politics. We'll lose every time."

"How can you be so sure?"

"Come one, Hugh—the lawyers have given so much money to politicians over the years, they own the state legislature. For Christ's sake, half the politicians in Salem were hatched as lawyers before they became the snakes they are. They'll never pass any laws that'll hurt their own profession."

"Voters control politicians, not lawyers," said Hugh. "Once they realize how this issue affects *them*, no amount of lawyer money is going to make any difference. You'll see."

"Voters aren't going to come to their senses until it's too late," said Richard. "By then, neurosurgeons will be extinct and nobody will know how to take out a brain tumor any more. I've *got* to figure out a good way to muzzle that woman—something quick, effective, and outside the political process."

Those words—quick, effective, and outside the political process—appealed to Hugh. Nevertheless, he felt compelled to issue his friend a warning. "Don't do anything illegal," he said. "You'll end up in prison."

Richard suddenly stood up and walked over to a full-length mirror he had personally mounted on one of the lounge's walls some years before. In the old days, he would spend his down time between cases flexing, posing, and checking his appearance to make sure he always looked his best. Now he just stared at himself glumly, his shoulders slumped, his beer paunch protruding, and his scrub shirt hanging sloppily outside his pants. "Did you know that doctors aren't the only people who hate her? *Everybody* does."

"Like who?"

"Her employees, her colleagues . . ."

"How do you know that?"

Richard sighed, turned away from the gaunt man in the mirror, and resumed his seat on the couch. "Don't forget—I sat in the same courtroom as she did for three weeks. I watched the people around her: the legal assistants, secretaries, other lawyers. I could tell they all despised her from the way they looked at her. Obviously, they had to follow orders, but given half a chance, I'm sure they would have liked to murder her. Only one of them seems to give her any respect: some meathead called Carl Zeiger."

"Tall, beefy, with silver hair?"

"That's right. Do you know him?"

"I remember seeing him once. He accompanied Maxine to the Emergency Room when her aneurysm ruptured that night in '98. He told everybody he was her chief of security."

The conversation was interrupted by the overhead speaker. "Ready for lifting help, Room 5! Ready for lifting help!"

"Sounds like they're waiting for us," said Hugh.

"I'll join you in a minute," said Richard, reaching for another soggy French fry. "All this talk about Maxine Doggett has upset me. I'll stay here a while longer until I feel better."

"Whatever you say."

When Hugh reached Room 5, he started preparing for the operation; he crowned himself with his headlight and slipped on his loupes. "I hope you've got plenty of blood on standby," he said to the anesthesiologist, Tom Harrison, whose owlish eyes appeared even larger than usual as he labored to organize his tubes and monitors.

"We've got four units in the fridge outside."

"Better hang 'em high and start transfusing now. I've got a bad feeling about this one."

Bonnie was the circulator for this operation and Denise the scrub tech. They scurried around, preparing the case.

"Make sure the suction is good and strong," Hugh said to Bonnie. "We'll need everything the system can give us. Denise, attach big suckers to begin with. Okay?"

"Yes, sir."

Hugh was shaving the head when he looked up and spotted Richard standing outside the door, beckoning urgently through a small, square window. Hugh dropped what he was doing, joined him in the hallway outside, and was immediately hustled into an out-of-the-way corner.

"One of those people in there is a goddamned spy!" Richard hissed, jerking his head in the direction of Room 5 and looking at Hugh with fear in his eyes.

"Excuse me?"

"Tom Harrison . . . Bonnie . . . Denise . . ." Richard croaked. "One of them is a spy! Maybe all of them are! You've got to believe me!"

"What the hell are you talking about?"

Richard glanced towards Room 5 for an instant, then his eyes locked onto Hugh once again. "They're the same three people who were in the room when Dan Silver and I operated on Mr. Brown, the jerk who sued me. Nobody in the world knew that Dan accidentally opened up the wrong side of the head, except *them*."

"So who do you think they're spying for?"

"Maxine Doggett. Who else?"

"Oh, come on," said Hugh, rolling his eyes. "You're imagining things. You think that woman is behind everything that goes on around here. The Brown family probably asked one too many questions."

"No, the Browns loved me," said Richard, his broad chest heaving up and down. "When I saw them in my office afterwards for a follow-up visit, his family couldn't express enough gratitude. They even brought gifts! It was only later that they suddenly turned on me and hired a lawyer. I'm telling you: we have an honest-to-God spy in our operating room. Maybe they're *all* spies!"

"You're being paranoid. Why would they do something like that?"

"How should I know? Maybe she's got some kind of hold on them. I'm sorry, Hugh, but I'm not stepping into that room."

"You're not going to help me?"

"No!"

"Richard, I *need* you!"

"No, you don't," said Richard, gently pushing Hugh away and taking a step back. "You've done plenty of cases like this on your own without any problems. You got me involved only because you wanted to try and breathe new life into me. Well, I appreciate the effort, but it's not going to work."

"Richard . . ."

"Good-bye, Hugh."

Richard retreated, and Hugh watched him go.

First depression, now paranoia.

What was going to be next?

Hugh sighed, then reached for a scrub brush and bumped the water control under the sink with his knee.

CHAPTER 15

Manfred Horman was heavy and drenched in sweat. Maxine was relieved when he had finally finished his ritual of thrusting and grunting and rolled off her like a walrus sliding into a hole in the ice. Without him grinding her into the mattress, she could think more clearly and there was plenty on her mind. She drew the bedclothes over her nakedness and stared at the vaulted ceiling of her bedroom as if the answers to her throbbing questions could be found there.

For a while, Maxine's principle neurosurgical expert witness lay incapacitated beside her, panting, wheezing, and reeking of garlic. When he eventually caught his breath, Maxine felt compelled to say something before he fell asleep and started snoring, which was his custom once spent. There were important things to discuss and not a whole lot of time.

"You were terrific," she said, running her long red fingernails through his greasy grey hair.

A single lid cracked open and a dark brown eye ringed with yellowish plaques of fat looked at her with mocking disbelief. Then it fell shut again and the corners of Horman's purplish lips curled up in a cynical smile. "Maxine, I know you well enough by now to know when you're lying."

"I'm not—"

"Yes, you are. Don't deny it."

Maxine sighed. Flattery, obviously, was not going to work. "Okay," she conceded, abruptly withdrawing her fingernails from his hair and wiping them across the sheets to clean them.

"You're such a disgusting pig, Manfred. Every time I have to have sex with you, I wish you'd accept money for your expert testimony like everybody else does. Is that better?"

"That sounds more like the truth."

"How long have we been doing business, Manfred?"

"Years."

"How many cases?"

"Dozens."

"How much money?"

"Enough."

"So, be honest with me. Why the *hell* won't you testify against Defendant Montrose?"

Horman's eyes flickered open once again and he stared into the distance as if he was in deep concentration. Then he drew in a deep breath and bore down. A wet raspberry of remarkable amplitude and duration erupted under the covers and shook the bed. "As I've already told you," said Horman, releasing his breath and grinning his satisfaction, "I've carefully reviewed the case and he did exactly the right thing."

"What difference does *that* make?" asked Maxine, instinctively using her arms to press the bedclothes against the mattress in an effort to trap the toxic gases underneath. "You've testified against plenty of neurosurgeons before who did 'exactly the right thing'. Right and wrong has never stopped you from saying what I wanted you to say."

"This time it's different. I can't say anything outrageous under oath anymore, at least not for a while, or I'll get into trouble."

"Now *you're* the one who's lying," cried Maxine. "I know what it is: you've grown tired of me."

"Nonsense."

"Then why won't you be my expert anymore?"

"I don't mind being your expert. Just not against *him*."

"In God's name, why not?"

Horman sighed, then shifted onto his side so he could look more directly at Maxine. "Do you remember *Larson vs. Ferris*?" he asked, rubbing a swampy armpit as if it helped him think.

Maxine had a remarkable capacity to remember all her cases, as many of them as there were. David Larson was a four year old who was given a Superman costume for Halloween by his parents. Unfortunately, they didn't warn him not to try flying in it, so the poor little boy jumped out of a second story window and landed square on his head. The CT scan afterwards showed severe brain swelling and, two days later, he died. The Larsons eventually hired her to represent them in a lawsuit against the neurosurgeon involved because he didn't give the child any steroids. She had won the case, as usual: a stunning $1.7 million dollars in lost future wages and $12 million in non-economic damages.

"Yes, I remember that case," she said, absent-mindedly sniffing the air and checking for any leaks through the seal she had made with her arms.

"Dr. Ferris ended up killing himself, didn't he?"

"The man was emotionally disturbed."

"Not surprising, after what you put him through."

"Don't forget your part in it. You were my expert."

"I really went out on a limb for you that time," said Horman. "I falsely testified that if the steroids had been given, David Larson would have made a full recovery. After his suicide, some of Dr. Ferris' colleagues filed a formal complaint against me with CANS' Professional Conduct Committee. An investigation was carried out and a hearing was held three months ago. They concluded that my testimony was flagrantly unprofessional and recommended that the Board suspend my membership for a year."

"No!" cried Maxine, sitting bolt upright. In her consternation, she forgot about Horman's recent contribution to global warming and broke her seal between the mattress and the bedclothes. A powerful stink of rotten eggs wafted into the room.

"I'm afraid so, Maxine," said Horman, taking no notice. "The Board will almost certainly approve the committee's recommendation. Any more bogus testimony and I could be kicked out permanently."

"That's terrible!" said Maxine, reaching for an aerosol can that was standing on her bed table. She shook it hard, aimed it directly at Horman, and compressed the button on top with her forefinger.

"You think so?" he said, momentarily engulfed in a billowing cloud of lemon fragrance. He waved his arms about and the spray dissipated. "How do you think *I* feel? I gave up my practice long ago so I could make my living as an expert witness. If I'm suspended from CANS, even for only a year, my credibility will be severely damaged and I might have trouble marketing my services in the future. No, I'm afraid I have no choice but to play it straight, at least for a while. When things have settled down a bit, I'll have more freedom with what I say. But right now, I've got to be careful. I definitely cannot get involved against Hugh Montrose. It would be far too risky. You'll have to find somebody else to be your expert." Manfred swept the bedclothes off his body, stiffly climbed to his feet, and reached for his shirt.

"This is a disaster!" cried Maxine, returning the air freshener to its place on her bed table.

"Relax, my dear. I'm sure you'll find somebody else willing and able."

"But Montrose's defense lawyer has filed a motion for Summary Judgment. There's a hearing in a couple of weeks. If I can't come up with some kind of sworn declaration from a neurosurgeon by then, the whole case will get thrown out."

"What's so disastrous about that? There are plenty of other doctors you can sink your fangs into."

"I don't want other doctors! I want Montrose!"

Horman paused as he was fastening the buttons on his shirt and looked at Maxine as she sat naked on the bed, her breasts like two droopy fried eggs hanging from her chest. "Now you're sounding like a spoiled child. Is it something personal?"

"No, of course not. It's just that . . . I'm convinced this is the big chance I've been waiting for."

"Big chance to do what?"

"To prove that I'm . . ." Maxine's voice trailed away as she remembered that Horman was the world's biggest slug and would never understand the concept of a superstar. "Oh, never mind."

"If you're desperate," he said, returning his attention to his last button, "I know somebody you might be able to use on short notice."

"Who?"

"An acquaintance. But a word of caution: you have to be *really* desperate."

"A neurosurgeon?"

"Of course he's a neurosurgeon," replied Horman, now holding his underwear open in front of him and peering into them with a frown on his face. He shrugged, then pulled them up over his hairy buttocks and snapped the elastic band. "In fact, he's accomplished many things throughout his career: wrote an important textbook, did tons of research. Quite a legend actually. He called me recently; he saw my name on the internet and wanted to know more about being a professional expert witness. He's never done much testifying before but thinks it's the kind of thing that he might be good at. Apparently, he's marooned in some VA lab, missing all the attention he used to enjoy. Personally, I think he's the neurosurgical equivalent of Norma Desmond."

"Norma Desmond? Who's that?"

"You know—the old forgotten movie star in Sunset Boulevard, desperate to make her come-back. This guy was a star himself once, but he hasn't done doodle-squat in years. Testifying would be his chance to regain the limelight and win back the audience he once enjoyed in the old days. The witness chair would be his stage, the jury his audience."

"What's his name?"

"Professor Charles Mortimer."

While Horman was putting on his trousers, Maxine reached for her bed table once again. This time, she extracted a notebook from the top drawer.

Horman raised an eyebrow. "What's that?"

"My directory of expert witnesses."

"You keep one by your bed?"

"Sure. I always keep one close at hand. You never know when I might need somebody. Where does he work now?"

"At the St. Petersburg VA, Florida."

Maxine licked a forefinger and leafed through the pages, then snapped the book shut and returned it to the drawer. "I don't see his name," she said, disappointed.

"He wouldn't be in your silly directory. Like I said: he's never testified before. Spends most of his time doing research, although he's officially retired. He must be at least ninety years old by now."

"*Ninety?*"

"Maybe older. I don't know exactly."

"But that's too old!"

"No expert is perfect."

Maxine shook her head. "The jury's not going to like that. They want somebody who's actively practicing, not some relic with one foot in the grave."

Horman put a knot in his tie and smoothed the hair on either side of his head with the palms of his hands. "Maxine, you're not going to *have* a jury if you don't find an expert." Then, he leant over, planted a soppy kiss on Maxine's cheek, and treated her olfactory system to a potpourri of garlic, sweat, and lemons. "It's time for me to go. Same time in two weeks then?"

"I suppose so," said Maxine with a sigh.

With a little wave of his hand, Horman left.

The next morning, Maxine stood on a street corner in St. Petersburg, Florida, craning her neck at the gigantic VA hospital in front of her. Even though it was early in the day, the air was warm and a pleasant breeze rustled through the palm trees overhead. Any normal woman visiting from the cold, rainy Pacific Northwest might have relished the exotic tropical atmosphere and imagined that she was on vacation, but Maxine was focused like a laser on her mission and cared nothing for the scenery around her. She *had* to find an expert witness for her case against Hugh Montrose and swore not to return home until she had persuaded Mortimer to work for her.

Maxine crossed the street with her black elephant bag trailing behind her, its small wheels squeaking along the ground. No good lawyer should leave home without the little square case with its long handle, she'd always believed, and hers was filled with a copy of Julie's medical records. She swept into the main lobby of the hospital and approached a grisly veteran standing behind the information desk.

"I'm here to see Dr. Charles Mortimer. Would you inform him that Ms. Doggett has arrived?"

"Inform *who*?"

"Dr. Mortimer."

The man flipped through a directory, then adjusted the badge-spangled cap he was wearing and scratched his head. "I'm sorry. We don't have any Dr. Mortimer working here."

"Yes, you do. I checked with the neurosurgery office at the university only yesterday and they assured me that this is where I'd find him. Can you look through your book again, please?"

He did, but the name definitely wasn't there. "I'm not sure what to tell you, ma'am," he said. "Every physician in this hospital can be found in this book and I don't see his name. Try the neurosurgery office upstairs. They might have an idea where he can be found."

Maxine was given directions and found her way to the hospital's top floor. The windows were large and allowed in plenty of bright light. A plush carpet covered the floors and everything was clean, smelling of fresh paint. She found the correct office without any difficulty and asked a secretary about Dr. Mortimer.

"Dr. *Who*?"

God, not this again, she thought. "Mortimer! M-O-R-T-I-M-E-R. He's a neurosurgeon who's *supposed* to be famous; wrote *the* textbook on neurosurgery. Surely you know who he is."

"Mortimer, Mortimer . . ." said the secretary, tapping her forefinger against her lips and looking pensive. "The name sounds familiar . . ."

A young doctor wearing a short white lab coat stood up

from a nearby couch and approached. "Excuse me, I couldn't help overhearing. Are you looking for Dr. Mortimer?"

"Yes! Do *you* know where he is?"

"Hi, I'm Mark Smith, one of the neurosurgery residents here. And you are . . ."

"Maxine Doggett," she told him as they shook hands. "I'm a lawyer from Portland, Oregon, and I'm here to discuss a very important legal case with the professor. I was told by the neurosurgery office at the university that I might be able to find him here."

"Yes, he works in the sub-basement."

"Finally somebody who knows what's going on! Can you take me to see him?"

The resident suddenly looked uncertain of himself. "I'm not sure about that. I've never actually ventured down there myself. . . ."

"Please!"

"I suppose there always a first time."

"Thank you so much!"

They walked to the elevator together, Maxine's elephant bag following like an obedient dog. Once the doors closed, she turned to Mark and asked, "Why do you suppose so few people know where he works?"

"He rarely comes out of his lab," said Mark, punching an elevator button. "I've been here three years and I've only met him once."

"What's he doing down there?"

"Research, I'm told."

"What I mean is . . . why are his research facilities in the *sub*-basement? Surely somebody of his stature should be working on the top floor."

Mark snickered. "The sub-basement is the best place for Dr. Mortimer; everybody around here agreed on that a long time ago."

The 'BB' sign, the one below the 'B', lit up and the elevator doors opened. Maxine was now deep in the bowels of the VA. A cluster of pipes ran along the ceiling of the hallway and the humming sound of heavy machinery reverberated behind cinder block walls. Large bins on wheels were scattered around, some filled with laundry, others with bags of medical waste. She and her guide threaded through them and headed down a long, empty corridor. Here, the smell of garbage grew stronger and so she fished a scented handkerchief out of a pocket and held it to her nose.

"If I'm not mistaken, he's in here," said Mark, stopping in front of a low doorway. He knocked gently, then stepped back as if he was afraid of what he might find inside.

Presently, the door cracked open. "What do you want?" barked a voice from within.

"Dr. Mortimer, this is Mark Smith, one of the neurosurgery residents. I have somebody here who wants to talk to you."

"Who?"

"A lawyer by the name of Maxine Doggett."

"I don't have time to talk to lawyers. Tell her to buzz off."

Mark exchanged glances with Maxine before he continued. "But she came all the way from Portland, Oregon to see you. She says it's very important."

"I don't care. I'm busy."

Maxine stretched her neck, but was unable to catch a glimpse of Mortimer through the narrow opening. "Sir," she piped up, putting away her handkerchief, "my client is victim of medical negligence. She's quadriplegic and needs your help as an expert witness against the doctor who did it to her."

"Get somebody else."

"There isn't anybody else. Dr. Manfred Horman said you would be willing to help."

There was a pause. "Who?"

"Dr. Manfred Horman."

"Horman?"

"Yes. He said he's an acquaintance of yours. When I told him I couldn't find an expert witness to testify on my client's behalf, he gave me your name. *Please* don't turn me away. You're my last hope."

The door opened wide and for the first time Maxine could see Charles Mortimer. And he was *ancient*.

Indeed, he was so old, parts of him appeared to have already died. His small eyes were cold and lifeless. Ash colored skin sagged beneath them like wax on a hot day and wrinkled its way around a grim mouth. A patchwork of white stubble sprung from his jaw, some areas much rougher than others. Either he was too blind to shave himself properly or he had been using the same razor for months. The skin on his knobby hands was dry, discolored, and stretched tight like old parchment. The network of veins underneath bulged out prominently and his fingernails had a greenish hue.

Could that be *mold*? wondered Maxine with alarm.

Mortimer wiped his hands on a very dirty lab coat, leaving smears of what looked like blood, and tottered back into his room. He left the door open behind him—a gesture that Maxine interpreted as an invitation to enter. She briefly thanked Mark for his help and bid him goodbye. Then she followed Mortimer, wondering whether this trip might have been a big mistake after all.

The lab was small and was lit with fluorescent lamps that emitted a low electrical hum. Workbenches with black slate surfaces were lined against the walls and the shelves above them were heavily laden with glassware, instruments, and books. A strong smell of animals pervaded the atmosphere. She quickly identified its source as a cage full of mice sitting on a wooden table in the middle of the room. The little creatures were scurrying around, climbing on top of each other, and squeaking with agitation. Dr. Mortimer lowered himself onto a stool next to the table. Then he sat hunched over the cage and stared at the mice with an empty expression.

"Thank you very much for agreeing to see me," said Maxine, approaching him with her elephant bag in tow. It got stuck on some rubber hoses that lay on the floor and she grunted as she wrenched it free. "I can't tell you how much this means to my client. Manfred spoke very highly of you. He said you used to be a great neurosurgeon—"

"I *am* a great neurosurgeon."

"Oh, of course, how silly of me! He said you *are* a great neurosurgeon and that you were the obvious choice for an expert witness. Would you like to hear about the case? My client is a woman—"

Maxine suddenly sneezed. She produced the handkerchief once again and dabbed her nose.

"Excuse me," she said. "Her name is Julie Winter . . ."

Maxine rambled on, but Mortimer wasn't listening. He reached out with a trembling hand and opened the door to the cage. With a movement that was surprisingly quick, he grabbed a mouse and withdrew it, keeping a firm grip on the little bundle of black fur, kicking legs, and twitching whiskers. Then, with the same vacant look that never seemed to change, he picked up a large pair of scissors with his other hand and cut off its head. Maxine's voice trailed off and she watched in horror, her mouth agape. Even without its head, the mouse continued to wriggle. Little squirts of blood pumped out of its body and sprayed the table below. He dropped the dying body into a garbage can by his feet and popped the mouse's head into a beaker. Maxine saw that there were other heads already inside.

"What on earth are you *doing*?"

"Research," replied Mortimer, wiping his bloody fingers again on the front of his lab coat.

"But why do you have to cut—" another violent sneeze "—their little heads off?"

"I need their brains."

"What would anybody want to do with a mouse's brain?"

"I crush them and extract the juices so I can do experiments," he explained.

"But that's utterly *disgusting!*"

Mortimer said nothing and reached for the cage door.

Maxine tried to resume her description of the case, but the carnage in front of her was causing her to lose her train of thought and she repeated over and over again, between sniffles, how she was sure that Defendant Montrose was guilty of gross negligence. Privately, she wanted to run from this cadaver in front of her and return to the world of the living, but was prevented from doing so by the sure knowledge that failure to procure him would certainly mean the end of *Winter vs. Montrose*. So she suppressed her feelings and reaffirmed her mission to recruit Mortimer, mold and all, to her cause.

"Ms. Doggett," said Mortimer after hearing for the sixth time that Defendant Montrose was bound to lose, "there's no point telling me the facts of the case. As far as I'm concerned, they're not in the least bit important."

"The facts aren't important?"

"No."

When she took a moment to give it some thought, Maxine

found that she was unable to disagree with him. "So, how much money do you want?" she asked.

"Money?"

"Somebody as important as yourself should be adequately compensated for your testimony. I'm always very generous when it comes to fees, but in your special case I'll give you whatever you want. Just name your price. How about five hundred dollars an hour for reviewing the case? Five . . . no, ten thousand dollars a day for courtroom testimony? Would that be sufficient?"

"The money's not important either."

"The money's not important?"

"Ms. Doggett, do you have to repeat everything I say? I told you the money's not important. Isn't that enough?"

"I suppose it is," said Maxine, puzzled. She had never met an expert witness who didn't think the money was the most important thing in the world.

The blades of the scissors closed once again and another furry head dropped into the beaker. The remaining mice in the cage could see the executions and they became even more frenzied.

"If it's not the case or the money," said Maxine, "perhaps you wouldn't mind telling me what *is* important to you."

"Is there going to be a trial?" asked Mortimer, looking away from his work for the first time and appearing genuinely interested in the answer.

"Most likely yes."

"And I'll be required to testify in front of a jury?"

"Yes."

"And there will be lots of publicity?"

"Of course. This will be one of the most sensational medical malpractice trials ever. The public benches will be crammed. The press should have it well covered. Front pages stories every day, I expect."

"*That's* what I care about, if you must know, Ms. Doggett," said Mortimer. "Spectators, publicity . . . I want to be at the center of attention. Can it be arranged?"

"I believe so," said Maxine, although she had no clue how.

"Do I have your word?"

"If it means you'll be my expert witness."

"It does."

"So we have a deal!" said Maxine, then sneezed again.

"What's the matter with you?" asked Mortimer, returning his attention to the mice. He swept his fingers around the inside of the cage, trying to pin down his next victim. "Why are you sneezing all the time?"

"I'm sorry," said Maxine, wiping her eyes. "I have a mold allergy."

"There's no mold in here."

"No, of course not," said Maxine, eyeing Mortimer's green fingernails.

"You're disturbing the mice and making my work more difficult."

"I'm dreadfully sorry. I promise not to sneeze anymore."

Mortimer's hands had begun to shake now and the next mouse was not as fortunate as the others. Instead of simply beheading the poor creature, he cut it in half. This time, both pieces fell wriggling to the table.

"Damn! Now look you made me do!"

Maxine preferred not to. She turned away, appalled, while Mortimer's bloody fingers groped for the half that was still attached to the head.

"I've written a declaration," she said, keeping her eyes averted. She heard the crunching sound of a knife bearing down on the wooden table, separating bones and meat, and cringed. "I need you to read and sign it as soon as possible. The defense has filed a Motion for Summary Judgment and the hearing is scheduled for next week."

"I'll sign it before then."

"You'll also need to review the records." Maxine sneezed once more, although this time she made a supreme effort to contain herself. The pressure inside her head soared and her eyes momentarily bugged out. "I brought you a set of them," she added, wiping her nose with her handkerchief and jerking a thumb towards her elephant bag.

"Leave them on the desk over there."

When the sounds of mutilation paused, Maxine peeked at Mortimer. "I can't thank you enough for this. My client will be very grateful."

"Ms. Doggett, I don't give a damn about your client," he said. "So put your papers where I told you and leave me alone."

Then he wiped his bloody fingers on his lab coat once again and reached for another mouse.

CHAPTER 16

Richard Forrester wallowed in *The Raven's Nest,* his glassy eyes sucking in a buxom crumpet draped over the chair opposite him. He was wondering if she could possibly be, in fact, a whore. She had been gabbing for a long time; exactly *how* long, he couldn't remember. Why would she bother with him if she wasn't expecting to be paid? Four beers had deluded him into believing that she was good-looking. She was wearing a red blouse which squeezed her mid-section. Plump breasts spilled out above and her belly button peeked from below. Her jeans were low-cut and the uppermost tufts of her pubic hair were out in the open. Her skin thus generously exposed, she sported a couple of outrageous tattoos that screamed for attention. He wanted to strip her clothes off and have her—*now.* Instead of acquiescing to the drunken schemes that whirled around in his mind like a slipping clutch, she wouldn't stop rambling on about herself. He wanted to tell her to shut up and make a quick business arrangement with him, if one was needed.

"So what do you do for a living?" asked the girl, sipping her own beer.

"Me?" asked Richard, caught off guard by the conversation's sudden change of direction. "I'm a brain surgeon."

Beer exploded from her lips as if she was a can of beer herself, shaken vigorously and opened at high altitude. Everything within a few feet was sprayed, especially the table and Richard's face. "Oh my God!" she cried in mock horror. "I'm so sorry!" Then, she erupted into vulgar laughter.

Anybody who sounds like that has *to be a whore*, thought Richard, wiping his face dry. He wondered how she might sound when he was upon her and imagined a squealing pig.

"You think I'm joking?"

"Of course not!" Then, she lowered her voice and leaned forward until her breasts brushed the table. "I'll tell you a secret too: I'm the Queen of England!" She laughed again, displaying rows of dark grey fillings.

"Why don't you believe me?"

"Well, look at you! Shaved head. A ring in your ear. Dressed in a dirty old tank-top and cut-off jeans. You look more like my biker friends than a brain surgeon. It was a good joke though."

"It's true. I work at Columbia Medical Center."

"Sure, Baby. If that's true, what are you doing in this shit-hole with me?"

"I've been down on my luck lately. I came here to forget."

"I'm real sorry to hear that," she said with a big smile. "Why don't you tell me about it?"

Why not? thought Richard. This girl had probably heard more down-and-out tales than any of the expensive counselors he had seen over the past few months.

"I got sued for ten million dollars . . . and lost the trial. Now, all the money I make goes to a little old lady who doesn't know what to do with it. To top everything off, my liability insurance company just pulled the plug on me and my partners. We appealed and they compromised, taking us back on condition that we would no longer serve as a trauma center. That didn't stop the premiums tripling, though. Are you listening to me?"

"Sure, I am."

But she wasn't. Now she was bored, her head cupped in her hands, tossing some chewing gum around the inside of her mouth with her tongue. Richard didn't care; it felt good to be doing the talking for a change.

"How can anybody's life fall apart so quickly? One minute I've got everything a person could ever want, the next, I'm practically begging on the streets. At least I've still got a job. Who knows how much longer that'll be the case? You wouldn't believe how quickly neurosurgery services at Columbia medical center are collapsing. My partners bailed out like rats abandoning the Titanic. One retired. The other went to California. If I had any sense I would follow him. The residents have all disappeared too; they've gone back to the university where they came from. Many of the nurses too. *Nobody* stayed . . . except me, of course. And my friend, Hugh Montrose. We're the sole survivors."

"Life can be pretty shitty, can't it?" said the girl, sounding as if she had first-hand knowledge.

Richard felt a vibration from his belt. Instinctively, he reached down for his pager. "Shit!" he muttered angrily. "Who wants me now?" He squinted at the LCD display, but the numbers were too blurry for him to read. "Here, Honey," he said, handing the pager to the girl. "You're not quite as drunk as I am. Tell me what it says."

"Sure." She leaned forward to get a closer look. As she did so, Richard peered down the front of her dress. Her breasts were pale, smooth, and puckered close to her nipples. "Five-one-five-five."

"That's the Emergency Room," said Richard absent-mindedly, his eyes glued to her cleavage.

She noticed his interest and leaned further forward, allowing him a more generous view. "What do you have on your mind, my big bold brain surgeon?"

"You. Isn't it obvious?"

"Kinda." Then she jerked upright and the heavenly vision abruptly vanished. "But I don't think you should be having such thoughts about a nice girl like me," she teased. "After all, we've never met before tonight and we hardly know each other."

"You can trust me. I'm a doctor."

"You're no doctor. Maybe you're an actor. I'd believe that. Why don't you answer your pager? It's probably your wife."

"I don't have a wife." Richard guzzled more beer, then pulled a cell-phone out of his pocket and punched the keys. "Hello? This is Dr. Forrester. . . .Yes?"

The girl slouched while she waited.

"Damn!" said Richard. "You could have picked a better time. Okay, I'll be right there." He hung up. "Sorry, Honey. I've got to go."

"Really?" she asked, rolling out her lower lip with genuine disappointment.

"That was the Emergency Room at Columbia. They've got some ninety-eight year old woman with a big bleed in her brain. I have to go and see her." Richard struggled to his feet and scattered some dollar bills onto the table. For a second, he considered reaching over and tucking some money into her blouse. Then, another stronger, overriding thought crossed his mind: if she wanted the proof that he was a neurosurgeon, now he had the means to deliver it to her. After she believed him and was in his power, he could *have* her—from the back, the front . . . any way he wanted.

"I have an idea . . ." he said, groping for her hand. "Come with me. I'll prove to you who I am."

"Where are we going?"

"To the hospital."

"Oh, sure. Don't you think you're carrying this act a little too far?"

"It's no act."

Once again, she laughed at him. "All right, then. I'll follow a brain surgeon anywhere. Let's go to the hospital." She drained her beer, wiped her mouth, and belched. Then she followed him through front door of *The Raven's Nest* and into the cool summer evening.

Richard knew he was too drunk to be driving, but the alarm bells that were ringing within his mind were drowned by his desire to add this girl to his conquests. When he climbed into his old Volkswagen Rabbit he was vaguely aware of her shrill voice cutting through the silence that hummed loudly around him.

"No brain surgeon drives a piece-of-shit car like this!"

Richard guided his car through traffic, but his judgment was skewed. On more than one occasion, he drifted into somebody else's lane, provoking blaring horns and jabbing middle fingers. The girl was oblivious to the danger. With each near-miss, she erupted into ever more obscene laughter. However, when she saw the towering hospital swing into view, she grew subdued.

"Okay," she said. "We don't really have to go into the hospital. If you want me to believe you, I'll believe you . . ."

"You wanted proof? I'll give you proof."

"Please . . . Let's just go back to the bar."

"Shut up and watch this."

Richard drove up the ambulance ramp to the Emergency Room and braked in front of a police officer. The sight of the dark blue uniform alarmed the girl and she sank deeper into her seat. Richard switched off the engine and climbed out of his car.

"Good evening. Dr. Forrester," greeted the officer with a friendly wave of the hand. "Your patient arrived about twenty minutes ago. She's inside."

"Thanks, Fred," Richard replied. "Do me a favor, will you?" He tossed his keys over to him.

"Sure, Doc. I'll park it in the physicians' lot. Can't keep the patient waiting, you know."

Richard opened the girl's door and she spilled out. With an arm firmly around her shoulders, he escorted her through the automatic doors and into the ER. At first, Richard had to pull her along behind him, but as they plunged deeper into the hospital, he felt the tug on his arm grow weaker. Soon, she was by his side. When they reached a door marked MALE LOCKER ROOM, Richard plunged through and she followed without hesitation.

Inside, they were alone, hidden amongst a labyrinth of lockers. For a minute, they leaned against them and caught their breath.

"So—do you believe I'm a neurosurgeon now?" asked Richard as his eyes flicked between the girl's face and her heaving chest.

"I've seen proof you're a doctor," she teased, "but not a brain surgeon."

"You're hard to convince." Richard reached for some scrubs on a nearby shelf and tossed them at her. "Put these on."

She slowly undid the buttons on her red blouse and slipped it off. Underneath, her ample breasts were barely restrained by a lacey bra. They became pendulous and swayed from side to side as she leaned forward to wriggle out of her jeans. Underneath, her skimpy panties did little to cover her crotch. Richard feasted on the sight for a few seconds before he could restrain himself no more. He moved towards her and kissed her with passion.

"No-o-o . . ." she moaned with pleasure. "No . . . I want proof. I'll only make love to a brain surgeon."

Richard's mind was spinning. He reached behind her back with his left hand and unhooked her bra. It fell to the floor and her breasts swung free.

"No . . . not until I've seen you operate," she whispered, running her fingers over his shoulders.

But Richard wasn't interested in surgery. His body was filled with ravenous desire for this girl. He was going to *have* her. Right *here*. Right *now*. Nothing else mattered.

The spell was shattered by the sound of the door to the locker room opening and of a couple of men talking noisily about baseball. They were distant, but the fear of discovery shattered the heat of the moment. The girl hurriedly hooked her bra back on and slipped into her scrubs. Richard cursed his rotten luck, then changed into scrubs himself. When they were both dressed, they slipped out through a back door.

"That was close!" said the girl breathlessly.

"Goddamn orderlies," said Richard. "Why did they have to show up right *then*?"

"What are we going to do now?"

"I'd better see this damn woman in the ER. Come with me."

"Will she mind if I'm there too?"

"I'm sure she's beyond caring."

A few moments later, the two of them were in the heart of the Emergency Room, immersed in a crowd of people wearing scrubs and white coats. An older nurse peeled off from the others and approached them.

"Hello, Dr. Forrester. Your patient is in Room 6."

"What's her name?"

"Louise Diamond. Her husband is in the Quiet Room and the CT scan is hanging on the wall." Then she looked pointedly at the girl and said, "I'm Doris, the charge nurse. And you are . . ."

Before she could answer, Richard interrupted, "This is . . . This is . . ." Then his voice faded away as it dawned on him that he didn't even know the girl's name.

"Candy," she told him.

"That's right!" said Richard, slapping his forehead with the palm of his hand. "Kennedy. *Doctor* Kennedy. How could it slip my mind? She's a medical student from the university. Just starting her third year. Never been in an ER before . . . have you, Dr. Kennedy?"

"Oh, yes," she replied. "Plenty of times."

"I mean, as a student doctor."

"No, I suppose not . . ."

"Welcome to Columbia Medical Center," said Doris, glancing at Richard with uncertainty. "Our Emergency Room is not what it used to be, but you ought to learn a lot anyway. Will you be rotating under Dr. Forrester?"

"You could say that," said Candy, putting her fingers to her lips in an unsuccessful attempt to suppress a giggle.

"Good. If you need anything, please let me know."

"Thanks. I will." After the nurse withdrew, Candy grabbed Richard's sleeve and pulled him closer. "Why did you tell her I'm a medical student?" she demanded between clenched teeth.

"It's the perfect cover."

"But I don't know a *goddamn* thing about medicine."

"Relax. I told her you were starting your third year."

"What's that supposed to mean?"

"Brand new third year students don't know a goddamn thing about medicine either."

"Shit! You're going to get me into so much trouble."

Richard patted her on the shoulder. "Just keep your mouth shut and your eyes open, just like any other medical student. You'll be fine."

Room 6 was full of people working on Mrs. Diamond. When Candy saw her, she realized that Richard had been right; the old woman was, indeed, beyond caring. Her eyes were closed and her skin was pale. A plastic tube emerged out of her mouth and was attached to a machine that was blowing air into her lungs. A cluster of IV bags and clear plastic tubes hung from poles at the head of her bed, delivering fluids and medicines into her body. Saliva drooled out of the corner of her mouth and trickled over her chin. Somebody was sitting next to the gurney and was sticking a long needle into her wrist. The procedure looked painful, yet she didn't move.

"So, Dr. Kennedy," said Richard, loud enough so everybody could hear. "What's your assessment?"

"My *what*?"

"Tell me what you think is going on."

Candy's voice was weak. "I'm not sure—"

"The first thing you do is obtain a history; you find out what happened. Does anybody know?"

One of the nurses in the room spoke up. "She's a ninety-eight year old who was having dinner with her husband when she suddenly collapsed," she said as she fiddled with some glass tubes filled with blood. "When the medics arrived, they intubated her airway and brought her here."

"So, Dr. Kennedy," Richard continued. "With that history, what do you think happened?"

"I—I don't know . . ."

"God, don't they teach you *anything* in medical school? She's had a bleed. Isn't it obvious? Now examine her and tell me what you find."

Candy swallowed hard, gingerly reached out to the woman, and laid her fingers on her skin.

"That's no way to examine a patient," said Richard, stepping forward. "*This* is how you examine a patient." He pulled down the sheet that covered the old woman's chest, grabbed one of her nipples between thumb and forefinger and twisted it sharply. The patient's reaction to the infliction of extreme pain was seen and heard everywhere. Her wrinkled face scrunched into a frightful grimace and she breathed hard against the ventilator. The steady . . . *beep* . . . *beep* . . . *beep* . . . on the heart monitor suddenly accelerated into a *bip-bip-bip-bip-bip-bip-bip-bip* and every alarm on every machine in the room exploded into life. She extended her arms down her sides and rotated her clenched hands outwards. Throughout all this, though, her eyes remained closed. When Richard let go, the nipple was blanched and bleeding.

Candy shrank away in horror and folded her arms protectively over her own chest.

"She's decerebrate," Richard explained blandly. "That means her brain is fried, but not quite dead. So, Dr. Kennedy, what are we going to do next?"

"Did . . . did she *feel* that?"

"Looks like she did. What now?"

"I—I . . ."

"It's quite simple: we look at the CT scan." Richard waved in the general direction of an X-ray view box hanging on the opposite wall. "In fact, the problem's so obvious I can even see it from this distance. See that big glob of white stuff on the right side of her brain? That's a clot. It's causing the pressure inside her skull to go up and that's why she's in a coma. So, given the dire situation, what do you suggest we do now?"

"I don't know."

Richard sighed impatiently as if any high school student should know the answer. "I'll tell you what we're going to do," he said. "We're going to ship her to the regular ward and let her croak in peace."

Candy looked at Mrs. Diamond with concern in her eyes. "You're not going to do *anything* for her?"

"What's the point? She's ninety-eight years old and already halfway to the Eternal Care Unit."

"You're just going to let her *die?*"

"That's the general idea."

Candy glared at Richard defiantly. "Well, I think you're wrong," she declared.

Richard was caught off balance by her dissent and found himself on the defensive. "You have any better ideas?"

"Sure. Somebody should operate on her and take the blood out of her brain."

"But her chance of survival is zilch, zippo, natta—"

"If I was her granddaughter and loved her, I would want everything possible to be done."

For a few moments, Richard stared blankly at Candy, and Candy stared back. A few moments into the stand-off, however, the beginnings of an idea seeped into Richard's mind and he backed down. "Let's go and talk to the husband," he said.

They found Mr. Diamond hunched on a couch in the family counseling room. He was also in his nineties and appeared very frail.

"We've been married seventy-one years," he whimpered. "I don't know what I'll do without her."

Richard explained the situation and told him that it would take a major operation to remove the clot. Was that what he really wanted?

The husband's voice grew louder. "I just want my girl back," he repeated, over and over again. "Do everything you can for her! *Please!*"

Richard appraised the 'I told you so' expression on Candy's face and the idea that had germinated inside his mind gathered strength.

Why not? he thought. *She's going to die anyway.*

"All right," he said aloud, reaching a decision. "I'll do as you wish." Then, he turned to Candy and said, "Let's go, Dr. Kennedy. We have an operation to perform."

Outside, Candy pulled Richard closer and whispered into his ear. "You can't operate when you're drunk!" she said. "Isn't there somebody else around who could do it?"

"All I have to do is saw a hole in her head and suck out the clot. I don't have to be sober to do that."

"But what about your patient? How do you think she would feel about having a drunk brain surgeon operating on her?"

"She won't feel anything."

"What about you? What do you feel?"

"I can't feel anything either. At least, not anymore."

"Can I have your attention, everybody?" said Richard as he swept into the operating room with Candy in his slipstream. "I would like to introduce Dr. Kennedy. She's a third year medical student from the university. She's never been in an operating room before, so please make her feel welcome and keep her away from anything sterile. Our anesthesiologist tonight is Dr. Steve Blake. Our scrub tech is Noel."

Noel grinned from behind his splash-guard, a sheet of clear plastic that hung in front of his face.

"Our circulator is Mel. Hi, Mel. How are you?"

A Philippino woman smiled pleasantly. "Just fine, Dr. Forrester. And you?"

"Couldn't be better." Richard stumbled over a cable on the floor and almost fell. He reached out to catch himself and his hand fell into a basin that was full of drills and air hoses. "Shit! Look what I've done. I've contaminated the goddamn craniotome. I'm sorry, Mel. Better get it all sterilized again."

"Are you sure you're feeling okay, Doctor," asked Mel.

"I'm fine. Really."

"Working too hard again," said Blake. "You really ought to lighten up a little, you know. It seems like you're always in here, operating in the middle of the night. One of these days you're going to run yourself into an early grave. Take some time off."

Candy hugged the walls of OR 5 with her back and looked around with wide eyes. "Where do you want me to stand?" she asked.

"You're going to be scrubbing with me," said Richard. "Up front and personal."

"You can't be serious!"

Both Mel and Noel looked up from their work. It was unusual for a third year to be anything but quiet and submissive in an OR.

"I'm perfectly serious," said Richard. "There has to be a first time, you know. It may as well be now."

"But I don't know if I can—"

"It's all right, Dr. Kennedy," said Blake with a reassuring voice. "You won't have to *do* anything. Dr. Forrester will be in control. Scrubbing is just a way of getting close to the action so you can see more. You'll be fine."

"Jesus, give me strength!"

Candy needed more than strength when she saw Richard drive the metal spikes of the Mayfield clamp into Mrs. Diamond's scalp. She shrank away, horrified, and turned a light shade of green. Once the old woman's head was firmly fixed to the table, clippers appeared and her hair was shaved off. Within seconds she was bald, looking like a scrawny buzzard with its feathers plucked.

"Let's go scrub," said Richard. "Do what I do."

Once outside, Candy leaned against the scrub sink for support and stammered, "I—I can't believe this is happening to me."

"Now do you believe I'm a brain surgeon?" asked Richard, washing his hands with a scrub brush.

"You're just a drunk."

"And you act like a whore."

"What if I am? At least I do my job the way it's supposed to be done. How do you think that husband outside would feel if he knew some drunk was operating on his wife? You're worse than a whore."

"These days I can't operate unless I *am* drunk," he responded flatly.

Once back inside the OR, Candy tried to follow Richard through the gowning and gloving procedure, but her sterile technique got muddled up and she was sent to scrub again. Third year medical students were not much better though, so no suspicion was aroused. When she returned, Richard was already slicing through the patient's scalp with a knife. Fine jets of blood squirted from the edges of the skin.

Candy teetered.

"Stand close to me, Dr. Kennedy," said Richard. "I want you to get a good whiff of this."

When Candy was near enough, he fired up the monopolar cautery. Pools of blood bubbled and boiled and clouds of stinking blue smoke swirled from the wound. Next, the newly sterilized craniotome was brought up, its head resembling the multi-fingered business end of an oil drill. Richard jammed it against the exposed skull, pulled the trigger, and the bone underneath disintegrated into paste. A hole appeared, and another, and another. Then he laid aside the smoking drill and picked up a cutting saw. He guided the oscillating blade between the holes. Bone dust kicked up behind it and swirled through the air.

The bone flap was lifted up and set aside. Through the opening, Richard glimpsed the dura. The scalpel in his hand plunged downwards and sliced it open.

"Behold—the human brain in all its glory," announced Richard in a deep, resonant voice.

Candy cracked open an eye. What she saw was an eruption of cream-colored mush that fungated out of the opening and poured over the outside of the head.

"The clot's in here somewhere!" Richard poked a large sucker into the brain and stirred it vigorously as though he was mixing a pudding. It whooshed up blenderized brain matter like a powerful vacuum cleaner and sent it foaming down coils of transparent tubing. "Where is it? What's wrong here?"

Then Richard froze.

He gently laid his suction down and quietly walked over to the X-ray view box. His eyes reflected bluish light as they searched the pictures, then rolled up into his head as he came to a shocking conclusion.

The writing on the films was *backwards*. They had been hung wrong.

It had happened *again*! He was on the wrong side of the head!

Richard took a deep breath, then, with all his considerable strength, he swore as violently as he knew how, a primordial explosion of noise that burst through the doors of OR 5 and echoed down the empty halls of Surgery.

Candy staggered away from the table, sank to the floor behind the anesthesia machine, and spewed into her mask. The vomit poured all over her face, up her nose, into her eyes, and through her hair. As she was retching she glimpsed Mel and the anesthesiologist rushing towards her.

"You've got to do something!" she cried, choking on her own gastric juices. "The man's drunk out of his mind. He's going to kill her!"

"What are you saying?" demanded Blake.

"He's been drinking all evening. I know because I've been with him!"

"She's right," whispered Mel. "I can smell it on his breath."

"And I'm not a medical student at all," continued Candy, wrenching off her mask and wiping the vomit from her face. "I'm just some hooker he picked up in a bar tonight. He brought me here because he wanted to prove to me he's a brain surgeon. I didn't ask for any of this. I swear it!"

"You're not a student?" asked Blake.

"No!" she wailed. "Of course not! I never even finished high school. This whole thing is scaring the shit out of me!"

Blake and Mel looked at each other with desperation. Their thoughts were interrupted by a fresh string of curses that came from the direction of the X-ray view box.

"*Who* put up these X-rays?" Richard demanded. "Her hemorrhage is on left, not the right!" He returned to the patient and grabbed his sucker. "Well, I'll be damned if I have to put another hole on the other side of her goddamn head! You won't catch me giving the game away *this* time, Maxine Doggett! I'm going clear across the middle. There'll still be only one incision. Nobody can say I screwed up. Hand me another big sucker. I'm going to need two of them."

Then, as Noel watched with disbelieving eyes, Richard thrust the suckers through the opening like a gunslinger with both barrels blazing and removed large swaths of brain.

"He's gone nuts!" said Blake to Mel and Candy as the three of them cowered behind the anesthesia machine.

Richard started shouting at the anesthetized patient. "You *bitch*! So you think you're going to sue me over this, do you? You want to try and make a little extra pocket money, do you? Well, this is what happens to people when they sue me! They get their *brains* sucked out! Whoa—there goes your frontal lobe! Still feel like suing me? How about some of your temporal lobe? You won't need *that* any longer . . ."

"He's going to take out her whole brain!" said Mel. "Dr. Blake, you've got to stop him!"

"*Me*?" cried Blake. "Why me?"

"You're a doctor."

"What if I am? Forrester is bigger than me. He'll crush me! *You* stop him!"

"Are you joking?" said Mel. "He's ten times my size!"

"I've sacrificed my whole life for people like you!" screamed Richard at the patient under the drapes, his eyes bulging out like those of a maniac as he continued to suck. "I've given up everything . . . I give . . . you sue . . . you take. . . . Now it's *my turn* to take, and I'm taking your goddamned brain!"

"Dr. Forrester!" cried Candy. "Dr. Forrester! You're sick! Get control of yourself!"

"You think I'm out of control, do you?" shouted Richard without taking his eyes off his work. "This is just a routine operation, something I do every day. Welcome to *brain* surgery, Dr. Kennedy. You wanted to see what it was like. Well, what do you think now? Still want to get laid by a brain surgeon?"

Candy sobbed.

Then Richard reached into the skull with his fingers and scooped out what was left of the temporal lobe.

"Here, why don't you take this home to feed your cat?" he cried. He flung the piece of quivering brain across the room at Candy and it splattered against her face.

"I don't have a cat!" she screamed.

Some more pieces of the old woman's brain flew in her direction. Under this withering onslaught, Candy scrambled to her feet, slipped in the slimy mess, steadied herself, then ran for the door in terror. A moment later, she was gone. More brain material sprayed across the door as it closed behind her.

Richard returned his attention to the patient and, muttering and mumbling to himself, he peered into her skull. Then he reached for a knife and slashed a hole in the falx, a thick membrane that hung down the middle of the cranial cavity and separated the left cerebral hemisphere from the right. When he spotted the clot, he shouted, "There it is!" With a little more work with the suckers, he delivered a large, dark red glob the size and color of a beet root. He dumped it with a loud *splat* in front of Noel who had turned as white as a sheet.

"There!" he said, satisfied. He paused and looked at Mel and Blake who were huddling in a corner. His heaving chest slowed and he blinked away sweat that had run into his eyes.

Then, he said, very quietly and calmly, "Ladies and gentlemen, the operation has been a complete success. Go and tell *that* to The Dog."

CHAPTER 17

"Mortimer, you slimy bastard!" Hugh shouted in the privacy of his old Volvo as he drove east on I-84. The setting sun cast dazzling light across the Columbia River and the billowing clouds in the sky were a flourish of pink and gold. Gathering thunderstorms in the east loomed dark and threatening, complimenting Hugh's mood perfectly. He paid no attention to the developing weather, but could only fume about a certain sworn declaration. Denmark had sent him a copy and now it was lying crumpled on the passenger seat next to him. He had made the mistake of reading it before the end of his clinic and its words had elicited a gut reaction that he had not felt since his early days of clipping aneurysms. Soon afterwards, he had given up trying to concentrate on his work and had ditched the rest of his clinic.

The harsh words were still reverberating throughout his brain:

Defendant Montrose should have performed surgical removal of the spinal cord tumor immediately, without any delay. His failure to perform immediate surgery proximately caused Julie Winter's paralysis to worsen and become permanent, with no hope or possibility for recovery. Indeed, his deliberate delay in performing surgery guaranteed that Julie Winter would become permanently paralyzed with no possibility for recovery or improvement. The decision to

delay surgical removal of the tumor in this case was a
breach in the standard of care expected of a reasonably
prudent neurosurgeon.

Winter vs. Montrose was taking shape and gaining momentum.
As it did so, it consumed ever increasing amounts of Hugh's
time. He was often summoned to the offices of Moscowitz,
Pursley & Boggs where Denmark would relentlessly grill him on
some new aspect of the case. As depositions of various witnesses
were taken, the two of them would dissect the endless tran-
scripts line by line, searching for inconsistencies. From Hugh's
point of view, this process gave the word 'dull' new meaning.
Most of the questions and answers didn't appear to be remotely
relevant. Another seemingly worthless exercise was called In-
terrogatories and Requests for Production, a process by which
the plaintiff's attorney posed written questions in an attempt to
extract as much information from the defense as possible. The
defense, of course, responded to the simpler questions with little
more than name, rank, and serial number, and to everything
else (for example: the identity of every textbook Hugh had ever
read in medical school) with the words 'Objection: vague, overly
broad, and unduly burdensome'. Hugh reviewed the literature
and found numerous journal articles and textbook chapters
that supported the way he had treated Julie Winter. He brought
them to these meetings and they pored through them. Hugh
expected to see Denmark's eyes glaze over in much the same
way as his own would when he tried to read legal documents,
but to his surprise his lawyer studied everything very closely,
never tiring and always asking questions. Potential expert witnesses were also discussed at length. By now, Denmark had established contact with neurologists, pathologists, radiologists,
and oncologists, and had taken depositions from the ones who

appeared most promising and supportive. The most important expert, however, would be the neurosurgeon who would testify that Hugh had met the standard of care. For this, Denmark was using an old colleague of Hugh's, a man by the name of Robert Bull, somebody who'd left Portland some years before. He was articulate over the telephone and held the strong opinion that Hugh had done absolutely nothing wrong. Like all good neurosurgeons, Bull paid more than average attention to detail and had discovered the abnormal CSF protein buried deep in Mrs. Winter's medical records. It was a critically important piece of evidence, showing that Clegg, predictably, had botched the one and only opportunity to save his patient from paralysis. If anybody should be the target of lawsuit, it was him.

Yet, strangely, Clegg had escaped being named.

How?

Hugh thought that attorney incompetence might be a good explanation. In her zeal to sink her claws into him, Maxine had overlooked the fact that other doctors might be guilty. Denmark, on the other hand, knew better and disagreed. Yes, there were plenty of incompetent medical malpractice lawyers around, but Maxine wasn't one of them. If she had omitted anybody else's name on the Summons and Complaint, there was a very good reason for it.

After reading Mortimer's declaration, Hugh had wanted to go home and shovel this shit into the back of his mind, but his plans were interrupted by a phone call from Richard, asking him to accompany him to a meeting.

"*Tonight?*" Hugh had asked.

"Yes, tonight."

"But that's impossible."

"It's important, Hugh."

"What kind of meeting?"

"It's too dangerous to discuss it over the phone. I'll meet you at Starbuck's in Parkrose Mall at eight and we can go together from there."

"You can't discuss it over the phone? What's going on, Richard?"

"I'll see you later."

Richard had occupied Hugh's thoughts more than usual in recent days, ever since a strange meeting Hugh had had with Ed Cleveland, Columbia's aging medical director. The big man had glowered at him from behind his desk, a long cigar sticking out of his mouth like the gun on the deck of a battleship. Smoking inside the hospital was a flagrant violation of all the rules, but, as Ed was fond of saying, he was there to make the rules, not follow them. As far as he was concerned, he was going to enjoy cigars in his office and everybody else, including his cardiologist and his pulmonologist, could go to hell. Tobacco was the only way he knew how to calm his nerves and as a hospital medical director, they needed all the soothing they could get these days.

In the meeting, Ed had expressed deep concern about Richard's recent behavior and, initially, Hugh thought that the man was talking about *The Incident* a few months ago.

"No, no—the business with that old woman is history now," Ed said. "Richard has paid his debt to society, having his privileges revoked for a while. He's very remorseful and swears he'll never do anything like that again. No, I'm thinking of something else—something *much* more serious."

Hugh had trouble imagining what could be more serious than getting drunk, inviting a prostitute to assist in surgery, and slinging bits of a little old lady's brain around the operating room.

Ed had glanced around, checking for unwelcome eavesdroppers, although he must have already known they were alone.

Then he had leaned closer to Hugh, lowered his voice, and told him that the hospital had a system for tracking surgeons' performances. "We keep statistics on *everything*," he said. "Admissions, discharges, caseload, complications, cost, and so on. You never know when you might need them. For years, Richard has had respectable numbers in all categories. Ever since that day in the OR, there's been a major change and the alarms on our computers haven't stopped ringing."

"What do you mean?"

"Richard's admissions for elective spine cases have dramatically increased, yet the number of outpatient visits hasn't changed. It's as though his threshold for operating has bottomed out."

"I hadn't noticed—"

"And it's not just the elective stuff either. These days, just about any soft-boiled egg in the ER gets its top lopped off and the yellow sucked out, if you follow my drift. There was a time when the old were allowed to die in peace. Now they are whisked to the OR to get holes drilled in their heads, then they're shipped to the ICU where—surprise, surprise—they don't wake up. *Then* they're allowed to die in peace."

"There are no rules against treating patients aggressively," Hugh said without conviction.

Ed had pulled the cigar out of the corner of his mouth and glowered at its end. The thing had gone out, and now he looked as if he didn't know whether to relight it or to chew it into a soggy pulp. Evidently, he decided on the latter course of action for he stuck it back into his mouth and worked his jaw. "All these worthless tests aren't doing anything to improve outcomes," he said.

"You and I know that," said Hugh, "but the patients don't."

"There's more," continued Ed. "The number of tests he orders has soared: labwork, X-rays . . . everything. It's no longer enough for him to get a lumbar MRI for somebody who has back pain. These days, he'll order the whole enchilada: cervical, thoracic, and brain too, if he's in the mood. Sometimes, he'll throw in electrical testing too, just for good measure. It's as though he trying to spend as much money as possible on patient care. And he's succeeding too. I've looked at the numbers and they're mind-boggling. The cost of his average admission has more than doubled. You're aware that the hospital only gets a fixed dollar amount for each diagnosis code. If he keeps this up much longer, he'll put Columbia out of business. Maybe the insurance companies too since they're paying for all this."

"Perhaps he wants to give patients and their families the kind of health care they expect."

"If the families knew what was *really* going on . . ." Ed had left his sentence unfinished and shuddered.

"Have you talked to Richard about this?"

"Yes, I have."

"So how does he explain it?"

"He vigorously defends himself. Says the patients love it when every cubic millimeter of their internal anatomy is being photographed and investigated. With respect to old folks with brain bleeds in the ER, he says every red-blooded American citizen has a God-given right to survive, even if the chance of that actually happening is infinitesimally small. Nobody can accuse him of doing anything wrong. That's just the point. He's playing it safe . . . super-safe"

"So why are you telling me all this?"

"I've tried talking to him and he just throws up a brick wall and justifies everything he's doing. He won't open up for me, but he trusts you. Talk to him. Find out what's going on and why.

What are his intentions? And tell him to stop before he bank-rupts the system!"

By the time Hugh reached Parkrose, the thunderstorm was unleashing itself upon the land below. Lightning crackled and boomed from one end of the sky to the other. Curtains of heavy rain poured down in a way that was not commonly seen in this part of the country. Richard emerged from the coffee shop dressed in a suit and hurried over to Hugh's car, holding a newspaper over his head. He quickly climbed in and sat on Mortimer's declaration, crushing it.

How appropriate, Hugh thought. *Fart on it while you're there.*

"Thanks for coming," said Richard, wiping water from his face with his fingers. He had lost some weight recently and had been seen quietly flexing his muscles and posing in front of mir-rors in the hospital once again. He was re-growing his hair too, only now his beard was grey.

"Where do you want me to go?" asked Hugh, driving out of the parking lot.

"Get back on I-84 and head east."

"So what's this all about?"

"There's a meeting tonight."

"You already told me. What kind of meeting?"

"Hugh, do you remember what BOHICA means?" asked Richard with a twinkle in his eye.

"How could I forget? Every first-year medical student knows the answer to that one. It's an acronym for Bend Over—Here It Comes Again."

"Medical school was all about getting shafted, wasn't it? One unfair test after another . . . struggling to keep a passing grade. At least, that's the way I felt about it. Private practice is no different, only this time it's the trial lawyers who are sticking the barbed harpoons up our butts and not the professors. Well, no more BOHICA for us. We're fighting back."

"Who's 'we'?"

"The organization I'm building: SOD'M."

"SODOM?"

"No . . . SOD THEM. Or SOD'M for short."

Hugh laughed and after a day like today, it felt good.

"Do you know what it means?" asked Richard.

"Of course. In Britain, 'sod' means—"

Richard interrupted before Hugh had a chance to elaborate. "I was quite certain you, of all people, would know," he said. "Now it's got a new meaning. Another acronym: the Society of Defensive Medicine."

Hugh took his eyes off the road for a moment and looked at his partner with consternation. "Richard, what the devil have you been up to?"

"You know what it's like, being sued and all that. Not much fun, is it?"

"No, definitely not."

"It's certainly the worst thing that's happened to me. My life has been hell on earth ever since my trial. Most lawsuits are frivolous, but if lawyers think there's even the remotest chance of hitting the jackpot, they'll try anything these days. For them, it's a risk-free business. There's no downside. So they sue like there's no tomorrow and *we're* forced to live through the misery of defending ourselves instead of doing our work. There's never been a good way to fight back, until now."

"What are you doing?"

"You met with Ed Cleveland the other day, didn't you?"

"Yes. He was complaining that you've suddenly become very expensive."

"He's right, you know. I *am* expensive. But I'm only giving patients and their families what they want—the most complete medical care money can buy. MRI's are critical to our campaign. They cost a lot, about fifteen hundred dollars apiece, but they're also harmless and everybody wants one." Richard looked at Hugh with a glint of eagerness in his eyes. "I bet you can't guess how many I ordered last month alone."

"I'm afraid to."

"Three hundred! That's nearly half a million dollars' worth. The MRI center at Columbia has been forced to open their doors twenty-four hours a day and hire extra people to accommodate the rush. And get this: the patients *love* it! They don't even care if their scan is scheduled for three in the morning or three in the afternoon. They are just delighted to be getting so much attention."

Hugh's cell phone rang and he spent the next few minutes talking to a nurse in the ICU about a head injury patient whose intracranial pressure was proving difficult to control.

"My volume of CT's has risen too," Richard continued when Hugh was finished. "I figured we can never get enough follow-up scans after surgery; a nasty complication might develop at any time. On average, I order about six of them after each craniotomy and that's before they've even left the hospital. Afterwards, they get another one every time they come to my clinic. There are other things I do too, like keeping patients in the ICU longer than usual. Why should I use the regular ward where beds only cost six hundred dollars a day when I can use an ICU bed which costs twice as much? You can't deny patients get closer attention in an ICU—one-on-one nursing care and all that. Everybody deserves their own nurse after an operation, don't you think?"

"Ed told me your threshold for operating is much lower. There's a rumor that you're doing unnecessary back surgery."

"It depends on your definition of unnecessary. Unnecessary from your point of view, or the patient's? People often come into my office wanting an operation because they believe it'll help them. Sometimes, they can be quite demanding, as you well know. When I lowered my threshold for cutting, I believed I would see a higher percentage of failed operations. I was right. But if that's what they want—"

"You might as well give them a sugar pill and tell them it'll cure their pain. You'd get the same results."

"Sugar pills don't cost very much. Operations do."

Hugh remained skeptical. "Ed also said you were operating on a lot of really old folks with major head bleeds," he said.

"That's how this whole idea got started in the first place. Remember that weekend in April when things got a little out of control in the OR?"

"A *little?*"

"I wasn't planning to operate on that poor old lady; I told the hooker that I was going to let her die in peace. That's when she became upset and told me I should be doing everything I could as long as there was the smallest chance the patient might survive. The husband wanted me to treat her aggressively too. So, after due consideration, I did. I gave them exactly what they wanted: a pointless operation. When she died three days later, her husband said he was very glad she'd had surgery. At least we had tried. Now he was sure it had been her time to go."

"Oh, come on, Richard—you know as well as I do that there are standards of decency in this world. The woman was ninety-eight years old, for Christ's sake."

"Standards of decency?" cried Richard with a look of disbelief. "Not any more, there aren't! Suppose, for a moment, I hadn't operated on her. You know as well as I do there's always a lawyer who'll pay an expert witness enough money to say that surgery would have saved her. Then who's going to get screwed? Me, of course. It doesn't matter if the lawsuit is so weak that it lasts only a few days before it's dropped or thrown out on Summary Judgment. As long as I have to file a claim with my insurance company, then my future is on the line. If people allow lawyers to pull off these stunts and get away with it, then, as far as I'm concerned, they can sit in the waiting room while Great-grandma gets her skull sawn open and the clot sucked out of her brain!"

It was raining harder now. The wipers on the Volvo protested noisily as they flipped from side to side, while inside, condensation accumulated on the windshield, worsening visibility. The de-mist fan whirred loudly but accomplished nothing. Hugh sat hunched forward as he drove, peering ahead like a blind man, intermittently wiping the glass with his sleeve.

"Look," continued Richard, mellowing. "You, of all people, should know all about defensive medicine. *You* practise it. *I* practise it. Every physician we know practises as if they expect to get sued at any moment. Defensive medicine is estimated to cost hundreds of billions of dollars a year—more than enough money to pay for the medical care of every uninsured person in this country. Put the costs of defensive medicine together with the costs of improved technology and *that's* why health care costs are spiraling out of control. The two have a synergistic effect on each other, ballooning the health care system beyond the country's capacity to support it and pushing it towards a precipice. SOD'M simply speeds up the system's demise so change can happen sooner. Just look at all the problems some businesses are having these days providing their employees with affordable health care coverage. Can you imagine what'll happen when *ev-*

erybody starts screaming? That's when we'll have the lawyers and their lackeys in the legislature by the balls. I can't wait—"

"You'll never be able to keep this up," said Hugh. "Ed Cleveland will come down on you like a ton of bricks. He'll have you thrown off the staff."

"What for? Practicing defensive medicine?"

"You're causing trouble and that may be reason enough." The fog and water on the windshield in front of Hugh turned into a dazzling kaleidoscope of reds and he braked. "You'll never succeed in changing the system, you know. You're a very small fish in a very big pond."

"I agree," said Richard. "By myself, I would never have much of an impact. So I started talking to some fellow physicians about my ideas. I was amazed how fed up everybody was, and how angry and frustrated they were about being so damned impotent. We decided to start getting organized and came up with the SOD'M concept. Appropriate name, don't you think? Now we've been meeting in small groups, like Alcoholics Anonymous, airing our nasty little lawyer problems out in the open."

The light turned green and Hugh pulled forward. "How many members do you have now?" he asked.

Richard smiled and glanced sideways at Hugh. "Not many, but our potential for growth is unlimited. You'll see."

Hugh was now driving east on I-84. It was still raining hard, and large puddles of water were accumulating by the sides of the road. As daylight faded, each flash of lightning burned brighter in his eyes, leaving jagged green shapes floating in the darkness. For the next half hour, he fielded three more phone calls from nurses, while Richard handled a similar number on his own phone. At one point, they were both simultaneously talking to different people in the hospital—all routine calls, except for one from the ER.

"No, I'm *not* available!" Richard had cried, trying to make himself heard above the weather and the noisy engine. "No, Dr. Montrose is not available either. . . . How do I know? Because he's *with* me, you moron! You'll have to send the patient somewhere else. . . . Where? How the hell do I know! Call around and see who'll take him. Try the university first."

Eventually, they reached their destination: Bridal Veil Lodge, a hotel perched at the edge of a precipice and a stone's throw from Bridal Veil Falls. Normally, the waterfall at this time of year was little more than a trickle, but the storm had swollen the river and Hugh could hear a distant roar when he climbed out of the car. Once inside the lobby, they shook off the rain and Hugh was quietly pleased when Richard took a moment to check his reflection in a highly polished grand piano and flex a bicep or two. When they were ready, they proceeded through a set of double doors and walked into the hotel's main conference room.

The large room contained about fifty people engaged in animated conversation. When Richard loomed large the doorway, the hubbub quickly faded. Faces turned towards him from all directions and broke into smiles. For a few moments, the leader and his followers silently regarded each other with mutual admiration. Then applause broke out and Richard plunged into the crowd like a politician on the campaign trail, giving high fives to the hands that were held up for him. He moved randomly across the floor from one knot of people to another, back-slapping his old friends and gripping the hands of new ones.

As Hugh was watching, he was quietly approached by Stan Reeder, the bespectacled neuroradiologist who had read Julie Winter's original MRI scan.

"Glad to see you could make it, Hugh," he said without taking his eyes from Richard. The big neurosurgeon had reached the center of the room and towered a head taller than anybody else. "Awful weather outside, isn't it?"

"Stan? What are you doing here?"

"Same as all these other doctors," said Stan, nudging his glasses higher on his nose. "Getting organized. Fighting back."

"Have *you* been sued?"

"Does it matter?"

"I suppose not," said Hugh, who knew that if a doctor hadn't yet gone through the experience of a lawsuit, the chances were good that he soon would. "So, how are you planning to fight back?"

Now, for the first time, Stan turned to look directly at Hugh and his eyes were shining as if he had seen a vision. "I have lots of ideas. My latest technique is to recommend lots more radiology studies in the final conclusion of my reports. If I get my wording exactly right, I can force referring doctors to order them. If they don't and something is missed, they know they could be held liable."

An obstetrician joined them, openly wondering what would happen when the last member of his specialty left the state. Most of the time, he supposed, things would be okay since women have been popping out babies for millions of years without a doctor in attendance. But tragedies were bound to happen. Only when women and their babies started dying would the politicians start noticing. SOD'M was going to head off this catastrophe-in-the-making by bringing the issue to a head *before* the last obstetrician closed his office.

Another obstetrician was far more animated. "I'm simply not going to use the vagina anymore!" he cried, gesticulating wildly with his arms. "It's just too risky. Every woman in my practice gets a C-section now. There's always some kind of excuse I can find. Did you know that the lawyers in my county have learned to be experts at reading fetal monitor recordings? If I can't find a reason why I should perform an emergency C-section, you can bet your bottom dollar *they* will!"

A psychiatrist whose big bald head and beard made him look especially brainy heaped praise on Richard for coming up with the idea of getting organized and rebelling against the system.

"I was so depressed," he said. "I didn't know anybody else felt the same way I did until Richard came along. It felt so good to get this off my chest. We are all very grateful to him."

A neurologist declared that he was doing electrical conduction studies on every patient who walked through his front door. It was a test that often made little difference to patient management, but at eight hundred dollars a pop, he was racking up the bills at an impressive rate. He swore it would continue until either he lost his license or was successful at changing the system, whichever came first.

"But those tests can be painful," said Hugh. "You're sticking little needles under the skin and zapping patients with electricity. I thought the objective was not to do any harm."

"What are a few volts between friends? Just a minor inconvenience. And it's *such* a good way to spend money."

Hugh frowned and wondered what other 'minor inconveniences' were being inflicted upon patients. He found his answer when he heard a neurosurgeon from Florida speaking. He was tall and wore a dark suit and bow tie. A neatly clipped moustache decorated his upper lip and fierce eyes glared down at his listeners. "I used to be a really conservative neurosurgeon," he said. "There was a time when I operated only on those who needed it. But a few years ago, with malpractice premium climbing out of control and reimbursement declining, I started taking liberties. Had to! I had a business to run. How was I going to pay my bills without increasing my volume? So, I operated on fringe patients; folks who didn't really need an operation but who'd say yes to anybody with a knife and a license to use it. In time, I did more and more sham cases, until pretty soon I was taking everybody who walked through my front door to surgery. Didn't matter what the MRI showed. It could be completely normal, for all I cared. If the patient was dumb enough to sign the permit, then I'd cut. Lumbar fusions were the best. They're the cases that pay the most. I put enough steel in people's backs to build a goddamn railroad from one end of the country to the other. If they already had steel in their backs, I'd take it all out again. Put it in one year, take it out the next. Put it in, take it out. Sometimes over and over again on the same patient. The money kept me afloat. Felt like crap inside, though. Then I heard about SOD'M and discovered there was help for knife-happy jerks like myself."

"So have you changed your ways?" asked one of his listeners.

"I'm trying as hard as I can to kick the habit. I've still got bills to pay, though."

Cutlery tinkered against wine glasses and the noise of conversation faded. Attention was directed towards Richard, whose eyes reflected the cool self-confidence of a natural leader as they surveyed the audience.

"Can I have your attention, please?" he called out. "Thank you. Thank you. Can somebody close the doors please? I want to thank everybody for coming tonight, despite the bad weather. Almost everybody who is a member of our organization managed to show up, which I believe shows how dedicated we all are to our cause. And it *is* a noble cause—"

Cheers and whistles erupted from the group.

Then, Richard shouted *"SOD'M! SOD'M!"* with such vehemence that Hugh was startled. This elicited even louder cheers, followed by ripples of laughter. When the noise subsided, he continued. "Sometimes I am amazed at how successful we've been. All this began three months ago. I felt beat-up and depressed. Couldn't eat. Couldn't sleep. I was wallowing around in the local watering-hole, drowning my sorrows in beer, when I got a call from the Emergency Room about an old woman, nearly brain dead from a big hemorrhage. As I was standing there at her side, deciding what to do, my philosophy of how to practise medicine suddenly changed. All my professional life, my primary function has been to do what was best for the patient. Now I realized I had a secondary function—to protect myself at all costs from any potential lawsuits so I can continue to carry out my primary function. So, I operated on her—the first conscious act of self-preservation made by a member of the Society of Defensive Medicine."

More cheers and whistles.

"The next day, after my hang-over had cleared, I had so many questions! Why have physicians allowed things to get to this point? Why were we behaving like lambs being led to the slaughter? Wasn't there a way to fight back? The answers came to me in clinic soon afterwards. I was talking to a woman about their back pain and the possibility of having surgery. While I was speaking with her, I saw a miniature lawyer with horns and a forked tail sitting on one of her shoulders, taking notes. Every time I said something a little risky—something that could be used in a court of law against me—the lawyer would write furiously with his pencil, taking it all down. When I said something that was safe, such as covering the risks of an operation, he would look up at me madder than hell. I figured that the angrier I made the little prick, the better off I was. Do you know what pissed him off the most?"

Heads shook from side to side.

"Ordering tests. Lots of them. The more I ordered, the angrier he became, until he was literally jumping up and down. I thought he was going to have a heart attack, keel over, and die. That's when the idea struck me and, before I knew it, SOD'M was born."

The crowd burst into applause.

"Seriously though, we've made tremendous progress. Our membership continues to grow exponentially, doubling every month. I see our growth as the best way to accomplish our mission. Let's face it: the more physicians practise safe, and *expensive*, medicine, the faster costs will go up, and the quicker the public, employers, and insurance companies will start getting upset. The politicians will have no choice but to act. So, my message to you is this: keep up the good work. Talk to colleagues in the lounges and locker rooms of your hospital. Tell them about our movement and invite them to the next meeting. Eventually, we'll restore some sanity to the system."

"Amen to that!" somebody cried.

"We're going to start our program this evening with a collection of the latest horror stories," continued Richard. "Dr. Griffith is a family physician who has kindly consented to share with us the details of his most recent lawsuit. Seems like one of his patients is blaming him for their rectal impaction, claiming he didn't prescribe enough stool-softeners. Dr. Griffith?"

A man with a flashy purple tie came forward and Richard stepped back to give him room. Hugh approached his partner and tugged on his sleeve.

"Yes, what is it?" asked Richard.

"I'm leaving."

"But we've only just got here!"

"I want to go."

"Why?"

"We can talk outside."

Richard turned to a woman nearby and murmured a few words quietly into her ear. Then, as Dr. Griffith started speaking, Richard and Hugh quietly left the room.

Outside, the rain had stopped and the clouds were breaking up. Now they were being driven across the black sky by the winds, their edges tinged silver by a rising moon. The steady roar of Bridal Veil Falls filled the night and as the two friends strolled away from the hotel, they entered a drifting mist that felt cold against their faces.

For a while neither of them said anything, as if they were both afraid to start an argument. Eventually, Richard spoke up first, raising his voice so he could be heard above the sound of falling water. "So, what do you think of SOD'M?" he asked, making his question sound casual.

"You really want to know?" said Hugh, realizing that the answer he wanted to give would offend his friend.

"Your opinion is important to me."

"Okay, then. I think you're frigging nuts."

Richard looked as if he had been slapped and his face hardened. "Why?"

"For one thing, SOD'M scares the hell out of me. You told me that you wouldn't harm a patient. Maybe *you* wouldn't, but can you say the same for some of your starry-eyed friends back there?" Hugh jerked his thumb towards the hotel.

"We all know the rules. No patients are to be harmed."

"Not everybody is as familiar with the rules as you are. The neurosurgeon from Florida, for instance . . . he admits to operating on as many people as he can. It doesn't matter to him what their X-rays look like, even if they're normal. If the patients are dumb enough to sign the permit, then he's willing to cut. *His* words!"

"Oh, don't worry about him," said Richard. "He's different."

"How?"

"He's not mainstream SOD'M; just some guy who's operating a lot so he can pay his bills. It's a very common problem, you know; you would be amazed how many surgeons are in the same predicament. Instead of shunning him, we welcomed him into our group so he can get the counseling he needs."

"Listen, Richard—I can see SOD'M developing into something sinister. Those people are pretty upset about what's been going on and some of them want to see blood. They'll use this to tear apart the whole medical system instead of just fixing the parts that need to be fixed. Patients are the ones who'll end up suffering, not the lawyers."

"So you believe in BOHICA instead?"

"No, we should fight back, but through the usual channels; through legislatures, lobbying efforts, political action. If we try to force a solution this way, it'll get ugly."

"What do you mean: 'ugly'?"

They had now reached a pergola; it was perched at the edge of a cliff and was used by tourists as a vantage point. From here, the falls came into view. Ghostly moonlight shone upon tons of white, frothing water that was slipping over the edge of a high bluff. A thick cloud of mist shrouded the gorge and bathed everything with cold, dripping wetness.

"SOD'M is clear fantasy. It's a cause for public fear and rejection, not sympathy. You'll give us all a rotten reputation and set back liability reform for years."

"Bullshit!"

"And that's not all," continued Hugh, wiping moisture

from his face. "Once the trial lawyers find out about this, they're not going to sit around and do nothing, you know. They'll get riled up like hornets and do *something* to stop you."

"Good!" cried Richard, expanding his chest and towering over Hugh. His arms were thrust deep into his pockets and his eyes blazed in the moonlight. "If they want a fight, let's have one! I'm ready. I've been ready for years. It'll be the moment I've been waiting for. And may the best side win. It'll be the voters who'll decide the winners—the teachers, the ordinary working men and women who've been desperately trying to keep the health benefits that they've worked hard for all their lives. And what do you think they'll decide? To keep padding the pockets of the rich scumbag trial lawyers? Or to restore decent medical care? I think I know the answer to that one."

"And in the process of proving your point, it doesn't matter if you hurt a few patients. Is that it?"

Richard tensed and, for a moment, Hugh thought his partner was going to pick him up and throw him into the gorge. However, whatever violent thoughts that might have crossed his mind quickly passed and he blinked the water from his eyes.

Or were they tears?

"Look," said Hugh, putting his hand on Richard's sleeve, "I'm really sorry about everything that's happened to you."

"You have no idea what it's been like!" cried Richard, shaking his friend loose.

"God knows, if it had happened to me," persisted Hugh, "I would have gone crazy long ago. Maybe it *will* happen to me. After all, I've got my own trial coming up and God knows how it'll end. But this *isn't* the solution. Sure—it's a way to satisfy your thirst for revenge, but in the final analysis, you'll only make things worse."

Richard was uncompromising. "They can't be any worse than they are right now," he said. "You're either with me, Hugh, or you're against me. Make your choice."

"I'm sorry, Richard," said Hugh, shaking his head. "I'm not going to be a part of SOD'M. I'll practise neurosurgery the way I always have."

"Even if it means getting creamed by that red-headed bitch and losing everything—and I mean *everything*, like I have?"

Hugh thought of Maxine Doggett gleefully taking possession of his home, auctioning his belongings, and banishing him and his family from the state forever. "Yes—even if it means that," he said with a cracking voice.

There was a long pause as Richard searched his friend's eyes. Finally, he said, "You've always been too good and kind for this world, Hugh, always following the rules and doing the right thing, no matter how painful. God knows how you manage."

"It's not easy. Sometimes I feel like a prude."

"Well, I'm not like you. When I get screwed, I fight back and save the things I love the most. I'm sorry you couldn't find it in your heart to give me any support. I suppose this is where we part company. I wish you well."

"It doesn't have to be this way, Richard," cried Hugh.

"Yes, it does. Don't worry about taking me home. I'll ask one of my *real* friends back there to give me a ride." Richard turned to leave, shrugging away Hugh's outstretched hand. He walked towards the hotel and was immediately swallowed by the swirling mist. Hugh called after him one last time, but his voice was carried away by the roar of Bridal Veil Falls.

CHAPTER 18

The couple on the television was copulating in a hotel room. The man was on his back and was middle-aged, balding and had a hairy pot-belly that wobbled with each thrust of his loins, sending shadows rippling across his skin. The woman straddled his hips with her thighs and dangled her arms up in the air, slowly waving them around as though they were the necks of flamingos. The hair that obscured her face was dark brown.

Yet, it was a dense tuft of *red* hair that sprouted between her legs.

Carl looked away and sank his face into the palm of one of his hands.

"What's the matter, Carl?" asked Maxine, dipping her fingers into a bag of popcorn as she watched the screen. "Never seen porn before?"

"You know how your sex videos always bother me."

"Just think of them as business," said Maxine, popping a couple of fluffy white and yellow pieces of popcorn into her mouth.

"Some day, this so-called business is going to get you into trouble."

"That's why I pay you so much—to keep me *out* of trouble." Crunch, crunch, crunch.

"I still don't like it," huffed Carl, crossing his arms in front of his chest. "You deserve more respect than this."

Maxine looked away from the television and studied Carl's face. He appeared as serious as ever and she was unable to detect the faintest trace of sarcasm or insincerity. Their eyes met for a fraction of a second before she quickly returned her attention to the screen and dipped her hand into the popcorn once again.

The Las Vegas operation had been a month ago. Maxine's memory of the gynecologist's fingers creeping over her skin was still as fresh as if it had happened yesterday. The doctor and his wife had been separated by two time zones and he had celebrated his freedom by having an erotic fling while attending the Third International Symposium of the Vagina. He had met Maxine at the opening banquet after he had spotted her wandering around by herself with a drink in her hand, looking bored and obviously seeking a tryst. She wasn't pretty; her eyes were luring in a creepy sort of way, her face narrow and witch-like. But the alcohol running through his veins softened her features, augmented her modest breasts and trimmed her buttocks until she resembled one of the babes he had been watching all day at the pool. He had approached her and found her receptive to meaningless conversation, corny jokes, and casual physical contact. Before the evening was over, his fingers were entwined in hers and he was escorting his new plaything to his hotel room.

"Do you think the video is ready to be used?" asked Maxine, wiping her mouth with a napkin. "I don't want any mistakes."

"I've been over it frame by frame and have done tons of editing," said Carl. "The lighting and sound are perfect. Nobody will be able to identify you. There are a few more adjustments I would like to make, though. How much time do I have?"

"The deadline for his sworn declaration is in about three weeks."

"Isn't there a simpler way to—"

"No, there isn't. I know you're not happy about this, Carl, but I have no choice. I've tried to make deals, but they've all fallen through. The trouble is that this guy is being paid an obscene amount of money to say these outrageous things against my client. Unfortunately, it's going to take a hard-hitting video like this one to silence him."

"It sounds like the defense attorney who hired him has been studying your techniques."

"There's nothing wrong with that," Maxine snapped. "But I simply cannot allow this hired gun to take the stand and ruin everything."

There was an urgent knock on the door.

"Wait!" Maxine cast aside her bag of popcorn, reached for the remote sitting on her desk, and aimed it at the television. The image of the two writhing bodies blipped into oblivion, leaving a fading impression of fleshy curves, tangled limbs, and titillations of pleasure. "You may enter now."

The door opened slightly and Maxine heard her secretary's raised voice outside. She was insisting that visitors couldn't simply barge into Ms. Doggett's private office whenever they wished.

"But I'm not a goddamn visitor," said a second voice—Billy's. "I'm Ms. Doggett's co-counsel. I *belong* here!"

"I'm sorry, sir," countered the secretary. "But Ms. Doggett's instructions are very implicit: she didn't wish to be disturbed by anybody."

"I must see her!"

Some scuffling ensued, then Billy advanced into the office. The secretary's plump face popped through the doorway behind him. She was wearing a low-cut dress and the swell of her breasts was rising up and down. "I'm sorry, ma'am," she said, pushing her glasses higher onto her nose. "I tried to tell him—"

"That's okay," said Maxine, waving her away. "I'll take

care of this. Why don't you go home now? It's almost quitting time."

"Yes, ma'am."

Now that Billy had won admittance, he approached slowly, his face pouting. "Is this the kind of reception I deserve?" he asked.

Maxine shot back a defiant look. A more appropriate reception would be to throw Billy out of the window. A fall from the sixty-fifth floor would solve at least one of her problems, perhaps not cleanly, but nonetheless effectively. He was supposed to be a fan of hers, yet the moment he became her co-counsel, his flattery ended and he acted as if he wasn't interested in the case any longer. She gave him plenty of work to do, but he dragged his feet and complained about everything. After considerable trial and error, she found she could assign him only the most menial work—the sort of trivial nonsense she might force upon her lowest paid legal assistants. The more he was given to do, the worse his attitude became. She wanted to fire him, but was uncertain how he might react. Now was not the time to get into a spat with him anyhow. The case was far more important and maintaining at least a sense of collegial congeniality was essential to winning.

Making a concerted effort to soothe his ruffled feathers, she said, "Of course you deserve better, Billy. It was boorish of my secretary to be so obstructive. I'll have a word with her later. Have you met Carl Zeiger? No? He works for me."

The two shook hands stiffly.

Maxine indicated a nearby chair with her hand. "Have a seat and make yourself comfortable. What can I do for you?" she asked.

His feelings were quickly mollified and Billy's chest expanded with pride. "Just wait until you hear what I just found out!" he said. Then, he glanced at Carl and hesitated.

"That's all right," said Maxine. "Carl and I don't have any secrets. Do we, Carl?"

"No, ma'am."

"You can speak freely, Billy. What have you found out?"

"Well, I have a doctor friend. . . . Actually, he's not really a friend," he added quickly as if he feared such an admission would diminish his standing in the room. "Just somebody I've known . . . for only a short time, that is. He's quite trustworthy, though—"

"Get on with it, Billy," said Maxine, gently strumming her bejeweled fingers on her desktop. "We don't have all day."

"Well, he told me about a secret physician organization called the Society of Defensive Medicine. SOD'M for short."

Maxine exchanged a brief glance with Carl.

"You'll never guess what they're up to!" continued Billy. "*Never!*"

"Let me try," said Maxine with a thinly disguised smile. "They're a small cult of malcontent physicians who agreed amongst themselves to order as many unnecessary tests as possible, send patients for endless specialist consultations, make hospital stays long and expensive, and so on. The purpose is to drive up the cost of medical care in the hope of triggering a crisis in the near future and forcing politicians to pass medical liability reform legislation."

Billy's eyes grew larger. "You already know about SOD'M?"

"Personally, I think Defendant Forrester is a sore loser," continued Maxine, "and now he's carrying out a personal vendetta against me. If you ask him, he'll deny it, of course. He'll claim it's for the common good, but it's obvious the only thing interests him is a taste of my blood."

Now, Billy's mouth was hanging open.

"The health insurance companies have already noticed a sudden increase in costs, but they don't have a clear idea what's causing it. Judging by the electronic chatter Carl's been monitoring, though, we know they're worried."

"How the hell do you know all this?"

"Oh, Billy—don't be so naïve! I wouldn't be any good at my job if I didn't know everything going on in this town. Defendant Forrester won't get very far. None of these puny little doctor rebellions against the trial lawyers ever accomplish much. We'll just remind our politician friends in Salem and Washington D.C. who's been sending them the big checks through thick and thin over the years and they'll squash this subversion for us like a bug. And that'll be the end of that."

"How can you be so sure?"

"Money talks, Billy, and we've been giving away a lot more of it than anybody else. Although," she added with regret, "sometimes our success works against us. If I hadn't won so many lawsuits over the last few years, those doctors would never have rebelled."

"Surely they're doing something illegal!"

"No," said Maxine. "They're practicing good, safe medicine, and the patients love it. We can't use the law against them."

Billy was unconvinced. "We can't let them get away with this!" he cried. "If we do nothing, their strength will grow. Maybe they don't have as much money as we do, but they've got a very powerful weapon we don't—and that's *respect*."

Maxine's eyes narrowed and she suppressed the urge to grab this little prick by his scrawny neck and throw him out of the window right then. She didn't want to be reminded by the two-bit runt that she had a significant problem earning other peoples' respect.

Carl made a threatening move towards Billy. Maxine waved him back into his seat.

"We're not going to let them get away with it," she said quietly. "A plan is beginning to take shape in my mind. It's still early on and I'm not sure how to develop it yet, but things look very promising."

"What kind of plan?" asked Billy.

"A confidential one."

Billy rolled his eyes. "Oh, for God's sake," he protested, "you never tell me anything important. You don't trust me. Is this any way to treat your co-counsel?"

"SOD'M has nothing to do with *Winter vs. Montrose.*"

"I know that, but you could at least treat me as if we're on the same side. I'm sick of being kept in the dark about everything."

"All right, then," said Maxine, who was never one to keep secrets amongst her senior staff, especially if they underscored her mastery of medical malpractice. "I'll divulge a few things about my plan, if it'll stop you from whining. Certain information about Defendant Forrester has come to my attention recently—*extremely* damaging information. If it ever becomes public, it'll certainly put an end to his career—and SOD'M too. The question remains: how best to make sure that every man, woman, and child in this state finds out about it. It's a delicate problem, one that needs to be handled in just the right way."

"Information?"

Maxine turned to Carl. "Would you fetch me the dossier, please," she asked.

"Are you sure it's wise to—" he began.

"The dossier, please," she insisted, flicking her fingers.

Carl shrugged and went to a filing cabinet. He unlocked it, withdrew a folder from one of the drawers, and handed it to Maxine. She licked her lips with the tip of her tongue and opened it to the first page.

"A few months ago, the ER at Columbia Medical Center received a certain Mrs. Louise Diamond—a ninety-eight year old lady from Cedar Hills with a large hemorrhage on the left side of her brain. Defendant Richard Forrester was on call for neurosurgery and responded promptly to the consultation."

"So what's wrong with that?"

"Defendant Forrester was drunk."

"Drunk?"

"Not only that, he was also accompanied by a certain young woman named Becky Briggs, a.k.a. Candy—a prostitute of the most common variety. After he evaluated the patient, he decided to operate on her head and remove the blood clot. He took the tart to the operating room and invited her to assist him in surgery—"

"He did brain surgery with a whore helping him? Hah!"

"Calm yourself, Billy," said Maxine, patiently leafing through some of the papers in the file. "We haven't reached the good stuff yet."

"Good stuff? What could be better than that?"

"It seems as if Defendant Forrester didn't learn anything at all from *Brown vs. Forrester*. You're familiar with that case of mine, aren't you?"

Billy suddenly looked bewildered. "I'm not sure if I remember that one specifically . . ."

"Really? You once told me that you studied all of my cases."

"I have!" said Billy, blushing as if he had been caught lying. "Remind me what that particular one was about."

Maxine didn't pursue it any further. "Defendant Forrester operated on the wrong side of somebody's head and tried to cover it up," she explained. "He paid dearly for it in the end, though. The jury's award was ten million dollars."

"Oh, yes!" said Billy, slapping his knee. "I remember now."

"Apparently, Defendant Forrester was drunk enough to repeat his mistake when he operated on Mrs. Diamond. He opened up the wrong side of the head again."

"No!"

"Yup. Only this time, when he realized what he had done, he didn't bother closing up and starting again on the correct side. He just burrowed right through the middle of her head like some bunker-busting bomb until he reached the blood clot on the other side. He sucked it out—along with most of the contents of her skull, I might add—then told the husband that the operation had been a complete success. The poor woman died the next day."

"Why don't you sue him, then?"

"I would," said Maxine, "except there are a couple of problems. First, Mr. Diamond is so old and senile he's told me he doesn't want to sue Defendant Forrester."

"He *doesn't*?"

"He knows nothing about the whore, the drunkenness, the wrong-side surgery . . . all that stuff. All he knows is that his wife was going to die anyway and that Defendant Forrester was kind enough to offer an operation only as a last ditch effort. Believe it or not, the stupid old man is actually grateful to him for trying."

"Can't somebody let him know what really happened?"

"Therein lays the second problem," said Maxine with a sigh. "All my information about this incident comes from internal quality assurance documents that belong to Columbia

Medical Center. They're privileged and inadmissible as evidence in a trial. I can't talk about all the really scandalous stuff or somebody will ask me how I obtained my information. And we don't want to divulge that, do we, Carl?"

"No, ma'am," said Carl, shaking his head. "We certainly don't."

Maxine closed the file and tossed it onto the desk in front of her. "So, I've got a neurosurgeon who is obviously guilty of the worst malpractice imaginable. The trick is: knowing how to nail him. You see, Billy, a successful medical malpractice case has to be massaged into existence with great care. They don't just drop out of heaven like manna. It takes skill and patience. Smart people have to be manipulated in a way so they don't even notice what's happening to them. Lies have to be made believable. Small, trivial incidents have to be identified so they can be blown completely out of proportion. Facts have to be created out of thin air. I've got plenty of time, though. The deadline for the statute of limitations isn't for at least another year. Mr. Diamond will be baying for Defendant Forrester's blood long before that. You'll see."

"So, when Forrester falls—"

"*Defendant* Forrester."

"Excuse me. When Defendant Forrester falls, then SOD'M will collapse too."

"Of course. The organization will be totally discredited in the eyes of the public. It'll fizzle with barely a whimper."

Billy leaned forward in his chair and reached for the file. Maxine quickly snatched it from his fingers.

"I can't look at it?"

"Definitely not," said Maxine, handing it back to Carl. "But if you're looking for something useful to do, I've got an idea."

"Yes?"

"We've got an important trial coming up, one that'll surely set a milestone in the history of medical malpractice litigation. It's essential that everybody knows about it well in advance, just so they can clear their calendars."

"Everybody? You mean the public?"

"No, not the public," said Maxine in an impatient tone as if Billy was missing the most obvious point in the world. "I mean the legal community here in Portland, and beyond. I want you to go out there and spread the word about *Winter vs. Montrose*. Pin special fliers to every notice board at the law school, send out mailings, talk to your colleagues, involve CATL. You get the idea. Do you think you can manage that?"

"I think so."

"Good." Maxine jerked her eyes towards the exit. "Run along now and get to work on it immediately. I want that courtroom to be full every day, starting from the beginning."

Taking his cue to leave, Billy backed out of the office. When the door had closed behind him, Maxine sighed. "Thank God, he's gone," she said. "Now let's go over this video one more time, Carl. I want to make *sure* we've made no mistakes."

She reached for her bag of popcorn.

CHAPTER 19

Creeping through the Multnomah County Courthouse, Hugh was in a different world—a sinister and unfamiliar one. This late in the afternoon, the usual throng of litigants had largely cleared out, leaving behind empty hallways and idle security guards. He felt like a criminal, guilty before proven innocent, with a trial in his future that seemed to him to be a mere formality on the road to punishment. Since his was a civil case, there would be no time behind bars if the jury affirmed his negligence. In this grim place, however, the subtle differences between civil and criminal law were lost on him.

Hugh was here to watch Denmark negotiate a settlement—a pay-off so they would piss off.

Not that a settlement conference was likely to succeed where a Motion for Summary Judgment failed, as it had. A meeting between the opposing camps was mandated by law in a feeble attempt to avoid the time and expense of a trial. A neutral judge would be batted between the parties like a shuttlecock, translating their threats and insults into a civilized language, trying to find common ground. Denmark had already told Hugh that he didn't expect any significant developments. Maxine was still demanding the full $14 million and not a penny less. Neither party had much incentive to settle, with the trial still four months away.

"Just what *is* the point of having this conference?" Hugh had asked his lawyer.

"We're just feeling each other out. Let me do all the talking."

Denmark had told his client that he wasn't obligated to attend the settlement conference, but a courthouse was as alien to Hugh as the surface of Mars and he was curious enough to see for himself what one looked like. He arrived early and peered into an empty courtroom with the same sense of awe as he'd experienced when he had seen his first operating room when he was a college student. The judge's bench was a throne—hallowed ground on high from which death sentences were delivered and windbag lawyers silenced with the wave of a hand. Two rows of seven chairs filled the jury box; twelve jurors and two alternates, ordinary citizens who were empowered to determine innocence or guilt. The public gallery was smaller than Hugh had expected. Perhaps the spectacle of lawyers scrapping amongst the ruins of their clients' lives wasn't as popular as TV shows suggested.

Hugh was ogling through a small window in a door, checking out his third courtroom, when he heard voices approaching. He turned and found himself suddenly face to face with the Winters. Julie was in a mechanized wheelchair, guiding her joystick with her hand, a hunched, shrunken figure starkly displaying all the ravages of her condition. Any hope for recovery she may have ever held was now extinguished and her eyes possessed the same vacant look as one of Hugh's coma vigil patients. Her husband was pushing her along. When he saw Hugh ahead, he froze.

Hugh also stiffened. For a few moments the two men looked at each other awkwardly, not sure how to react. Hugh had not seen Julie since her follow-up visit years before. On that day, at least she had smiled at him and had thanked him for trying his best. Now, he imagined that she would curse him and blame him for everything that had gone wrong with her life. He felt his heart pounding within his chest and looked around for an escape. He couldn't find one and there were no lawyers nearby to tell him what to do, so he did what came naturally: he said hello and extended his hand. After a brief hesitation, Gary did what must have felt natural for him: he shook the hand that was offered.

Julie looked up. The angry explosion that Hugh was expecting never occurred. Instead, she appeared resigned, or, more accurately, *defeated.*

"I didn't know about the high protein," she said in a halting voice that was barely audible.

"The protein?" asked Hugh.

"The abnormally high spinal fluid protein," she explained. "Your expert witness, Dr. . . ."

"Bull?"

"Yes. He testified about it at his deposition yesterday. Ms. Doggett passed the news along to my husband and me today. She told us it was the first she'd ever heard about it." Even after three years, her breathing was still labored and she had to struggle to construct every sentence. "Did you know about it, Dr. Montrose?"

"Yes. Dr. Bull pointed it out some time ago."

"Nobody told me. I am always the last to know. Tell me something, Dr. Montrose . . ."

"I'll do the best I can."

"If you had known about the high protein before I had my lumbar fusion, you would have found the tumor. Right?"

"Julie," said Gary, touching one of her shoulders with his hand. "There's no point going into this."

"I have to *know*, Gary," she said, shrugging him off. She turned her head towards Hugh and looked into his eyes. "Dr. Montrose, you would have found the tumor. Isn't that correct?"

"I don't . . ."

"Tell me the truth."

"I would have looked for a tumor. An MRI would have shown it."

"If you had discovered my tumor, you would have operated on it. Right?"

"Yes, that's right."

"And I wouldn't be like this now?"

"Julie . . ." began her husband.

"*Gary!*" Julie's eyes flashed with anger. "Answer my question, please, Dr. Montrose."

Hugh hesitated. The answer was not one that required much thought, but nonetheless, it was still difficult to give. "Most probably not, I'm afraid," he said eventually. "No, you wouldn't be paralyzed."

Julie gently closed her eyes and sighed away a valuable breath. Then, after gathering another, she said, "Thank you for being truthful with me, Dr. Montrose. I believe you are an honest man."

"And I believe you've suffered more than anybody could ever know," said Hugh, lowering himself to Julie's level so he could look directly into her moistening eyes and take her withered hand into his own. "But you've *got* to be strong and keep going. Life still has so much to offer. You have your husband and your children. They love you, and you must surely love them. As long as that's the case, there's hope. One day, all this will make some sense."

"You cannot even imagine how terrible my life is," said Julie, hardly audible. "Can you even guess the worst part? Not the total dependency on others, not the bowel protocol, not the loneliness . . . It's knowing that a medical mistake was made and my condition could have been avoided. If I hadn't started this lawsuit, I'd still be paralyzed, but at least I wouldn't know the details. I suppose it's what I deserve for stirring up trouble. It was never my intention to sue you and now I'm sorry I did. Isn't that right, Gary?"

"It's true," said her husband, stepping forward a pace. "We *are* sorry. We resisted as long as possible, but you have to understand our situation. It costs a lot of money to care for Julie and our insurance money and savings are quickly drying up. We were going to lose our home. Julie and I could probably manage somehow, but we have two children and, naturally, we have to think of them. We were becoming desperate. Maxine Doggett came to our house and persuaded us to put the whole matter in her hands."

"Why didn't she know about the protein?" asked Julie. "Why did she advise us to sue you, and not Dr. Clegg? I don't understand anything anymore. It's all so confusing."

Hugh wanted to tell Julie that he had been asking identical questions over and over again. Instead, he simply said, "I'm sure your lawyer knows what she's doing. You have to put your trust in her, and perhaps, one day, everything will become clear."

A tear trickled down Julie's cheek. "Do you really think so, Dr. Montrose?"

"There's no doubt in my—"

"*Jesus Christ!* What the *hell* are you doing?"

Hugh dropped Julie's hand, straightened up, and saw another of his former patients, Maxine Doggett. She was wearing a fluffy black and white outfit that made her look like a dead ostrich. Her eyes, though, were very much alive and brimmed with fiery indignation. Her chin jutted out a mile and her hands were planted firmly on her ample hips. Standing behind her and eclipsed by her was a young weasel of a man, presumably Billy Funk. He was staggering under a stack of heavy legal files.

"Just what do you think you're doing?" Maxine repeated, addressing her clients.

"We were talking," said Gary.

"Never, *never* talk to the defendant!" cried Maxine. She strutted over to Julie's wheelchair, her high heels tapping loudly on the floor. "You could screw up everything! What, precisely, did you say to him?"

"We were just—" began Hugh.

"I'm not talking to you!" interrupted Maxine, pummeling him into silence. "I was speaking with my clients. Come on, what did you tell him?"

"Dr. Montrose was just giving us some words of encouragement," said Gary, shrinking from his lawyer.

"You are not to refer to him as *Doctor* Montrose! He is *Defendant* Montrose."

"You don't have to be so—" began Hugh.

"And *you!*" snapped Maxine, wagging a crooked finger at Hugh. "If you've got any messages for me, you can deliver them through your attorney! Is that clear?"

Hugh was lost for words.

"*Is that clear?*"

"I'll have to speak to him about that," said Hugh, retreating.

"You can speak to that blithering fool all you want," said Maxine. "It won't do you any good." Then, she turned to her clients. "Come on, you two. We're wasting our time here. Let's go and find some place where we can talk privately." She left with them while Billy obediently followed.

***

As expected, the settlement conference yielded no settlement. Hugh stayed with Denmark in one jury room while the plaintiffs sat with their own attorneys in another. An amiable judge bounced between the two camps like a ping pong ball, carrying messages and trying to reason with the parties. Denmark made an offer of fifty thousand dollars. Maxine scoffed that such a ridiculously small amount wouldn't even cover her copying costs. She grudgingly lowered the demand from fourteen to ten million dollars, then it was Denmark's turn to reject the offer. Julie became emotionally upset and had a bowel movement in her pants and Gary spent most of the conference cleaning her in the restroom. In the end, everybody went home frustrated and empty-handed. The prospect for a showdown in court loomed larger.

From Hugh's perspective, the settlement conference had been a failure, but not a total waste of time. For the first time since the beginning of the lawsuit, he had met the plaintiffs. He could no longer feel such blind anger towards them for suing him. They were just a couple trying to survive in a society that often showed no mercy to those struck down by catastrophic illness. Who could blame them for resorting to the legal system for help? They were right to seek full compensation for such a horrible screw-up in their medical care.

Bonehead's screw-up.

No, Gary and Julie were normal, decent people. He could not fault them.

The Dog, on the other hand, was something entirely different.

CHAPTER 20

A signature—that's all it would take; a scrawl of ink at the bottom of a settlement agreement, its illegibility betraying the frustration and anger of the defendant. Hugh carried the papers in his pocket everywhere he went in the vague hope that, one day, he would suddenly whip them out, sign them, then throw them into a mailbox before he had a chance to change his mind. With the trial only about seven weeks away, the plaintiffs had suddenly lowered their price. Now, it would cost two million dollars, the limit on his insurance policy, to make the lawsuit go away.

"Why do they demand fourteen million dollars so passionately when they're obviously willing to settle for two?" Hugh had asked Denmark one day.

"It's called bargaining."

"I call it 'screwing with my mind'."

"Most trial attorneys aren't interested in putting doctors out of business," explained Denmark. "For them, it would be counter-productive. They would much prefer to keep you around so they can keep filing lawsuits year after year, like leeches slowly bleeding you dry."

"Like they taught us in medical school: no good parasite kills its host."

"Precisely."

To settle or not to settle, that was the question. Was it better to fork over the dough and get on with life, or fight for one's reputation and risk losing everything? Hugh had been agonizing over the question for weeks and now felt that he had finally reached a conclusion.

Settle.

A familiar voice interrupted his brooding. "It's Christmas Eve, Hugh. Can't you put the lawsuit out of your mind for just a few hours?"

Hugh emerged from his trance and focused on Michelle. She was sitting beside him on the couch in their family room. It was late; the children were in bed and all was quiet. A Christmas tree stood in a corner, laden with glittering ornaments and multicolored lights, its silver star at the top tickling the ceiling. Santa Clauses, elves, angels and cute, furry animals portrayed a fantasy world which can only fully exist in the minds of children. Scattered across the carpet were gifts that had been wrapped and were ready to be put underneath the tree—toys, games, books, clothes, electronic gadgets, all the material trappings of a prosperous family. Around the room, most of the candles that had burned brightly earlier in the evening were now extinguished. Those that remained were mere stubs of wax and their flames were growing small. Embers glowed in the fireplace, providing little warmth.

Hugh saw the settlement papers lying on the coffee table, a nasty eyesore amid the Christmas spirit.

"I'm sorry, Michelle," he sighed. "No matter how hard I try, I just can't think of anything else."

"I know."

"Is it *that* obvious?"

Michelle nodded. "You've been going around all evening like you're in another world. You burned the fish we were supposed to eat for dinner and poured so much brandy over the Christmas pudding I was afraid to light it in case it exploded. Look, Hugh, I know you're consumed by this, but aren't you carrying things a little too far? I'm looking after the children and running the home while you're stumbling around in your own little world. I don't know how much longer I'll be able to cope. I want my husband back."

Hugh sighed. "The trial's only a couple of weeks away. I think I'm going to tell my insurance company to settle."

"*Non!*"

Hugh was startled by the depth of Michelle's feelings. "But, Honey—"

"Ne fais pas de transaction!" insisted Michelle. Don't settle!

"I *have* to—"

"No, you don't! You can fight this thing and win. Then you can put it into the past and start being my husband again."

"But if I settle, I can avoid a court battle and return to normal so much sooner."

"If you settle, you'll *never* return to normal," said Michelle. "You'll go around for the rest of your life with a big chip on your shoulder, always wondering how things might have been different. The Hugh Montrose I fell in love with in France when I was young will be gone forever."

"It's just not worth fighting the system," said Hugh, sounding as if he was trying to convince himself, rather than his wife. "Robert Bull, the expert witness who's testifying in my defense, told me so himself."

"What does *he* know?"

"Quite a lot, actually. Years ago, he decided *not* to settle a case against him. He went to trial and for three weeks he was forced to listen to the lawyers spout all kinds of garbage. They didn't bother to give the jury any relevant facts. Instead, they fed them diatribe, bullshit, and lies. They had fancy clothes and bad haircuts. They told tasteless jokes and acted as though they were

271

everybody's best friends. Bob said it was nauseating to watch. By the end of it, he felt that he had been gang-raped. And do you know what? He actually won the case. Did he feel vindicated? Not at all. In fact, quite the opposite. He wished he had settled right in the beginning. At least he would have spared himself the humiliation."

"And look what happened to him," said Michelle. "He divorced his wife, became a drunk, and nearly killed himself."

"I would never do things like that," said Hugh quickly.

"How can you be so sure?"

"Look, Michelle," said Hugh with a trace of desperation. "This trial has absolutely nothing to do with me."

"Vraiment?" Really? "Until now, that fact has escaped my attention."

"I lost any relevance I had as a person a long time ago. The only important thing now is *money*—who pays it, who gets it, and how much changes hands. This is something to be decided between the lawyers and the insurance company. I might as well put it out of my mind and get on with my work. Now it's time for bed."

Hugh started to get up from the couch, but was pulled back down.

"Have you seriously thought what may happen if you demand a settlement from your insurance company?" asked Michelle, gripping his shirt tightly and shaking it.

"Sure—the insurance company will do one of two things: either they'll follow my wishes and settle, or they'll refuse and make me go through a trial. If they settle, it'll go on my permanent record. I know a million dollars won't look good, but what does under these circumstances? The next time my policy is up for renewal, the insurance company will probably drop me like a rock. Hopefully, I'll find another company that will sell me insurance."

"Don't be so certain about that," said Michelle, releasing her grip on her husband. "Some of your friends have had to retire or move to other states. And don't think you'll be retiring any time soon, not with the number of children we have." She poked him in the side lest he forget too easily.

"I have no intentions of—"

"And what happens if the insurance company forces you to go through a trial and you end up losing?"

"If I lose any amount of money up to my policy limit, then the insurance pays. If the jury awards a judgment against me in excess of my policy limits, then I can sue your insurance company for bad faith and they might have to cough up the extra money. At least I won't lose my home and the rest of my assets, but try getting liability coverage again. It'll be damned near impossible. No carrier will want to insure somebody who has filed a lawsuit against them for bad faith. Again, retire or move."

"So you've got no choice but go to trial and win the damn thing!" cried Michelle.

"But it's too dangerous!" retorted Hugh. "Denmark told me that quadriplegics never lose. The award from a sympathetic jury could be huge. Better to pay a million or two now, than risk a much bigger loss later on."

"Capitulation would run against every grain in your body," said Michelle. "You did nothing wrong and the only neurosurgeon who speaks against you is a ninety year old crackpot who hasn't practised in decades. This lawsuit is the fanciful creation of a trial lawyer with some twisted agenda of her own. You've even told me the plaintiffs don't have their hearts into it. All this hardly makes a strong case against you. If you settle, you'll forever change the way you think about yourself, Hugh. From now on you'll be Dr. Montrose, the coward and the loser—somebody who put money ahead of his principles."

"If the verdict is against me, we could lose everything, including our own home!"

"Do you honestly believe I give a damn about losing our home?" blurted Michelle, taking a tack Hugh had never heard before. "It's *you* I don't want to lose."

"Me?"

"Oui! Je t'aime!" I love you! "And I'm terrified you'll end up dead like Richard, or a burned-out drunk like Robert Bull. Then what will happen to us? And the children? I don't even want to think about it."

Hugh reached out for Michelle's hand, but she pulled away, choking back tears. "I want you to fight back!" she cried, jumping from the couch and backing away. "Go to trial! Win! Then return to me as you *were*, not as you *are*!" She turned, and, without another word, stormed from the room.

Hugh blew out a lungful of air. Evidently, the decision whether or not to settle was not going to be difficult after all. He reached for the settlement papers, crumpled them in his hands, and threw them into the fireplace. They landed amid the embers and, for a few moments, lay there, smoking. Then, as he watched, flames erupted with the sound of a soft puff. Within seconds they were consumed until nothing remained except for dancing ashes, fluttering to and fro amongst the currents of hot air.

CHAPTER 21

Hugh blinked away his weariness and studied the freshly shaved head before him, judging every angle and carefully planning how to make the plunge. He held a plastic white catheter about the thickness of a piece of spaghetti delicately between his thumb and his forefinger. It was eighteen inches long, perforated with a number of small openings at one end, open at the other, and had a stylette inside its lumen which kept it straight and stiff. He placed the perforated end into the small hole in the skull that he had just created with a hand drill and took careful aim.

The head belonged to Mr. Rice, a sixty year-old man with high blood pressure. He was having dinner with his wife when he suddenly cried out, staggered from the table, and collapsed in a heap. The medics tubed his airway, scooped him off the floor, and rushed him to the ER at Columbia. A CT scan showed a large clot deep inside his brain. Some of the blood had broken through to the ventricles and plugged up the normal drainage of CSF. The pressure inside his head was rising quickly and his level of consciousness was deteriorating. He needed a ventriculostomy—a drain to the outside so the CSF could escape—and he needed it quickly.

"I wouldn't stand there if I were you," Hugh murmured to a wide-eyed nursing student standing behind his right shoulder. "You might get wet."

She promptly backed away.

Hugh checked his angles one last time, sighting along the catheter as if he was trying to sink an eight ball.

"Well, here goes . . ."

A piercing scream erupted from the next room.

"No! Please, God! Stop it! I can't take any more!"

"What the *hell* was that?" cried Hugh, suddenly straightening up.

Doris, the charge nurse, provided a quick explanation. "Dr. Pagonis is next door. He's trying to reduce a dislocated neck."

"Pagonis? Who's Pagonis?"

"He's the neurosurgeon you hired."

"Somebody I . . ." Then Hugh remembered a recent meeting with Ed Cleveland, the medical director. The blustery man had blown clouds of blue cigar smoke at him and thrust a file in his direction, saying it belonged to a neurosurgeon who would help to cover the service while Hugh was on trial.

"He's not exactly the man I'd pick to remove my own brain tumor," he had admitted, sotto voce. "Excitable little bugger, originally from Greece. Still has a strong accent. Hard for me to understand him when he speaks fast. But he's got all the right qualifications. With any luck, we'll survive until you get back."

Hugh had flipped through the file without paying much attention to the details. Pagonis was thirty-four years old and had trained at a small, struggling program in Montana. However, his license and other credentials were in order and no lawsuits were pending. With only three thousand of them in the entire country, neurosurgeons were an endangered species and were becoming much harder to find. Emergency rooms, on the other hand, were busier than ever and screaming for coverage. Obviously, there weren't enough neurosurgeons to go around and so it was becoming increasingly more common for hospitals to hire itinerant ones to fulfill their needs. It was an expensive proposition and they could never be sure of the quality of who they were getting, but at least they could keep their doors open. Pagonis was obviously one of these neurosurgeons—no family commitments, short of money, and harboring a desire never to stay in one place long enough to grow any roots.

Hugh had supposed there was no need to be picky and had nodded his assent.

Another scream, even louder and more piercing.

"For God's sake!" cried Hugh. Without further delay, he thrust the catheter deep into Mr. Rice's brain and withdrew the stylette. Bloody spinal fluid ejaculated from the open end and sprinkled across the floor a few inches in front of the nursing student's feet. The flow quickly ebbed once the pressure was released and soon the fluid was only dripping. Hugh attached the catheter to a sharp metal skewer, tunneled it under the scalp three inches, and hooked it up to a drainage bag system. He sewed the tubing to the scalp so it couldn't be accidentally pulled out, popped off his gloves, and hurried into the next room to see what was going on.

A large man was stretched out on a gurney and Gardner-Wells tongs, a C-shaped arc of metal with a sharp spike pointing inwards at either end, were clamped to his head. A rope was tied to the tongs, threaded through a pulley, and hung over the end of the bed. A cluster of weights had been added, at least one hundred pounds, Hugh estimated, and they hung from the end of the rope like a bunch of giant iron grapes. The man's face was contorted in pain and he was noisily sucking air in and out between two rows of clenched teeth like a pair of bellows. Sweat was pouring from his face.

Pagonis was poring over about a dozen neck X-rays that were hanging on a viewing screen, repeatedly tapping on the films with his index finger and thoughtfully shaking his head. He was a small, thin man with an olive-skinned face, a stubbly jaw, and big brown eyes. He was wearing scrubs and a white lab coat. Thick, matted chest hair sprouted from his neckline.

Hugh approached and introduced himself. "Hi. I'm Hugh Montrose."

Pagonis was preoccupied by the X-rays in front of him and didn't answer.

"Excuse me—" said Hugh.

Pagonis jumped as if he had been startled and a couple of X-rays spiraled to the floor. "Yes?" he said, regarding his visitor with alarm.

"I'm Hugh Montrose. You must be Dr. Pagonis."

The man suddenly grinned at Hugh. "Yes, yes!" he said, speaking with a heavy Greek accent. "Pagonis. Petros Pagonis. Very pleased to meet you." They shook hands. "Very pleased!"

"Welcome to Columbia. What are you up to?"

"Dislocated neck," Pagonis explained, the expression on his face becoming serious again as he swept an arm across the X-rays on the viewing board. "Maybe traction works. Very, very difficult."

Hugh wondered how best to break the news that unlocking facets using traction in the ER was an outmoded method of treatment that belonged in medieval torture chambers and not in modern hospitals. From his point of view, it was far more humane to fix the problem under general anesthetic using one of the many different kinds of instrumentation available these days. However, he didn't want to start off his relationship with this man on the wrong foot and stifled his objections. Before he could offer help, however, Hugh heard his name being announced on an overhead speaker. He excused himself and went to a phone. Trish was calling from the office.

"I just heard a nasty rumor," she said. "There's actually going to be a *trial?*"

"I'm afraid so," replied Hugh. "All last minute efforts for a settlement have failed. There's no avoiding it now."

"Starting *tomorrow?*"

"Starting tomorrow."

"It's going to last *five* weeks?"

"That's Maxine's estimate. Denmark says such a long trial is totally unnecessary; dragging things out is one of The Dog's tactics for winning. She figures that the longer the jury hears about quadriplegia, the more sympathy it'll have for the plaintiff."

"So how the hell are your patients going to manage for five weeks without you?" asked Trish.

"Give them Maxine Doggett's home phone number and tell them to call *her*. It's her goddamned fault!"

Trish was in no mood for humor. "It's going to be a disaster!" she said.

Hugh found himself privately agreeing with her. He had spent weeks imagining the worst case scenario: hundreds of patients suddenly abandoned and forced to find care elsewhere. It was bound to get ugly. Under normal circumstances, Richard Forrester would take a deep breath, shift into warp drive, and save the day. However, since their argument at the SOD'M meeting eight months ago, Hugh felt that he could no longer rely on him. Richard had somehow changed inside and was deliberately avoiding him. The two of them never made rounds together anymore, would sit apart at conferences, and made no time for the collegial chit-chat in the office that was so vital for every healthy group practice. When confronted about the deteriorating relationship, Richard claimed that he was far too busy operating, ordering tests, and spending other peoples' money on health care to have any time for socializing. Hugh knew that it was a flimsy excuse; in the past, Richard would always find time to pay him impromptu visits in the operating room, no matter how inundated he was. Hugh found the chill deeply upsetting;

Richard had always been his close friend and he grieved to see him change like this. At the same time, he knew that there was little he could do about it and hoped that he didn't have long to wait before the big man burned through his grief and returned to normal.

"Dr. Forrester will handle it," said Hugh, without conviction.

"Talking about Dr. Forrester," said Trish, "I've been trying to contact him all day long and I haven't been able to find him anywhere. I had to reschedule all his morning patients and he didn't show up for his operation this afternoon."

"He missed an *operation*?"

"Yes. I've never known that to happen before."

For all Richard's erratic behavior in recent years, he had always shown up for surgery when he was supposed to. This was something new and troubling. "You've looked everywhere for him?"

"Everywhere. He's gone; totally disappeared. What should I do?"

"Let me handle it. I'll try to find him when I get off from work"

When Hugh hung up, he felt a tugging on his sleeve. It was Doris. "Come and see your patient!" she said.

"What is it?"

She led him into the treatment area where he was lying. "Mr. Rice!" she called loudly. "Say hello to the doctor."

Mr. Rice was intubated and unable to speak. He wouldn't open his eyes either. But as he lay there, buried under a jungle of IV poles, monitors and tubes, he slowly raised his hand off the bed . . .

. . . and flipped Hugh a bird.

✳✳✳

Rounds that evening were slow and painful. Hugh had fifteen patients; five in the ICU and the rest on the floor. To those that weren't in a coma, he gently broke the news that he was turning over their care to a neurosurgeon whom they'd never met. He told them that his partner, Dr. Forrester, would take good care of them, as well as he could himself, but few were reassured. One intelligent and perceptive patient in the ICU, Mrs. Peabody, took the news particularly hard. She'd had a complicated hospital course involving multiple operations on a recurring blood clot on the surface of her brain and over time she had developed a deep trust for Hugh. When he told her that he would be suddenly withdrawing from her care, he watched concern and fear filling her eyes as though an invisible dyke in her mind had been breached.

"You're *leaving?*"

"Yes, I'm afraid so."

"Where are you going?"

"I—I have to do some work outside the hospital for a while."

The fear in Mrs. Peabody's eyes changed into suspicion as if she knew he was keeping something from her—something embarrassing. "What kind of work?"

"Just . . . work."

Mrs. Peabody frowned at his evasive answer and looked as if she was about to ask more questions along the same lines when an alarm on one of her monitors suddenly exploded into life. Hugh stabbed at a button with his finger and cut off the noise, grateful for the diversion.

"So, what's going to happen to me?" asked Mrs. Peabody.

"My partner, Dr. Forrester, will assume your care. You'll like him. There's another neurosurgeon: Dr. Pagonis. You might be seeing him also."

"He's your partner too?"

"No. He's just filling in."

"Do you know him?"

Hugh wanted to tell her that he knew the locums well and that he was a very good surgeon, but he was never a very good liar. "Actually, I met him for the first time this afternoon."

"So you don't know whether he's any good."

"He has all the qualifications—"

"But is he any good?" Mrs. Peabody stubbornly insisted.

Hugh remembered the patient being tortured at the hands of the Greek in the ER and said nothing. He shifted around his feet, hoping some other alarm might choose this moment to get tripped. But he had no such luck and there was a long, difficult silence while Mrs. Peabody studied him closely. Then, with a knowing look, she said, "You're being sued, aren't you?"

Hugh's face tinged with warmth and he nodded.

"And you have to go away for a trial."

Hugh nodded again.

Mrs. Peabody gently shook her head with bitter disappointment. "A cousin of mine was a doctor, you know. He once had the same deer-in-the-crosshairs expression on his face as you do."

"I didn't think it would be so obvious."

"It is to me. I'll never forget that look as long as I live. Walter retired right after his trial and never spoke about medicine again. A couple of years later, he died, of a broken heart, I think."

"I'm sorry to hear it."

"I hope the same doesn't happen to you."

Another alarm went off and Hugh silenced it too. "How does anybody sleep in this place when alarms are going off all the time?" he asked.

Mrs. Peabody didn't take the opportunity to follow a different thread of conversation. Instead, she looked at Hugh sharply and said, "You're leaving a lot of patients in the lurch, aren't you?"

"I'm afraid so."

"How many patients depend on a single neurosurgeon at any one time, do you suppose?"

"Hundreds, at least."

"And I just happen to be one of them. Now, after I *believe* in you—*trust* in you—you're forced to abandon me too."

"Mrs. Peabody—Dr. Forrester is a very good neurosurgeon. I'll be checking out my list of patients to him tonight. I promise I'll go over your case in detail and make sure he understands everything. You have nothing to worry about. Doesn't that make you feel better?"

"No."

Hugh felt something was seriously wrong as soon as he stepped out of his car in front of Richard's house.

The night was cold and the wind was gathering new strength as yet another Pacific storm rolled in from the coast. The evergreens along the street looked like dark giants, dancing to some grotesque choreography as their trunks and branches writhed around in slow motion. Low clouds scurried across the sky from the south, reflecting the city lights with an eerie yellowish glow. A jet screamed overhead against the wind as it headed for a landing at the airport ten miles away. The small house where Richard had lived appeared abandoned; no lights burned, the front lawn was uncut and ill-kept, and a plastic garbage container had fallen over and was rocking to and fro in the driveway. Hugh gripped the collar of his raincoat closely around his neck and shuddered.

Of all nights, this was one he would have preferred to spend at home. After it became clear Richard was nowhere to be found at the hospital, Hugh had made a tour of his partner's usual watering holes, asking the barmen and waitresses whether they had seen him. None had, so he decided to check his home. Taking care not to slip on the slick sidewalk, he made his way to the front door and knocked.

He listened carefully, but only heard the bark of a startled dog nearby.

He knocked again, louder this time.

Still no answer.

Hugh gripped the doorknob and twisted it. The door was unlocked and creaked as it swung open. He stepped inside and flipped a switch on the inside wall. The weight-lifting machine he had given Richard a few years ago stood in the middle of the living room floor. It had been a thoughtful present; Hugh had never forgotten the look of sheer joy on his friend's face when he had first seen it. A picture of a boy in a baseball uniform stood on a mantelpiece. He bore a striking resemblance to Richard himself and Hugh knew that it must be the nephew he often spoke about.

And there was an odor . . . .

Hugh immediately recognized it and felt the skin crawl at the back of his neck. He had smelled it in the ICU or the surgical ward. Sometimes in the ER. Almost never in the operating room.

And *always* in the morgue.

It was the smell of death.

"Richard? Are you here?"

A stupid question, for Hugh already knew the answer. Yes—he was here, somewhere. He moved slowly and silently through the house, occasionally kicking an empty beer can with his foot. Every time he turned on a light, his thumping heart felt as though it was going to burst in his chest.

Hugh found the body in the bedroom. It was sprawled diagonally across the bed, belly up, with the head hanging over the edge of the mattress. Richard was only wearing pajama bottoms. His skin of his massive torso was a ghostly white, mottled with a bluish hue that only a corpse can have. His eyes were wide open, bulging out in horror at some unseen devil. His lips were separated and out of the corner of his mouth hung a long tongue that was caked with dry blood. On the floor below his head was more blood, pooled and splattered across the wooden floor.

Hugh staggered against the edge of the doorway and leaned forward, resting his hands on his knees while revulsion rose in his gut. For a few moments, he remained in the same position, taking deep breaths and fighting the shock that threatened to overwhelm him. He had witnessed far more gruesome scenes at the hospital and had always maintained a certain measure of cool, professional detachment. But this was quite different.

Richard had been his best friend.

When the initial waves of nausea had receded, Hugh crept towards the corpse and cautiously looked it over. Richard's right arm was stretched out and in his hand he saw a handgun—a .38 Special. The index finger was still curled around the trigger.

Had he shot himself? At first glance, it certainly looked that way. Had he owned a gun? Hugh wasn't sure and Richard certainly had never mentioned one. Hugh looked for a bullet hole hidden in his hair, but was unable to find one. His eyes once again focused on the tongue which looked as if it had been dipped into a can of dark red paint.

The truth dawned in a horrific revelation: Richard had shot himself in the back of the mouth. Hugh leaned closer and saw the exit wound at the back of the neck—a small, meaty crater with jagged wound edges that resembled the teeth of a saw. Amongst the ribbons of flesh he saw cream-colored flecks of tissue, all that was left of Richard's brainstem.

At least this part made sense. No neurosurgeon would take his own life by pointing a gun at the side of his head. He would know the risks only too well, having operated on too many of the failures. Often people ended up blind, paralyzed, mute, or even vegetative, but not quite dead. Richard knew the proper way to kill himself. He had pushed the barrel past his lips and aimed it at the back of his mouth where death was assured.

But *why*?

What terrible thing had happened to drive him to this? Sure, he'd been depressed ever since his trial, but he had showed signs of recovery since SOD'M had been born. The physician revolt had galvanized his mind. He was beginning to lose weight and grow his hair longer. Hugh had even noticed him flex his muscles once again in front of reflective surfaces, a ritual he hadn't performed in a long time.

So why had he committed suicide?

Hugh could make no sense of it. He sank to his knees beside the bed and slid into a sitting position on the floor. He buried his face in his hands and yielded to his grief.

CHAPTER 22

Hugh's trial began on Monday, February 21st, 2005.

"All rise!" cried the bailiff, a beefy-looking woman dressed in uniform. "The Court is in session."

Hugh blinked and shook his head, clearing the recurring and haunting images of Richard lying spread-eagled across his bed, his mouth caked with blood and remnants of his brainstem seeping out the back of his neck. He climbed to his feet and watched as the portly, white-haired Judge Jenkins entered the courtroom from his chambers. Flowing black robes magnified his importance in much the same way as a white lab coat and scrubs did for a neurosurgeon, and Hugh felt humbled. In his clinic, though, his own mild demeanor put the most nervous patients at ease. This judge, on the other hand, was no friend. He was stern, humorless, and seemed ready to hand out maximum sentences at the minimum of provocations. When he settled into his leather seat and peered over his half-moon spectacles, Hugh felt sure he was being scrutinized by those dark, intense eyes, made all the more fearsome by bushy eyebrows, grim mouth, and heavy square jaw.

Hugh was standing behind the defense table next to Denmark. To their right, at the plaintiff's table, Maxine and Billy had also risen to their feet, although neither of them bothered to show deference to the judge and continued to read documents spread below them. Their clients, Julie and Gary, were not present. Aside from the bailiff, the only other person in the courtroom was the clerk, a middle-aged women with her desk situated immediately below the bench. Cameras and microphones were placed in strategic positions throughout the room, silently recording everything that transpired. Empty wooden benches, resembling the pews in a church, stood at the back of the courtroom. A jury box with its fourteen chairs ran along one wall. Bookshelves on either side sagged under a couple of hundred volumes of the Oregon Legal Code, books dating back to the state's earliest days.

"Please be seated," said the judge with a firm, business-like voice.

"I'm telling you," whispered Hugh into Denmark's ear after they had settled into their own chairs. "Richard is dead, and there's the *bitch* who's responsible." He stabbed his finger towards Maxine.

"That's the tenth time you've told me," his lawyer whispered back. "You keep forgetting: it was suicide, not murder."

"Doesn't matter. If it wasn't for her, he would still be alive. There's a connection somewhere. I just haven't figured it out yet."

"Richard was depressed," said Denmark. "That's all there is to it. You're just suffering from a slight touch of juris psychosis."

"Juris psychosis?"

"JP for short: a psychiatric condition physicians get when they're overexposed to the legal profession. Don't worry: it'll pass. It always does. Now pay attention to the judge."

Judge Jenkins cleared his throat loudly. "Are there any matters that Counsel would like to bring up before we bring in the jury?" he asked.

Matters? thought Hugh bitterly. *There are* always *matters.*

Indeed, so far, there had been far more 'matters' than actual substance to this trial and things were proceeding at a snail's pace. For the first two days, Hugh was catatonic from the shock of Richard's death. As he sat with his head buried in his hands, staring at the floor, the lawyers argued over the Motions and Sublimine, each trying to outmaneuver the other as they set the rules under which the trial would be conducted. Maxine's strategy was clear: to be as obstreperous as possible. She succeeded brilliantly, giving long-winded speeches, pitching fits when she didn't get her way, and introducing so many irrelevant motions that even the tough judge seemed to wilt like a parched plant. For another three days afterwards, Hugh watched the process of jury selection. Sixty ordinary citizens were herded like cattle into the public benches and were asked numerous questions by the opposing lawyers. Had they ever sued anybody? (Half said they had.) Were they satisfied with their medical care? (*All* said they weren't.) Was there anybody who would suffer an undue hardship if they were asked to sit through a trial that was likely to last for five weeks? (Hands shot up all over the room: people with back-aches, jobs that wouldn't wait for them, and vacations that had already been paid for; they were all excused.) The questions droned on until both sides developed a clear idea of whom they wanted and whom they did not. Denmark was searching for educated jurors who could see through the deception and lies and render a verdict based on the facts. Maxine wanted people who never had any hope of understanding the science and medicine of the case and would more likely be swayed on a gut level by the sight of a crippled victim. Her perfect juror: an old man who had looked like he was press-ganged from the local park bench to be in the jury pool. Despite having been told nothing about the case, he already held a strong opinion.

"Is this somet'ing the doc done?" he asked loudly, shaking his fist in the air. "'Cos my wife was lost the same way!"

The man was dismissed by the judge before Maxine could get her sticky hands on him.

Once the obvious undesirables were weeded out, the surviving members of the jury pool were presented one by one to plaintiff and defense counselors. Each side was allowed to eject four of them for whatever reason they wished—the manner in which they looked at the defendant, their age, their race, the answers they had given. When the final fourteen, twelve jurors and two alternates, were eventually seated in the jury box, Denmark seemed pleased with the result.

Hugh was aghast.

"I have a right under the constitution to be tried by a jury of my peers," he said during one of the breaks. "Just *look* at those people! Four are high school drop-outs. Only two graduated from college. None of them have any experience with medical matters. How the hell are they going to understand the intricacies of a cervical intramedullary ependymoma case?"

"What did you expect?" asked Denmark, scribbling notes. "Fourteen neurosurgeons?"

"Three would be enough. One picked by the plaintiff, one by the defense, and the third by the first two. They could review the case and quickly come to some fair conclusion, then this circus would be over. It's the way they do it in Indiana. Makes a lot of sense to me."

"This isn't Indiana," said Denmark without looking up. "All things considered, I think we've been pretty lucky."

"Lucky to have an unemployed construction worker who can barely read, a student who is failing in college because he plays video games all day long, and a tree-hugger who straps magnets to his body because he believes they'll make his personality more attractive to women? Give me a break!"

"Things could be worse. At least most of the jurors have high school diplomas."

Far from being reassured, Hugh imagined what Maxine must surely be thinking: *Look at all the brain-dead people I managed to get onto the jury! They'll give me whatever I ask for.*

Now that the jury had been selected, it was time for the trial to get underway.

Judge Jenkins repeated his question. "Mr. Denmark? Ms. Doggett? Any other *matters?*"

Denmark stood up and, like all lawyers, buttoned his jacket as he did so. "Defense is ready to get this trial on the road, Your Honor. We have nothing to bring up at this time."

"Ms. Doggett?"

"I'm ready too."

"Good. Then the bailiff will fetch the jury."

While everybody waited, Hugh leant so close to Denmark he could smell shaving cream. "Maxine had motive too," he continued. "SOD'M was a grave threat to her business. She had to make sure it failed, so she planned a way of pushing Richard over the edge. I'm going to find out how she did it, if it's the last thing I do!"

"Don't do anything without discussing it with me first!" Denmark hissed, giving Hugh his undivided attention. "If the judge finds out you're snooping around the plaintiff's counselor, he'll lock you in jail and throw away the keys. If that doesn't scare you enough, just wait until you hear what *I'll* do to you if you ever get out. For God's sake, drop it! You can only cause more trouble."

Hugh nodded his acquiescence, but, inside, he was burning with fury. There was no way he was ever going to 'drop it'. Discovering the truth behind Richard's death had become his top priority—even greater than winning the trial, so it seemed right now. No—Denmark's warning didn't bother him in the least. There were only two things that had him concerned: exactly how far he would have to go in order to get some answers, and what he was going to learn when he got there.

As if he felt he had made his warning clear enough, Denmark returned his gaze to the bench and said, "Did you know that Judge Jenkins has never tried a medical malpractice case before?"

Hugh was shocked. *"Never?"*

"Nope. He's a total greenhorn. There's a rumor going around that he fought hard to avoid making this his first. None of his illustrious colleagues wanted it either and so they drew straws. Jenkins lost, and so here he is."

"Why didn't they want it?"

Denmark nodded towards Maxine; the simple gesture explained everything. "Judges are human too, you know," he added for good measure.

"Oh, great," said Hugh. "We've got a jury with an average IQ bordering on mental retardation and a pissed judge. What else could go wrong?"

"Plenty."

"Please rise for the jury!"

Once again, everybody climbed to their feet, Judge Jenkins included. As the fourteen men and women filed into the room, the judge's stern expression magically melted into one of benevolence as he offered his official gratitude for the invaluable service that these citizens were providing. The lawyers in the room followed his example. They plastered smiles onto their own faces and, no doubt, would have said 'Good morning', 'Thank you for being here', and 'Please don't pay any attention to what the other side has to say because they're a bunch of lying scumbags' had they been permitted to speak. The jurors looked resolutely ahead and avoided eye contact. When they sat down, they reached for their notepads and pencils.

The pleasant expression on Judge Jenkins' quickly faded and he curtly invited Maxine to begin her Opening Statements.

"Ladies and gentlemen of the jury," said Maxine, leaving her chair and approaching the jury box, "my name is Maxine Doggett and I am an attorney. The young man assisting me . . ." —she jerked a thumb towards her co-counsel, who suddenly swelled with indignation as if he had just suffered the worst insult—". . . is Billy Funk. I represent my clients, Mr. and Mrs. Winter, who haven't yet arrived this morning. They're late because Mrs. Winter is paralyzed from the neck down and her husband takes three hours to get her ready in the mornings, *every* morning now for almost four years. Why is she paralyzed? Because she had the misfortune of being treated once by the man sitting before you in this courtroom: Defendant Montrose!"

A crooked finger pointed at Hugh and he shrank from her accusing eyes. He wanted to point his own finger back at her and blame her for Richard Forrester's death in front of everybody.

But he was paralyzed and unable to utter a word.

Maxine went on to tell the jury that her clients were once two of the nicest people that they were ever likely to meet: a couple of beautiful children, steady jobs, everybody's idea of the perfect family. There was one problem though: Mrs. Winter had chronic low back pain, severe enough to have an operation. The night after surgery, a tumor in her spinal cord that nobody had known about caused weakness in her arms and legs. Her orthopedic surgeon, Dr. Bruno Clegg, was an excellent clinician. He ordered some tests and when he discovered the problem, he called the defendant for an urgent consultation.

"Now, the defendant is not just *any* doctor," continued Maxine. "He's a neurosurgeon—somebody who specializes in operating on the spinal cord. I understand the issues. You see, not only am I an attorney, but I'm also a fully qualified registered nurse—"

"Objection!" shouted Denmark, leaping to his feet and startling Hugh.

Judge Jenkins puffed up and turned crimson. "Counselors to the sidebar!"

Denmark, Maxine, and Billy hurriedly assembled in a place to the side of the bench, out of earshot from the jury. Hugh watched as the judge lectured them, angrily prodding the air with his finger. When he was finished, the attorneys resumed their places.

"What was all that about?" whispered Hugh.

"During Motions and Sublimine," explained Denmark, "the judge ruled that Maxine couldn't tell the jurors she's a nurse. Now they're going to think she's some kind of medical expert, which she is definitely not. It's nothing new; she does the same thing at every trial—at least, the ones I've been involved with. By now, I've come to expect it."

Judge Jenkins composed himself and addressed the jury. "As you heard, Ms. Doggett has a nursing degree in addition to her law degree. I would like to caution you, however, that this fact has no bearing on the case whatsoever and you are to disregard it completely. Continue, Ms. Doggett."

Maxine thanked the judge and proceeded to give her own version of Hugh's consultation. Dr. Clegg requested his emergency consultation close to noon on June 29th, yet Defendant Montrose delayed three hours before leaving his office. Defendant Montrose also misinterpreted the MRI scan, obtained a history from a confused and medicated patient, performed an inadequate exam, and, most negligent of all, chose not to offer Mrs. Winter the only option that might have saved her from becoming permanently paralyzed: an immediate operation to remove the tumor from her neck. He didn't run the problem past any of his colleagues, nor did he go to the library and research the medical literature. No discussions. No questions. While she talked, Maxine prowled up and down in front of the jury box. Billy had set aside his anger at the way Maxine had introduced him to the jury and was furiously scribbled notes.

"Mr. and Mrs. Winter trusted their doctor and waited. And waited. For *two* whole days they waited for Defendant Montrose to act. Finally, Defendant Montrose made his move. He took his patient to the operating room and removed her tumor. Of course, by then, it was too late. *Far* too late. Any chance of reversing her paralysis was long gone and Mrs. Winter was cruelly condemned to spend the rest of her life in a wheelchair."

Listening to this diatribe, Hugh had difficulty sitting still. He had been instructed by Denmark to keep his face neutral, and for the most part he was succeeding. Inside, however, he was burning up like a furnace.

"Ladies and gentlemen of the jury!" Maxine cried, sweeping her arms into the air in one final dramatic gesture after a long discourse. "I urge you to listen carefully to all the evidence that is presented to you. Weigh all the facts carefully in your minds. I am convinced that you can come to only one conclusion: Julie Winter was the victim of *monstrous* incompetence, *shocking* negligence, and *pure, unadulterated* callousness. Maybe you don't have the power to restore her limbs to their former strength, but you *do* have the power to put right what is so obviously wrong. Do not turn a blind eye to her pleas for justice! Do not ignore the cries of her deprived children. Give her family every dime to which they are entitled! I implore you to find the defendant *negligent.*

"I humbly thank you for your attention."

During the lunch break, Hugh and his attorney retreated to a small, windowless conference room on the fourth floor of the courthouse. Denmark pulled out a magazine with a big ugly fish displayed on its front cover.

"A *fishing* magazine?" said Hugh with a disapproving look.

"Sure," said Denmark, biting into an apple. "Fishing helps me relax. Do you fish?"

"No."

"Too bad. You're missing a wonderful sport."

Hugh grunted as though he didn't believe a word of it. As his attorney became absorbed by his magazine, Hugh discreetly distanced himself, pulled out his cell phone, and called his office.

"How are things?" he asked Trish.

"Not so good."

"What's the matter?"

"Where did you find that guy, Pagonis?"

"Why?"

"He's horrible!"

Hugh was filled with dismay. "What's he done?" he asked, dreading the answer.

"This morning he was called to the Emergency Room and I haven't heard from him since. He doesn't answer his pages. Our phone has been ringing off the hook. Patients are in pain. They want drug refills. They want appointments. They're desperate to be *seen*. I tell them you're not available. So they say they'll see Richard instead. I tell them he's dead. Then they start crying, and *I* start crying. . . . How am I going to survive five weeks of *this*?"

Somehow, Hugh wasn't surprised and he wished he had spent more time selecting a stand-in for himself. "We'll all manage, one way or the other," he said, sounding as if he didn't believe his own words.

"Another thing," added Trish. "Call Dr. Harrison, the anesthesiologist. He says it's urgent."

"What's it about?"

"He wouldn't say, but I wouldn't be surprised if it's about Pagonis. Everybody's talking about him."

After Hugh gave Trish some more words of encouragement, he hung up, called Tom in the OR, and pictured his owlish face in his mind.

"Sorry to disturb you while you're in trial," said Tom. "But I thought you ought to know what's going on around here. Last night one of your patients, Mrs. Peabody, died."

"No!"

"I was on call. Two o'clock this morning she had a seizure. At first, it was nothing big; just some twitching in her face—"

"That's how her hemorrhage presented last time."

"Her nurse called Pagonis at home and told him what was happening. He ordered her to be fitted with a neck brace."

"What?"

"I know. Even I know enough about neurosurgery to realize that doesn't make any sense at all. Obviously, he hadn't completely woken up. Then the seizures started getting worse. The nurse called again and, this time, Pagonis did the right thing and ordered a CT scan, only now it was too late."

"It showed another recurrence?"

"That's right. By the time Pagonis arrived at the hospital, four hours after the first phone call, Mrs. Peabody was brain dead."

"Oh, God—the poor woman."

"That's not all," continued Tom. "Later on, he ordered an EEG to prove brain death. You know how much paper that test produces?"

Hugh indicated that he did, and imagined a thick wad of computer print-out paper covered in squiggles of ink indicating brain waves.

"Well, he unfolded the paper all the way down the long hallway outside the ICU, right in front of the family."

"On the floor?"

"Yes! Then he took them on a guided tour of the EEG, from one end to the other, stabbing his finger at the thing and repeating over and over again: 'It's flat! It's flat! It's completely flat!'"

"Poor family."

"I'm telling you: Pagonis is a lot different than you. He's supposed to be a neurosurgeon, so you might expect him to know where the spine is, right? I'm even beginning to have my doubts about that. The other day he was doing a neck fusion, and he spent an hour—an *hour* digging around, just trying to find his way. You should have heard him jabbering to himself in Greek, growing more and more flustered as time passed."

"Oh, boy."

"He can't do anything right. A regular lumbar disc operation usually takes him about four hours. Both aneurysms he's attempted woke up dead. There are plenty of people around here who already want to get rid of him."

After he hung up, Hugh sat quietly, remembering Mrs. Peabody, the trial lawyers' latest victim. A while passed before he noticed Denmark on the other side of the room. His magazine was open on his knee and he was holding up both his hands as though he was gripping a fishing rod. Without taking his eyes off the pages in front of him, he lifted his hands up and over his right shoulder, and suddenly thrust them forward as if he was casting into some beautiful mountain river teaming with fish.

An expression of profound satisfaction filled his face.

"Ladies and gentlemen of the jury, my name is John Denmark and I have the privilege of representing Dr. Hugh Montrose and his wife, Mrs. Michelle Montrose, the defendants in this case."

Denmark was standing behind his special podium with wheels, gently caressing its smooth, dark wood with his hands. Earlier that morning, he had carefully unloaded it from the trunk of his car and had pushed it through the corridors of the courthouse as if it was an old friend. On this day, he needed every bit of reassurance it could offer. He had rehearsed his speech countless times and was well prepared, but at the same time he knew from experience that Maxine would try whatever dirty trick she could dream up to disrupt his train of thought. So, while one eye surveyed his prepared text, the other looked around warily. He noticed that she had changed clothes and was now wearing a skirt that ended above her knees, unusual for a female attorney making an appearance in court.

A red flag waved frantically in his mind.

It was not a question of *whether* she would try something, but *when*.

"I've met Mr. and Mrs. Winter," Denmark began, "and I want you to know that I agree with Ms. Doggett; they are indeed nice people. When you meet them yourselves, I'm sure you'll agree. I'll also be the first to admit that a terrible thing happened to Mrs. Winter; she's now paralyzed and she's not going to get any better. These are facts that are not in dispute. However, it's also true that when Dr. Montrose was called to help Mrs. Winter, she was *already* paralyzed and there was nothing he could have done to change that. In fact, if Dr. Montrose had performed surgery at that time, as the plaintiffs contend, not only would she *not* have improved, it was very likely she would have gotten worse. And by 'worse', I mean she could have completely lost the ability to breathe on her own or use her arms."

Denmark then proceeded to give a lecture on the anatomy of the nervous system, using poster boards that cost, Hugh later learned, as much as fifty thousand dollars for SPI to produce. Then he displayed Julie's MRI and the jurors craned their heads forward in an attempt to have a closer look at the tumor. Just in case any of them were unable to appreciate its gigantic size, he had put up an MRI of a normal spinal cord next to the sick one, and the contrast between the two was striking.

Denmark went through the specifics of Julie's history, making remarks about the high CSF protein, how the tumor must have been slowly growing over the years, and about the disastrous events on the day she was paralyzed. While he was speaking, he sometimes wandered away from his podium. On one of these occasions, when he was standing next to Hugh, he suddenly began to sound like a broken record; he became stuck on the words 'When you're talking about . . .' as though he had completely lost his concentration and didn't know what to say next. Hugh looked up and immediately spotted the cause for his attorney's confusion.

While she had been listening to Denmark's speech, Maxine had been slouching behind her table, her body turned towards the defense. She was twiddling a pencil between two of her fingers, looking bored. She had just raised one of her legs so she might rest a foot on her elephant bag, presenting those sitting at the defense table—and nobody else—with a direct view up her short skirt.

And she wasn't wearing any underwear.

"W—when you're talking about . . ." stuttered Denmark. "When you're talking about . . . sixteen hours. Long time for neurological tissue, you know. . . . Let's see . . . What was I saying? A *very* long time . . .When you're talking about . . ." Then he tore his eyes away from Maxine, hurried back to his podium, and hung onto it like a drowning man clinging to a life preserver.

"Mr. Denmark, are you all right?" asked Judge Jenkins.

"Yes, Your Honor . . . I'm fine."

"Your face has lost all its color."

"Just a touch of the flu, Your Honor."

"Shall I order a recess?"

"No, no, Your Honor. I already feel better. If I stay here, I'll be okay."

"Then continue, Mr. Denmark."

Maxine suddenly sat up and straightened herself out. Denmark picked up the frayed thread of his argument. He hadn't resumed speaking for more than five minutes when the door at the back of the courtroom abruptly opened and Julie appeared, propped up in her elaborate wheelchair for all to see. For anybody who wasn't accustomed to quads, the sight of her withered hands and legs, bloated stomach, and pale skin must have been a shock and a subtle gasp arose from the jury box. Julie nudged the joystick on her wheelchair with a gnarled knuckle and lurched into the courtroom, followed by her husband. They passed by the defense table, causing a major disruption since all the elephant bags that were scattered across the floor had to be moved. They settled next to Maxine and Billy, neither of whom showed the slightest acknowledgement of their clients' arrival.

"Did you see what she did to me?" whispered Denmark, bending low to help Hugh move files around. "The Dog flashed me! In open court! She'll do anything, I'm telling you. *Anything!*"

"Mr. Denmark," said Judge Jenkins. "Are you ready to resume your Opening Statement?"

"Yes, Your Honor."

Once again, Denmark picked up again from where he had left off, but it was clear that the jurors' concentration, as well as his own, had been shattered by Julie's arrival. He waffled on for another twenty minutes, often hesitating and obviously distracted, before he was interrupted for a third time. Maxine quietly informed the judge that her client had had an accidental bowel movement. Would he graciously allow her and her husband to be excused? Permission was granted and the jury was treated once again to the spectacle of a quad lumbering past it at close quarters, this time heading in the opposite direction.

"I'll bet you anything there isn't a turd within ten miles of her," Denmark angrily whispered to Hugh. "She just wants the jury to get a good, close look at the victim. It's a well-known technique, especially with paralyzed people and children with cerebral palsy. Been known to add lots of zeros to the end of a jury verdict."

When she was gone, Denmark resumed his Opening Statements, but the jury had had enough and was no longer listening. He quickly puttered to a close and fell dejectedly into his seat next to his client.

"This is going to be worse than I thought," he moaned.

CHAPTER 23

Billy was aghast. "You're not going to put *him* on the stand, are you?" he cried.

Maxine dealt Billy one of her signature withering looks. Once again, her assistant had barged into her office uninvited. Her patience with this moron was wearing thin. He was disrespectful, rude, and, worst of all, he'd utterly failed to fill the courtroom benches with lawyers as she'd told him to do. For somebody who claimed to have so many friends in law school who were admirers of hers, his efforts were pathetic and disappointing.

"By any chance, you wouldn't be talking about Professor Charles Mortimer, would you?" she asked, using a tissue to wipe Billy's saliva off some documents lying on her desk.

"Of course I'm talking about Mortimer. I went to his hotel like you told me to and found him in his room. You won't believe what he was doing!"

"I'm sure I won't."

"He had brought a cage full of mice with him from Florida. He was sitting at a table and was cutting their heads off, one after the other, with a pair of scissors. It was totally gross! The poor creatures were squeaking with terror and there was blood everywhere."

"Oh, no," Maxine groaned, remembering the chamber of horrors in the basement of the St. Petersburg VA hospital.

"He was only saving the heads; he had a glass beaker full of them. The bodies . . . he was flushing *them* down the toilet."

Maxine slapped her hands over her eyes in an effort to block her vision of the bloody scene. "I never imagined that weirdo would bring his mice with him," she moaned.

"When I asked him what the hell he was doing," continued Billy, putting both his hands on Maxine's desk and leaning towards her, "he told me he was conducting *important* research and that he never went anywhere without his mice."

Maxine gave Billy's hands a disapproving look and he immediately withdrew them. "Did you bring him here like I told you?" she asked.

"Yes," replied Billy, "although I had a hard time persuading him to leave his damned mice behind. We came in a taxi, but I should have stuffed him into a coffin and hauled him over here in a hearse; it would have been more appropriate. He looks just like a cadaver! And what's more: he's had a stroke since you last saw him and now he drools out of the corner of his mouth. You *can't* put him on the stand!"

"That's exactly what I intend to do," said Maxine with grim determination.

"The judge will think you've lost your marbles."

"I don't care what the judge thinks. It's the jury that matters."

"Come on, Ms. Doggett—be serious! Is he the best you could do for an expert witness?"

"Billy . . ." said Maxine in a low, threatening voice. "You're forgetting who I am."

Billy ploughed on, paying no attention to the threatening tone in Maxine's voice. "I didn't think a trial lawyer would ever have to resort to using somebody like *him*."

"Charles Mortimer is the only neurosurgeon I could get my hands on," Maxine explained icily. "It was either him or nobody. Besides, you should know me better by now. I have a plan."

"A plan? What do you mean?"

"Bring him in and I'll show you. Where is he?"

"I parked him in front of the bird exhibit in your waiting room."

A look of horror suddenly filled Maxine's face. "You left him *alone* with my canaries?"

"Well, yes—"

"Oh, my God!" Maxine leapt to her feet, knocking the documents off her desk. She ran from her office, into the waiting room, and found Mortimer in front of the bird cage. He had opened its door, inserted his arm, and was groping around with his hand, trying to catch one of the canaries inside. The little birds were flying around in a high state of agitation, cheeping loudly and scattering little yellow feathers in all directions.

"Leave my darlings alone!" cried Maxine, pulling Mortimer away from the cage and slamming the door shut.

"Hello, Ms. Doggett," said Mortimer, waving a pair of scissors at Maxine.

"Good morning, Professor," said Maxine, snatching the scissors away from him and tossing them aside. With a sickening feeling in her stomach, she realized Billy had been making a valid point; Mortimer did indeed look awful, an Egyptian mummy stripped of its bandages. The left-hand side of his waxy, pale face was now drooping. A string of spittle hung from the corner of his mouth and traced a small circle in synchrony with the slight tremor of his head. He was looking around vacantly as if he had no idea where he was.

They shook hands. Maxine gripped frigid skin and bones; his tendons felt as though they were the strings of a guitar. She didn't bother to introduce him to Billy who had followed Maxine into the waiting room. "Did you have a good trip from Florida?" she asked instead.

"Yes, thank you."

"We're glad you made it safely. Why don't you come into my office?"

Once seated at Maxine's desk, Mortimer asked, "How has your pre-trial publicity been?"

"Pre-trial publicity?"

"You told me the trial was going to be one of the most important in the history of medical malpractice and that you were expecting a lot of attention. Remember?"

"Oh, yes—"

"Front page stories, the public benches filled with spectators . . ."

"Quite."

"I don't want to be disappointed, you know," said Mortimer, wagging a bony finger at Maxine. "I'm an important neurosurgeon with a very busy schedule. I'll be very angry if it turns out I came all this way for nothing. Under such circumstances, who knows what I might be inclined to say from the stand—"

"I can guarantee you won't be disappointed," interrupted Maxine quickly. "The courtroom will be full of people hanging onto every word of your testimony. Some of them will be from the national media. I can already visualize your picture on the covers of Time and Newsweek."

Maxine noticed Billy looking like a bug-eyed fish and neutralized him with an urgent wave of her hand. Then, remembering Horman's Norma Desmond theory on why the old man wanted to be a plaintiff's expert witness, she said, "Testifying in a court these days is not unlike being on stage, you know. You have to perform in front of an audience, which, in a court of law, happens to be a jury. You must remember your lines, look sad when you feel happy, and look happy when you feel sad. If you have to lie, be unabashed about it. Nobody will know the difference."

As he listened, Mortimer's eyes remained vacant and lifeless.

"And if you're going to be an actor, you'll need make-up."

"Make-up?" said Billy, doing a double-take.

"Yes, make-up. All actors wear make-up. Our own expert could certainly use a little. Sit down here, Professor." Maxine put her hands onto his bony shoulders and coaxed him into a chair. Then she opened a case, pulled out some brushes, compacts and tubes of cream, and laid them out on her desk. "You're very pale. Probably spending too much time in the basement of the St. Petersburg VA."

"Sub-basement."

"Not enough nice Florida sun. So, with your permission, I'm going to fix that right now."

"I want to look my best in the courtroom," said Mortimer.

"You're going to put *make-up* on him?" repeated Billy. "This is a farce!"

"Shut up, Billy," Maxine intoned in a pleasant, musical voice in an effort to disguise her anger at him. "You're going to spoil things."

Billy fell into a grudging silence. Maxine dabbed a cotton ball into a bottle and smeared foundation across Mortimer's ghostly skin, brushing away the spittle. His blemishes magically melted away. She dipped a brush into a compact, then, with vigorous movements of her wrist, she applied powder to Mortimer's scrunched-up face until white clouds filled the air. A layer of rouge for his cheeks was the last step, just enough to give the jury the impression that some blood ran under his skin.

"There!" she said when she was finished. "Maybe he's not

thirty years younger, but he's at least ten. Pity his hair is so white."

"So what are you going to do about that?" asked Billy. "Grecian formula?"

"Not enough time. I bought something the other day that will work quicker." Maxine rummaged around in her desk draw and pulled out a can of Kiwi brown shoe polish.

"*Shoe polish?*"

"That's right. Works like a charm every time." Maxine opened it and scooped out a small amount of the waxy substance with a rag. She smeared it into Mortimer's hair and spread it around in little circles with the tips of her fingers. Within minutes, the whiteness was replaced by a rich dark brown luster.

"That's better," she said. "Now he passes as a real expert witness, as long as the jurors don't get too close. And now it's time for his shot."

"His *shot?*"

"Yes, his shot." Maxine opened a tool box that was sitting on a side table. Inside were assorted vials of medicine sitting in separate compartments. She picked one of them out, took the wrapping off a small syringe, and twisted a needle onto its end.

"What does he need a shot for?"

"I'll give him some Robinul. It'll dry out his mouth so he doesn't drool while he's testifying. A small detail perhaps, but I can assure you: jurors don't like to be distracted by things like that. Could easily make the difference between a win and a loss. Professor, can you roll up your sleeve, please?"

"I'm going to have a shot?" he asked, eyeing the needle with uncertainty.

"Yes, sir. It'll improve your performance."

"*You're* going to give it to me?"

"Don't worry," said Maxine. "I *am* a fully qualified registered nurse, you know. I've given thousands of shots before."

"Well, okay—if you think it's important."

While Billy rolled his eyes and shook his head with disbelief, Maxine rolled up Mortimer's sleeve, exposing a withered arm. She gripped it, searched long and hard for some muscle fibers, then plunged with the needle. When she was finished, she suddenly clapped her hands together and asked, "Now, are you ready to testify?"

"Yes. I'm looking forward to it."

Maxine suddenly sneezed.

"Your mold allergy again, Ms. Doggett?" asked Mortimer.

"I suppose so." She dabbed her nose with a handkerchief. "Anyhow, we talked a lot about your testimony over the phone, but I need to remind you about a couple of really important things before we leave for the courthouse. Remember to speak loudly and clearly so the members of the jury can hear you. When you're answering questions, look directly at *them*, not at me or Mr. Denmark, even if it feels awkward."

"I understand."

"Whenever you mention Montrose's name," she sniffed, "don't call him 'Doctor'. Refer to him as 'Defendant' Montrose instead. Okay?"

"Okay."

"And whatever you do, don't say anything against Dr. Clegg. As far as you're concerned, he's an angel. Is that clear?"

"Dr. Clegg? The orthopedic surgeon? That man is guilty of gross incompetence. He should have known about the CSF protein."

"Yes, yes—I know," said Maxine, flapping her hand impatiently. "But I still don't want you to criticize him in front of the jury. Keep your true feelings private. Okay?"

"If you say so."

"Just stick to the things you said in your declaration, especially the part about Julie Winter. You have to make it very clear that she would be walking today if Montrose had operated on her without delay. Okay?"

"Okay."

"You *must* sound convincing! Everything depends on it."

"I will, Ms. Doggett."

Maxine smiled her satisfaction. "Good. Now wait in here . . ."—Maxine opened the door to a closet—". . . while Mr. Funk and I have a private chat."

"As you say, Ms. Doggett."

Mortimer tottered into the closet. The door was barely closed behind him when Billy whipped around and faced Maxine. "I can't *believe* you smeared that shit all over his hair!" he said.

"Don't you agree it makes him look better?"

"I suppose it does," admitted Billy. "But what difference will it make when he sees nothing but an empty courtroom in front of him? Nobody's shown up to watch since the beginning of the trial! He'll go ballistic!"

"I know," said Maxine, her face turning grim as she tried to concentrate. "Filling the courtroom with law students was supposed to be your job."

"What are we going to do?"

Maxine opened a desk drawer and took out a wad of cash. "Go outside the courthouse and gather as many homeless people as you can," she said. "Give them twenty dollars each. Tell them to come to Judge Jenkins' court and to sit quietly in the public benches. There'll be another twenty for each of them at the end of the day, but they won't get a dime unless they sit still and behave themselves."

"I don't believe it! You want me to fill up the court with a bunch of bums? Mortimer will be insulted."

"That blind old fool will never know the difference," said Maxine, handing Billy the money and pushing him none too gently towards the exit. "Go and do as I say. There are at least three flophouses within two blocks of here. Get a minimum of fifty people to come. Hurry!"

Billy took off. After her co-counsel was gone, Maxine took a moment to gather herself, then went to the closet to collect her precious expert.

Charles Mortimer sat next to Maxine at the plaintiffs' table, quietly biting his green fingernails and frowning as if he was displeased. Aside from the defendant and his lawyer, the bailiff, and the court reporter, the courtroom was empty.

"Where *is* everybody, Ms. Doggett?" he asked grumpily. "You promised me that the public benches would be full of spectators."

Maxine sneezed into her handkerchief. "Don't worry," she said. "They'll be here in a few minutes."

"Are you quite certain?"

"Absolutely." She wiped her nose and sniffed.

"If there aren't any, I won't—"

"Goddamnit! They'll be here!"

Sure enough, at that moment, the doors at the back of the courtroom cracked open and a man with a long grey beard, ragged clothes, and woolen blue cap poked his head through.

"Is this Judge Jenkins' courtroom?" he asked.

"Yes, it is," replied Maxine, recognizing a bum when she saw one. "Come in!"

The man gave a toothless grin and pushed the doors wide open. He entered the room, followed by a flood of his friends, similarly disheveled men wearing tattered clothes and carrying blankets, brown paper bags, and twenty dollar bills. They poured into the public benches in an orderly fashion and took their seats, jostling only a little amongst themselves. Soon, they occupied every available spot and strong odor of unwashed bodies filled the courtroom. Flies buzzed in circles over their heads.

Maxine anxiously looked at Mortimer beside her and was relieved to see that he was smiling his satisfaction. When Billy eventually sat down next to her, she quietly nodded her approval of his work and took a moment to enjoy the looks of utter bewilderment that were coming from the defense table.

"All rise!"

Everybody obediently climbed to their feet as Judge Jenkins swept in from his chambers. When he saw the large crowd, he looked around himself with uncertainty as if he had walked into the wrong courtroom. He quickly confirmed his bearings and sat down in his tall, leather seat.

"Counselors to the sidebar!" he barked as everybody resumed their seats. When Denmark and Maxine were huddled close with him, he asked quietly, "What *the hell* is the meaning of this?"

"What is the meaning of what, Your Honor?" asked Maxine innocently, as if she had no idea what he was talking about.

"All these people! They're off the street!"

"Every one of them is a red-white-and-blue American citizen, Your Honor," said Maxine, casually inspecting her long, red fingernails for any irregularities.

Denmark pointed at Maxine. "She's up to no good, Your Honor. She has stuffed the courtroom with hobos for some devious reason!"

"Ms. Doggett—*are* you up to no good?" asked the judge.

"*Moi*? Of course not!"

"If you are—"

"These citizens are fully entitled to exercise their rights under the United States Constitution, Your Honor."

"You may be right, Ms. Doggett," growled the judge, "but if there are any disturbances, I'll throw them out of here . . . you included!"

"I promise there won't be any trouble, Your Honor."

"Meantime, for God's sake, will somebody *please* get some air freshener?"

When the jurors took their seats, they looked at the new spectators with puzzled looks. However, the spectator benches were orderly and the trial moved forward without delay.

Charles Mortimer was called to the stand.

"Good morning, Professor Mortimer," said Maxine, approaching him with a notepad in her hand, yet taking care not to get too close; she didn't want to start sneezing in front of the jury. "Will you state your full name for the record and your professional address?"

"My name is Charles Hollingsworth Mortimer," he answered, looking directly at the jury directly as he spoke. "And my professional address is 4200 Austin Boulevard, St. Petersburg, Florida."

"And what is your profession, Doctor?"

"I'm a neurosurgeon."

"Have you reviewed the medical records of Mrs. Winter in this case?"

"I have."

"Do you know the standard of care for a reasonably prudent neurosurgeon in the State of Oregon?"

"I do."

"Have you formed any opinion as to the care that Mrs. Winter received from Defendant Montrose?"

"I have."

"And what is your opinion, Doctor?"

Mortimer hesitated and Maxine waited. He smacked his lips and worked his gums. Then he asked, slowly and deliberately, "I'm very thirsty. May I have a glass of water?"

"Of course, Doctor."

Maxine wagged an impatient hand at the bailiff who reluctantly climbed to her feet and provided the witness with a jug of water and some paper cups. Mortimer poured some out and drank deeply.

"So what is your opinion, Dr. Mortimer?" asked Maxine, hoping she hadn't accidentally overdosed her witness on Robinul.

"Clearly, Defendant Montrose practised below the standard of care," said Mortimer, putting his cup down.

"Can you tell the members of the jury in what ways Defendant Montrose breached the standard of care?"

"Of course. When he first saw the patient, he did an incomplete neurological exam, he misinterpreted the MRI scan, and he made an inappropriate decision not to operate based on his completely unfounded fear of making her worse. Everybody knows that spinal cord tumors will only make the patient worse if they're not properly removed without delay."

"Doctor, do you have an opinion, to a reasonable degree of medical certainty, whether the breaches in the standard of care that you've outlined for us caused injuries to Mrs. Winter?"

"I do."

"And what *is* your opinion?"

"They did, because they deprived her of having any chance of recovery."

Maxine smiled. The man may have looked like a relic, but his voice was strong and spoke with conviction. He was following her instructions perfectly.

She launched into extensive questions about her witness's background, beginning with his graduation from medical school before the Second World War. He told the jury that when he finished his residency in neurosurgery in 1942, he went to work in Florida at the University of St. Petersburg. From then until 1985 he worked as a professor of neurosurgery, teaching residents, performing research and cranking out enough literature to fill a couple of shelves in the medical library; there were over four hundred papers and eight textbooks in all. And, of course, he wasn't finished yet. He was currently in the midst of *important* research that could lead to the cure for brain cancer and the Nobel Prize. Maxine asked him about all his accomplishments throughout his life and they were legion: the first surgeon to perform *this* operation, the man who pioneered *that* operation, the Chairman of *this* medical society, the President of *that* one, the recipient of dozens of awards, a world expert in the use of the operating microscope . . . The list went on and on. As each accomplishment was described, Maxine asked carefully worded follow-up questions in an attempt to sculpt her moldy fossil into a hero larger than life.

As he talked, he drank more water and scratched his hair with fingers that were slowly changing from green to brown.

By now, Maxine had cast aside her notepad and was strutting in front of the jury box. She had her witness testify how Defendant Montrose had done an incomplete exam on June 29th, 2001. Some postoperative burning Julie experienced in her legs that night was an obvious sign of intact sensory function and an isolated toe reflex observed by the nurses the next day was a similar sign of preserved motor function. With more questions, Maxine developed the theory that her client was never completely quadriplegic.

"Since Mrs. Winter wasn't paralyzed, she could have been helped by early intervention. Is that what you're saying?"

"That's exactly what I'm saying. I think she would have had a functional recovery."

"What do you mean by functional?"

"She would be walking right now." Mortimer went on to say that not only would Mrs. Winter be walking, but she would also be able to feed herself without a special device attached to her arm, brush her teeth with an old-fashioned toothbrush, comb her hair, use her bladder without a catheter, and have a normally functioning anal sphincter.

"Do you hold all these opinions to a reasonable degree of medical certainty?" asked Maxine, hovering over her expert like a dragonfly.

"I do."

"Thank you, Dr. Mortimer."

***

After lunch, Denmark stood behind his beloved podium, leafing through his carefully arranged notes and trying to ignore the odors coming from the filled spectator benches. When he was ready, he looked up and stared at Mortimer with the same intense concentration written on his face as he might have had sitting in a boat in the middle of a lake, trying to catch the monster bass that would win the top prize.

Mortimer appeared to be enjoying him for his eyes now reflected the faintest gleam of life. Brown smudges from his fingers and food stains from his lunch had appeared all over his clothes since the midday break. The flies that had been circling the homeless crowd had moved to more fly-friendly pastures and were now buzzing around his head. A jug of water stood within his reach, the second of the day. Unused paper cups were stacked next to it, while a pile of used ones were lying jumbled in a nearby wastepaper basket.

Maxine's fingernails had evidently failed their earlier inspection for she had produced a small file from her handbag and was now working on them.

"My name is John Denmark," said Denmark, addressing Mortimer, "and I represent Dr. Montrose. Do you practise neurosurgery?"

"I'm a neurosurgeon."

"Do you still operate on people?"

"No."

"When was the last time you performed an operation on a patient?"

"About twenty-five years ago."

"When was the last time you had to make any kind of clinical decision about patient care?"

"In 1980, when I retired."

"Now, if a neurosurgeon stopped operating and caring for patients for a quarter of a century, would he be able to return when he felt like it, just like that?" He snapped his fingers.

"I don't think so."

"Why not?"

"Because he might be a little rusty."

"Would he have to repeat some of his training?"

"Some."

"Some, or all?"

"After twenty-five years? Probably all."

"His hands would be unaccustomed to tying knots? Is that what you mean?"

"I suppose so, but in neurosurgery, the hands do a lot more than simply tie knots. Dissecting out an aneurysm is very delicate work. It takes a certain touch, and after twenty-five years, that touch might be lost."

"What about day-to-day problem-solving? Patient care? Making decisions? Wouldn't that be more difficult too?"

"Yes, it would."

"So, in your case; if you haven't practised neurosurgery in twenty-five years and wouldn't be allowed to return without remedial training, how can you possibly purport yourself to be an expert?"

"I'm a board-certified neurosurgeon," said Mortimer, proudly puffing up his hollow chest and smiling his defiance with the right side of his face. "I can still give valid opinions even if I'm not actively involved in patient care."

"What, in fact, *do* you spend most of your time doing these days, Dr. Mortimer?"

"Research."

"Research? That's very interesting. How many papers have you published in the last twenty-five years?"

There was a pause as though Mortimer was calculating some astronomical figure. Then he said, "None."

Hugh looked scornfully at this witness. Surely the jurors would see him for what he was: a charlatan, a joke, an embarrassment to the neurosurgical profession.

Taking his cue from his notes, Denmark began an indictment of the care Julie had received from Bruno Clegg. Mortimer admitted that a tumor must have elevated the CSF protein and that the finding should have been investigated. An MRI of the cervical spinal cord would have discovered it and an operation might have prevented her paralysis.

"Dr. Mortimer, is it your opinion that Dr. Clegg was negligent in his care of Mrs. Winter?"

Before he could answer, a piercing shriek filled the courtroom. Hugh whirled around in time to see a shriveled-up old hag behind him collapse onto the floor. Her eyes rolled up into her bony sockets, her eyelids fluttered rapidly, and her scrawny arms and legs shook violently as though she was having a seizure. The people around her were backing away, expressions of horror on their faces.

From Hugh's perspective, something didn't look right.

Denmark gave Hugh a violent jab with his elbow. His client was the only warm-blooded physician in the courtroom and the entire jury was watching. Hugh needed no further prompting. He leapt out of his chair and rushed to her side, crying, "She's having a seizure! Everybody stand back!" He fell to his knees, cradled her head in his hands, and gently extended her neck while the rest of her body thrashed around. Within seconds, Maxine was at his side, loudly reminding everybody that she was a fully qualified registered nurse and highly experienced in such medical emergencies. Hugh blocked her from getting close to the old woman and issued instructions with authority. "Somebody call 911 and tell them to send some medics! I need somebody to go through her purse and find out who she is. Phone number, address . . . anything. Maybe we can get a medical history." Denmark joined the huddle, trying to appear involved while at the same time keeping a close eye on Maxine. Mortimer remained in the witness chair, his droopy eyes showing no reaction whatsoever.

Judge Jenkins was determined not to allow this incident to jeopardize the integrity of the trial. He ordered the bailiff to clear the jury from his courtroom. After they had abandoned their notepads and pencils and had been herded out, he loudly declared a recess and bolted for his chambers.

When Hugh saw that the jury had left, he backed away from the shaking woman. He tugged at Denmark's sleeve and the two of them retreated to the defense table.

"The old bag is faking," Hugh whispered into his attorney's ear. "I've seen plenty of seizures in my lifetime and that's nothing like the real thing."

"She's *faking*?"

"I'm sure of it."

"So why is she . . ." Denmark eyes widened, as though a terrible thought had crossed his mind. "The Dog! She's up to something! This is classic Doggett! Keep your eyes peeled, Hugh!"

By the time the medics arrived, the woman had finished jerking around her limbs and was lying in a trembling heap. While the crowd of spectators craned their necks to see, the medics loaded her onto a stretcher and carted her away. The judge re-emerged from his chambers and asked the bailiff to retrieve the jury.

When all had settled back to some semblance of normalcy, Denmark received a nod from the judge and once again approached his podium. He picked up his papers. "Dr. Mortimer," he said, "I believe we were discussing your experience with . . ." He peered closer at the papers and frowned. Then, he started leafing through them, at first slowly, then his fingers gradually moved faster and faster. Finally, he slapped them noisily onto the podium and glared angrily at Maxine.

"Mr. Denmark," said the judge. "I said you may continue."

"I—I . . ."

"Is something the matter?"

Denmark waved his papers in the air, but was unable to utter a word. Finally, he said, "If I could have a moment with my client, Your Honor."

"As you wish."

Denmark huddled beside Hugh and whispered angrily, "That *bitch* has taken all my notes!"

"What do you mean?"

"My notes, my questions, my references . . . *Everything* . . . Gone! She stole them during the confusion."

"It couldn't have been Maxine. She was next to me the whole time."

"Then it must have been Billy!"

"Inform the judge about it at the sidebar."

Denmark shook his head. "I can't possibly do that. Maxine will deny everything."

"Then you'll just have to carry on without them."

"I don't know if I can. I've always depended on my notes."

"You *have* to, John!"

"I *knew* Maxine was up to something, and I was right!"

Denmark resumed his cross-examination, but he was rudderless and his questions lacked venom and potency. The rhythm of his delivery was disrupted by lengthy pauses while he thumbed through textbooks and journals, looking for the relevant excerpts that supported his client. Sometimes he jumped from one subject to another without warning. Just as the jury was beginning to understand the subtleties of Julie's neurological examination, they suddenly found themselves in the middle of a discussion about research on paralyzed dogs. They grew restless, fidgety, and started yawning. Hugh's head sank lower and lower. Confused and disheartened, Denmark eventually ground to a finish, ending with questions that he had planned to ask at the beginning.

The day Charles Mortimer testified was the blackest day of Hugh's life. For months, he had wondered what kind of man would invent the trash he had read in the sworn declaration, but he had never fully prepared himself for the specimen he saw teetering in the courtroom that day. He was *pathetic*, deserving pity, not hatred.

Why?

Why was he ruining his legacy at the end of his life when he should have been above the fray, basking in the glow of his accomplishments? Why did he risk making himself the laughing stock of all reputable neurosurgeons? The money? Not likely. After operating for at least five hundred years, he was bound to be very wealthy. Did he feel that it was his sacred mission to put right all the wrongs in the world, or was it an attempt to resurrect the glories of the past—to step into the spotlight one last time before dying? Whatever the reason, there was absolutely no justification, not from any quarter.

Mortimer was the most pathetic creature Hugh had ever laid eyes on.

Pathetic and sad.

And, unfortunately, effective.

Walking back from the courthouse to the law offices of Moscowitz, Pursely & Boggs when it was over, Hugh and his lawyer exchanged few words as if the Grand Canyon had opened up between them. At one point, Hugh blurted, "I used to really love neurosurgery!" Then he remembered that Richard had once uttered exactly the same words and fell silent again, his mind boiling in a cauldron of anger and frustration.

As soon as the door to Denmark's office was firmly closed, he whirled around and confronted his attorney.

"You once told me Mortimer would never survive!"

"How was I to know Maxine would pull a stunt with my notes?" Denmark shot back. "I told you how much I depend on them."

"Not only did he survive, I thought he came across rather well. He had a ready answer for all your questions and gave the impression he actually believed what he was saying. I was watching the jury. They absolutely loved him."

"You don't know that."

"Yes, I do. I saw it in their faces." Hugh collapsed into a seat and stared through the dark windows with weary eyes. From this height, Portland seemed to be spread out beneath him like a carpet of twinkling lights. A river of white headlights flowed from regions in the north, changing into red tail-lights as I-5 passed downtown and twisted its way south in long sweeping curves. Another river ran parallel to it; traffic heading in the opposite direction. Every one of those cars was packed with lawyers, Hugh imagined, returning home from their offices after a hard day of suing. It was a depressing view, symbolizing a culture run amok as it lurched into the future.

The red and white lights slowly twisted out of focus and he wiped away the tears that had begun to well in his eyes. "I can't believe this is happening," he said, his voice hollow and cracked. "I'm actually *losing* this case. I made a big mistake. I should never have listened to Michelle."

"Hugh—"

"There's more going on right now than I can handle.... More than *anybody* could handle. All my life I've made big sacrifices so I could be the best possible doctor I could be. For me, it was a calling. Most physicians feel the same way. I guess that's why getting sued is so bloody painful. And now *this!*" Hugh thumped the top of Denmark's desk hard with his fist. "This...this *evil monster* says whatever he damn well pleases on the stand and the jury *actually believes him!*"

Denmark put a hand on Hugh's shoulder. The personal contact served as a trigger, destroying what little was left of his deep-seated British reserve. Despair boiled over into a string of gut-wrenching sobs, each more intense than the one before. Embarrassed and ashamed at his display of emotions, he buried his face in his hands and the carpet below him turned fuzzy and distorted. Warmth and wetness ran down his cheeks and dripped from his quivering lips. "Michelle was wrong!" he cried, gently rocking back and forth. "I should have settled!"

Why was he weeping? He was a *neurosurgeon*, for God's sake—somebody who had suffered terrible defeats over the years and had held his patients' hands while they died. He had seen more pain in his clinic than anybody could imagine, shared the suffering in the Quiet Room as families learned about the fate of their loved ones, broken news to parents that their children were no more. Most recently he had endured the shock of seeing his close friend, Richard, dead in his home, and had grieved like never before. He had done it all without losing control.

But now, a crazy old fart had pointed his gnarled finger at him and had accused him of gross negligence, incompetence, not caring . . .

The tears flowed as if all the bottled-up emotions over the years had been finally set free.

CHAPTER 24

By all accounts, the incident on the soccer field was trivial—one of many harmless collisions during a match when two young girls are sent sprawling in the mud while the ball rolls away. They simply picked themselves up, shook themselves off, and waved away the concerns of on-looking parents. For a while, they continued to play, running circles around each other and fighting for possession of the ball. Nothing seemed to be out of order . . .

. . . until one of them, Miriam, began to slow down.

Bonnie Davidson noticed it first, perhaps because she was an OR nurse at Columbia Medical Center, but more likely because she was Miriam's mother. She approached the coach, who was standing on the touch line with a clipboard in his hand.

"My daughter's hurt," she said simply.

"Miriam? She got a pretty hard knock, but she looks okay—"

"I'm telling you: something's wrong. She's unsteady on her feet and seems confused. She may have been concussed. Pull her off the field and let's check her out."

At the next whistle, Miriam was withdrawn from the game and a substitute was sent in.

"My head . . ." she groaned as she approached her mother. "I feel so dizzy. That knee hit me really hard."

Bonnie examined her daughter closely and was filled with a sense of unease.

Miriam sat down on the grass and held her head in her

hands. As time passed, she complained of headaches and nausea. The worst-case scenario slipped effortlessly into Bonnie's mind and she debated how long she should wait before she called for an ambulance.

The answer came quickly.

"Mom . . ." whimpered Miriam, "I'm getting so confused."

"Speak to me, Miriam! Can you tell me where you are?"

"I'm . . . I'm . . . I don't know."

The coach ambled over. "Is there anything wrong?" he asked.

Bonnie shook Miriam gently. "What day is it today?" she asked.

"I—I don't . . . Monday?" Miriam was chalky white and her eyes were half-closed.

"No, it's Wednesday," said Bonnie, pulling out her cell phone and dialing 911.

***

Dr. Petros Pagonis stood behind the anesthesiologist, Heidi Cunningham, looking over her shoulder as she applied EKG leads to Mr. Cartwright's chest in preparation for surgery. The middle-aged truck driver had suffered a ruptured lumbar disc while changing a tire and the pain down his leg had become intolerable. He had come to Columbia's neurosurgery clinic for treatment and had consented to have it fixed. Now he was lying on a gurney next to the operating table, while nursing staff bustled around, getting everything ready.

A phone call arrived from Dr. Holz in the Emergency Room and was patched through to the speaker phone. "Can anybody hear me?" he asked.

"Please . . . What do you want?" asked Pagonis.

"I've got Bonnie Davidson's daughter down here. She's a twelve year-old who was hit on the left side of her head a couple of hours ago playing soccer."

Everybody in the room, except Pagonis, knew Bonnie. They fell silent and moved as if in slow motion.

"She complains of headaches and nausea and her mother says she been getting sleepier ever since it happened," continued Holz. "Now she's obtunded, although she wakes up when aroused and readily follows commands. A little weakness on the right. Otherwise she's neurologically intact."

"Very bad," said Pagonis, shaking his head gravely.

"The CT scan shows a small hairline fracture through the left temporal bone. Underneath there's an epidural blood clot about two centimeters thick."

"*Very* bad."

"There some mass effect," added Holz. "The midline of the brain is shifted about three millimeters to the opposite side."

Pagonis' brown eyes darted nervously from the speakerphone to Mr. Cartwright, then back again. Behind them, his sausage grinder was churning through the information and was cranking out a decision. "Watch her, please," he said eventually. "We see what happens."

"You're not going to take her to surgery?"

"To be perfectly honest with you, I don't think so."

"Are you *sure*?"

Once again, Pagonis hesitated and his eyes shifted around some more.

"It's not too late to back off," said Heidi Cunningham, looking concerned. "We can do this later, if you wish."

"No, thank you very much," said Pagonis. "This case won't take long, I promise you that."

***

Bonnie stood in the hallway of a crowded Emergency Room. Beside her, Miriam was lying on a gurney—one of a long line of gurneys that seemed to stretch forever, each with its own patient . . . waiting . . . waiting . . . waiting for treatment. Bonnie clutched her daughter's hand and squirmed with anxiety. Six hours had passed since the two of them had arrived in this chaotic place, and, in the beginning, things had moved at a glacial pace. When she complained about it, she was told to have more patience; waiting times of up to forty-eight hours were not unusual when it was busy. After the CT was done, however, there was a noticeable improvement in the level of care she was getting; Dr. Holz promptly explained the findings to her and said he would try to honor her special request that Dr. Montrose be the consultant neurosurgeon. The color in her face faded to a chalky white when Holz returned soon after, only to inform her that Montrose was not available.

"Where is he, then?" she cried.

"It wouldn't be proper for me to say."

Bonnie glared at Holz, but refrained from giving him the tongue-lashing he deserved for being so cagey. "So you're telling me there's only Pagonis, and he's in the middle of a case upstairs?"

"Yes, that's right. Don't worry, though. Dr. Pagonis says your daughter will be fine."

"What the hell does *he* know? He hasn't seen either my daughter or the CT scan. Everybody in the hospital knows he's useless anyhow. Sweet Jesus—my daughter has an epidural clot in her head and we're just going to sit around forever in this damned hallway and see what happens?"

"We gave her some steroids a while ago. The medicine is supposed to help with the swelling."

"*Bullshit!* Even *I* know she needs to go to surgery and have the clot taken out . . . *now!*"

Nearby people turned to look at Bonnie. When their eyes met hers, they quickly returned to minding their own business.

Miriam moaned and Bonnie drew close to her. "What is it, my darling?"

"My head—it's killing me," she murmured. "Please do something for my head. The pain is *so* bad."

"We're doing everything we can, my love," said Bonnie, gently wiping her daughter's forehead with a cloth. "You'll be better in no time. I promise." Then she motioned Holz to accompany her down the hallway. Once she was out of earshot from Miriam she said, "Listen very carefully because I'm only going to say this once. My daughter is getting worse and you're doing absolutely *nothing* to save her. Tell me what the hell's going on! Where's Dr. Montrose?"

"I—I . . ."

"For God's sake, *tell me!*"

"All right, all right," cried Holz, throwing up his arms in surrender. "He's at the Multnomah County Courthouse."

"The Multnomah . . . What the hell is he doing *there*?"

"He's . . . defending himself in a lawsuit."

Bonnie's eyes suddenly filled with alarm. "A lawsuit? Oh, no! Who—who's the plaintiff's attorney?" she asked.

Holz's eyebrow lifted in surprise. "What difference does it make?"

"*I want to know!*"

"She's some sleazy tart named Maxine Doggett," said Holz. "I met her myself once. She ruptured an aneurysm a few years ago and was brought to this ER."

Bonnie clutched her face with her hands. "*Maxine Doggett?*"

"Do you know her?"

"Of course I know her! Everybody knows her—especially around here. Listen . . ." Bonnie reached for Holz with a trembling hand, "we've got to get Dr. Montrose out of that courthouse or my daughter doesn't have a chance!"

"What's Maxine Doggett got to do with it?"

"She's got *everything* to do with it! But that's not important right now. We need Dr. Montrose here right away! *That's* what's important!"

Holz was evidently persuaded for he squeezed Bonnie's hand reassuringly and said, "I'll do what I can."

"Call Montrose's office and find out which judge is trying his case," said Bonnie, taking the initiative. "Then call the judge's office and ask to speak to him. Don't take no for an answer. Explain the situation. Tell them it's a real medical emergency!"

A loud crash was heard down the hallway. Bonnie and Holz rushed back to Miriam and saw her body convulsing on the gurney. Every muscle had taken on a life of its own, contracting into violent spasms that tightened her skin and sent her limbs flailing around. Her eyes were turned upwards until only the whites were showing while her teeth clenched shut and foam dribbled out of the corners of her mouth. An urgent, high-pitched moan was coming from her throat, as though her brain itself was screaming for help in the only way it knew how.

"She's having a seizure!" Holz shouted to a nurse as nearby families scattered. "Get me some IV Valium and tell the pharmacist to bring some Dilantin. A thousand milligrams. Hurry! I'll see if I can protect her airway."

Bonnie stood with her mouth hanging open.

"And get her mother out of here!"

Bonnie was ushered away, her mind numbed by the image of her seizing daughter. She went to the nurse's station and lurched against it.

***

Pagonis looked up from the moist, meaty trench in front of him and glared at Monica, an Advanced Registered Nurse Practitioner who was assisting him. "What you doing?" he cried with a shrill voice. "Hold retractor *this* way!"

"I—I'm sorry . . ." Monica stammered.

"I'm trying to go fast. You slow me down."

"I'm doing my best."

"Well, try harder! I not want to be here all day, please."

The circulating nurse hung up the telephone. "That was the ER," she said. "The girl with the epidural just had a seizure. They want to know what to do next."

"I hurry as fast as I can!" screamed Pagonis. "What more do they want?" He turned his attention to Monica. "You see dura in there?" he jabbered. "Hold aside with a retractor while I drill on bone next to it. Be careful now! Very, very careful! Lots of fragile nerves. No damage, please. You can do?"

"I think so."

"Very good." Pagonis reached for the high speed drill and stuck its business end into the spinal canal. Then he pushed down on a pedal with his foot. Compressed air stiffened the black hose that snaked across the floor and the finely sculpted drill-bit emitted a shrill whine as it rotated at forty-five thousand revolutions per minute. The bone disintegrated into paste and, for a while, everything proceeded smoothly.

Then, in the blink of an eye, disaster struck.

Without any warning, the spinning drill skipped out of Pagonis' hand, knocked the protective retractor out of the way, and ripped into the dura. The bundles of nerves underneath were instantaneously chopped and mangled as though somebody had plunged an egg-beater into a bowl of spaghetti.

"Turn it off! Turn it off!"

"Take your foot off the pedal!" shouted the scrub tech.

"Σκατά!" Shit! Pagonis' foot recoiled as if the pedal had suddenly become red hot, and the drill stopped. He saw a rent in the dura that might have been as long and ragged as the one along the bow of the Titanic. Spinal fluid was pouring out, carrying with it debris from the destruction inside.

"Σκατά! Σκατά! Σκατά!"

✳✳✳

Mortimer returned to his sub-basement in Florida, the homeless spectators shuffled back to the streets, and Judge Jenkins' court was once again virtually empty. As the plaintiffs' case plodded on, Hugh was dying from boredom. The trial had entered a lethally dull phase and he had little else to do but stare out of the courtroom windows, watch the leaden clouds slowly drift by, and ponder Richard's death. Hugh had resolved to do whatever was necessary to uncover the truth, but, after nearly three weeks, he was no closer to achieving his goal. He had the sinking feeling that he was no match for Maxine. She and her security chief, Carl Zeiger, were far too clever for him and would have no trouble hiding their complicity in the tragedy. Hugh worried about the extremes to which he might go in order to uncover the truth if it looked as if those two were going to get away with their crimes.

While Hugh suffered, Denmark occasionally poked him in the ribs and passed him notes ordering him to look interested even if he wasn't.

One by one, Julie's family friends were sworn in. They described how she was once a happy, vibrant person; fun to have around and full of life. Now she was mere shell of her former self and her social life was dead. One of them who claimed to have been her best friend prior to her paralysis confessed that she no longer visited her because she couldn't bear to see her in such a terrible state. John Denmark scowled and wrote yet another note to Hugh, this one saying: SOME FRIEND! After more of Julie's 'friends' were called to the stand to repeat the same sad story, Judge Jenkins became impatient and cut off the repetitious testimony. Maxine fussed and sulked, then told her cadre of lay witnesses to pack up and go home.

Next, a certified life care planning expert testified. She was a short, fussy nurse named Constance Payne, M.N., R.N., C.R.R.N., C.L.C.P., C.C.M. Armed with so many badges of self-grandiosity, she had visited the Winters one day with a clip-board in hand and had busily assessed, as described in the disclosure document, 'the extent of Julie's quadriplegic paralysis, the extent of her inability to perform functions and activities of daily living, prognosis considering her condition, both short-term and long-term needs for Julie Winter, and the short-term and long-term costs associated and expected for treatment and care of Julie Winter, both with and without assistance from family members and other.' Her report was numbing in its thoroughness. Every conceivable contingency was accounted for, right down to the number of bedsores per year she was projected to develop over the next couple of decades, how much hydrogen peroxide that would be consumed per bedsore, and the estimated cost of hydrogen peroxide in 2025.

"None of the jurors are writing down the amounts!" Denmark had whispered excitedly into Hugh's ear. "I've never seen this happen before!"

"So bloody what?" Hugh had asked, picking up his sagging head and wearily confirming Denmark's statement with blood-shot eyes.

"When I've been in cases like this before, the jurors *always* write down the dollar amounts onto their little notepads. It means only one thing: they're as bored as you are! Wow! This is big! This is really *big!*"

At the end of her report, Nurse Constance suggested various care options (24 hour home health aide, live-in attendant, or nursing home) and declared that without one of them soon, Julie was not likely to survive very long. She paid no attention to the fact that for the past four years, Julie had been living without the benefit of any of those options and seemed to have done admirably well.

An economist was even worse. He was as dull and colorless as the endless columns of numbers in the life expectancy tables that he brought with him. His main function was to add up all the figures that the M.N., R.N., C.R.R.N., C.L.C.P., C.C.P. had generated, multiply them by the number of years estimated to remain in Julie's life (36.2), factor in adjustments for inflation and interest rates, and come up with a total that the jury should award for all future economic damages. The number turned out to be $8,392,873.36 *exactly*. Not a penny less.

Hugh thanked God he didn't make his living as either a life care planner or an economist.

Shortly after three in the afternoon, Hugh noticed that the court clerk was having a quiet but animated conversation on the telephone. He watched as the woman put the line on hold and scribbled a note to the judge. His Honor's expression quickly changed from thinly disguised boredom to one of great alarm.

"Excuse me," said Judge Jenkins as soon as the witness had finished a long-winded answer to yet another of Maxine's many irrelevant questions. "I have to take an urgent phone call from the bench. Everybody must stay in their places."

Hugh and Denmark exchanged glances and shrugged. Maxine and Billy watched with suspicion. The jurors waited patiently, their faces as enigmatic as ever. When the judge was finished, he curtly ordered the bailiff to take the jurors back to the jury room.

"Your Honor!" cried Maxine, rising to her feet as soon as the door had closed behind them. "May I ask what this is all about? I was in the middle of a critical line of questioning for this witness."

Judge Jenkins ignored Maxine and addressed Denmark instead. "There's a doctor on the line who says your client is urgently needed at Columbia Medical Center," he said. "A young girl in the Emergency Room is dying from a hemorrhage in her head."

Hugh was thunderstruck and jumped to his feet. "Dr. Pagonis is supposed to be covering!"

"He's busy in the operating room and won't be free to take care of it for a while."

"Then transfer her to the university!"

"The doctor says she's not stable enough."

Forgetting where he was, Hugh left the defense table and hurriedly approached the bench. "Who do you have on the phone?"

"Somebody called Holz."

"Let me speak to him!"

"Your Honor," objected Maxine. "This is *most* irregular! This is nothing more than a ruse cooked up by the defense counsel to distract the jurors from this pivotal testimony!"

Hugh grabbed the phone from the clerk, identified himself, and listened closely with one ear while he kept the other plugged with a finger; Maxine, Denmark, and the judge had become embroiled in a verbal skirmish and were making it difficult for him to hear. "Has she gotten any Mannitol?" he asked. "No? Give her fifty grams right away. That'll buy us some time. Call the operating room and tell them to get ready for a crash craniotomy. Don't wait for me. Get the patient up there and on the table as quickly as you can. Have the nurses prep and drape her. Bonnie is good; she knows what to do. . . . The patient is Bonnie's *daughter*? Oh, my God! Then get another nurse to circulate. They're all experienced. Don't waste any time. Have them hang the CT's on the viewing board so I don't have to go looking for them. When I arrive, I want to cut right away. . . . Yes, I'll be there as soon as I can!"

Hugh slammed down the phone. Without waiting for permission from anybody, he ran from the courtroom.

***

Bonnie sat in the surgery waiting room. Her alert mind was tuned into everything going on around her while her nerves twisted themselves into knots. She had become so accustomed to working in the OR, she had very little appreciation of the emotions that ran through the families that gathered in this place. Now, with her daughter's life in the balance, she knew first-hand what it was like to sit with a lead brick in her stomach, listening out for the slightest sign that the operation had ended. When she saw Hugh approach, she leapt out of her seat and rushed over to him, searching his face for the slightest clues as to how the operation went.

"Dr. Montrose!" she cried. "How is she?"

"She's going to be all right, Bonnie," said Hugh, sweeping a blue surgical cap off his head. "We got the clot out pretty quickly. When Dr. Harrison woke her up she opened her eyes and started moving both sides."

Bonnie fell against Hugh, put her head on his shoulder, and started to cry. Hugh held her, patted her gently on the back, and repeated his assurances that Miriam was going to be fine.

"I know Miriam's going to be okay," she sobbed. "That's not why I'm crying."

Hugh looked puzzled. "Then . . . what's the matter?"

She pulled away from Hugh. "I have a confession to make," she said, her green eyes sparkling from her tears.

"A confession?"

"Yes. I should have told somebody a long time ago, but I was a coward and never had the courage. I can't keep it a secret any longer, not after what happened today. You see, for many years now, I've been Maxine Doggett's eyes and ears in the operating room at Columbia Medical Center."

"Her eyes and ears?"

"I've been spying for her."

After a grim silence, Hugh said, slowly and deliberately, "So Richard was right! He always believed that somebody inside the hospital had ratted on him when he and a resident operated on the wrong side of a patient's head. How else could Maxine Doggett have found out about such a mistake? Nobody *outside* the OR suspected anything—not the nurses, not the family. Not even the patient. Nobody at all."

"His suspicions were correct," Bonnie whimpered. "There *was* an informant, and it was me."

"But *why?*"

"Maxine had a hold on me."

"A hold?"

"That's right," she continued, sounding pitiful. "There was a time when my dream was to be a nurse, but I didn't have the money for the schooling. One day, I saw an ad in the newspaper offering financial aid to attend nursing school in return for certain obligations after graduation. I went for a couple of interviews, first with a man called Mr. Zeiger who did some basic screening, then with Maxine herself. I must have answered her questions to her satisfaction because she offered to pay full tuition for four years. That was a lot of money for me. There was one condition, though: once I graduated and was working in a hospital, I would have to inform her of any medical errors I witnessed on the job. Being an informant was hard to swallow, but she gave me certain guarantees: I wouldn't have to do it for long and would be free as soon as her winnings from the settlements and judgments covered the expenses for my education. Nobody would ever have to find out the truth. There was no other way I was going to fulfill my dreams of attending nursing school, so I agreed."

"So, what prevented you from reneging on your obligations once you got your degree?" asked Hugh.

"She made it very clear to me what would happen if I didn't fulfill my end of the bargain," said Bonnie, wiping her cheeks with the back of her hand. "She would hound me with lawsuits until no hospital would ever hire me again. Double-crossing her would mean the end of my nursing career."

"Supposing you didn't witness any errors?"

"There are always errors. You know that as well as I do."

Hugh nodded solemnly.

"If I didn't perform," continued Bonnie, "she made it clear she was going to make my life hell. You know something? I never doubted her."

"So, was Dr. Forrester's ten million dollars enough to get you off the hook?"

"Yes. After that, she told me there were others at Columbia that could take over now and that she was finished with me. So, you see, when I betrayed Dr. Forrester, I won my own freedom."

"Who else is a spy for her?"

"She didn't say and I never found out. There's more than one—maybe lots of them. They're not all nurses either; all kinds of different health care workers are involved. OR techs, X-ray techs, lab techs, orderlies, administrators, supervisors, maybe even doctors. . . . I'm so sorry, Dr. Montrose! I never realized how much damage I had done until today. God—my daughter was dying and she needed you so badly! Then Holz told me you were in court, defending yourself from *that woman*, and that you couldn't come. It was terrible . . ."

Everything made perfect sense. A system of secret informants fit Maxine's modus operandi very well and it explained why she always had so much work. The quality of the information she received was obviously very good since it was coming from the inside; her dollar winnings per lawsuit ratio was much higher than any other trial lawyer's in the country. It was also a system that would be very difficult to expose.

Then, another thought occurred to Hugh: Richard would probably still be alive now if it hadn't been for Bonnie Davidson.

As if Bonnie could read his thoughts, her face flushed and her eyes dropped to the floor. "I'm so sorry about Dr. Forrester," she murmured. "Somehow, I feel partly responsible for his death. After all, he was emotionally stable until he got sued. And Miriam . . . I could have easily killed her too! I don't think I'll ever forgive myself."

At this particular moment in time, Hugh didn't think he could forgive her either. He stepped away from her and looked at her with cold, hard eyes. "At least you got your daughter back," he said. "How many other people out there aren't going to be so lucky?"

Without waiting to hear the answer, he left.

CHAPTER 25

Bruno Clegg raised his right hand.

Judge Jenkins peered down at him from the Bench and administered the oath. "Do you swear to tell the truth, the whole truth, and nothing but the truth?"

"I certainly do."

"You may take your seat."

Clegg lowered his bulk into the witness chair and it groaned underneath him. His black eyes surveyed the courtroom before him.

To his right, sitting at the defense table, he spotted his neurosurgical colleague, Hugh Montrose. The two hadn't spoken since the early days of this lawsuit and had studiously steered clear of each other in the hospital. Even now, Montrose was avoiding eye contact. Whatever friendship they might have had in the past was clearly a casualty of this lawsuit. No matter. As far as Clegg was concerned, trouble of this magnitude for Montrose only meant one thing: the neurosurgeon's eventual departure from Oregon and even more spine cases for himself.

To his left, he saw Maxine Doggett, the attorney who had asked him to testify on behalf of the Winters. She was wearing a bright red jacket and skirt as she stood in front of the plaintiffs' table. Her shoulders were adorned by thick gold epaulets that looked like scrub brushes. Gaudy braids ran along the seams and cuffs of her outfit, making little loops at every turn. Like most physicians, Clegg was afraid of medical malpractice attorneys and this rare specimen especially disturbed him. She had flitted around him like a gadfly, forcing him to rehearse his testimony a hundred times and fussing over every word. Until now, he had suppressed his fear and had played along with her stupid games. The time had arrived, however, to make a departure from the role she expected of him and win a certain little bet he had made.

Julie and Gary had made a rare appearance in court this day and were sitting behind the plaintiffs' table next to Billy. Clegg hadn't seen them since the day Julie had become paralyzed and cracked a toothy smile at them. Gary smiled back, then quickly resumed courtroom seriousness when Maxine whisked around to check on him.

A big man with blonde hair and alert, blue eyes sat amongst a handful of spectators at the back of the room: Bent Olufsen, fellow orthopedic surgeon, latter-day Viking, and Clegg's long time betting buddy. "If I don't witness your testimony myself," he had told Clegg a few days earlier in the surgeons' lounge, "I'll never believe it actually happened."

"Then come and watch," Clegg had replied. "I can guarantee you'll be revolted."

Maxine approached Clegg, her curly hair bobbing up and down like springs as she walked.

"Dr. Clegg, would you tell the jury your full name and business address?"

Clegg grunted the information.

"What kind of doctor are you?"

"I'm an orthopedic surgeon."

"Would you tell the jury about your education and experience?"

Clegg spent the next few minutes describing his extensive training. Maxine frequently interrupted him in order to polish certain milestones in his career and make her witness shine. Despite his sloping forehead, flat nose and chunky jaw, she wanted the jury to think he was brilliant and believe whatever he had to say today.

"When did you first see Mrs. Winter?" asked Maxine.

"I saw her on June 22nd, 2001, in my clinic at Columbia Medical Center." Clegg stuck a finger in his ear and excavated.

"What history did she give you?"

"She told me about her problems with chronic low back pain."

"Did you then examine her?"

"No." Clegg flicked a tiny ball of wax into the courtroom in front of him.

Maxine paused, cocked her head slightly, and looked puzzled. "Don't you really mean 'yes'?"

"No. I mean 'no'."

"You *didn't* examine her?"

"No, I didn't." Clegg shook his head to make himself clear.

"Why—why not?"

"Because it wouldn't have made any difference," explained Clegg. "None of these chronic back pain patients ever have anything on their exams, so I didn't bother."

Maxine stared at her witness for a few moments, apparently not knowing what to make of his answer. It certainly wasn't anything they had rehearsed. He was supposed to tell her that he had thoroughly examined Mrs. Winter like all highly qualified specialists should and that he hadn't found any signs of a spinal cord problem in her neck. "Let's move on," she said quickly, shrugging off his answer with one of her epaulets and hoping that Denmark and the jury hadn't been paying close attention. "So, what recommendations did you make?"

"I suggested we order a lumbar myelogram to see what was wrong with her back."

"That's one of those tests when a radiologist sticks a needle in a patient's back, injects dye, and takes X-rays, is it not?" asked Maxine, eagerly displaying her knowledge of medical matters.

"Yes."

"And what did it show?"

"A lot of degenerative disease in one of the lumbar discs."

"For the benefit of the jury, could you explain what you mean by degenerative disease?"

"Wear and tear."

"And this was the cause of Mrs. Winter's back pain?"

"Most likely, yes."

After a long discussion on the relationship between back pain and disc problems, Maxine asked her witness what happened next.

"I recommended an operation to fuse her back."

"What do you mean by that?"

"I'd put some metal implants and bone graft into her back so the bones on either side of the bad disc would fuse together, like turning two bones into one. It's a generally accepted way to fix problems like this."

Next, Maxine asked Clegg questions about Mrs. Winter's hospitalization. How did the operation go? (Very well.) Why did Mrs. Winter suddenly become quadriplegic in the middle of the night? (He had no idea, aside from the fact that the tumor in her neck had something to do with it.) Who called him about it, and when? (Betty, the head nurse, at about five in the morning.) With her line of questioning, she made it abundantly clear that he had rushed to the hospital without delay as soon as he knew something was wrong. Then, having portrayed her witness as an exceptionally conscientious doctor, somebody who could be trusted by his patients (and especially by the jury), she popped her most critical question:

"At what time did you call Defendant Montrose for a neurosurgical consultation?"

Clegg looked at Hugh, who quickly averted his eyes. "I called him at about three o'clock in the afternoon."

Maxine had been pacing up and down in front of the witness box, but now she suddenly stopped and stared at Clegg. "*Three?*" she gasped. "Don't you mean: twelve o'clock, as soon as the MRI was finished?"

"No. I mean three o'clock."

"But that's not what we agreed you would say!" blurted Maxine, then quickly pressed her hand to her mouth.

"It's what I'm telling you now," said Clegg, unperturbed by Maxine's rancor. "I know I should have called him a lot earlier, but, to tell you the truth, I got busy in my clinic and completely forgot about Mrs. Winter." Clegg noticed that Montrose whispering rapidly into Denmark's ear, gesticulating with his hands. Gary and Julie were exchanging confused looks. Olufsen was staring at his fellow orthopod with wide, unbelieving eyes. Some of the jurors had put down their notepads and pencils and were leaning forward in their seats, listening closely.

Maxine seemed dazed.

"Your Honor," she said, "may I ask for a short recess so I might confer with the witness?"

"Mr. Denmark?"

"No objections, Your Honor."

"All right, Ms. Doggett. You have fifteen minutes."

"Thank you, Your Honor."

When Maxine and Clegg were alone in a stairwell, she grabbed the big man by the lapels and pushed him against a wall. "What the *hell* are you doing?" she demanded, thrusting her face into his and shaking him.

"Telling the truth," replied Clegg, his defiant eyes unable to hide his dislike for this woman.

"But you're under oath! You're not supposed to be telling the truth!"

"I thought I would, for a change."

"And what's this crap about not examining the patient?"

"I didn't."

"It's okay to tell me that, but not the damn jury! Now they'll think Julie's tumor could have been discovered and treated before she was paralyzed."

"They would have been right."

Maxine released Clegg and backed away, clenching and relaxing her fists over and over again as her frustration boiled inside her. "And you were supposed to say that you called Defendant Montrose at noon."

"That's not how it happened," said Clegg, brushing off his lapel with his fingers.

"Damn it! We rehearsed your testimony for days! We had a script! Don't you see how this makes *you* look negligent, not Defendant Montrose?"

"What's wrong with that?"

"What's gotten into you?" shouted Maxine, turning the same color as her clothes. "Are you *sick*?"

"No."

"Do you want to ruin everything for me?"

"No."

"Have you made a little deal with that worm Denmark?"

"No."

"So, what *the hell* is going on?"

Clegg looked at her sullenly and said nothing.

"How much more of the truth are you planning to divulge?"

"As much as they want to hear."

"*Everything?*"

"Maybe I'll tell them things that even *you* don't know about, Maxine," replied Clegg.

"God in heaven, help me. Why are you doing this to me?"

"You'll never guess," said Clegg with a mischievous smile. "Not in a million years."

Maxine's eyes rolled back into her head and she clutched onto a railing for support. "I don't believe this is happening to me!" she moaned. "I've put a *rogue witness* on the stand!"

***

"Do you wish to resume your questioning, Ms. Doggett?" asked Judge Jenkins once the court had reconvened.

"No, Your Honor," said Maxine angrily from her chair behind the plaintiffs' table. "I have no further questions . . ." Then, dropping her voice so the judge wouldn't hear, she added, ". . . for this miserable traitor."

"Mr. Denmark?"

"I have plenty, Your Honor," said Denmark, enthusiastically bouncing to his feet and buttoning his jacket. He had been listening closely throughout Maxine's examination of this witness and had scarcely believed his testimony. The man was behaving like an enemy missile that had lost control after launch, only there was no self-destruct button. Denmark had no idea why this was happening, but wasn't going to look at a gift horse in the mouth either. Barely able to contain his excitement, he fetched his podium from a corner of the courtroom and extracted a wad of notes from his jacket pocket, holding them tightly in his hands so he wouldn't lose them again.

"Dr. Clegg—my name is John Denmark and I represent Dr. Montrose. Earlier you said that you didn't perform an exam on Mrs. Winter when you first saw her on June 22nd, 2001. Isn't that correct?"

"Yes."

"When she returned for follow-up on June 26th after the myelogram, did you perform an exam on her then?"

"No."

"So, you *never* performed *any* kind of exam on her before she had back surgery?"

"No."

"In retrospect, if you had, might you have found evidence that Mrs. Winter had a very dangerous tumor in her spinal cord?"

"Objection!" cried Maxine, who, by now, must have been having visions of her errant missile destroying an entire city. "Calls for speculation."

"Overruled," said the judge. "I would like to hear the answer to that one."

"In retrospect, considering the size of the tumor, I'm sure I would have found it."

"Dr. Clegg—do you admit to negligence in Mrs. Winter's care?"

"Objection!" cried Maxine, jumping to her feet in one last attempt to avert disaster.

"Overruled."

Clegg appeared eager to answer the question. "Yes, I was negligent all right," he admitted. "I should have examined her. If I had, she might never have been paralyzed."

A buzz arose in the courtroom. The Winters had both turned white. Olufsen buried his face into his hands. Maxine sank back into her seat, horrified.

"Order in the courtroom!" said Judge Jenkins, banging his gavel.

When the spectators had settled down, Denmark, beaming from ear to ear at his good fortune, continued. "We've heard you testify that after you first saw Mrs. Winter, you ordered a myelogram. Did you know that spinal fluid was drawn off at the time of that test and was sent to the lab for analysis?"

"Yes. It's done routinely."

"Did you look at the results of those tests when Mrs. Winter returned to see you on June 26th?"

"Yes."

"Did you notice anything abnormal?"

"Yes. The protein was 140—three times the upper limit of normal."

"Did you know what this meant?"

Clegg shrugged. "Not immediately, no."

"So what did you do about it?"

"While Mr. and Mrs. Winter were waiting in the examination room, I went to the clinic library and looked it up."

"And what did you find?"

"I learned there was a possibility she had a tumor somewhere in her brain or spinal cord."

"When you returned to the examination room, did you tell them about your discovery?"

"No."

Denmark looked genuinely puzzled. "In God's name, why not?"

Clegg fixed his eyes on Julie. "Because I wanted to operate on Mrs. Winter as soon as possible," he said without hesitation. "Investigating an elevated spinal fluid protein would have delayed things."

"Why were you in such a hurry?" asked Denmark, gripping his podium as if he knew the answer might blow him away. "Did Mrs. Winter request quick treatment?"

"No. It was because I wanted to win my bet."

"*Bet?*"

"Yes. I made one with an orthopedic colleague of mine that I could perform fifty back operations in a single month. So far that June, I'd done forty-nine of them. Mrs. Winter would be number fifty. I had to get her surgery done before the end of the month or I'd lose."

Julie screamed.

Gary, ashen-faced and trembling, grabbed the handles to his wife's wheelchair and propelled her towards the exit, knocking aside elephant bags as he went and running over the papers that spewed out of them. Her shrieks could be heard beyond the doors and eventually faded into the distance.

The jurors sat frozen in their seats, horrified by what they had heard and seen.

Dazed, Maxine slowly hoisted an arm into the air and flapped it around to get the judge's attention. "My witness has obviously lost his marbles, Your Honor," she said. "I make a motion to call for an emergency psychiatric consultation."

"Motion denied," said the judge. "Mr. Denmark, you may continue your questioning."

"Thank you, Your Honor," said Denmark, recovering his train of thought with some difficulty. "Dr. Clegg, you were telling the jury about the bet you made with your orthopedic colleague. Can you give us his name?"

"Of course. Dr. Bent Olufsen."

"Is . . . is he in this courtroom today?"

Clegg nodded and pointed. All eyes followed the direction of his finger. Olufsen suddenly became the focus of attention in the courtroom and he shrank a couple of sizes smaller.

"And what were the stakes in this bet?" asked Denmark.

"A cheeseburger."

"A *what*?"

"A cheeseburger," repeated Clegg.

"You risked Mrs. Winter's life for the sake of a *cheeseburger*?"

"Not just *any* cheeseburger, Mr. Denmark," said Clegg. "I'm talking about a half-pounder with super sized French fries and a root beer, from Frank's diner . . . you know—that place down the street from the hospital. Dr. Olufsen and I often make wagers and the prize is always the same."

For a few moments, Denmark was lost for words. When he found his footing again, he looked at the witness with disgust and asked, "How does it make you feel, knowing that your little bet was responsible for Mrs. Winter's paralysis?"

"I didn't know about her tumor in her spinal cord," said Clegg without a trace of guilt in his voice. "As far as I was concerned the high spinal fluid protein was not likely to mean anything; one of those common abnormalities that deserves a work-up, but not right away. It's easy for us to sit here and make judgments with the benefit of hindsight, but, at the time, I didn't think I was risking anything. In fact, I thought I was doing Mrs. Winter a favor by giving her what she so obviously wanted—a quick operation."

"I have no more questions, Your Honor," said Denmark. Then he turned his back on Clegg and returned to his seat.

"Ms. Doggett?" said Judge Jenkins. "Do you wish to redirect on this witness? *Ms. Doggett*?"

Maxine had wilted behind the plaintiffs' table and appeared as if she no longer had the will to live. Her missile had exploded upon impact and a major city was burning to the ground. She fluttered her eyelashes and croaked something in the negative.

The judge looked at Clegg as if he was putrefying road-kill somebody had dragged into his courtroom. "The witness may step down," he said, unable to disguise the contempt in his voice.

As everybody silently watched, Clegg left the stand and strode towards the exit. Without looking back, he ploughed through the heavy wooden doors—a free man.

Olufsen caught up with Clegg on the sidewalk outside the courthouse. Oncoming pedestrians divided in front of the two big orthopods as they lumbered along side-by-side.

"Congratulations!" cried Olufsen, slapping Clegg on the back. "You won our bet!"

"Thanks."

"You actually told the truth!"

"I said I would."

"I didn't think you had the balls."

Clegg waved off his friend's lack of faith. "It was perfectly safe," he said. "The statute of limitations expired long ago. Mrs. Winter can't touch me now. So, why not? Besides, it was fun to watch what my testimony was doing to that revolting lawyer of hers."

Olufsen shook his head in wonder. "Everybody was *really* grossed out by your performance, you know . . . even the judge. You should have seen his face."

"They were meant to be."

"I never thought we would ever find a wager more tasteless than the last one—you know, when you said you could do fifty cases in a month. Looks like I was wrong. How are we ever going to top *this*?"

"Right now, I don't know, but we'll think of something."

"If you say so," said Olufsen doubtfully. "In the meantime, let's eat."

"Good idea."

"How do you feel like going for a cheeseburger?"

"Super sized French fries and a root beer too?"

"Sure."

"Great! Let's go!"

They both laughed, gave each other a high five, and steered a course for Frank's diner.

CHAPTER 26

The evening of Clegg's catastrophic testimony, Maxine bundled up against the cold, rainy weather and paid her second visit to the Winter home. She hated to go out on a night as foul as this one, but, after all of Julie's screaming and shrieking in court that day, she was deeply worried about the state of her client's mind and wanted to be sure she was still committed to the cause. When she arrived, the place was dark except for a single dim light in one of the windows. She walked up a wheelchair ramp, stepped across the porch, and rapped loudly on the front door with her knuckles.

A small animal scurried away into the night.

Was that . . . *a rat*?

She knocked again, more urgently this time. A few moments later, the door creaked open a few inches and odoriferous air wafted out of the house. Gary peered through the opening. He was wearing a plaid shirt with rolled-up sleeves.

"Maxine?" he said. "What are you doing here?"

"May I come in?"

"That wouldn't be a very good idea" he said, keeping a firm hand on the door. "Julie is not in any condition to receive any visitors right now."

"I can understand how she feels—"

"Can you?" interrupted Gary. "Can you *really*?"

Maxine didn't answer the question. Instead, she asked, "Are *you* able, at least, to talk with me?"

Gary glanced over his shoulder, then stepped out of the

house and closed the front door firmly behind him. He took Maxine to the camper parked in the front yard. "We can talk in here," he said, opening the side door for her. "Climb in."

"I'm . . . not sure if this is such a good idea," she said, hesitating. "You see, I have mold allergies."

"Would you prefer to talk out in the cold and wet?"

The weather and her allergies didn't bother Maxine as much as the rat she had just heard scurrying from the porch. The little beast sounded as if it might have headed in this direction too, so, without much more thought about it, she stepped up into the camper. She suddenly screamed and clawed wildly at the air.

"Watch out for spider webs," said Gary, following her in and pulling the door closed behind him.

"Ugh!" cried Maxine, sweeping fine filaments from her face with her fingers. "*Ugh!* Turn on a light!"

"I can't. The batteries died a long time ago."

Maxine cleared the last of the web from her hair and looked around her with disgust. Yellowish light from a street lamp outside filtered through blinds that hung in front of the windows, bathing the interior with an eerie glow. There was a bedroom at the back where Julie and Gary must have once slept, with a bathroom and a shower nearby. In the middle, a table was set up between two sets of seats—a place where meals were enjoyed and games played. Now it was bare. Rivulets of shadows streamed across its surface as rain dripped down the windows outside. The children's sleeping area was above the driver's seat. A forgotten doll with a missing arm lay on the mattress. Pieces of Lego were scattered nearby.

Water leaked through a hole in the ceiling and dripped into a puddle on the floor.

It was cold, dirty . . . and *very moldy*.

"Brr!" said Maxine, gripping her elbows and shivering.

"There was a time when things were very different," said Gary with a sad, distant look in his eyes. "We actually thought of this camper as a member of the family. Called it Harvey the RV. I can almost see and hear my family around me . . . Julie, standing over there by the cooker, smiling, laughing, preparing some fantastic meal in the middle of the wilderness . . . me, planning the next day's itinerary with Patrick at this table . . . Jennifer up there, playing with her dolls . . . music coming from the CD player . . . warmth . . . love . . . Seems like it was only yesterday. Now this place is nothing more than a monument to our happiness."

"Look, Gary," said Maxine, anxious to move on to business. "About today . . . I had no idea Clegg was going to say all those horrible things."

Gary snapped out of his trance and shuddered. "What a nightmare that was!" he exclaimed. "And I suppose he's safe from all lawsuits too."

"The statute of limitations expired long ago," said Maxine. "He's untouchable and he knows it too, otherwise he wouldn't have confessed his negligence in such a brazen manner. If I had only known about the CSF protein much earlier . . ." Maxine's eyes grew large and puppy-dog innocent as she remembered her special deal with Grand National. "But the result was printed on one tiny little lab slip, tucked deep in a medical record that must have been at *least* a foot thick." She suddenly sneezed, then pulled a handkerchief from her sleeve and dabbed her nose. "Clegg deliberately hid the information from me and Charles Mortimer didn't even notice it—the blind, old fool! I still depend on specialists to tell me what's going on, even if I *am* a nurse. What am I supposed to do if my people let me down?"

"Maxine," said Gary in a soothing tone. "We're not blaming *you*. We know you've been very good to us and have tried to help us in any way you can."

"Yes, I *have* tried," said Maxine, dabbing her eyes now.

"And we really appreciate it, you know."

"I'm so relieved."

"But we're wondering . . . if we could drop the case against Dr. Montrose."

"*Drop the* . . ." Maxine blinked her disbelief.

"By now, it's pretty clear that Dr. Clegg was the negligent one, not Montrose."

"What difference does it make?" cried Maxine, waving her handkerchief around. "As long as you have a defendant and a sympathetic jury in the same courtroom, why should you care who's negligent and who's not?"

"But we don't want to keep persecuting an innocent doctor," Gary persisted. "It's not right."

"Defendant Montrose is . . ."—Maxine sneezed again—". . . far from innocent!" She blew her nose with a loud honk.

"I'm sorry, but you can't convince us of that any longer," said Gary. "He did what he could for Julie after Clegg was finished with her. It wasn't his fault he couldn't save her. The circumstances were obviously very difficult."

"What are you telling me?" Another honk. "Have you actually become *friendly* with the defense?"

"No. Simply put: we've lost interest in pursuing this case." Gary paused for a few moments, presumably debating how to put his thoughts into words. Then he sighed and said, "You see, we would like to try a different way of bringing some comfort to our lives—something that doesn't involved lawsuits."

"A different way?" she asked incredulously as if litigation was the only thing in the world that mattered. "What other way is there?"

"As a last resort, we thought we might try . . ." Gary faltered, then drew a deep breath as if he was making an embarrassing confession. "We thought we would try putting our faith in God. If He really exists, maybe He'll help us through these hard times."

"You've gotten *religion*?"

"I wouldn't put it quite *that* strongly," said Gary, holding his ground against the look of utter dismay in Maxine's face, "but we're desperate enough to give it a try."

"I can't believe this!" Maxine moaned. There was a rustling sound underneath the camper, but she paid no attention.

"Look—this lawsuit isn't going anywhere, so why not?" continued Gary. "The whole thing has been difficult and emotional for us and today was by far the worst day. When we got home this evening, Julie and I finally broke down and did something we've never done before: I fell to my knees in front of her wheelchair, she bowed her head, and we prayed like nobody's ever prayed before. We poured our hearts out to God, asking Him, if He really exists and was listening, to forgive all the bad things we've done in our lives and grant us peace in our hearts."

"You're wasting your time," said Maxine flatly. "For all the good it's going to do, you might have asked Him to cure your wife's paralysis and make her whole again. Rise up and walk! Hah!"

"Maybe you're right," said Gary. "If you ask me, I would be surprised if He pays us any kind of attention after all the nasty names we've called Him since Julie was paralyzed. But we figured there was nothing to lose; we can't do much worse than we're doing now."

"Personally, I find birds much more helpful," Maxine muttered. "At least you can *see* them."

"*Birds?*"

359

"I don't expect you to understand. It's an acquired taste."

"I see . . ." said Gary, obviously not seeing at all.

Maxine took a step closer to Gary and prodded him in the chest with her finger. "However, I hope you *do* understand how much work I've put into this lawsuit," she said, returning to the subject that concerned her most right now.

"Yes—"

"The *thousands* of hours of my own precious time (prod, prod) I have invested in your cause so you'll win?"

"Yes—"

"Not to mention all the money I've already spent on office labor (prod), copying (prod, prod), and expert witnesses (prod, prod, prod)?"

"We realize—"

"And now you want me to drop everything and give up?"

"Well—"

Maxine suddenly exploded. "No client of mine has *ever* walked away in the middle of a trial!" she shouted.

Gary cringed. "I'm sorry—"

"Wait until you hear the verdict, then you can do whatever you like."

"But if we win, we don't want Montrose's money."

"Then give your share back to the insurance company," replied Maxine, waving an arm in the general direction of the SPI corporate offices downtown. "Donate it to the church." The other arm waved in the opposite direction. "Do whatever the hell you want with it, but don't deprive other people of their hard-earned due! Especially me!"

"I didn't—"

"Quite right," interrupted Maxine. "You didn't *think*. Have you considered, for example, what would happen to you if you don't win this trial?"

"We're prepared to accept bankruptcy."

"*And* you'll lose your home. Have you thought about that too? Where will you go then? You'll be forced to park this old crate in a rat-infested field somewhere and live in it. Personally, I couldn't imagine anything worse." Another sneeze, more dainty dabbing. "And think of your poor kids. No college, no future. A life of abject poverty, groveling in the gutter. Is that what you really want for them?"

"No, of course not."

"Then you'd better listen to me . . . very carefully," said Maxine, drawing closer to Gary and glaring at him with red, swollen eyes. "I don't want to hear any more of this 'we want to drop the lawsuit' nonsense. Whether you like it or not, you're stuck with this trial until the end. As long as I'm your attorney, I'm going to try my best to win. And I'm not going to win if you and your wife go mushy on me. Understand?"

Gary gulped and said nothing.

"Tomorrow, Julie will be taking the stand. She'll have to put on the best performance of her life. She *must* make Dr. Clegg look like a hero, despite all the crap he said today. When she first went to see him, he obtained a thorough history from her and performed a detailed exam. He wanted her to have conservative treatment like physical therapy, but she insisted on fast-track treatment. Since she could not be persuaded otherwise, he went over all the risks of surgery in detail, including the risk of paralysis. When the unthinkable happened in the hospital, Clegg rushed in to take care of the problem and was very kind to her. She's *got* to say all those things!"

"But Julie remembers hardly anything about the day she was paralyzed."

"And she *must* make Defendant Montrose look like a quack," continued Maxine, ignoring what Gary had to say. "When he came to see Julie in the hospital, he told her there was nothing he could do. He was in a hurry and barely examined her. He wanted to delay things before he took the tumor out, but didn't explain why. He didn't even give her any choice in the matter. It was 'my way or the highway'. Then, he rushed off to play a round of golf before she had a chance to ask any questions or consent to his plan."

"But—"

Maxine silenced Gary with a wave of her hand. "I know. You've already told me: Julie doesn't remember. Well, pray for something useful for a change, like a miraculous return of her memory before she takes the stand tomorrow. Her testimony will carry a lot of weight with the jury and will be critically important."

Gary shook his head. "She won't like it."

"I don't care whether she likes it or not," said Maxine. "Dr. Clegg is her hero, and Defendant Montrose is a quack. Have her repeat those words over and over again between now and tomorrow morning. If she hears herself say them often enough, maybe she'll start believing them."

"Dr. Clegg is—?"

"Don't start until I'm gone," said Maxine, reaching for the door. "I'll see you tomorrow morning in court." Ducking her head to avoid any more spider webs, she stepped out of the camper, sneezed violently one last time, and let the screen door slam behind her.

As she splashed back to her car through the puddles and the rain, Maxine heard an owl hoot from a nearby clump of trees and her tense face melted into a smile. No doubt, the bird was giving approval of the way she had handled this difficult situation. Birds were always so nice—always there whenever she needed them, predicting the future, advising on business decisions, or simply being good company. The same couldn't be said for God, who seemed to make such a sport out of playing hide-and-seek and never failed to be so tiresome and demanding when it came to one's own personal conduct. However, if Gary and Julie wanted to bark up the wrong tree and start getting chummy with some figment of their imagination, there was nothing she could do to stop them. Frankly, she didn't care what they did as long as they didn't make good on their threat to drop the case.

The owl hooted again.

"Sue, sue, to you too!" Maxine called over her shoulder, waving good-bye with her hand. Then she climbed into her car and drove away.

CHAPTER 27

For months now, Maxine had been eagerly anticipating Julie's testimony. She had thought about it every morning in the shower and had felt electricity, not water, run over her skin. She knew nothing more professionally exhilarating than a massacre of the defense and no weapon more lethal than a quad with which to carry it out. However, when the big day arrived, her nervous anticipation was replaced with a profound sense of unease. Her visit to the Winter home the night before had not given her the reassurance she had been looking for; the Winters' insane desire to drop the case was a worrisome development—unprecedented in all the years of her practice. If Julie actually did the unthinkable and told the jury she was persecuting an innocent doctor, the massacre taking place in court this day would not be of the defense, but of Maxine herself.

As if client reticence was not enough, another problem arose that put an even bigger damper on Maxine's mood. As she sat at her desk preparing to receive Carl's usual 7 a.m. Daily Brief on the affairs of her empire, Billy invaded her office again and insisted on handling Julie's testimony, saying that he hadn't attended law school for four years so he could photocopy documents all day long. If he was going to spend so much time on *Winter vs. Montrose*, he wanted to do something useful.

Maxine bluntly told him that as a junior lawyer, he should lower his expectations. Then, as if to prove her point, she thrust yet another stack of papers into his arms and told him to take them to the copying machine.

With a wild sweep of his arm, Billy scattered the papers across the floor. He called Maxine names and accused her of driving him mad with her bossy, condescending behavior. When he took a couple of threatening steps towards her with his fist raised, Carl quickly intervened. He grabbed Billy by the scruff of the neck and lifted him until his feet were dangling six inches above the floor. Then he carried him, wriggling like a worm, to the door and threw him out of the office.

In court, Maxine sat with her clients at the plaintiffs' table, bubbling and steaming like a mud pot at Yellowstone.

Everything was going wrong. Clegg had dared to tell the truth under oath, the Winters wanted to drop the case against Montrose, and now Billy had disappeared and wouldn't respond to any phone calls. Her fight with that little runt in her office that morning had been an unfortunate incident—the kind of internal spat that detracted from the main mission. In retrospect, caving in and letting him handle Julie's testimony might have been the wiser thing to do. It didn't matter what questions were asked of the quad, what answers she gave, or whether the attorney doing the interrogation was any good. Her physical appearance alone was enough to elicit oodles of sympathy. Even so, Maxine had been having nightmares of that little creep Billy somehow wrestling control of the case from her, alienating the jury, and ruining everything. When those fourteen men and women filed into the courtroom, she struggled to calm herself and offered them the same expansive smile as usual, hoping they wouldn't notice the empty seat beside her.

Julie, accompanied by her husband, arrived in court that day with her customary tardiness and, as always, made a spectacle of herself as she trundled past the jurors in her wheelchair. Normally, Maxine would watch her client with pride and admiration; nobody played the part of a negligently damaged cripple as well as Julie—the sufferance in her face, the slumped shoulders, the laborious breathing. Maxine felt she had trained her well. However, on this particular morning, Maxine was preoccupied and paid no attention to her client's entrance. As soon as Julie was within whispering range, she drew close and cupped her hand alongside her mouth in case anybody at the defense table had suddenly learned how to read lips.

"How are you doing today?" she asked.

"Okay," replied Julie.

"Better than yesterday?"

"Yes, thank you, Ms. Doggett."

Maxine didn't waste any more time arriving at her core concern. "Did your husband talk to you about my visit last night?" she asked, batting her eyelashes to underline the importance of her question.

"Yes, he did."

Gary intervened. "Julie knows very well what she must do," he said quietly. "Everything will be all right."

Despite Gary's words of reassurance, Maxine felt a compulsion to remind her client the main points of her upcoming testimony. "Don't forget," she said, "Dr. Clegg is your hero, and Defendant Montrose is a quack! Make this clear to the jurors every opportunity you get. Okay?"

"Ms. Doggett!" hissed Gary. "I already told you that Julie is ready. There's no point harassing her about it."

Maxine sniffed at the admonition, then reluctantly nodded her satisfaction.

When it was time for her to testify, Julie edged her wheelchair forward and positioned herself in front of the jurors. They looked at her with obvious sympathy; the memories of her anguish the day before must have been fresh in their minds. Maxine extracted a yellow notepad and pencil from her elephant bag, perched herself on a nearby wooden railing like a bird of prey, and peered at her client with narrow, analytical eyes.

To begin with, Maxine asked endless questions about Julie's family life before she was paralyzed. After an hour of slogging through the daily activities of a typical American middle-class family, she moved on to her disastrous battle with back pain.

"Who referred you originally to Dr. Clegg?"

"My family physician, Dr. Taylor."

"You liked Dr. Clegg when you saw him in his office, didn't you?" asked Maxine, smiling and nodding so as to suck the most positive answer possible out of her client.

"He was okay."

"He took a long, detailed history from you, didn't he?"

"He asked me what was wrong with me."

"He thoroughly examined you, didn't he?"

"I suppose so."

"You *suppose* so?" asked Maxine, traces of impatience creeping around the edges of her mouth; her client wasn't being effusive enough about Clegg. "Don't you remember?"

"It was a long time ago. My memory is not perfect."

Maxine glared at her client for making an unauthorized admission regarding the accuracy of her memory, then impatiently flipped over a page of the notepad she was holding and hurried on to the next question. "Do you remember what Dr. Clegg advised you to do about your back?"

"He wanted me to have a test."

"And after your test?"

"He told me surgery was an option."

"And what was your opinion about that?"

"I didn't know what to do," said Julie, shrugging. "I just wanted to stop hurting. I was ready to listen to any kind of advice."

"Didn't he want you to pursue conservative treatment first? Physical therapy? Massage?"

"He only offered an operation."

The pencil in Maxine's hand snapped. Now it was obvious that her client wasn't sticking to the script; she was supposed to say that Clegg had offered numerous non-surgical options and, being the careful, conservative orthopod that he was, had only reluctantly agreed to operate on her. "Are you sure about that?" asked Maxine.

"I think so"

"So, you turned down the conservative options he offered and insisted on an operation instead—"

"Objection!" cried Denmark. "Ms. Doggett is mischaracterizing the witness' testimony."

"Sustained," said the judge. "Ms. Doggett, do you wish to rephrase your question?"

"No! I mean . . . I suppose so, Your Honor," said Maxine. She climbed off her perch, took a couple of steps closer to Julie, and peered down at her along her nose. "Mrs. Winter, didn't Dr. Clegg talk to you about the risks of surgery?"

"I don't remember."

"Didn't he mention the possibility of paralysis?"

"I don't remember."

"Are you *sure* you don't remember?"

"Objection!" cried Denmark once again. "Ms. Doggett is badgering the witness."

"Sustained," ruled the judge. "Move on, Ms. Doggett."

"Yes, Your Honor." Maxine strode back to the wooden railing, found her place in her notes, and continued, "Mrs. Winter, I would like to ask you some questions about Defendant Montrose. On the day following your lumbar fusion, what time *exactly* did he see you at your bedside?"

"I don't remember—"

"And what did he do at your bedside?"

"I don't remember—"

"He didn't examine you, did he?"

"I don't—"

"Oh, for heaven's sake!" cried Maxine, throwing her notepad onto the floor and balling her hands into fists. "Don't you remember *anything?*"

"Ms. Doggett!" thundered Judge Jenkins.

"I'm sorry, Your Honor," said Maxine, quickly picking up her scattered papers. "I don't know what came over me. It won't happen again."

"It had better not. Carry on."

"So you don't remember much about Defendant Montrose's visit to you that day?" continued Maxine.

"That's right," said Julie in a small voice. "I don't. I wish I could be more helpful, Ms. Doggett, but I'm sworn to tell the truth. All these things happened a long time ago and I was under a lot of emotional strain. I can't be expected to remember every small detail."

Maxine felt like tearing her beautiful hair out. Why did her most important witnesses feel compelled to tell the truth? What was wrong with them? A few well-placed, white lies would have served Julie very nicely at this point. As it was, she was risking the entire case by admitting to a faulty memory on so many critical issues. Instead of pursuing this hopeless course, Maxine decided to change tack and asked Julie to describe her current daily life in excruciating detail—a line of questioning that lasted another couple of hours, brought her frustration under control, and provoked stifled yawns from the jury. Things picked up, however, when Maxine tucked in her big chin, lowered her voice a couple of octaves, and said, "Now I want to ask you some extremely important questions about things that most people consider to be very private and personal. Please understand that I wouldn't be doing this if there wasn't a very good reason for it. Do you understand, Mrs. Winter?"

"Yes, I believe I do."

"Good." Satisfied that she had recaptured the jury's flagging attention, she asked, "Can you tell me how often you had *intimate* relations with your husband before you became paralyzed?"

Maxine had warned Julie long ago to expect this question and had fully prepped her.

"On average, about—"

Suddenly, the doors at the back of the courtroom flew open with a crash and Billy entered. His hands were thrust into his pockets and he stared straight ahead with a stony expression. Every man and woman on the jury shifted their attention from Julie to Billy, and Maxine sizzled with fury. His interruption at this particular moment was incredibly bad timing. He was ruining one of her most important plays of the trial: the exposition of a quad's sex life, or, rather, the lack thereof.

"I'm sorry, Mrs. Winter," said Maxine hurriedly. "I didn't hear your answer to my question."

"About once or twice a week."

"Would you say that intimacy was an important part of your marriage?"

Julie nodded. "Yes."

Billy shuffled in front of the jury, momentarily blocking its view of the proceedings, and made his way to the plaintiffs' table.

"You were saying, Mrs. Winter?" said Maxine, having difficulty maintaining her concentration. "What was your answer?"

"What was your question?"

"Was *intimacy* an important part of your marriage?"

"Yes. Very important."

"And how are things now? Are you able to be intimate with your husband?"

Julie cast her eyes down as she had been coached to do.

"I'm sorry that we have to—" began Maxine.

"No, no . . . It's okay," said Julie, her cheeks tingeing red. "My husband and I no longer share the same bed and we are unable—"

Billy plopped down into his usual chair beside Maxine. She shot him a sideways look intended to freeze him on the spot. What she saw, however, was enough to give her pause. Her co-counsel appeared as if he had just mounted the stairs to a scaffold and somebody had slipped a noose over his head. His eyes were glazed with a far-away look and his skin was pale and clammy. Something was wrong with him and she wanted to know what, but now was not the time to find out; she could feel the jury's gaze locked onto every move she made.

Maxine scrambled back to her questions. "You are unable to do *what*, Mrs. Winter?"

"We are unable to have intimate relations."

Having finally established Gary's loss of consortium, Maxine said she had no further questions and called for a midday recess so she could deal with Billy. The judge gave his consent and the jury was dismissed. While the defendant and his lawyer looked on with great interest, she bustled her co-counsel out of the courtroom.

Maxine confronted him at the end of a remote hallway. "What's happened to you?" she demanded to know.

"Happened?"

"Just what *the hell* do you think you're doing?"

Billy paled under the onslaught and murmured an inaudible reply.

"You could have ruined the case!" she hissed. "Maybe you already have!"

"I'm sorry—"

"You're *sorry?*"

"I'm sorry for losing my temper this morning and for not showing up in court," said Billy, wringing his hands together.

"I don't think the jury noticed your absence until you came bumbling in right in the middle of the consortium testimony! Your timing was atrocious!"

"I know—"

"Jesus! Are you working with me or against me?"

"*With* you."

"You could have fooled me." Maxine gripped Billy by the collar and dragged him closer. "Listen to me, you little prick. I'd love to kick your ass out of here and never lay eyes on you again, but the jury might interpret your departure as weakness in the plaintiffs' case. So I'm stuck with you, at least until the end of the trial. Do me a favor: show up on time every day, keep your mouth shut, and stay out of my way. Is that understood?"

"Y—yes . . ." stammered Billy.

"Yes what?"

"Yes, ma'am."

Maxine stared after Billy as he beat a hasty retreat, angrily wondering what had happened to the kid.

***

In the afternoon, Judge Jenkins was delayed in his office by some urgent business. Hugh and Denmark conducted a quiet conversation while Maxine, Billy and the Winters sat in silence.

"What do you think is going on between them?" whispered Hugh into Denmark's ear.

"Between who?"

"Maxine, that monkey of hers, and her clients. Haven't you noticed? They're barely looking at each other."

Denmark risked a sideways glance in the direction of the plaintiffs' table and rubbed his chin. "Hmmm—now that you mention it . . ."

Hugh leaned even closer and lowered his voice further. By now, he had discovered that, in a courtroom, the quieter he talked, the more urgent he sounded. "They must have had some kind of argument. I can just feel the tension in the air."

"It's about time *something* broke down between them," Denmark mused. "How would *you* like to be within perfume range of that woman, day after day, for weeks on end?"

"And another thing," continued Hugh. "Julie keeps looking at me with those sad eyes of hers, over and over again. I get the impression she's trying to tell me something."

"Don't bet on it," scoffed Denmark. "More likely she's sorry for not suing you sooner. Or perhaps she wishes your insurance policy was bigger."

"You know, I actually feel sorry for the poor woman," said Hugh, ignoring Denmark's cynical remarks. "Don't be too rough on her when you start your cross-examination . . . please."

"Don't worry—I won't be. The jury wouldn't like it."

When judge and jury were ready, Julie was once again nudged forward in her wheelchair. Denmark pulled up a chair and sat close to her. He put a cup of water in her wheelchair's cup holder and promised that he wouldn't take long for he could see that she was tired. She nodded her head with appreciation for his thoughtfulness.

"Mrs. Winter," he said, "you were in court yesterday, weren't you?"

"Yes, I was," said Julie. Staring at some unseen object in the distance, she lifted her right hand slowly to her mouth, put the knuckle of her forefinger between her lips, and nibbled nervously at her skin.

Hugh wondered why even good lawyers ask some of the dumbest questions in the world. Of course Julie was in court yesterday; everybody had seen her there.

Denmark continued with his questions. "Did you hear Dr. Clegg testify about your treatment?" he asked.

She mumbled something unintelligible.

"Can you speak louder please, so the jury can hear?"

Julie lowered her right arm back to her wheelchair's armrest. "I'm sorry. Yes."

"As you must recall, he testified that he made a wager with one of his colleagues about the number of operations he could do in June, 2001. That was the month you had your back fusion, wasn't it?"

"Yes, it was."

"He also testified that the reason why he operated on you so quickly, without trying conservative treatments first, was so he could win his bet. Apparently, you were the last patient of the month . . . the fiftieth one. Do you remember that too?"

"Yes."

"Do you have any reason to believe he was lying?"

"No."

"I would imagine hearing something like that would be very upsetting for you."

"It was . . . devastating."

"Is that why you left the courtroom in such obvious distress yesterday?"

"Yes, it was."

"I can't say I blame you," said Denmark kindly. "Would you like me to give you a drink?"

"Yes, I need one."

With compassion in his blue eyes, Denmark took the cup of water from the cup holder and raised it to Julie's lips. There was silence as she took a few gulps, spilling a few drops down her front. Then she nodded her thanks and he took it away.

"Isn't it true you've suspected all along that Dr. Clegg hadn't been completely open and honest with you?" asked Denmark, putting the cup down.

Maxine stiffened. "Objection!" she cried.

"Overruled."

"Haven't you and your husband suspected something about him all along?"

"Objection again!"

"Overruled again. The witness may answer."

"I confess we had a lot of questions about Dr. Clegg," Julie admitted.

"But a little harmless gambling is not what really upsets you, is it?" continued Denmark.

"I don't know what you mean."

"What if it turns out that the gambling wasn't so harmless after all? What if it directly results in your paralysis? That would *really* upset you, wouldn't it?"

"Please, this is difficult . . ."

"I know it is, and I'm very sorry for this line of questioning, but it's very important. Mrs. Winter, do you believe Dr. Clegg deliberately ignored the high CSF protein?"

"Objection!" cried Maxine.

"Overruled."

"But, Your Honor—"

"*Overruled!*"

"Yes . . . I do," answered Julie.

"Has anybody told you that a high CSF protein is a sign that a tumor might have been present?" continued Denmark.

"Yes, they have."

"And if that tumor had been recognized and removed before your lumbar fusion, you wouldn't be paralyzed right now?"

"No, I wouldn't."

"That's what really upset you yesterday, wasn't it? If Dr. Clegg hadn't treated you so callously, your paralysis would have been avoided. Yes?"

"Yes."

Panic was filling Maxine's eyes and she jumped to her feet. "Your Honor," she began, "I really must—"

"Forget it, Ms. Doggett," said Judge Jenkins. "You've used up your quota of objections for this trial."

"Your Honor?"

"Your objection is overruled."

"But I didn't make one!"

"You were going to. Sit down."

Maxine put her hands on her hips, pouted for a second or two, then reluctantly did as she was told.

Denmark continued. "Do you believe, Mrs. Winter, that Dr. Clegg has been negligent in your care?"

"Yes, I'm afraid I do."

Maxine gasped, but said nothing.

"And meantime, my client, Dr. Hugh Montrose, is paying the price!" cried Denmark, bringing his fist down hard onto the arm of his chair. "Is that not correct?"

Julie recoiled as if she had been wounded, then spoke into the microphone with her usual labored breaths. "Your client, Mr. Denmark, is a good doctor—"

"Objection!" cried Maxine, unable to restrain herself. "The witness is forgetting she's the plaintiff!"

"You're overruled, again," growled the judge. "Mrs. Winter may continue."

"I am truly, *truly* sorry if this lawsuit has hurt him," said Julie. "If I could start from the beginning again, I would not name him as a defendant . . ."

"Objection!"

"Overruled, Ms. Doggett."

". . . because it's obvious to me, and should be obvious to the jury, that Dr. Montrose wasn't negligent—"

"*Objection!*" screeched Maxine, who, by now, was as white as a sheet. "My client is *sick!*"

"Your objection is overruled!"

"—and if I had to do it all over again," continued Julie, "I would certainly choose Dr. Montrose to be my surgeon, and not Dr. Clegg."

Maxine made a gurgling noise that sounded like a waste disposal unit.

"Counselors to the sidebar!" commanded the judge.

Maxine and Denmark scurried over to the judge like children and huddled heads with him while Hugh watched closely from the defense table. The three of them whispered and gesticulated with each other while their faces shot from one end of the color spectrum to the other, and back again. Then they broke up and returned to their places.

When Maxine reached her table, and before Hugh had a chance to ask his lawyer what was going on, she suddenly whisked around and faced the judge. "The plaintiffs rest their case, Your Honor," she said loudly and clearly this time. "The plaintiffs rest!"

"Ms. Doggett," said Judge Jenkins, "are you sure? Don't you want time to confer with your clients about something as important as this?"

"My clients and I have already discussed it in great detail. *The plaintiffs rest!*"

"As you wish," said the judge, shaking his head and no doubt wondering if he could recall such a thing ever happening in his courtroom before. With a bang of his gavel, he officially ruled that the plaintiffs had rested their case. Gary and Julie looked at each other; it was clear from their puzzled expressions that they hadn't discussed anything with Maxine as she had purported and had no clue what was going on.

"What the hell is this all about?" Hugh asked Denmark.

"The plaintiff just testified on behalf of the defendant!" he replied. "I've never seen such a thing! *Never!* Not in all my years."

"That much I gathered," said Hugh. "But what's The Dog up to now?"

"In our little sidebar," explained Denmark, "the judge wanted to know if Maxine was going to declare a nonsuit."

"A nonsuit?"

"In other words, he wanted to know if she was going to drop the case against you, considering how damaging Julie's testimony was."

"Drop the case now? Just like that? After all we've been through?"

"The plaintiffs have the right, you know, so long as they haven't rested their case yet," said Denmark with a learned smile. "You're not off the hook, though; they can start over and sue you again in the future if they wish. Sometimes lawyers use this tactic if they see their case is collapsing. Maxine wasn't interested in declaring a nonsuit, though. In fact, she just did exactly the opposite: as you just heard, she went ahead and rested her case, forcing this trial to its natural conclusion."

"*Why?*"

"Because she knows that her client is a quad, the most powerful plaintiff known to mankind," explained Denmark. "If the jurors feel that Julie deserves money, they'll give it to her, no matter what crazy things are said in court."

"Or maybe it's because she can't bear the thought of starting over," suggested Hugh.

"Either way, don't start getting complacent. This trial isn't over yet."

Hugh glanced in Maxine's direction and confirmed what Denmark had just said; she appeared far from defeated, busily pulling some files out of her elephant bag and searching through them. She must have felt Hugh's gaze upon her for she inexplicably chose this moment to look up. Her cold, grey eyes met his, and a crafty smile spread across her face.

After the jury had been dismissed and the judge had escaped to his chambers, Julie nudged the joystick on her wheelchair and made a move to leave the courtroom. When she was passing in front of the defense table, she stopped and smiled wearily at Denmark and Hugh. The two men exchanged glances with each other, uncertain how to react to her gesture, then did what felt natural: they returned her smile.

"Looks like I've been given no choice, again," she said quietly, jerking her head towards her lawyer. "Well, no matter. I'm sure it won't take you gentlemen long to present your case, then this terrible ordeal will be over for all of us. I want to wish you the best, and I really mean it."

Before either of them could respond, Maxine noticed what was going on. She dropped the files she was holding and marched over to her client. "Excuse me!" she cried. "You can't speak to *them*! They're the enemy!"

"I was only—"

"You could ruin everything!"

"But—"

"What did you say to them?"

"I was wishing them—"

"Not another word!" Maxine grabbed the handles to Julie's wheelchair, spun her around, and propelled her forward.

"What are you doing?" cried Julie. "Stop! I don't want to leave!"

"Yes, you do," said Maxine, picking up her pace with longer strides. "It's past time for you to go home."

Julie continued her objections, but was ignored. As she was pushed out of the courtroom, Billy and her husband following close behind, she turned her head sideways and shouted, "Good luck, Dr. Montrose!"

After Julie and her entourage were gone, stunned silence reigned in the courtroom.

Hugh wasn't sure which was more shocking—Julie raising her voice for the first time in his memory or hearing her wish him luck. "That poor woman deserves better," he muttered to himself. "Sometimes I wish she would win this case."

Denmark overheard him and scowled. "If she wins," he said, "that means I lose . . . again. We *don't* want that to happen, do we?"

"No, I suppose we don't."

"*Definitely* not. Come on—we've got things to do. Get your coat. We need to see the man who's going to save your neck."

Hugh sighed. "As you wish."

CHAPTER 28

When Hugh and Denmark left the courthouse, the wind had picked up and heavy clouds were racing northwards above the city. Rain was falling, streaking the black streets with a dazzling display of colors. Denmark hailed a taxi and told the driver to take them to the Sheraton.

Hugh was warmed by the memory of his old friend, Robert Bull, a first-class neurosurgeon who was good with his hands, his brain, and his bedside manner. A few years ago, the poor man had become embroiled in a couple of pointless lawsuits and responded to his stress by drinking excessively. Portland had lost one of its finest when he suddenly abandoned his practice and moved to Indiana. Surely Bob would know how to testify effectively from the stand. Thinking about the strong support he would shortly be receiving from him, Hugh felt encouraged and no longer so lonely.

When the taxi arrived at the hotel, Denmark paid the driver and led Hugh into the lobby. He searched the cavernous marble spaces, saw nobody he recognized, and shrugged his shoulders.

"Is he expecting us?" asked Hugh.

"Yes. He let me know he would be waiting downstairs. We were supposed to meet and get acquainted."

"You mean you've never met him?" said Hugh with surprise.

"No, but I feel like I know him very well by now. We've had a number of long conversations on the telephone."

"Aren't you nervous relying on somebody you've never met?"

"No. Should I be?"

"What if he doesn't meet your expectations?"

"That's not likely. Anyhow, you know him well enough, don't you? Isn't he a good guy?"

"Yes, but I haven't seen him in years."

"Don't worry. I guarantee he'll be the perfect expert witness." Denmark looked around the lobby again. "I wonder where he could be. . . ."

"Perhaps he changed his mind and decided not to come?"

As though this possibility struck Denmark as being plausible, he hurried over to the reception desk and made enquiries. Yes—Dr. Bull had indeed checked in and was staying on the twentieth floor. Denmark and Hugh caught an elevator and were whisked into the sky. A few moments later, they knocked on his door.

No response.

Denmark knocked again and exchanged an anxious glance with Hugh as he waited. The small point of light that shone through the spy hole abruptly went out and Hugh knew they were being watched.

"Who's there?" demanded a voice from inside the room.

"It's John . . . John Denmark. Open up, Bob. Hugh and I have come to welcome you to Portland."

The door swung open wide.

Bull's short, heavy body teetered in the doorway. His graying hair was disheveled and stuck up from his head as though he had been lying on it for a long time. The collar of his shirt was undone and his tie was hanging at half-mast. A cigarette hung from his lips, the column of ash at its end perilously long. His bloodshot eyes lurched from one visitor to the other. There was a flicker of recognition, then he swiveled on one heel and headed back into his room, setting a direct course for a half-empty bottle of Johnny Walker Blue Label that stood on the bed table.

"You're drunk!" said Denmark with dismay.

"Yes, thanks to you."

Denmark hurried into the room and Hugh followed him, grimacing at the pungent cigarette smoke that filled the air.

"Thanks to me?" said Denmark. "What do you mean by that?"

"If you hadn't been so thoughtful and generous, I'd be sober right now."

"Thoughtful and generous?"

Bull waved his arm in the direction of a small wooden box sitting on a table. Its lid was lying to one side. Inside were two more bottles of Blue Label that hadn't yet been opened. "I suppose you didn't know I'm a recovering alcoholic—"

"I didn't send this!" cried Denmark.

"Your name was on the card. *Welcome back to Portland*, it said. You knew how emotionally difficult it would be for me to return to this lousy lawyer-infested shit hole, so you thought you'd make it a little easier on me by sending over the finest and most expensive scotch available."

"But I didn't!"

"Then who did?"

Denmark and Hugh exchanged looks; the answer was written in each others' eyes.

The Dog!

"You're not here to get drunk!" sputtered Denmark. "You're being paid to testify in a critically important trial."

"Not any more, I'm not," said Bull, lifting the bottle to his lips. Before he took a swig though, he caught Hugh's eye and said with bitter disappointment, "I'm sorry, Hugh—I simply can't do it."

"What do you mean by that?" demanded Denmark, snatching the bottle away and handing it to Hugh.

"Hey! I want that back!" said Bull.

Hugh turned the bottle upside down over the bathroom sink and scotch gurgled down the drain.

"I asked you a question," said Denmark, prodding Bull on the chest provocatively with his finger. "What do you mean you can't do it?"

Bull sank heavily onto his bed. The ash at the end of his cigarette broke off and dusted his lap. "I can't be your expert," he said.

"The *hell* you can't!"

"Look—I never asked to be Hugh's expert witness. You called me. I didn't call you. Sure, I told you I would like to help. God knows I owe him. But getting involved means testifying in a Portland courtroom again. I'm sure I'll never be able to go through that *hell* again."

"I know about that lawsuit of yours, *Mead vs. Bull*," said Denmark. "Something like that shouldn't prevent you from taking the stand."

"You know about that lawsuit, do you?" said Bull. "Just how much do you know about it? Did you know that the patient was a fat pig who ruptured a lumbar disc while she was at work?"

"I didn't know she was fat," Denmark murmured, acting surprised that he had missed that one small detail.

"Did you know I operated on her back and made her completely well again?"

"I heard something like that."

"I bet you didn't know that she and her husband were happy with her surgery until the minute I declared her fixed and stable and told her to return to work. That's when they decided they didn't like me anymore. You see, Mrs. Mead had been feeding out of the government trough for so long, she had no intention of ever earning a living again. So, she claimed her back had never gotten well and sued my ass out of spite."

"On what grounds?"

"Her lawyer went through the medical records very carefully and dug up an excuse. At the beginning of her operation I stuck a spinal needle into her back and took an X-ray. It's a routine thing to do in order to make sure you're operating at the correct level. Only in her case, there was so much blubber between her skin and her spine, I veered off course after making the incision and began the bone removal at the wrong place. Ever done that before, Hugh?"

"More times than I would ever admit to," said Hugh.

"So, I reached through the little opening with a probe, felt around, but could find no ruptured disc. I realized the error and took another X-ray. It turned out I was too high. Is that a big deal, Hugh?"

"No. Such a small amount of bone removal makes no difference to the spine," Hugh explained to Denmark. "It's not important if a surgeon starts operating at the wrong level. What *is* important is that he quickly realizes the mistake and makes the appropriate correction."

"Bravo!" cried Bull, clapping his hands together. "I couldn't have put it better myself. So, I moved one level further south and took out the ruptured disc fragment. It's all there in black and white in the operation summary which I dictated. I didn't try to hide anything because there was nothing to hide. She did great and went home later that day, telling everybody she was miraculously cured. Hey—I'm thirsty! I want another drink!"

"You've had enough, Bob," said Denmark. "Hugh—make some coffee."

Hugh started fumbling with a coffee machine that was sitting on a chest-of-drawers.

"That's not the kind of drink I had in mind," said Bull, dragging on his cigarette and narrowing his eyes. However, his thoughts were unanchored and he quickly forgot about his thirst. "So, the fat pig found herself a lawyer," he continued. "I find it amazing he actually bothered to take the case. There are just so many of the creepy little vermin around, I suppose they all have to make a living somehow. The lawyer hired one of those so-called expert witnesses—some whore of a neurosurgeon who testifies for a living. The bastard even has his own website touting his special courtroom skills and promising favorable verdicts every time. Of course, he didn't offer any money-back guarantees. So the lawyer threw a ton of money at this blood-sucking liar so he'd say anything he was told to say, then demanded five hundred thousand dollars in damages . . . for operating at the wrong level, causing 'irreparable damage', *and*, get this, giving the plaintiff's husband PTSD—Post-Traumatic Stress Disorder. The whole business stank. I've never heard of anything so disgusting in my life. The trial was held in the Multnomah County Courthouse. It went on for two weeks—two weeks of hell! I sweated it out day after day, hardly believing the circus that was going on around me. People who might have been reasonable human beings outside the courtroom turned into goddamn freaks once they stepped inside. The expert blew all kinds of shit out of his ass. None of it could be backed up by the literature, of course. I hope and pray he burns in hell."

"Coffee's brewing," announced Hugh.

Bull paid no attention. "The jury handed down a verdict in my favor," he continued. "I won the case, but it was still the worst experience of my life. Later, I had horrible arguments with my wife who couldn't understand why I was falling apart. Within months, I was separated from her. Then I started drinking. Things got so bad, I came close to . . . taking my own life. You *think* you know about my lawsuit. . . . You don't know a *damned thing* about my lawsuit!"

Bull was breathing more heavily now and wiped his brow with his sleeve.

"I turned things around by getting the hell out of Portland. I moved to Indiana and put my life back together again. I dried out at AA, and things improved. By the time you contacted me, John, I really thought the demons were gone for good and that I would be able to return here to help my old friend Hugh Montrose. I was wrong. God, I was really wrong! As soon as my plane touched down, all those memories flooded back into my mind as if I had never left. Then my taxi drove past Gestapo headquarters—"

"Gestapo headquarters?"

"The Multnomah County courthouse. I felt my pain just like the old days. I can't step into that goddamn building again without risking a mental break-down. I know I gave you a commitment. I swear to God, I can no longer do it! I'm sorry. I'm so sorry!" Bull toppled sideways onto the bed and started sobbing.

Hugh turned to face Denmark. "Still think he's the perfect expert witness?" he asked.

Denmark was unable to reply.

"He even makes Mortimer look good," said Hugh. "I suppose I shouldn't have gotten my hopes up. This means we've lost the trial, doesn't it? I mean, nobody's going to believe me if I don't have a neurosurgeon testifying on my behalf."

"Hugh . . ." said Denmark, wrenching his eyes from Bull who, by now, was blubbering into a pillow like a child. "I didn't know he was so emotionally fragile. Maxine Doggett must have discovered his weakness and sabotaged him with the booze. I'm really sorry—"

"Don't be," said Hugh, heading for the door. "It doesn't matter any longer. Nothing matters. The coffee will be ready in a few minutes. Good luck sobering him up. I'll see you in court tomorrow."

CHAPTER 29

The following morning, for the first time in his career, John Denmark was late to court.

Maxine was slouching with one elbow on the plaintiffs' table and her head propped in the palm of her hand. Her other hand was stretched across the shiny wood, her long painted fingernails tapping a silent tune. Billy sat next to her, staring into space. Hugh was alone at the defense table, feeling vulnerable without his lawyer sitting nearby. The jury box was empty. The court clerk loitered by the door to the judge's chambers, waiting to announce the defense attorney's arrival.

When Denmark eventually made his entrance, he crept up to the defense table and slid quietly into his seat.

"Shall I inform the judge you're ready now?" asked the clerk, loudly.

Denmark was startled. "Yes . . . that'll be fine," he said.

"What about Bull?" Hugh asked Denmark in an urgent whisper.

"I spent the whole night at the hotel, trying to sober him up. This morning I thought he was feeling better, but—"

The judge swept onto the bench and everybody stood up. "Do you have a good reason for keeping the Court waiting this morning?" he demanded, addressing Denmark directly.

"I'm very sorry about my tardiness," said Denmark, straightening his tie. "I was . . . *detained* by a problem concerning the defense's neurosurgical expert witness, Your Honor."

"You mean Dr. Bull?"

"Yes, Your Honor."

"A problem you wish to share with the Court?"

"I was trying to dissuade him from . . ." Denmark caught sight of Maxine and his voice trailed away. She was watching him like a hungry wolf that had just whiffed the scent of its dinner.

"Speak up, Counselor! I can't hear you!"

"I was trying to dissuade Dr. Bull from . . . leaving town."

Maxine suddenly sat bolt upright and her eyelashes fluttered with excitement.

Billy didn't react at all.

"Your expert was trying to skip town?" asked the judge.

"I'm afraid so, Your Honor. It seems like he changed his mind about giving testimony today . . . not because he didn't believe in the defense's case," he added quickly. "He's still quite sure that Dr. Montrose did exactly the right thing. No, it was for personal reasons."

Maxine shifted forward and balanced herself at the edge of her seat.

"Were your efforts successful?" asked Judge Jenkins.

"No, I'm afraid not. The last I saw of him, he was climbing into a cab and making a dash for the airport."

"Is he aware of the fact that he's under court order to appear today?"

"Yes, I told him that, but he didn't seem to care. He just wanted to leave town as soon as possible."

The judge grunted his irritation and said, "That's still no excuse for your own lateness this morning. You may have forgotten that we have a jury and they're not very happy about being here for five long weeks. If they're not happy, then I'm not either. Do you see where I'm going with this, Mr. Denmark?"

"Yes, Your Honor. I won't let it happen again."

"Do you have any other witnesses you can call upon today? We can't waste any more time, you know."

"The only witness I have available right now is Dr. Montrose himself."

Hugh looked at his lawyer sharply and felt his pulse race. He wasn't expecting to take the stand for at least a week and had done nothing to prepare.

"Ms. Doggett?" said Judge Jenkins, seeking the opinion of plaintiffs' counsel.

"This is totally unacceptable, Your Honor!" she cried, springing to her feet. "Defense counsel has invented this cock-and-bull story about his expert's so-called emotional distress for his own devious purposes, and I'm afraid to guess what those may be. Plaintiffs' counsel is unprepared for the defendant's testimony at this time. If Defendant Montrose is allowed to take the stand today, it will amount to nothing more than a deliberate attempt to sandbag me and Mr. Funk."

"Sandbag?" asked the judge.

"Yes, Your Honor. *Sandbag.*"

"Mr. Denmark?"

"The defense can proceed with some motions that we were planning to make anyhow. That could take an hour or two. Perhaps when we've finished, my office will find another witness more acceptable to Ms. Doggett."

"Any objections, Ms. Doggett?"

"It sounds like hocus-pocus to me."

"Any *objections?*"

"I suppose not, Your Honor."

For the next two hours, Maxine and Denmark argued several motions that twisted themselves into knots and went nowhere. After the last one, Denmark obtained permission to step outside to call his office, but was told by his secretary that none of his other witnesses were available to testify.

The case for the defense had run dry before it had even started.

"Well, Mr. Denmark?" said the judge when he returned to the courtroom. One bushy eyebrow was cocked up and the eye underneath was dark and probing.

"I have no available witnesses at this time, Your Honor, except the defendant himself."

"Objection, Your Honor!" cried Maxine. "Mr. Denmark won't give up his tricks, not as long as he believes he can call Defendant Montrose to the stand today. *Of course* his other experts are available to testify. He just doesn't want them to."

"Ms. Doggett, I can understand your displeasure at this turn of events, but sometimes I wish you would——"

The doors to the courtroom suddenly opened and Bull appeared. Everybody watched as he slowly approached the bar, his arms slightly extended from his sides as though he was undergoing a sobriety test. His eyes were red, swollen, and stared resolutely at the floor, not daring to take in the scene around him. The stench of stale alcohol reached the defense table before he did.

"I'm sorry I bolted," he breathed into Denmark's ear. "Is it too late for me to testify?"

Denmark backed away from the fumes and whispered, "You look like crap."

"Not so loud. My head is killing me."

"Mr. Denmark," called the judge from the bench. "Is *this* your witness?"

"Yes, Your Honor."

Hugh gently kicked his lawyer under the table to get his attention. "You can't put *him* on the stand!" he hissed. "He'll ruin everything."

"I *have* to," replied Denmark.

"Mr. Denmark!" said Judge Jenkins. "Is your witness planning to testify?"

"He is, Your Honor."

The judge looked pleased. "Then the bailiff will fetch the jury and we'll get this trial on the road."

Hugh's face fell into his hands.

After the jurors had settled in, Denmark called his neurosurgical expert to the stand. After the judge administered the oath, Bull reached for a nearby pitcher of water, poured himself a glass, and drank. He began by answering Denmark's questions about his qualifications. He was a board certified neurosurgeon who had been in practice twenty-five years and had performed thousands of operations. Tumors of the spinal cord were very rare, but he had seen more of them than average since his old professor during his residency had sub-specialized in them and had drawn patients from all over the country.

Once he had established his witness's credentials, Denmark moved on to the subject of CSF proteins. Bull told the jury that a level over one hundred meant that Mrs. Winter had a tumor until proven otherwise. If she'd had surgery on her neck before her back fusion, she'd be walking today.

"Do you feel that Dr. Clegg followed the standard of care for a reasonably competent orthopedic surgeon?"

"Objection!" cried Maxine. "Dr. Bull is a neurosurgeon, not an orthopedic surgeon.

"Sustained."

"Do you feel that Dr. Clegg followed the standard of care for a reasonably competent *spine* surgeon?"

"Objection! For the same reason, Your Honor."

"Overruled. They are both spine surgeons. The witness may answer."

"No, he didn't," declared Bull without hesitation. "Dr. Clegg should be the defendant in this case, not Dr. Montrose."

Hugh smiled his tentative approval. Despite Bull's ragged appearance, he spoke with conviction.

"When I first heard about this lawsuit, I thought my ears were deceiving me," Bull continued. "Here is a highly competent and experienced neurosurgeon who was faced with an impossible situation. If he operates immediately, somebody might accuse him of being reckless and sue him for jeopardizing Mrs. Winter's life. If he delays in order to let the swelling decrease, somebody else might accuse him of not operating soon enough. It was a no-win situation. In the end, he did what he believed was right; what he had learned through his own training and experience. He did what the literature said ought to be done. He played it safe and operated at the appropriate time. So what happens? As predicted, instead of being applauded for making the right decision, he got sued."

Bull's testimony continued throughout the morning and he never missed an opportunity to express his outrage at what he called 'a ludicrous lawsuit'. After a while, however, he began to sound repetitive and shifted his focus onto the inadequacies of the system and away from Hugh's innocence. His round face turned the crimson hue of a cardiac patient who smokes and drinks too much, and his eyes grew glassy. He became more indignant, poking his finger at the jury and referring to them as 'those people', words that made Denmark cringe and prompted him to scribble a note to Hugh.

Do not—EVER—refer to the jury as 'those people', it read.

Shortly after eleven, Denmark decided that he was pushing his luck with this emotionally unstable witness and abruptly ended the direct examination.

After the jury had been excused for lunch, Bull left the stand and gently lowered himself into a seat behind the defense table.

Denmark approached the bench. "There is one matter I would like to discuss before this witness' cross-examination, Your Honor."

"Yes, Counselor. What is it?"

"A long time ago, Dr. Bull was a defendant in a medical malpractice lawsuit here in Portland. It involved a patient by the name of Mrs. Mead on whom he performed a back operation. There was a trial and the jury rendered a defense verdict. Shortly afterwards, Dr. Bull left the state of Oregon and started a practice in Indiana where he now resides." Denmark stole a glance at the plaintiff's table. Maxine had a pencil in hand and was once again scribbling notes. "Plaintiff's counsel is going to try to use this incident to discredit my witness. I would like a ruling from the Court, precluding her from even mentioning *Mead vs. Bull* in front of the jury, since it has absolutely no relevance to this case."

"Ms. Doggett?"

Maxine laid aside her pencil and looked up. "I totally disagree, Your Honor. Mr. Denmark didn't hesitate asking Dr. Mortimer embarrassing questions about his own past—"

"I never asked him about his history of malpractice!" interrupted Denmark.

"You demanded to know how many operations he's done in the last twenty-five years!"

"That's not the same thing!"

"You're implying incompetence!"

"*Counselors!*" boomed Judge Jenkins.

"I believe prior lawsuits have every relevance, Your Honor," said Maxine. "They speak to the character and competence of the witness—"

"That's a lie!" shouted Bull, jumping to his feet and butting into the argument. "Lawsuits don't have anything to do with character or incompetence—"

"*Dr. Bull!*" said the judge. "Any more outbursts like that and I'll cite you for contempt of court. Mr. Denmark—curb your witness, sir!"

"Yes, Your Honor," said Denmark, then ordered Bull to sit down and shut up.

"As I was saying," continued Maxine, pressing her case, "the jury should be allowed to consider Dr. Bull's lawsuit during their deliberations. There are volumes of precedence. If you like, I can quote—"

"No, thank you, Counselor. I can do without your quotes. Mr. Denmark?"

"Your Honor, Dr. Bull's malpractice lawsuit had nothing to do with tumors of the spinal cord. It was a ruptured lumbar disc and has no relevance."

"The Court is ready to make a ruling on this matter," said Judge Jenkins. "I do not need to hear further arguments. Ms. Doggett—during your cross-examination, you will make no reference at all to *Mead vs. Bull*. Is that clear?"

"Yes, Your Honor," pouted Maxine.

"Good. And now, let's adjourn for lunch."

"All rise!"

During the lunch break, Denmark cast aside his customary fishing magazine and grilled his expert with questions that he believed Maxine might ask. They rehearsed the answers over and over again until Bull started complaining of double vision. Hugh escaped from the conference room, found a private corner, and called his office to check on things. Trish told him bluntly that the money was drying up. Although there was enough in the bank to cover his employees' payroll and the hefty quarterly malpractice premium, there was not enough left over for his own paycheck.

When Bull returned to the stand, Maxine eagerly began her cross-examination. She approached him and softened him up with a well-rehearsed stare. After a few preliminary questions, a jab here and there to test her victim, she went straight for the jugular.

"Did you have a patient once by the name of Mrs. Metzler?"

Robert Bull's face suddenly went pale. "Y—yes . . ." he stammered.

Denmark leaned forward in his chair and was like a coiled spring, ready to jump to his feet.

"She was a patient of yours that you caused to be quadriplegic after performing a neck operation—"

"*Objection!*" cried Denmark, catapulting himself into the air.

"Ms. Doggett!" bellowed Judge Jenkins.

"That's not true, Your Honor!" shouted Bull.

"The witness will not say another word!" ordered Judge Jenkins. "Bailiff—return the jury to the jury room."

The jurors filed out of the courtroom. When they were gone, the judge turned to Maxine.

"Explain yourself, Ms. Doggett," he said. His purple face completed the second half of his sentence for him: *before I tear you apart with my bare hands.*

"Dr. Bull has a darker history than we've been led to believe," she said, sneering triumphantly at Denmark. "We've already been told about the witness' bungling of the lumbar disc case, but at about the same time there was another lawsuit, wasn't there?"

"It's not as she says!" cried Bull.

"Go on, Ms. Doggett."

"Dr. Bull had a patient called Mrs. Metzler who had a ruptured disc in her neck. He performed an elective operation on her and removed it. After surgery she developed a clot which he missed. By the time he re-entered the incision, the woman was paralyzed—"

"That's not true!" shouted Bull. "It was a nursing error and the delay was only fourteen minutes!"

"Dr. Bull!" cried Judge Jenkins.

Bull fell silent, but continued to pour forth righteous indignation with his eyes.

"Carry on, Ms. Doggett."

"I understand we're not here to determine Dr. Bull's guilt or innocence, but *Metzler vs. Bull* is a relevant case to this trial, especially since it also resulted in a patient becoming quadriplegic. It calls in question the competence of this witness, Your Honor."

"Mr. Denmark?"

Denmark quickly approached the bench, pointing an angry finger towards Maxine. "She's dug up an old lawsuit that has *nothing* to do with the current case, Your Honor. It is ancient history, dragged into court today purely for the purpose of making my client look bad. You have already ruled that old lawsuits have no relevance and they cannot be brought to discredit the witness—"

"The Court is respectfully reminded that it prohibited any mention of *Mead vs. Bull*," said Maxine, "not *Metzler vs. Bull*."

"I wasn't aware of any other lawsuits, Your Honor," said Denmark. "If I had been, I would have asked for the same prohibition against them."

"Can I help it if the defense counsel is too incompetent to do his homework?" countered Maxine.

"Enough of this!" said Judge Jenkins. "Ms. Doggett—you are *not* to introduce evidence regarding *any* prior lawsuits against this witness. Is that clear?"

Maxine did not immediately answer, then sat down and said sulkily, "Yes, Your Honor."

"We'll have a fifteen minute recess so we can all calm down before bringing back the jury. Mr. Denmark—I suggest you use the time wisely. Perhaps you might like to become better acquainted with your own expert."

"Yes, Your Honor."

In the short recess, it became obvious to Denmark that Maxine's primary objective hadn't been to drag up muck that would embarrass Dr. Bull and cause the jury to call into question his competency. Instead, she had recognized his principle vulnerabilities, his emotional instability and his drinking, and was exploiting them to the fullest extent.

To a large measure, she was succeeding. Bull had been visibly shaken by the introduction of Mrs. Metzler's name. Sweat drenched his forehead and his hands now had a visible tremor. He followed Denmark and Hugh out of the courtroom and joined them in the privacy of a nearby stairwell where he groped at Denmark's arms.

"Don't make me go back to the stand!" he begged, his voice echoing up and down the marble walls of the stairwell.

"Why didn't you tell me about that lawsuit?" demanded Denmark.

"I—I didn't think it was important."

"Of course it was important! Everything's important! Is there anything else you've kept from me?"

"No . . . no, that's it. There haven't been any other lawsuits. I'm sorry if I screwed up. Just keep that awful woman away from me. *Please!*"

"I'm sorry," said Denmark. "You're in the middle of being cross-examined. You have no choice but to answer her remaining questions."

Once everybody had resumed their seats in the courtroom, Maxine moved in for the kill.

"Dr. Bull—you once practised in Portland, did you not?" she asked.

"Yes," he replied, shrinking away from her.

"And now you practise in Indiana?"

"Yes."

"How long ago did you make the move?"

Bull counted the fingers of his right hand. "About five years."

"Why did you move?"

Bull hesitated and nervously glanced around himself. "It was time for a change."

"Is that all? Or were there other factors?"

"Objection!" said Denmark firmly. "This line of questioning is not relevant to this trial, Your Honor."

"Overruled."

"Could it be because you were about to lose your privileges at Columbia Medical Center?"

"Objection!"

"And your medical malpractice insurance company was about to drop your coverage?"

"*Objection!*"

"All because of a serious drinking problem?"

"*Objection!*"

Before Judge Jenkins could silence Maxine, Bull jumped to

his feet and gripped the wooden railing in front of him. *"No! No! No!"* he shouted, his face turning deep red.

The judge hammered his gavel as though he was trying to drive a nail into the bench.

"It's all lies," continued Bull. *"Lies!* I've always been a good neurosurgeon! It's the lawyers; they did this to me! The *bastards!* Nobody would have cared if it hadn't been for *them!* I should never have agreed to come back to Portland. I don't deserve this! *Nobody* deserves this!"

Then, as Hugh watched in horror, Bull stumbled from the stand and fled from the courtroom.

With utmost grace and poise, Maxine looked up from a row of red fingernails, smiled at Judge Jenkins, and said with perfect non-chalance, "I have no more questions for this witness, Your Honor."

CHAPTER 30

Denmark had prepared a long list of witnesses. Now was the time for him to unwrap them, display them on a pedestal in front of the jury, and try to erase some of the damage inflicted by 'Dr. Bull-in-a-china-shop', as he now referred to his principle expert.

The medical experts were mostly eggheads recruited from the university faculty. They gracefully consented to exchange their exalted opinions for the maximum amount of dough they could squeeze out of the insurance company. Denmark quietly acknowledged to Hugh that this was no different than what that tottering corpse, Mortimer, had done, but at least *his* experts were reputable, in active practice, and gave testimony that could be supported by the scientific literature. A neuropathologist described in detail the microscopic appearance of Julie's tumor and then attempted to educate the jurors on the subtle differences between ependymomas and astrocytomas, a lecture that went straight over their heads, leaving them looking bewildered and confused. A neuroradiologist set up huge posters of Julie's MRI's, then, peering through the bifocals perched at the end of his long nose, he pointed out the ugly mess that represented the tumor. A neurologist sniffed that orthopods had no business operating on spines since they hadn't a clue how to perform a proper neurological exam. A rehabilitation doctor was asked questions about rehabilitation, a physiatrist about physiatrics, a psychologist about psychology. Finally, another life care manager and economist took the stand and, as if it was possible, the two of them were even more boring than their counterparts on the plaintiffs' side. Using monotone voices and long-winded sentences, they presented estimates for Julie's future care costs which were sharply lower than the ones the jury had already heard.

The factual witnesses were also paraded through court and they testified about the events that had occurred four years earlier. Bogdana and Betty, the two nurses on duty the night after Julie's back surgery, swore that they had been highly vigilant and that there had been absolutely no delay in recognizing her paralysis. Dr. Stan Reeder answered questions about Hugh's visit to his cave in radiology later on that day. Others were put on the stand too: the pale-faced pathologist with dark shadows under his eyes who had read Julie's slides, the pimply pharmacist who had provided the steroids, the muscular orderly who had rushed Julie to radiology, first to have a myelogram, then later for an MRI, all trying to remember what had taken place on a perfectly ordinary day four years before. When they finished their testimony, each of them gave Hugh a look as if to say 'I'm glad you're the poor bastard sitting there and not me', then bolted from the courtroom.

Hugh paid no attention to any of this. His thoughts dwelled at the bottom of a pit. Ever since this lawsuit had started, nothing had gone right.

Richard, he had to keep reminding himself, was dead. For all his bravado, the big neurosurgeon had been a good and decent man, totally connected to his patients. He loved to spend extra time with them, explaining their problems in a way they could understand, never growing tired of answering questions. This special relationship must have been why his lawsuit had wounded him so badly. It was a vicious, unexpected attack that had blind-sided him and he hadn't known how to cope. His response had been a natural one for a person of his physical strength: he had violently rattled the bars of his cage, hoping the door would fall off its hinges. SOD'M had, indeed, set him free, at least for a while. Then, obviously, something radical had happened to change everything—something real, terrible, and devastating. Short of hearing her make some sort of miraculous confession, Hugh doubted he would ever prove that Maxine was involved. His dreams of a SWAT team bursting into court one day and frog-marching the red-headed bitch away were likely to remain just that—dreams.

"If you really want to investigate her," said Denmark after patiently listening to yet another bizarre cloak-and-dagger theory from Hugh, "wait until the trial is over. You can do anything you like with that woman, but not until then."

Things at the hospital were going badly too. The scrawny little Greek, Petros Pagonis, was single-handedly driving what was left of the Columbia neurosurgery program into the ground. Word of his incompetence continued to find ways to Hugh's ears and each successive story was even more chilling than the one before. Everybody on the medical staff wanted to tie a block of concrete around his ankles and drop him into the Columbia River even though his dismissal would leave the entire hospital without any neurosurgical coverage at all. The issues were hotly debated in the surgery lounge and in the halls of the administration. In the end, the controversial decision was taken to grin and bear it just a little longer until his scheduled departure at the end of Hugh's trial.

Most depressing of all was Hugh's deteriorating relationship with Michelle. With each successive setback he suffered in the courtroom, he found himself blaming her more often for his misfortune. After all, *she* was the one who had forced him to fight the case rather than settling; *she* was responsible for all those sleepless nights when his thoughts pinged and popped around his head like the ball inside a pinball machine. If it hadn't been for her, he wouldn't have to experience frequent tension headaches and the misery of sitting in court every day, week after week. By now, they were having nasty arguments, sometimes in front of the children. They often ended when Michelle broke into tears and said that she was watching a rerun of a vampire movie. Richard had originally been Dracula's victim, and now her own husband had that part. She already knew the ending and it terrified her more than ever. Her frayed nerves led to more arguments, incriminations, and fear.

"Win or lose, things will get better at the end of the trial," Hugh had tried to reassure her.

Non cela ne s'arrangera pas, she thought with a trembling heart. *Tu es marqué à vie et tu ne seras plus jamais le même.* No, they won't. You're scarred and will never be the same again.

Being the eldest of Hugh's children, Marie and Renee were the only ones who had some understanding of what was going on, and, with time, they also began to show signs of being negatively affected: flagging grades, more than the average rebellious teenager behavior, and occasional tantrums of their own. One day, they returned from school, pale and shaken, saying that the cat was out of the bag; some busybody had dug up information about the lawsuit on the web and had gossiped about it. Now all their classmates were snickering that their father was being sued for medical malpractice and that he must be a no-good quack if he had gotten himself into so much trouble. Marie and Renee had bravely tried to defend him. Eventually, though, peer cruelty had proven too much for them and they had fled home in tears.

When the last day of testimony arrived, it was Hugh's turn to take the stand. He walked slowly to the wooden witness chair, his head stuffed to capacity with all the answers to Denmark's upcoming questions. His mouth was dry, his heart was hammering within his chest, and when he took the oath from the judge, he stumbled over the words. He sat down, looked as pleasantly as he could at the jury without making it obvious he was faking, and prepared to give his own version of events.

Denmark retrieved his podium from a corner of the courtroom, wheeled it into position, and produced some notes from his inside pocket. When it was quiet, he cleared his throat and began.

"Dr. Montrose—kindly tell the members of the jury your full name and what kind of work you do."

"My name is Hugh Montrose and I'm a board certified neurosurgeon at Columbia Medical Center."

Denmark then asked a series of introductory questions, designed to make his client look less like a stuffed mannequin that had been propped behind the defense table for the past few weeks and more like a normal human being with his own feelings, thoughts, and aspirations. The jury learned that Hugh had been born and raised in Scotland and had wanted to be a neurosurgeon ever since he had met one named Sir John Worthington when he lived in Edinburgh. The distinguished old gentleman had shown him a skull that had once belonged to somebody called Matilda, a woman who had wanted to make her mark in the world by donating her body to science. Hugh told the jury that Matilda had influenced his own life in a major way; if he hadn't caught sight of her skull in Sir John's gripsack that day many years ago, he might never have become a neurosurgeon himself.

"Did Sir John do anything else aside from showing you the

skull," asked Denmark, teeing up a carefully planned humorous moment for the jury.

"Oh, yes," answered Hugh. "He explained to me how neurosurgeons operate on peoples' brains by sawing holes in their skulls. When I heard *that*, I knew I didn't want to be anything else when I grew up." He grinned in exactly the manner prescribed by his lawyer.

The faces of the jurors remained carved in granite.

"But as an adult," said Denmark, moving on quickly as if he wanted to put some distance between himself and his failed joke, "you wanted to be a neurosurgeon for different reasons, didn't you?"

"Of course," replied Hugh. "Like Matilda, I felt a compelling need to do something useful and worthwhile; to make a difference in peoples' lives. Everybody has a gift, and it's up to an individual to discover what theirs is. I realized early on that I had a knack at working with living tissue. This confirmed to me that neurosurgery was my calling and not some childhood fantasy."

Denmark delivered another salvo of questions, enabling Hugh to describe how he immigrated to the United States with his parents when he was eighteen and attended college and medical school with the hope of becoming a neurosurgeon. The competition to be accepted to a training program was intense, but, in the end, his determination prevailed. After slaving in a residency program for seven years, he achieved his lifelong dream and began his work at Columbia. He was married to a French woman named Michelle, his co-defendant, and now they were raising five children.

"Tell me when you first met the plaintiffs, Mr. and Mrs. Winter."

"It was June 29th, 2001."

"Could you relate the circumstances under which this meeting took place?"

Hugh described how Dr. Clegg had called him in the middle of the afternoon, inviting him to consult on the case. He had dropped what he was doing once he understood the urgency of the situation and had rushed straight to the MRI scanner.

Denmark left his podium and wandered in the general direction of the jury. "What were your thoughts as you were walking over to take a look at the films?" he asked, his eyes skipping over the faces of the fourteen men and women as he slowly moved in front of them.

"Judging from what I'd been told, I knew the situation was very serious. The unfortunate woman had been quadriplegic for many hours. No matter what I did, I was not going to be able to reverse her paralysis, not after so much time. I also knew that I couldn't take anybody else's word on a matter so serious, so I was obligated to carefully check things out myself."

"Tell us about the scans."

Hugh described how he reviewed the pictures with the radiologist, Dr. Reeder, and saw a large tumor inside the cervical spinal cord that looked benign. It must have been a very slow grower. How else could it have grown to such proportions with the minimum of symptoms? The exact pathology, whether it was an ependymoma or an astrocytoma, was not known, but neither did it matter; the management was the same either way. With so much swelling inside the spinal cord, the only prudent thing to do was to give the patient high doses of steroids, control the swelling, and remove the tumor at a later date when it would be much safer.

"What were you thinking when you left the scanner and were on your way to see Mrs. Winter?"

"There was only one thing on my mind," said Hugh in the

most serious voice he could muster. "By now I was certain that this woman was going to be paralyzed for the rest of her life, so I was figuring out how best to break the news."

"I see." Denmark broke away from his engagement with the jury, returned to his podium, and patiently thumbed through a few sheets of notes. Somewhere outside the window, a garbage truck was making its rounds along the street below. The straining sound of a hydraulic lift was punctuated by tinkling and crashing of trash as it emptied into the collection bin. Men shouted, refuse containers were dropped back onto the street with a clatter, and the truck moved on. Denmark looked as if he heard none of this. Without looking up, he asked, "What did you do when you reached the hospital?"

"First of all, I had to verify all the information I had been given. I looked through the chart and read all the progress notes and reports. Then I introduced myself to the patient and her husband and obtained a thorough history. After that, I examined her."

Denmark turned another page. "Was the history she gave you consistent with Dr. Clegg's?"

"Yes, it was. She said that she had been completely paralyzed in her hands and legs since the early hours of the morning. She had stayed the same since then; neither improving nor deteriorating."

Now Denmark looked up and fixed his clear blue eyes on his client. "Did you do a *thorough* exam?"

"Yes."

"And what did you find?"

"My examination of the patient confirmed the history. She was indeed quadriplegic."

"What did you do then? Did you give her any options?"

"There was only one option that made any sense."

"What was that?"

"I told Julie . . . Mrs. Winter and her husband, that in my opinion, the risks of early surgery far outweighed any potential benefit and that she would be better off having the swelling first brought under control with some steroids. Operating on her at that time wasn't really a realistic option, to my deep regret, of course. It might spread her paralysis, or even make her dependant on a ventilator."

Denmark's stepped closer. "But what if she and her husband had insisted on surgery at that time?"

"I would have refused . . . politely, of course. I wasn't about to do something that clearly wasn't in her best interest. Maybe I would have called around town to see if there was a willing neurosurgeon, but I seriously doubt I would have found anybody. The Winters didn't insist on surgery. They trusted my judgment."

"So, Dr. Montrose, after all this time you've been given to reflect on your actions that day, is it still your belief that you made the right decision when you chose not to immediately operate on Mrs. Winter?"

"I am *convinced* I made the right decision!" said Hugh, his eyes moistening as he looked directly at the jury. "I had spent my whole life preparing to make that decision. All those years working around the clock during my neurosurgical residency were for a reason, you know; memorizing the textbooks, studying the literature . . . so I could develop as much experience and judgment as possible . . . so I could make the right decisions for the Mrs. Winters of this world . . . so I could sit here and say that I did *nothing* wrong, and *everything* right."

"One more question, Dr. Montrose," said Denmark with

a reassuring smile. "If you were faced with the same situation again today, what would you do?"

"I would save myself a great deal of misery by operating immediately, but that would only serve my own interests, not those of my patient. The patient's needs always come first. No . . ." Hugh's gripped the wooden railing in front of him. "Under the same circumstances, I would do *exactly* the same things over again."

"Thank you, Dr. Montrose," said Denmark. He gathered together the papers on his podium, held them upright, and gently tapped them against the polished wood. "Your Honor, I have no further questions."

After lunch, Maxine launched into her long-anticipated cross-examination.

Hugh lurched from a friendly interrogation to one that filled him with terror. Old memories from his days at Helmsdale Manor flooded into his mind on a wave of pipe tobacco and musty books. He could picture a partner's desk laden with homework, a flowery armchair, and a gym shoe with a large hole in its sole.

Hugh gritted his teeth and avoided Maxine's eyes, afraid that if he fell under their wicked spell, his mind would be paralyzed and he would stutter like a fool. He also tried not to pay any attention to the sarcasm and loathing in her honey-filled voice. Instead, he focused on her thin pale lips and wondered, absurdly, if they had ever tasted the tenderness of a loving kiss. When he came through her initial questions unscathed, her eyes narrowed with determination and she cranked up the intensity of her offensive. The questions came in faster and with sharper barbs and were like arrows flying across the courtroom. Denmark's voice echoed in his head: 'Remember: just be yourself. The jury is on your side. They *want* to believe you.'

An hour of questions passed, then another. He spoke what he believed to be the truth, but after eighteen months of discovery, the truth had been badly mauled and what little left was hardly recognizable. It had become a rotting corpse hanging from a noose, gently twisting one way and then another, depending on the direction of the wind. Sometimes, he became befuddled. Maxine wedged open the cracks and made him appear weak and incompetent. Unaccustomed to being assaulted in this manner, Hugh grew panicky and he prayed that she would soon finish. After the second hour, his mind was screaming:

Oh, my God! No more! Please!

But there was much more to come, each question carefully aimed and specifically designed to inflict maximum carnage. He fought back, but weeks of this trial had drained him, dulled his powers of reason, and robbed him of strength. His emotions were walking a tightrope; with each stinging accusation his breathing grew more labored and his eyes once again moistened. After the third hour, his ears were playing tricks on him and he thought he was being dismissed. He started to rise from his chair.

"Where are you going?" Maxine demanded. "I haven't finished with you yet!"

That's enough! That's enough!

The judge's voice rang out: "The defendant will answer the question!" and Hugh felt an invisible hand shoving him down back onto the arm of the flowery chair.

The relentless questioning resumed.

What is the definition of quadriplegia? How's quadriplegia different from quadriparesis? Can you be quadriplegic if you have feeling in your legs? Can you be quadriparetic if you have numbness in your hands? Was Mrs. Winter complete or partial? Is there such thing as a complete quadriparesis or a partial quadriplegia? How about partially complete? Or completely partial?

The riddles kept coming in rapid succession like bullets spitting out of the barrel of a machine gun. Words melted together into an unintelligible blur and his answers became automatic, unthinking. In the midst of the maelstrom, Hugh felt those grey eyes boring through his body with an intensity that was supernatural, sapping his will to fight back . . . the big chin . . . the infamous sneer . . . the pale and almost imperceptible scar from her aneurysm surgery. Then Maxine's mouth was open too and Hugh could see the back of her throat as she screeched more questions. The golden hummingbird on her chest came to life; its long tongue flickered towards him as if he was a flower dripping with nectar. He felt a dash of stickiness against his cheek and an irresistible tug. He was being winched inexorably towards a foaming chasm that yawned before him.

The gym shoe in his mind was beating him hard. Six of the Best—the maximum sentence.

"Don't let me ever catch you being *negligent* again!" screamed Maxine.

"Yes, I promise, I *promise*. Just don't hurt me any more . . ."

". . . *negligent, negligent, negligent, negligent* . . ."

Then, thank God, it was over.

CHAPTER 31

For John Denmark, the last day of the trial began with a disaster that eclipsed all the others that had bedeviled him since the beginning. This one was especially personal and hit him in the gut so powerfully that he might have given up altogether if he hadn't been so close to the end of the trial. He had planned to practise his speech in front of an empty jury box. With Hugh in tow, he showed up at the courtroom early in the morning, anxious to warm up.

At first, they didn't notice it.

They hung up their coats by the doorway and unloaded files, papers, and books onto the defense table. Denmark leafed through his notes, cleared his mind, and concentrated on the task at hand. When he was ready, he stood up, and started for the far corner of the courtroom to fetch his podium.

That's when he spotted the pile of splintered wood.

Denmark stopped dead, saying nothing, his jaw hanging. Hugh looked up from a neurosurgical journal. His eyes followed his lawyer's shocked gaze and saw the wreckage in the corner.

"Is . . . *was* that your podium?" Hugh asked.

"*No!*" cried Denmark, rushing forward. He sank to his knees, grabbed a splintered piece of wood, and shook it in the air. "Smashed to bits! Who did this?" Then his eyes narrowed. "Classic Doggett!" He flung away the wood; it clattered across the floor. "That *witch!* She did this! I know it!"

"Maxine?" said Hugh. "Why?"

"She knew it would hurt me."

"Why would she bother? She's already got this trial in the bag."

"Maybe she just wants to be sure," said Denmark, his face drawn and grim.

"Don't be ridiculous!" said Hugh. "How can you be so dependant on a stupid podium? You can deliver Closing Arguments without it."

"*Stupid podium?*" shouted Denmark with such force that Hugh dropped his journal and almost fell out of his chair. "You don't understand what that thing meant to me! I've *never* been in a courtroom without it!"

Hugh realized that Denmark was in no frame of mind to rehearse Closing Arguments, so he apologized for his insensitive remarks and suggested that the two of them withdraw to a café across the street from the courthouse.

"Look, Hugh," said Denmark a short while later, nursing a cup of coffee, "I'm sorry about how things have turned out. After all these years of battling Maxine in court, I thought I knew how to win a case against her. Turns out I was wrong. I'm simply not up to it. She lies and cheats all the time, things I'm unable to do."

Hugh gazed out of the café's windows and at the courthouse opposite, his home for the past few weeks. It was a big, imposing building, built in the early twentieth century and specifically designed to impress with its elaborately carved façade.

And that's exactly what it is—a façade, Hugh thought bitterly. *Formal and pompous on the outside, rotten on the inside.*

In the street, a group of grimy homeless people were standing around and lying on the sidewalk, passing the time. Hugh thought he recognized some of them from the day Mortimer had testified in court.

"So you're saying the trial's over and we've lost?" he asked Denmark, fingering a glass of orange juice.

"We haven't lost yet, but—"

"We soon will," said Hugh, finishing his lawyer's sentence for him. "Frankly, at this point, I no longer care."

"You can't really mean that!"

"I'm being serious. The maximum damage has already been done. The jury can't make it any worse for me."

"What damage?"

"I've lost all interest in neurosurgery."

"Oh, come now—don't feel so bad about it. You can get back to operating as soon as the trial's over."

"And act as if nothing happened? It's not that easy, you know. You see, I don't want to be a neurosurgeon anymore if it means there's a chance I could go through this particular version of hell again. It's just not worth it. Grant me just a little human dignity. There are better things I could do with my life."

"It's not hell. It's the system—*our* system. Like it or not, it's the only one we have."

"It needs changing."

"Easier said than done."

"I've got an idea how to do it."

"Oh, yes?" Denmark leaned forward. "Tell how, then."

"I've been thinking . . ." said Hugh, taking a sip from his orange juice. "It's very difficult to target the trial lawyers, limiting their fees, capping non-economic damages, and so on. Politically, they're far too powerful. They own the legislative and judicial branches of government. Half of all politicians and judges were once trial lawyers. Maybe more. If they don't like something, all they have to do is have a back room conversation with their friends. If that doesn't work, they just write a few checks with lots of zeros on them and the problem usually disappears. No, the biggest and most vulnerable villains in the system are these so-called expert witnesses—monsters like Charles Mortimer who have absolutely no business testifying. They're the Achilles' heel we should go after."

"How?"

"This is my idea, John: our national organization, CANS, should certify neurosurgeons to act as expert witnesses. They must be well-respected professionals, engaged in active practice, don't testify for a living, and believe in using the scientific literature as a basis for their opinions. Make it a requirement that they must work for both sides, plaintiffs and defendants, so they don't become partisan. And they must be volunteers too."

"You want them to do all that legal work for free?"

"Why not? I would be the first to sign up if I knew I was doing something to save the system from destroying itself. We've *got* to take money out of the equation in order to make it fair. The certified expert witnesses will be proud of the work they're doing. Hell, they could even make a coat-of-arms for themselves like the shining white knights of old: a Crusader's shield emblazoned with a scalpel and a gavel crossed together. They should have a Latin motto to live by: Veritatis Defensor, Protector of the Truth."

"You've got this all worked out, haven't you?"

"The point is: let's give the experts some real credibility. Surely that's something both plaintiffs and defendants want! I especially like the fact that it wouldn't take a political battle to make this happen; CANS can forge ahead regardless what anybody else thinks."

"Don't think it'll be so simple," said Denmark. "The trial lawyers are sure to torpedo your efforts. Any change from the current system wouldn't be in their best interests."

"How can they fight back if CANS decides to certify expert witnesses?"

"They'll think of something."

"Of course, the trial lawyers are free to continue business as usual, hiring loony crackpots like Mortimer if that's what they want. However, the fact that a witness is *certified* should be admissible and weighed by the jury."

"I don't know about this, Hugh," said Denmark, shaking his head. "You've no idea how powerful the trial lawyers are. CATL will squash you like a bug."

Hugh waved away Denmark's concern with his hand. "I contacted CANS about a week ago and talked with the president, an acquaintance of mine named Chuck Graham. He sounded interested in the idea of starting a certified expert witness program and promised to get back to me. Of course, one never knows if he really will."

"Talking about getting back," said Denmark, suddenly glancing at his watch. "It's time we got back to court. I can't wait to see what Maxine will do to us next."

Back at the defense table, Denmark traded places with Hugh, positioning himself on the leeward side of his client for the first time. When a wheezing workman entered with a wheelbarrow and unceremoniously shoveled the wreckage of the podium into it, he blanched and pretended not to notice. When Maxine gave him the predictable sadistic leer, he averted his eyes and busily rearranged his notes.

Julie and Gary were back in court. Sitting in her wheelchair, Julie was positioned next to her lawyer. Her husband was directly behind them, looking pensive. When the jurors were seated, Hugh and Denmark scanned their faces, but were unable to discern what they might be thinking.

Maxine delivered her Closing Arguments flawlessly. She wore a deep blue suit with the ever-present golden frills and braids, and paraded up and down in front of the jurors, wiggling her hips for the men amongst them, gesticulating with her arms and rattling her gold bracelets. After she had summarized the case for them from her own point of view, she told them that her clients had been grievously harmed and richly deserved the maximum compensation. Of course, there had to be millions—*many* millions of dollars changing hands for justice to be properly served. She accused Defendant Montrose of being a monster on the loose, guilty of every crime in the book short of genocide, making it abundantly clear that if anybody didn't agree with her, they must either be a fool or an idiot. Maybe the defendant was a slick talker on the stand, but his weepy eyes had been nothing but a show and he cared absolutely nothing for the people he had damaged so badly. She claimed that Professor Charles Mortimer was God's gift to the world of neurosurgery and expounded upon his qualifications. Wasn't it wonderful that there were still doctors of his caliber in this country? The neurosurgery expert for the defense, on the other hand—Maxine pointed her finger at her temple and slowly circled it around, a gesture that elicited a few chuckles from the jurors—who could trust anything *he* had said on the stand? She ended by begging them to have pity on her clients and render a plaintiffs' verdict so Mr. and Mrs. Winter could start picking up the pieces of their lives.

Maxine took an hour to deliver her performance. When she was finished, she strutted past the defense table, giving the defendant and his lawyer a look drenched with contempt. Then she settled into her seat next to Julie, grasped Billy's limp hand, and gave herself a congratulatory handshake.

Denmark rose to his feet and appeared awkward as he stood in front of the jury, like a schoolboy who was about to deliver a recital. For a few moments his arms flopped around as though he was uncertain what to do with them. In the end, he kept one hanging by his side, while he held his notes in the other.

"Ladies and gentlemen of the jury," he began, "there's no doubt that Mrs. Winter has suffered a terrible misfortune. She's quadriplegic and that's something that can never be changed. But my client is not responsible for her paralysis. He arrived on the scene more than twelve hours too late. Quite frankly, the plaintiff's attorney has made a colossal mistake in this case: she sued the wrong doctor."

"*Objection!*" screamed Maxine, shooting to her feet and crashing her fist down on the joystick to her client's wheelchair. Julie and her chair were suddenly launched backwards into her husband, sending him sprawling. In a wild attempt to save herself, Julie hit the joystick with her hand, but miscalculated and struck it too hard. Her wheelchair leapt forward and careened into the table in front. She was catapulted out of her seat and landed on the floor in front of the jury box with a sickening thud.

For an instant, there was a horrified silence. Julie lay in a heap in the middle of the floor as pathetic and helpless as a beached whale. Her husband was clutching his ankle, grimacing in pain. Maxine stood with her arm frozen in mid-air, an expression of shock written all over her face. Then everybody started moving at once. Hugh started for Julie, but Maxine reached her first and blocked his path.

"Stay away from my client before you do any more damage to her!" she hissed. "I'm a fully qualified registered nurse, you know. I can handle this!"

Billy helped Gary back into his chair and prodded his ankle to give the impression that he was doing something useful. Denmark held the wheelchair steady while Maxine and the bailiff hoisted Julie off the floor and heaved her back into it.

Judge Jenkins watched the scene below him with incredulity. When the bailiff was free, he sent the jury back to their room and ordered a fifteen minute recess. Denmark and Hugh retreated to their secret conference room on the fourth floor.

"She did that on purpose!" cried Denmark, slamming the door behind him.

"She did *what?*" asked Hugh. "Hit the joystick *on purpose?*"

"Yes! I saw her! When she finished her Closing Arguments and returned to her table, she adjusted the position of her chair. She moved closer to Julie just so she could pull something like this."

"Classic Doggett, huh?" Hugh asked.

"Exactly!"

"But why?"

"To disrupt my own Closing Arguments, of course," cried Denmark. "Don't you see? No matter what I say from now on, the jury will only remember the fiasco that just happened. The image of a quad flying through the air is far more powerful than anything I can conjure up. How could Maxine illustrate Julie's helplessness better than by having her lie like a lump on the floor of the courtroom? It'll bring more sympathy points than a week of testimony. The whole thing was planned from the very beginning, every detail choreographed to have maximum effect."

"Choreographed?"

"Of course!"

"You think the Winters were in on it?" asked Hugh.

"I bet they rehearsed until it was perfect. Goddamn *witch!* How am I supposed to defend a client against somebody like her?"

After the recess, the courtroom was restored to some semblance of normality. Gary's ankle wasn't that badly injured after all and Julie had also recovered. Maxine was seated at the plaintiff's table and was flipping quietly through her notes as if nothing had happened. Billy was at her side, yanking errant hairs from his nostrils with his thumb and forefinger.

Judge Jenkins ordered the jury back and the trial resumed. He sustained Maxine's objection and cautioned Denmark to stay within the accepted limits of Closing Arguments.

Once again, Denmark stood in front of the jury, this time without his podium. He fingered his notes, deep in thought.

"Mr. Denmark," said the judge impatiently. "We are waiting for you to resume."

"Thank you . . . Your Honor." Another long pause, then Denmark appeared to have reached a conclusion. He tossed his notes onto the defense table and approached the jury. "I've been a lawyer for a very long time," he said, his blue eyes gleaming with inspiration. "When I've spoken in court, I've always stood behind a podium with notes in front of me. I've always been thoroughly programmed to say exactly the right things at exactly the right times. Kind of contrived, don't you think? Well, in case you haven't noticed, this whole trial has been contrived. Certainly the defense has been. As the defendant's attorney, I can vouch for that."

Maxine smiled broadly and vigorously nodded her agreement behind Denmark's back.

"I strongly suspect the plaintiffs' side has been too," added Denmark, jerking his thumb over his shoulder.

The smile on Maxine's face promptly vanished.

"You might ask yourselves what I mean by 'contrived'," Denmark continued, surveying the fourteen faces that were watching him intently. "Let me briefly explain myself: I spent weeks preparing for Dr. Montrose's testimony and knew the answer to every question before I even asked it. The same is true for Dr. Bull and all the other expert witnesses. However, just because I knew the questions and answers, that doesn't mean I really understood what was being said. The truth is: I don't really have a good comprehension of any of this neurosurgery business simply because it's far too complicated for me. Look how long it took him to learn." Denmark raised an arm and pointed towards his client. "Dr. Montrose had to go through *seven* years of training before he became a neurosurgeon, and that was *after* four years of medical school."

Even after all that training, Hugh reflected, he still wasn't fully qualified; he didn't receive his board certification until three more years after the end of his residency. And it was another ten years of busy practice before he felt truly settled into his profession.

Denmark put his arms out in front of himself as if he was instinctively reaching for his podium, then quickly dropped them by his side again. "If I was a member of this jury, I would be unhappy about being here," he went on. "God knows you have enough to put up with, showing up every day, and all that. But that's not what I would be especially unhappy about. I'll tell you what would really fry my goose: being asked to look at a neurosurgical case and determine whether or not the standard of care was met. How the *heck* would I know? I'm a lawyer, not a neurosurgeon. None of you are neurosurgeons either."

More than one juror shook their head emphatically.

Denmark smiled, pleased that he had elicited some kind of response out of his audience, then said, "So we have to rely on experts to explain these complicated things to folks like ourselves. But here's another problem: one expert says one thing; the other side has an expert who says exactly the opposite. Between

Dr. Mortimer and Dr. Bull, who are we to believe? When it comes down to it, we don't *really* know and, in the end, we're more confused than ever."

At least three jurors gave subtle nods of agreement. Billy did too, until Maxine kicked him under the table.

"I could spend the next hour going over the testimony, like Ms. Doggett did, trying to sort things out for you and explaining what's important from my own point of view. I could repeat some of the finer details you may have missed and reiterate for the hundredth time why Dr. Montrose delayed his surgery instead of operating right away. Maybe some of you may have no trouble taking in all this stuff. But if you find the reams and reams of evidence overwhelming, I want you to remember one important thing: most of you have, at one time or other, been a *patient*. And so, at the conclusion of this trial, I want you, the members of this jury, to make a decision about Dr. Montrose based on your expertise as *patients*. What kind of impression do you get from having been in the same room with him for the past few weeks? You've heard him testify from the stand. Form an opinion about him. Is he somebody that can be trusted? Would you see him if something was wrong with your own health? That shouldn't be too hard to determine; most of you have been to a doctor's office and came home thinking: I liked Dr. So-and-so, he seemed to care. Or: Dr. So-and-so was a jerk; he wasn't interested in me as person at all. People often have to make life-and-death judgments about their doctors. After all, these guys are going to open them up on the operating table. I want you to apply the same principles when trying to decide how you feel about Dr. Montrose."

Now Denmark circled away from the jury box and approached the plaintiffs' table. As he drew closer, Maxine bristled with hostility like a hyena protecting its kill.

"Here, I think, is a person who knows how she feels about Dr. Montrose," said Denmark, pointing at Julie from safe distance. "The plaintiff herself! In her testimony, she told us all kinds of things about him: he's a good doctor . . . she's sorry if the lawsuit hurt him . . . if she could start over again, she would not name him as a defendant . . . it should be obvious that he wasn't negligent . . . and if she had to do it all over again, she would choose Dr. Montrose to be her surgeon, and not Dr. Clegg. Isn't it amazing she would say all those kind things about the doctor she's suing? If she—the quadriplegic plaintiff—feels that way about Dr. Montrose, how should you, the jury?"

With a parting look of triumph, Denmark turned away from the plaintiffs' table and circled back to his position in front of the jurors. "My client was not negligent when he cared for Julie Winter," he told them with conviction. "I urge you to return a verdict in his favor.

"Ladies and gentlemen, thank you very much for your attention."

CHAPTER 32

Late the following afternoon, after hours of legal maneuvers between Maxine and Denmark, Judge Jenkins placed *Winter vs. Montrose* in the hands of the jurors. He chose two of the fourteen at random and informed them that they were the designated alternates. He thanked them for their service and gave them permission to go home. He handed the rest a set of jury instructions that both sides had agreed on and told them to begin their deliberations without delay.

Fifteen minutes later, Hugh arrived back at his office. The phone on his desk was ringing. His lawyer was at the other end of the line.

"Hugh, get down to the courthouse right away!" cried Denmark breathlessly. "The jury has reached a verdict! Already!"

"What the hell are you going on about?" asked Hugh.

"It took them only five minutes to decide the case! This must be a record! I've never seen anything like it! *Never!*"

"What do you mean: it took them only five minutes?" he asked, throwing his coat into a corner.

"They went into the jury room, closed the door behind them, and almost immediately the door was open again and the foreman was asking for the bailiff."

"What can anybody decide in only five minutes?"

"They must have taken a quick vote right at the start. This can only mean one thing: that we've won the case. They would have certainly taken much longer if they'd had to decide on an award."

Hugh's annoyance deteriorated into anger. "I've been suffering through this lawsuit for the last two years," he shouted, "and the jury only takes *five minutes* to reach a verdict?"

"For Christ's sake—you *could* sound a little less pissed and little more enthusiastic! This is big! This is *really big!*"

"For you, perhaps," growled Hugh through clenched teeth. "For me, this just confirms everything I've ever believed about this lousy case."

"What are you talking about?" cried Denmark. "This is the moment when you get to put it all behind you."

"That's something I'll never be able to do."

"Goddamn it—stop moaning and hurry down here before I come to your office and wring your neck!"

"All right, all right. I'm coming."

Click.

Five minutes! What a fitting commentary on the pathetic quality of the case against him! Infuriated and feeling numb all over, he swept his arm across the top of his desk, sending papers, pens, telephone, and prescription pads crashing to the floor. Then, swearing softly under his breath, he left one last time for the Multnomah County Courthouse.

Winded and pink-cheeked, Denmark was waiting impatiently for Hugh underneath the tall, arched entrance to the courthouse. "You took enough time getting here!" he complained.

Hugh didn't bother answering.

"Look, I'm sorry if your case didn't get longer deliberations," said Denmark, "but you don't have to act as if *I'm* responsible. Let's go in and find out what happened."

They muddled through the metal detectors and past the

watchful gaze of Sheriff's deputies. An elevator whisked them to the third floor. They entered the courtroom and settled behind the familiar defense table.

Five minutes later, Maxine arrived with Billy in tow. Both of them were looking stunned at the brevity of the jury's deliberations.

Judge Jenkins entered his courtroom and everybody stood up. "Ms. Doggett," he said, spreading his black gown and lowering himself into his chair on a pillow of air, "are your clients planning to be present?"

"No, Your Honor. Mrs. Winter cannot be here and her devoted husband doesn't want to leave her side at this time."

"I understand. Mr. Denmark, I see Dr. Montrose is here. Does his wife plan to come too?"

"No, Your Honor. She's at home taking care of children."

"In that case, I will ask the bailiff to fetch the jury."

After a few minutes, the twelve remaining jurors entered the courtroom and took their places. They were keeping their enigmatic masks in place right to the last moment. Not one of those men and women so much as smiled or winked at the defendant.

"I understand you have reached a verdict," Judge Jenkins said, addressing the jury.

"Yes, we have, Your Honor," replied the spokesman, a young man with a goatee and blue-tinged spectacles.

The bailiff took the verdict form from him and passed it on to the clerk, who in turn handed it to the judge. Judge Jenkins looked it over and passed it back to the clerk. She stood up and started reading.

"We, the jury, make the following answers to the questions

submitted by the Court: Question #1—Was the defendant negligent? Answer . . ."

Hugh heard his lawyer draw a deep breath.

"No."

"*Yes!*" exploded Denmark, punching his fist in the air. With a blatant disregard for courtroom decorum, he gripped his client by the shoulders, shook him hard, threw his arms around him, hugged him, then shook him again. "We won, Hugh! We won!"

"Mr. Denmark!" boomed the judge from the bench. "Control yourself!"

"After so many years, I've finally beaten *The Dog! Yeah!*"

As his head rattled back and forth, Hugh caught sight of Maxine sitting ramrod straight at the plaintiff's table. All color had drained from her face and she was staring vacantly into space. Billy was slumped next to her.

"What a victory!" said Denmark. "God, what an incredible victory!"

Now the judge was banging his gavel. "Mr. Denmark, if you can't control your exuberance, I'll have you removed from the courtroom!"

The loud hammering brought Denmark back to his senses. With a sheepish expression, he obediently released his grip on Hugh's lapels, straightened out the crumpled jacket, dusted the fabric with his fingers, and resumed his seat.

Once he had restored order, the judge rattled on, but his words were distant and Hugh didn't listen. Eventually, the jurors filed out of the room and Denmark watched them leave, his eyes filled with adoration. The judge soon left too, no doubt delighted that this crazy medical malpractice trial was finally over and he could get back to the simple stuff like rape, armed robbery, and murder. Maxine, Billy, Denmark, and Hugh found themselves alone together.

A powder keg waiting to explode.

Denmark lit the match. He stood up and sauntered over to Maxine with an outstretched hand and a smirk plastered across his face. "Counselor," he crowed, "I have to admit you made a valiant effort. I thought you would score yet another victory against me right up until the end—"

"You son-of-a-bitch!" Maxine hissed. "You lied and cheated and now you dare to offer me consolation!"

"*I* lied and cheated?" said Denmark, retracting his hand as if he'd just been stung by a hornet. "Jesus, Maxine—you're the one who broke all the rules! You paid that old bag to have a seizure so you could steal my notes. You smashed my podium to pieces. You sent your poor client flying across the courtroom—"

"That was an accident!"

"Bullshit! It was carefully planned, just like all your other tricks."

"*Tricks*? How dare you call them 'tricks'!"

"How else am I to call them?"

"'Tactics' will do."

"You call exposing yourself in court, 'tactics'?"

"Pervert!" cried Maxine. "You had no business looking up my skirt!"

"How could I avoid it? You spread apart your legs right in front of me!"

"One day, you'll regret this, Denmark. I swear it!"

"Is that a threat?"

The venom that filled Maxine's eyes confirmed that it was. "Things are never going to be the same for your client again," she snarled. "I may have missed burying him this time, but I'll always be around, watching carefully, waiting for him to make another mistake. And when he does, you can expect the biggest, nastiest battle you've ever seen in your life; one so large, it'll make the one he just survived seem like a parking ticket! You're sure to be representing him, and when you do, I'll beat you so badly—"

"Maxine, you've inflicted enough pain and suffering," said Denmark, taking a step closer to her. "Why don't you leave everybody alone for a change?"

"You don't know anything about pain and suffering," snapped Maxine. "Not like I do. I know all about hunger and poverty, being cold and lonely. I had to fight to get ahead in the world, waiting tables in nursing school and then working the night shift in hospitals so I could pay for law school. *You* talk to me about pain and suffering . . ."

With Denmark's next step towards her, Maxine urgently prodded Billy, her gold bracelets jingling with alarm. "Get up, Billy!" she cried. "The defense counselor is a dangerous man. I need protection."

Billy slowly rose to his feet and with his face inches from Maxine, he said through gritted teeth, "I hope the defense counselor tears you apart, limb from limb." Then, without another word, he left the courtroom.

Maxine forgot about Denmark and stared after Billy, speechless.

"Come on, John," said Hugh, tugging at his lawyer's sleeve. "Let's get out of this dump."

At first, Denmark resisted Hugh and mouthed a stream of soundless vindictive in Maxine's direction. Evidently, he had a lot more things to say to her, but didn't want to waste good insults if she was no longer paying attention. He gave her one final rude gesture—slapping his left hand hard into the crook of his right elbow—then turned on his heel and followed Hugh outside. Once they had reached the street, he began to smile again as the warmth of his victory seeped back into him.

"Let's go and celebrate!" he said, clamping his hand on Hugh's shoulder.

"I don't feel like celebrating," replied Hugh, shaking him off.

"Oh, come on!" said Denmark. "You've just won a spectacular trial. You *have* to celebrate!"

"I didn't win anything. *You* did."

"How can you say that?" cried Denmark, exasperated. "You were the defendant, the jury ruled in your favor, and now it's all over, except for the guzzling champagne part. Call your wife and tell her to join us. I know a great place—"

"Michelle won't feel like celebrating either."

"What *is* this?" shouted Denmark, spreading his hands out wide and shaking them at the sky. "We just scored the biggest upset in the history of medical malpractice litigation and the winner is acting as if he's at a funeral. Oh, I know! You already told me: you don't like neurosurgery anymore, not if means you have to get bullied once in a while by a bunch of mean trial lawyers. And what's the point of life without your precious neurosurgery?"

"Stop taunting me, John. There's more to it than that."

"What else is it then? Are you still mad the jury took only five minutes to come to a decision? Don't tell me they made you feel like you've wasted the last two years of your life?"

"There's even more."

"Even more? What are you talking about?"

Hugh fixed his eyes on Denmark and said, "Julie and her husband; the Winters . . . and their children. What's going to happen to *them*?"

"The Winters?" Denmark looked puzzled as if he had already forgotten who they were. "How the hell should I know?"

"I *wish* I could do something to make things a little easier on them."

"Forget it, Hugh," said Denmark, rapidly waving a hand back and forth as if he was sweeping the absurd thought under a carpet. "I know they're good people, but they almost succeeded in ruining your career. Put them out of your mind."

"I'll never be able to do that."

"Come on—get over it, Hugh! You'll feel better in the morning, as soon as you realize you no longer have to face that bitch's ugly mug in the courtroom every single day and smell her disgusting perfume. Think of it: you're now free to investigate any possible connection between her and Richard's death. Isn't that what you've always wanted to do? First, though, we need to celebrate our victory."

"No."

"Not even for one evening?" said Denmark, smiling. He looked like a friendly dog, wagging his tail and begging for a treat.

Hugh finally broke into a smile and gave his lawyer's shoulder a gentle jostle. "All right, John. If you insist . . ."

"That's more like it!" cried Denmark triumphantly. "Now, let me tell you about this little place I found recently. . . ."

Denmark swept Hugh's arm into his own and guided him swiftly towards the parking lot before he changed his mind.

CHAPTER 33

Gary slammed Harvey's hood shut and slowly straight-ened up, grimacing from the stiffness in his back. He wiped his greasy hands on a rag, then rolled down his sleeves and fastened his buttons. He had been working on the camper all day, trying to coax it into running condition. First, he'd had to clear the brambles away so he could get close to it without shredding his skin. Then he had replaced the belts, spark plugs, hoses, and battery, changed the oil, and pumped up the flat tires. Theoreti-cally, everything was ready. Turn the key in the ignition and the engine should start.

Theoretically . . .

Gary's children were working on Harvey's interior. Jenni-fer, armed with an assortment of cleaners, was removing buckets of mold and dirt while a radio played rock music. Patrick had volunteered to tackle the plumbing and electrical systems and was last seen trying to make the toilet flush properly. Julie was sitting on a couch, quietly watching her family as they worked. Her family had carried her there earlier in the day and had se-curely tied her in place with seat belts so she wouldn't tip over.

The light was fading fast. Gary decided it was time to see what, if anything, he had accomplished. "Okay, everybody . . ." he said, climbing aboard and settling into the driver's seat. "It's time to crank the engine. Turn off the radio. Jennifer, Patrick— sit on either side of your mother and make sure she doesn't fall if . . . *when* we start moving."

The music died and Julie found herself sandwiched between her two children, their hands on her shoulders. They frequently touched her there for they knew it was one of the few places on her skin where her sensation was still normal. She smiled at their thoughtfulness and wished she could return their affectionate squeezes.

Gary was poised to insert the key into the ignition when a black Bentley rolled up next to the camper. Maxine stepped out and strutted towards the house. Gary wound down the window and called to her.

She stopped and looked around. When she realized from where the voice had come, she approached. "What are you doing in *there*?" she asked.

"We're fixing things up," said Gary.

"Is it really worth it?" asked Maxine, frowning at the dilapidated camper.

"We think so."

"Where's Julie? I want to talk to both of you."

"She's inside with me. Why don't you join us?" Gary nodded towards the side door.

"Oh, no, I can't possibly do that," said Maxine, recoiling. "Remember—I have terrible mold allergies."

"It's quite all right," said Gary. "Jennifer has done a thorough cleaning job today. There isn't any mold in here anymore. I'm quite sure of it."

Maxine walked around to the side of the camper and cracked open the door. She tentatively poked her nose through the gap and sniffed, her nostrils flaring as she inhaled a small sample of air. When she was quite certain she wasn't going to explode in a fit of sneezing, she cautiously climbed inside and gave Julie and the children a perfunctory greeting with her hand.

"I have something to talk to your parents about," she said to Patrick and Jennifer as she helped herself to an armchair. "Why don't you run along?"

"That won't be necessary," said Julie. "We all have an idea why you're here."

Maxine hesitated, then shrugged. "If you say so," she conceded. "I'm afraid I've got some disappointing news for you: we've suffered a temporary setback. Those idiotic jurors just bungled everything and returned a verdict in favor of the defense." She braced herself as if she was expecting screams of anguish and perhaps a string of bowel movements, but they never came. "Don't you understand what I just told you?" she asked, sounding annoyed. "We lost the trial and won't be getting any money—at least, not quite yet. Not until after we've won our appeal."

"We don't want to file an appeal," said Julie, quietly and firmly.

Maxine did not appear to have heard, for she proceeded to give a long, rambling description of the appeal process. "There are excellent grounds for one," she added at the end. "Some of that idiotic judge's rulings were totally incomprehensible."

Julie patiently listened, then said, "Ms. Doggett, I don't think you understood me correctly. My husband and I are not planning to file an appeal."

"Huh?"

"There won't be any appeal."

Maxine's eyes widened with disbelief. "You don't want to file an appeal?" she asked.

"No, we don't."

"Why—why *the hell* not?"

"We've had enough of this awful lawsuit business," said Julie with a shudder. "It has been much more stressful than we expected. The last straw was when you accidentally hit the joystick to my wheelchair with your hand the other day. I've never been so embarrassed in my life."

Maxine couldn't help a brief burst of laughter as she remembered the incident, then quickly resumed a serious expression. "But I've already apologized for that!"

"We know, and we accepted your apology. But there's more . . ."

"Like what?"

Julie sighed; her belly rounded from the effort. "We've told you before: it wouldn't be right to take money from an innocent doctor."

Maxine stared at Julie as if she had gone mad. "It's only insurance money. SPI will survive."

"What about Dr. Montrose? Will he?

"He doesn't care."

"That's what you told us when we first met," said Julie, "but we're afraid we no longer believe that's true. From my point of view in the courtroom, he looked as if he cared a great deal. Besides, why would he go through all the trouble of defending himself if he didn't? No, Ms. Doggett—my family decided yesterday it was better to live the way we do than accept an obvious injustice. We are all comfortable with our decision."

"But you're kissing good-bye to millions of dollars!" whined Maxine, who might have been having visions of money bags slipping through her fingers.

"We know."

"What about your future?"

"Don't worry about us," replied Julie. "Gary and I have decided that we're not going to sit around the house all day feeling sorry for ourselves any longer. It's time to put the past behind us and move on with life. We're fixing up Harvey so we can go camping again, just like the old days. We'll get far more enjoyment from being together in our camper than winning all the money in the world."

Maxine looked from Julie to Gary, to Jennifer, then Patrick. They all had the same look on their faces, one of agreement and resolve. "There's something you're not telling me," she said suspiciously. "Let me guess. . . . You're still on some ridiculous religious binge and God told you to forgive your enemies."

"No. God doesn't have anything to do with—"

"I know!" Maxine's eyes suddenly grew big and round. "You've hired another lawyer!"

"No—"

"Yes, you have! You don't trust me any longer and you've been secretly looking through the yellow pages for my replacement."

"That's not true!" cried Gary. "We've always trusted you, Ms. Doggett. As far as we're concerned, you're the best."

Now Maxine's eyes bulged even more as another, more troubling, truth dawned on her. "Not just *any* lawyer . . . You've hired a legal malpractice lawyer!"

"A what?"

"You're planning to sue me for legal malpractice, aren't you? Admit it!"

"Why would we want to do something like that?"

"Because I didn't include that fool Clegg in the lawsuit."

Gary shook his head. "How were you supposed to know about the spinal fluid protein? Like you said—your experts let you down. It's not your fault we didn't win anything."

Julie spoke up in support of her husband. "Please don't think we're not grateful for everything you've done for us. We know you tried hard and we appreciate all your efforts."

Maxine puffed herself up with indignation. "Well, I'm not going to stay here, listening to you deny what I know must be true," she said, abruptly rising to her feet. "You can try suing me, if you dare. There's nothing to stop you. But I promise you one thing: you'll never get a penny out of me!"

"Maxine . . ."

"Not one penny!" screeched Maxine, shooting an index finger towards the ceiling to emphasize her point. "I have nothing more to say; plaintiffs and defendants must *never* speak with each other directly. It's one of the most basic rules." She headed for the door.

"If you're leaving," said Julie, "I want to say good-bye as friends."

"*Friends?*" said Maxine as if she had no idea what they were.

"Of course."

Maxine shook her head.

"What's wrong with being—?"

The camper's door slammed shut and Maxine was gone. Moments later, the Bentley roared into life and sped away.

"Why did she leave in such a hurry?" asked Patrick.

"She was just a little upset about losing the case," explained Jennifer to her little brother. "She'll feel better tomorrow."

"No matter," said Gary, flourishing a key in the air. "It's time for the big moment. Let's see if this old rattletrap will start. Everybody assume your positions!" He inserted it into the ignition and twisted it clockwise.

The engine whirred for a few moments, then burst into life. Harvey shuddered and shook all over and everybody cheered. Before there was any time to exchange congratulatory hugs, however, an almighty *KA-THONK* came from underneath them and the engine immediately died. The silence afterwards was deafening.

"That didn't sound very good," Jennifer ventured to say.

"Definitely not," agreed Gary. He turned the key once again, but nothing happened. "Maybe I ought to take a look." He climbed out, dropped to his knees, and peered underneath the camper. A puddle of black oil was rapidly expanding directly underneath the engine.

Harvey's heart was broken and he was hemorrhaging to death.

Gary climbed back into the driver's seat, his face dark and angry. "Nothing serious," he said, trying unsuccessfully to make his trembling voice sound casual.

"Are you sure?" asked Julie, searching her husband's face with a disbelieving eye.

"I'll take a closer look tomorrow morning. It's getting too dark to do any more work now."

"That noise sounded *really* bad," said Jennifer.

"I said it's nothing serious!" Gary snapped, striking the steering wheel with the palm of his hand and startling his family.

Julie knew that Harvey would never run again. Instead of arguing with her husband, however, she said, "Yes, take a closer look in the morning, Gary. Tomorrow will be a better day."

"Tomorrow *has* to be better," murmured Gary.

Over the next twenty minutes, Gary, Patrick and Jennifer labored to carry Julie through the door of the camper and place her in the wheelchair parked outside. Then, without looking back or exchanging a word, they pushed her up the front driveway and back to the house.

CHAPTER 34

When Maxine arrived home, Toby, the macaw, was hungry, in a rotten mood, and loudly demanding his dinner. As she passed him by, she hissed at him like a cat, ruffling his feathers and forcing him to beat a hasty retreat to the far end of his perch. Then, she wrenched open her refrigerator, snatched a bottle of wine, and poured herself a glass. After the third refill, her mind was sufficiently numb and the world was starting to slowly revolve around her. She staggered outside onto her veranda with her glass and glared at the lake below her.

She couldn't honestly believe she had lost *Winter vs. Montrose*, the first time she had suffered a defeat in years. She had blown the Ace of Spades and allowed a neurosurgeon to wriggle free from her hook. The Winters were stubbornly refusing to file an appeal, despite Judge Jenkins' abundant blunders. Worst of all, they had almost certainly hired some slick trial lawyer to sue her for legal malpractice; a lawsuit against her would be certain to cause a sensation within the ranks of CATL. Instead of being hailed as a superstar, she would now be laughed at like a bumbling circus clown.

What diabolical madness had gotten control of her clients, or, rather—her *ex*-clients? How could they be so incredibly dumb? Who ever heard of refusing to appeal because 'it wasn't right to take money from an innocent doctor'? If everybody felt the same way, the whole system of medical malpractice litigation in the country would collapse in a great cloud of dust. Why were the Winters willing to sacrifice themselves for the sake of something as abstract and intangible as justice? Or, even worse, was it religion, even more abstract and intangible, that had gotten its grip on them? Had they become soft in the head and were now going around forgiving their enemies and offering the other cheek? Surely they knew the insurance company was loaded with money and was actually *looking* for a place to stash it. The absurdity of it all!

"Awk! Toby wants a cracker!" screeched the macaw from inside the house. "Toby wants a cracker!"

Maxine screeched back with twice the decibels, "Not now! Can't you see I've got other things on my mind?"

To be sure, there was plenty to think about. Maxine's mind was locked onto the image of Gary and Julie, a couple tossed around by the eddies and currents of a cruel world. The poor sods had never even guessed that Maxine had known about the high CSF protein right from the beginning. Now they had nothing left in the world except their children, a run-down home, and a rusting camper in their front yard. Their future had never looked bleaker. However, the deuce of it: when Maxine had visited them, they had seemed to be happy and at peace, enjoying each other's company and making plans for a vacation. Maxine, on the other hand, had everything: a mansion to live in, a successful law practice (despite the day's loss), and robust health. Why, then, did she feel so desperately lonely and empty inside? It was the same old theme that had dogged her since her youth: her desire to give her life some meaning and direction so, one day, she might be remembered for something.

Except . . . she wasn't getting anywhere.

"Augustus!" Maxine shouted across the lake as loud as she could. "Where are you? Why are you hiding from me?"

Maxine scoured the trees along the shore for the mighty bald eagle, but had difficulty focusing and could not spot him. She guzzled more wine from her glass.

"I know you're there somewhere! Come out where I can see you!"

Still no response. The water was as smooth and still as glass. Mount Hood silently floated around the sky.

Maxine flung her glass away and gripped the wooden balustrade in front of her with both hands.

"*Why?*" she screamed, shaking the rail. "Why did you tell me to sue Montrose? *Huh?* What was your purpose? Was it so you could see me lose? Does it give you *so . . . much . . . pleasure* to smash my dreams? Or are you just punishing me for who I am?"

Maxine's eyes desperately searched the sky.

"Augustus!" she screamed again. "Where are you when I need you? What is it you want from me? How do you want me to live my life? Give me another sign! *Please!* I *need* another sign!"

The macaw inside the house started screeching again, only now he sounded alarmed, not angry.

Maxine raised her voice even more in an attempt to make herself heard over the ruckus. "Augustus! *Augustus!* You've never abandoned me before! Why now, when I need you the most?"

A voice, cool and suave, spoke behind her. "Having eagle problems, Maxine?"

Maxine whirled around, almost losing her footing. She came face-to-face with Billy, who looked as if he had aged ten years in one day. The wavy curls of his hair were no longer raking the air. Its flatness and the neat parting on the left gave him a certain maturity that she was unaccustomed to. His eyes were looking at her with a cold intensity that sent a chill down her spine.

"What are you doing here?"

"I came to talk."

"How did you get in?"

"Your front door was open. I took it as an invitation."

"You're mistaken. You're not welcome here."

"That doesn't matter. I would have come anyway."

"No wonder my macaw is making so much noise!" cried Maxine. "There was an intruder in my house!"

Toby's stopped his wild screeching and once again returned his attention to his hunger. "Maxine is a superstar!" he squawked, now trying some flattery to get his dinner. "Maxine is a superstar!" He was making so much noise, Billy and Maxine would have trouble hearing each other, even on the veranda. Maxine stepped past Billy into the kitchen, snapped her teeth at Toby to shut him up, and poured herself some more wine into a fresh glass.

"You and I are going to have a talk," said Billy, following her.

"So—after spending the last couple of weeks sulking like a spoiled brat, you want to talk now? Well, I don't." She poured herself a fresh glass of wine, raised it to her lips, and drained it. "Besides, there's nothing to talk about. We lost and that's that. Shit happens, you know. I'm sorry if I didn't meet your expectations."

"On the contrary, you performed exactly as I expected."

Maxine glared at Billy. "What's this?" she sneered. "No longer the skulking bottom feeder who knows his lowly position in the world?"

Billy smiled. "That's right, Maxine. From now on, you'll have to find somebody else to torment. This is where we part company."

"Thank God! You're the worst lawyer I've ever known! You couldn't do *anything* right. I asked you to go out into the legal community and spread the word about this case, yet not a single lawyer showed up to watch. Nobody! And you think you've got a future in medical malpractice? Hah! What a joke!"

"The joke's on you, Maxine," said Billy.

"What, precisely, do you mean by that?"

"I've *never* wanted to go into medical malpractice law," said Billy, his eyes blazing. "And I've *never* been a fan of yours. You don't have *any* fans, Maxine. Everybody hates you. And do you know why? Because you single-handedly give all trial lawyers a dirty name. We're trying to carry out a very important function in America, fighting against oppression and incompetence . . . and it only takes single, solitary bitch like you to make us the butt of everybody's jokes!"

"If you're not a fan of mine," Maxine snapped, "then why the hell did you volunteer to do this case with me?"

"I didn't volunteer," said Billy. "I was forced."

"*Forced?*"

"That's right. Those bastards at Grand National made me do it."

"I don't understand."

"You think you're so damn smart, Maxine, and yet you don't understand *anything* of what's going on around you. Grand National is always looking for ways to save money. When that ugly mug, Bruno Clegg, called them in a frenzy early one morning to tell them how he butchered Julie Winter, they scrambled to find a way to get their client, and themselves, off the hook. One of their executives had a bright idea: leak information about the case to some trial lawyer who would, in return, be willing to overlook Clegg's involvement and sue Montrose instead. But just *any* trial lawyer wouldn't do. They needed the most unethical, sleazy, piece-of-shit lawyer they could get their hands on— somebody who wouldn't think twice about screwing a client of theirs. Naturally, your name was the first to come up."

"You little runt."

"Grand National didn't trust you one millimeter though. They were afraid that somebody with your moral compass would double-cross them in a flash and sue Clegg anyway. So they built some security into the deal: you'd have to agree to have a co-counsel—one that would secretly keep an eye on you and keep them informed what was going on."

"You were . . . a spy?"

"There was a problem, though," continued Billy. "All of Grand National's lawyers were aware of your reputation and flatly refused to work with you. None of them would step forward and volunteer for a suicide mission like this one. Not one! So they decided to hire somebody new—somebody young and naïve who'd never heard of you. That's where I came in. I'd just graduated from law school and was looking for a job. The money was great. All I had to do was to introduce myself to you and pretend that I was your biggest fan. 'Flatter her', they said, 'and you'll have her feeding out of the palm of your hand.' Once I had gained your confidence, I was to tell you about the business going on at Columbia Medical Center, then ask you to take me on as co-counsel. It all seemed easy enough. God—what a dumb fool I was to fall for it! Now it's obvious to me why no other lawyer would touch this assignment."

Maxine splashed more wine into her glass and guzzled it down.

"It wasn't so bad in the beginning," continued Billy. "I learned a lot about the basic anatomy of the spine and shared your excitement when we signed on Gary and Julie as clients. After that, it started to go downhill. Jesus—I never heard so much nagging and complaining in my life." Now Billy raised his voice a couple of octaves, wagged his head form side to side, and batted his eyelids as if he was imitating Maxine. "Do this, don't do that. Go here, go there. Photocopy this, photocopy that." His face returned to normal and he lowered his voice once again. "How do people put up with you? Hell, I know *I* couldn't. You were driving stark raving nuts. It got so bad I finally snapped and did something really stupid."

Maxine slowly lowered her glass and stared at Billy.

"I'm sure Forrester's suicide was as much a mystery to you as it was for everybody else," continued Billy, now shifting uncomfortably. "Unfortunately, it was no mystery to me—"

"What did you do?" asked Maxine hoarsely, dreading the answer she might hear.

"Remember when you told me that you were planning to sue Forrester over an incident in the operating room when he operated on a ninety-eight year old woman?"

"Yes?"

"And you were hoping that your lawsuit would eventually expose his scandalous behavior and strike a fatal blow against SOD'M?"

"*Yes?*"

"Well, I decided to prove to you that you were wrong to treat me like an errand boy. I typed up a Summons and Complaint, *Diamond vs. Forrester*, and forged your signature. Then I went to his house before he had left for work and served him."

"You did *what?*"

"I only wanted to give him a nasty scare. How the hell was I supposed to know he was so emotionally unstable? Who would have guessed he was going to kill himself?"

"Y—you served Forrester with a bogus lawsuit?" Maxine stammered.

"Later on, I had second thoughts about it and returned to his house to confess and apologize. Maybe even laugh with him about it. That's when I found him dead in his bedroom, his cold fingers still gripping the Summons. I panicked, Maxine; I took the papers from him and destroyed them."

"Oh, no! A cover-up on top of everything else! How could you *do* such a thing?"

"What would be the point of telling the police?" Billy demanded. "I would only get into trouble and it wouldn't bring Forrester back to life. If you had given me something useful to do during the discovery phase, it would never have happened! Even during the trial itself, you still treated me badly. At least you could have let me handle Julie's testimony."

"You would have messed it up!"

"That's crap! I could have done it! Everything would have been okay. But how did you respond to my request? You ordered me back to the copying machine. That's when I realized I just couldn't take it anymore."

"You spineless jellyfish."

"That morning, I crawled back to Grand National and begged them to change my assignment," continued Billy. "I told them I'd do anything for them; just keep me away from the red-headed bitch! They refused. . . . *Damn their eyes!* They told me to get back to work and finish the trial with you. If I didn't, they'd fire me and make sure I never worked again as a lawyer. What choice did I have? I was forced to return to court."

"You're so pathetic."

"And you're a loser!"

With a single rapid movement of her arm, Maxine threw her drink into Billy's face. "Do not—*ever*—call me a loser!"

Billy appeared taken aback, but only for a moment. Then he smiled; he had discovered one of Maxine's vulnerabilities. He slowly, calmly wiped his face with his sleeve and drew closer to her. "Even if you'd won the case today, you'd still be a loser. You've always been a loser and you always will be a loser! *Loser!*"

At this moment, Toby broke his brooding silence. By now, he must have been very hungry, for he joined in, squawking, "Loser! Loser!" in his loudest, angriest parrot voice.

Maxine suddenly picked up a bottle of wine that was standing on the counter next to her and threw it as hard as she could at Billy. He dodged the missile and it shattered against the stove on the other side of the kitchen.

"Loser!" shouted Billy. "*Loser!*"

"Awk! Maxine is a loser!" squawked Toby.

Maxine's groping hands found a frying pan. It, too, flew across the room, narrowly missing its target.

"See, you can't even hit me!"

Moving fast despite her drunkenness, Maxine wrenched a short knife from a wooden block, sprang at Billy, and swiped at him. She barely missed.

"Oh, my God! You tried to stab me!" he gasped, his eyes wide with disbelief.

With a loud shriek, Maxine lunged again. This time, Billy caught her wrist with his hand and after a brief struggle, he twisted the knife out of her grip and it fell to the floor. He quickly snatched it up and advanced upon Maxine, gently waving its point in the air.

"This time you've gone *too far!*" he snarled.

"No, Billy!" said Maxine, backing away. "I didn't mean it; I've had too much to drink! You've got to believe me! *Billy!*"

"Maxine is a loser!" screeched Toby.

"No human being should have to put up with the things I did, not even a dog! It was hell, Maxine. *Pure hell!* Do you know what hell is like?"

"No, Billy! *No!*"

"Here—let me send you there, Maxine, so you can see for yourself. . . ."

A flash of steel. Maxine heard the ghastly sound of breaking bones and ripping flesh, terrifyingly close . . . *Inside* her. A bolt of searing pain exploded on the left side of her head and she felt herself falling. Through half-closed eyes, she saw the wavering image of a madman standing above her, shaking his fist and screaming obscenities.

Then, his face faded, and everything went dark.

***

"Ms. Doggett! Ms. Doggett! What happened?"

Maxine opened her eyes and saw two faces making circles around each other, both belonging to the same man. Carl was kneeling over her and was staring in horror at the left side of her head. She groaned from the pain.

"I'm here, Ms. Doggett," said Carl. "I'll take care of you."

"What are you staring at?" she murmured.

At first, her security chief didn't answer. Her fingers instinctively reached up to her left temple, but he quickly reached forward and restrained her wrist.

"*No!*" he cried. "Don't touch it!"

"Don't touch *what?*"

"The knife!"

Maxine swallowed hard and felt her blood turn to ice. "What has that little creep done?"

"What little creep?"

"Billy . . ."

"*Billy?*"

"Yes, it was him. He was here."

"There's nobody here except us."

"He must have run away. What has he done to me?"

"He's—"

"*What has he done?*"

"He's stabbed you in the head," said Carl. "The blade is in as far as the hilt. We've got to get you to the Emergency Room—*fast!*"

Toby was still hurling insults in the background. "Loser! Loser!"

Maxine reached up again with her hand, slowly and cautiously. When Carl tried to restrain her once more, she shook him off. Her fingers explored the skin of her cheek and felt the warmth and stickiness of fresh blood. Then they crept further up, tarantula-like, until they brushed lightly against something cold and hard—the knife. She pushed very gently and another lightening bolt of pain exploded through her head.

"*Oh, my God!*" she shrieked, sucking in air through clenched teeth. "I'm going to die!"

"No, you're not," said Carl. "We're going to get some help. You're going to do just fine."

"I've got a goddamn knife in my brain! I tell you I'm going to die!"

"Calm yourself, Ms. Doggett! You'll only drive it in deeper!"

Maxine moaned and her body became limp in Carl's arms. For a heart-wrenching moment, he thought she was gone. Then, he heard a weak voice stirring deep within her. "Save me, Augustus," she was praying, so quietly he had to put his ear to her lips. "Save me!"

"Don't worry, Ms. Doggett!" Carl cried. "I'll take you to Dr. Montrose!"

"He'll never agree to see me, not after . . . Take me . . . to the . . . university. . . ."

"No! I'm taking you to Dr. Montrose. He's the best there is, and right now, he's who you need."

"Augustus . . . Augustus . . ."

Paying special attention to her head, Carl gathered Maxine into his arms, stood up, and carried her towards his car parked outside. The last sound he heard as he left the house was Toby, loudly repeating over and over again:

"Loser! Loser! Loser!"

✳✳✳

Billy had barely escaped the Doggett mansion through its front door when he saw the headlights of a car coming down the long driveway. Without a moment to lose, he plunged into the surrounding dark woods and crouched behind a large clump of bushes—precisely the same place where he had hidden earlier in the evening and had carefully weighed the risks of paying Maxine a surprise visit. He watched the scene before him again, only this time his heartbeat was hammering three times louder in his ears. With gravel crunching underneath its tires, the car drew up in front of the mansion. Carl climbed out, walked over to Maxine's front door, and let himself in.

As he waited to see what would happen next, Billy replayed in his mind what it had been like to sink a knife into Maxine's brain and found that, no matter how many times he reviewed the images, he could not get enough of them: the sharp blade flashing into her red curls and slicing through her scalp underneath, his momentary surprise that it didn't glance off her skull, the headlong plunge into the vital areas underneath. Had he killed her? He prayed he had; nothing less than her permanent removal from the face of the planet would give him the sense of relief that he craved right now.

Suddenly, the front door of the mansion flew open and Carl appeared, looking grim and carrying Maxine in his arms. Her eyes were closed, her face was as pale as the moon, and her body was completely flaccid. At this distance, she looked as if she was dead and Billy's heart soared. However, when Carl opened the back door of his car and slid Maxine into the seat, she stirred and then shrieked from pain. The awful sound cut through Billy like a hailstorm of glass, instantaneously shredding his fantasies. Long after the car was gone, he was still staring at the empty driveway in front of him, wide-eyed and in shock.

The miserable bitch was still alive. Carl was taking her to hospital for emergency treatment, no doubt.

Billy knew what he had to do: it was time to use his quail-hunting skills to finish off Maxine. He left his hiding place and headed for home . . .

. . . and for the cupboard where he kept his shotgun.

CHAPTER 35

Hugh and Denmark sat together at Luigi's restaurant on First Avenue in downtown Portland. The lights were low, the music soft, and the Italian cuisine excellent. Hugh imagined it was the sort of place he might have liked to take Michelle on a romantic date, but knew he never would do so in the future for fear of reliving unpleasant memories.

"So, have you heard anything from CANS?" asked Denmark, chasing the last of his tiramisu with a spoon.

Hugh had already finished his and was trying to catch the waiter's attention so he could pay the bill and go home. "CANS?"

"You remember: a few days ago you were telling me all about your solution for the medical liability crisis. You wanted CANS to certify expert witnesses."

"I've heard nothing from them," said Hugh with disappointment in his voice. "Absolutely nothing."

"I shouldn't be so bothered about it," said Denmark, pushing his empty desert bowl away and wiping his lips with a napkin. "These things take time, you know. Nothing happens as fast as you want it to."

"Meanwhile, the problem continues," said Hugh. "It's so frustrating! I feel like I'm up against a brick wall."

Hugh's cell phone chimed. It was Ed Cleveland. The medical director was in the ER and Hugh could hear the usual hustle and bustle in the background. The reason the blustery old medical director had left gastroenterology for his current administrative job was so the rivers of diarrhea in the ER would never interrupt his sleep again and he still avoided the place like the plague. It was highly unusual for him to be there and Hugh knew that something big must be happening.

"Hello, Hugh!" he said cheerfully. "There's a patient here with a knife sticking in her head. I may be sadly mistaken, but, to me, it looks like a case for Neurosurgery."

Hugh reassured Denmark with a nonchalant wave of his hand that he would soon get rid of this rude interruption. He had seen similar injuries before: knives, turn signal indicators, hammers, screw-drivers, almost every tool that can be found in the average handyman's toolbox. When they rolled in through the doors, invariably the ER staff would become very excited and would fall over one another to be the first to give him the gory details. Usually, he was good-natured enough to play along. This time, however, somebody else could have the fun.

"Where's Pagonis?" asked Hugh.

"The Greek? Oh, he's around somewhere . . ."

"Then tell *him* to take care of it. I'm busy celebrating. We won the trial, you know."

"So she told me."

"So *who* told you?"

"The patient in the ER I'm calling you about—the one with the butcher block head."

"Was she at my trial?"

"You could say so," tittered Ed. "Her name is Maxine Dog-breath . . . Dog-face . . . Whatever the hell her name is."

"*What?*"

"You know: your good friend, *Maxine.*"

"Maxine *Doggett?*"

"That's it!" Cleveland erupted into laughter and it was a while before he could calm down enough to explain himself.

"After the verdict, she says she went home and got into a fight with her co-counsel, Billy Funk. He stabbed her in the head with a knife and ran off."

"*This is a joke!*"

"No, it isn't!" cried Cleveland. "I'm being deadly serious." More laughter.

For a few moments, Hugh's mind was in turmoil and he wasn't sure whether to believe Ed. Things as crazy as this simply didn't happen. Then years of training suddenly kicked in. "What's her neurological status?" he asked.

"She's awake and looking around. Doesn't look too comfortable with her surroundings, though. I don't suppose you'd be either if you were a medical malpractice attorney getting treatment in a hospital. Somebody might be tempted to do you in. How about something that's even harder to believe? She wants *you* to remove the knife from her brain!" As if this was the punch line to the funniest joke in the world, Ed burst out laughing louder than ever.

"She wants *me* to operate on her? After everything that's happened?"

"She insists on it!" Ed roared with renewed vigor.

"Why me?"

"She says you're the best there is!" More howls of laughter.

"Me? *Defendant* Montrose? The best there is? Has she already forgotten? She's been spending the last couple of years trying to prove that I'm the world's most incompetent neurosurgeon. Tell Pagonis to take the case. It'll be an enlightening experience for her."

Ed suddenly grew serious. "Be reasonable, Hugh. Our little Greek friend doesn't have the skill to do a difficult case like this."

"Then send her to the university."

"She doesn't want to go anywhere else."

"Not everybody gets the neurosurgeon they want."

"She's not just 'anybody'," countered Ed. "She's Maxine Doggett, the most successful medical malpractice lawyer in history. Do you know how many lawsuits she has pending against this hospital right now? *Five!* Imagine what might happen if we take good care of her. With a bit of luck, they'll go all away. And what, do you suppose, will happen if we kick her ass out of here? Within months, I promise you, we'll be flooded with lawsuits."

Hugh thought for a moment, then said, "Can you hold for a minute, Ed?"

"Sure."

Hugh explained the situation to Denmark, who stammered disbelief at the turn of events.

"Don't think for a minute you've got any obligation to treat that woman!" he spluttered. "You're not on call and there's another fully qualified neurosurgeon in the hospital. If Pagonis doesn't feel up to it, he can transfer her somewhere else. Have you already forgotten her threats? Not more than four hours ago she was telling me that she can't wait to face you in the courtroom again and thoroughly destroy you. She'll always be looking over your shoulder, waiting for you to make a mistake. No! No! No! Tell her to piss off! Maxine doesn't get the neurosurgeon of her choice. She gets Pagonis. Or she can go to the university. It's her choice. Take yourself out of the picture, Hugh."

Hugh said nothing.

"You're not actually considering it, are you?" said Denmark. "Because if you are, I forbid it! As your lawyer . . . as your *friend*, I absolutely forbid it!"

Hugh had no desire to operate on Maxine. In fact, at this particular moment in his career, he didn't feel like picking up another scalpel again. The lawsuit had taken too much out of him and he no longer possessed the spark that kept all neurosurgeons going through thick and thin. Besides, a long time had passed since he had performed a difficult case such as this. One could not simply grab the knife and yank it out of there. A full craniotomy was required—complete exposure along the length of the blade in case any bleeding started. A high-tension case, to be sure—the kind he used to especially enjoy, but now the prospect only frightened him.

Just as he was about to acquiesce to his lawyer's advice, Hugh suddenly remembered words Richard had once uttered in the surgeon's lounge at Columbia: *I've got to figure out a good way to muzzle that woman; something quick, effective, and outside the political process.* His friend had eventually come up with the idea of SOD'M, an organization that was still rapidly strengthening despite its founder's death. An alternative idea struck Hugh, perhaps a much more effective one, and a shiver ran up and down his spine. He turned and looked as his lawyer, his eyes charged with new purpose. "I know what I'll do, John," he said. "I know *exactly* what I'm going to do."

"What?" asked Denmark suspiciously.

"I think I know a way to get some answers; perhaps even cripple Maxine for good. This is the chance I've been waiting for ever since Richard died!" Before Denmark could say another word, Hugh lifted the phone back to his ear. "Ed? Are you still there?"

"Yes, Hugh. Will you come?"

"I'll be there as soon as I can. First, I'll have to swing by my office to pick something up."

"Good man! Columbia Medical Center will never forget this. We'll be waiting for you."

When Hugh hung up, Denmark was staring at him with astonishment. Hugh felt as if he owed him an explanation, but instead he simply said, "I know what I'm doing. Trust me."

Denmark was far from mollified. He grumpily declared that if his client wasn't going to listen to his advice any more, he might as well celebrate his victory with somebody else and rose to leave.

Hugh put a hand on his lawyer's arm. "Let's not end the evening like this," he said. "I want to thank you for everything you've done for me, especially for teaching me not all lawyers are bad."

The compliment softened up Denmark and he smiled faintly.

"Another thing," continued Hugh, "when are you next going fishing?"

"I don't know. Why?"

"Because when you go out, I want to come with you."

"I thought you hated fishing."

"Actually I've never really tried it. But I'm ready for you to teach me everything you know."

Denmark suddenly beamed from ear to ear. He thrust out his hand, but it didn't seem enough. The two of them gripped each other tightly and hugged. When they broke up, Denmark declared, "If it's the last thing I do, Hugh, I'll make you the best fisherman in the state of Oregon!"

Ten minutes later, Hugh hurried through the entrance to Columbia Medical Center's ER, with his hands thrust into the pockets of his coat and his face etched with anxious determination. He was met inside by the medical director.

"Hugh—thanks for coming!" said Ed, vigorously shaking his hand. A cold, soggy cigar protruded from his mouth; it must have died hours before. "I really appreciate you interrupting your celebration and coming in like this. It's always best to avoid an ugly scene, you know. This is a time when Columbia Medical Center must put its best foot forward."

"Obviously, you only care about the hospital getting sued," said Hugh, sounding not in the least bit surprised.

"What responsible medical director wouldn't be?" protested Ed. Then he lowered his voice, drew closer, and said, "To tell you the truth, there's much more to it than that. Personally, I'm terrified of *her*. She's the devil incarnate. When I look at her, my blood freezes, especially with that knife sticking out of her head. It's as if I'm watching an updated version of The Exorcist. Yech!"

"I know what you mean," said Hugh with a shudder. "So where is she?"

"In there," said Ed, waving in the general direction of the trauma room. "Dr. Pagonis had a chance to take a quick look at her—"

"Before she threw me out," interrupted Pagonis, scurrying over from the nurse's station. "Awake and drunk. *Very* drunk. Big kitchen knife in her left temporal area. Very bad. Very, very bad!"

"Got any X-rays?" asked Hugh.

"Sure. Please."

With an outstretched arm, Pagonis guided the group to a viewing box that was attached at eye level on a wall. On it were hanging two skull X-rays, one taken from the front and the other from the side. The wispy images of Maxine's bones stood in stark contrast to the solid, jagged whiteness of the metal knife. Judging from the perspective given by the two views, its point was deep inside her head at the base of her brain, not far from what looked like a miniature pair of scissors.

"She's had aneurysm operation before," observed Pagonis.

"It's a Yasargil clip," said Hugh.

"Really? How you know?"

"I put it there."

Ed looked at Hugh with astonishment. "You've operated the woman *before*?" he asked.

"Yes—a few years ago. She ruptured an aneurysm and I clipped it. See that defect on the side of her skull? That's where I cut through the bone with a saw and opened up a flap. At the end of the operation, I replaced the bone. It has all healed up now, except for a bit at the bottom. By a stroke of misfortune, that's exactly where she was stabbed. The blade passed through the narrow opening and penetrated her cranial cavity."

"You saved her life, yet she still filed a lawsuit against you?"

"She promised to put me on her 'Do Not Sue' list, but sued me anyway."

Ed yanked the cigar stub out of his mouth and threw it into a garbage can with a dark scowl.

Hugh approached the trauma room and saw a tall, silvery haired man anxiously pacing up and down outside. When the man spotted him, he abruptly headed for Hugh.

"I'm Carl Zeiger," he said, introducing himself and offering his hand. "Thank you for coming, sir. I knew you would."

Hugh hesitated. He knew who this man was from his conversations with Richard. Undoubtedly, he was intricately involved in all his boss's misdeeds and at first Hugh hesitated to shake hands with him. But the man was polite and did not seem threatening in the least, so he relented, took his hand, and felt a powerful grip. "I remember you," he said. "You're the one who brought Maxine here when her aneurysm ruptured back in '98."

"Yes, sir. I did."

"Looks like she's in trouble again."

"She is, sir. Terrible trouble. In all my years, I've never seen anything like this."

"Fortunately for her, I have, lots of times," said Hugh grimly. Then he remembered Richard calling this man a meathead and felt the urge to move on. He was about to brush past him when Carl stepped in his way.

"Dr. Montrose . . ."

"Yes?"

"It's probably not necessary, but I wanted to ask you . . . no, *implore* you to do something for me."

"What?"

"Please . . . *please* look after her. Don't let her die."

Hugh hadn't expected such a heart-felt request and he searched Carl's eyes. The pain he saw behind them was startling. "You actually *care* for her?"

"Yes, I do," confessed Carl. "Very much so. Is that such a bad thing? I know she's difficult sometimes, but once you get to know her, she's really quite a good person deep inside. I don't know what I would do if something happened to her. Please do whatever you can . . . if not for her, then for me."

Hugh was confused. How could any reasonable man actually like The Dog? In his deranged state of mind during the years he was being sued, had he misjudged her? Was there another side to her—a human one—that he had missed? If he had done so, he wasn't the only person who had made the same mistake; Denmark hated her even more than he did. Surely both of them hadn't been wrong.

Once Hugh had regained his equilibrium, the inquisitive side of him took over. He wanted to know more about the relationship between Carl and Maxine and grabbed at the opportunity to find out. "Does she feel the same way about you?" he asked.

Carl shook his head. "She doesn't know how to get close to anybody. Her life hasn't exactly been very easy, you know, especially when she was growing up. I think some experiences in her childhood scarred her for life."

"Have you talked to her about your feelings for her?"

"No," said Carl. "I'm afraid to. There's no telling how she might respond, especially considering that I'm officially one of her employees. You know how she can be sometimes."

Hugh certainly did and could understand Carl's concern. If she discovered that her chief of security had been deceiving her, she would likely call him a pervert, fire him on the spot, and refuse to talk to him ever again. Hugh had no trouble picturing the scene in his mind. He squeezed Carl's shoulder, gave him a reassuring smile, and said, "Don't worry—I'll take care of her the best way I know how. You can count on me."

"Thank you, sir," said Carl, stepping aside. "I trust you completely. Her life is in good hands."

Hugh entered the trauma room. Ed, Pagonis, and Carl made attempts to follow him, but he closed the door firmly behind himself.

Maxine was lying with her eyes closed on a gurney, surrounded by electronic monitors and IV bags. Her head was resting on a pillow; red curls tumbled around her face and over the blankets. Hugh focused on a black knife handle that stuck out of the hair on the left side of her head like some bizarre stage prop. It was a jarring sight, even for somebody who was no stranger to these types of injury. As gruesome as it looked, though, Maxine appeared to be strangely at peace and in no pain; her arms were folded over her chest and her breathing was smooth and regular. When he drew closer, her eyes fluttered open and she looked directly at him.

"You came . . ." she whispered when she recognized her visitor.

Hugh took a cautious step closer . . .

"I never thought you would," she added.

. . . and the smell of alcohol grew stronger.

"I've really messed up this time, haven't I? Can you do something for me . . . again?"

Hugh remembered promising Carl that he would take good care of her. Yes—he would keep his word, but not before he had executed the plan he'd carefully devised. So instead of offering the customary reassurance for patients in such a plight, he replied, just a little harshly and with an edge of genuine fear in his voice, "I'm not sure I want to do anything for you."

Maxine eyelashes batted, showing her lack of understanding.

"Have you already forgotten what happened the last time I stuck my neck out for you?" explained Hugh, creeping closer. "I saved your life and you showed your gratitude by suing me until I was puking my guts out with terror."

Maxine shrank into her covers "It was nothing personal," she said in a tiny voice.

"*Nothing personal*? How the hell do you expect me to believe that?"

"It wasn't! I've always treated you fairly."

Hugh was speechless for a moment, then shook that insane statement out of his mind where there was no room for it and said, "Anyway—I'm not on call tonight, so you're not my responsibility."

"You're here, aren't you? Isn't that enough?"

"Dr. Petros Pagonis is here too, waiting just outside this room. And he's the neurosurgeon who's on duty—not me."

"*Pagonis?*" cried Maxine with alarm, suddenly raising herself onto her elbows. "That horrid little Greek will kill me! I want *you! Please!*"

Obviously, Maxine's network of spies had kept her well informed of the scandals currently rocking Columbia Medical Center.

"And if I refuse?" asked Hugh.

Maxine sank back into her pillow. Soft sounds of weeping began deep within her and slowly rose with the force and strength of magma beneath a volcano. Her body started quaking, gently at first, then with ever increasing force until even the gurney underneath her was rocking back and forth. When the eruption came, it was violent and filled with anguish. She cried out to the ceiling and then buried her face into the blankets and sobbed her heart out. When she eventually looked up at him again, her eyes were red, swollen, and smudged with mascara. Tears were trickling down her cheeks.

"I've been so blind and stupid!" she moaned. "It's true! I can see it clearly now; all my life I've been so . . . ugh! God—the knife hurts!"

Hugh was unmoved. "Don't waste your time playing any more games with me," he said. Denmark had taught him well; by now, he could recognize *classic Doggett* when he saw it. "I don't care how many crocodile tears you shed. I won't be the one taking out that knife . . . unless—"

Maxine quickly brightened. "Yes? Unless what?"

"Unless you give me something in return."

Maxine wiped her tears away. "All right," she said, composing herself. "How much money do you want? Twenty thousand? Fifty?"

"Not money. Information."

"What kind of information?"

Hugh crept closer still to Maxine and now he was only a

couple of feet away. From here, he could see how liquefied brain tissue had welled up from inside her head and had dried around the entry point of the knife blade. Jagged fingers of blood had flowed in different directions from her glistening scalp wound and then had clotted, turning black and flakey.

Hugh lowered his voice as if he was afraid somebody was eavesdropping. "I want information on the things you've been up to," he said. "I want to know how you found out Dan Silver operated on the wrong side of Mr. Brown's head. And what you were doing at the CANS meeting the night your aneurysm ruptured back in '98? And that's not all. I've always wanted to know why you never included Dr. Clegg in that lawsuit against me. And I'm especially interested if you can shed any light on why Richard Forrester killed himself. As you can see, I have a lot of questions."

Maxine's eyes roved aimlessly around the room as she tried to replay the string of questions in her mind. Then she said, "I'm really sorry, but those are things I can't talk about."

"No, I suppose not," said Hugh. Even though Maxine had ingested a lot of alcohol, she was evidently not drunk enough to reveal the things he wanted to know and needed some nudging in the right direction. This was the moment in his plan that he had dreaded. With his heart pounding in his chest, he pulled a syringe out of his pocket and took the cap off the needle. He nudged the plunger with his thumb and a small jet of clear liquid squirted out of the end of the needle, arcing gracefully in the air.

"What's that?" asked Maxine.

"Just some antibiotics," Hugh lied, feeling the warm tinge of shame in his face as he did so. "We wouldn't want that dirty old knife causing an infection, would we? There's no telling what you've been cutting with it. Garlic? Liver sausage? Fish guts?" He found the injection port in Maxine's IV tubing and emptied the contents of the syringe into her vein. He knew that this particular 'antibiotic' wouldn't kill a single bacterium in a million years, seeing that it was really midazolam hydrochloride—a synthetic compound manufactured by Hoffman-LaRoche, also known by its brand name, Versed. It belonged to a class of compounds called diazepines, all sedatives, hypnotics and muscle relaxants; the perfect drug in an anesthesiologist's armamentarium, given freely to patients before operations to allay their anxiety. It was fast-acting and famous for two major side-effects: loosening tongues and erasing short-term memory.

Under its influence, patients would sometimes tell all their innermost secrets and never remember *a thing* afterwards.

"Now, where were we?" said Hugh, tossing the spent syringe into a red plastic bucket. "Oh, yes—I had just a few simple questions."

"I told you: you're asking too much from me."

Hugh started with a question for which he already knew the answer. "Tell me how did you find out Dan Silver operated on the wrong side of Mr. Brown's head?"

Maxine calculated silently for a few moments, then said, "I don't see why you shouldn't know the answer to that one. The Brown family had a friend who was a retired surgeon. He suspected something when they told him about the two incisions—"

"You're lying," interrupted Hugh. "*Lying!* Pagonis can do what he wants with you, for all I care." He started for the door. "Good-bye, Maxine. I can't say it's been a great pleasure knowing you—"

"No, wait! Don't go!"

Hugh stopped and waited, his head half turned.

"Okay, okay," said Maxine. "I'll tell you the truth, but

you've got to swear to me that it doesn't go beyond the four walls of this room."

"Of course I'll never tell anybody," said Hugh. He returned to the bedside and leaned as close as the alcohol fumes would permit. "You can trust me," he breathed.

"There are people in this hospital who keep me . . . informed," said Maxine.

Hugh manufactured a surprised look for his face. "Really? Like who?"

"Bonnie Davidson told me everything about Dr. Silver and Mr. Brown."

"Bonnie? The OR nurse? Why?"

"I paid her nursing school tuition. In return, she passes me information once in a while. One good turn deserves another, don't you think?"

Hugh shook his head to show disbelief, then asked a follow-up question. "How many informants do you have?"

"I'm not going to tell you *all* my secrets."

"There are other people involved?"

"Lots."

"That's how you know about Dr. Pagonis?"

"I've been getting a steady stream of reports on him since the trial began," said Maxine with a shudder.

Hugh knew his time was limited and that there were other, more important, questions to be answered, so he quickly moved on. "Tell me what you were doing at the Sheraton hotel that night your aneurysm ruptured."

"Oh, God—we don't have to go into that, do we?"

"Yes, we do," said Hugh. He noticed a glassy look in Maxine's eyes and knew the midazolam had taken control of her mind.

"God, I feel weird. What did you give me?"

"What were you doing?" Hugh asked again.

"Oh, hell—what's the big deal anyhow? Defendant Dickey was there . . . at the CANS meeting."

"*Frank* Dickey, the neurosurgeon from Astoria?"

"I had named him in a lawsuit," said Maxine, her speech slurring badly, "but he was being pigheaded and was refusing to settle. I was getting desperate, so I . . . made a video so I could blackmail him—a video of him and me having sex. That's when my aneurysm ruptured."

"My God!" muttered Hugh. "I had no idea . . ."

"Shocking, isn't it?" said Maxine. One of her eyes was moving in one direction while the other went in another.

"I know Frank Dickey," said Hugh. "Whatever else he might be, he's a good neurosurgeon."

"Since then, I've used the same method on many other doctors over the years. Not just neurosurgeons either. Gynecologists, pathologists, urologists . . . so many of them, I lost count. Carl would know; he keeps all the videos in my office. It never fails to amaze me how weak and vulnerable doctors are when it comes to carnal pleasures."

Hugh wanted to learn some names, but since time was short he quickly moved on to the next question. "Why didn't you sue Bonehead . . . Dr. Clegg? You must have known—"

"Bonehead? You call him *Bonehead*?"

"It's just a nickname—"

Maxine erupted into vulgar laughter and for a moment Hugh was concerned that she might draw somebody from outside the room. "Bonehead! What an appropriate name for him! I wanted to sue the bastard, but they wouldn't let me."

"*Who* wouldn't?"

"Grand National."

"I don't understand."

"I suppose it doesn't matter any more, does it? Why do we have to keep these silly little secrets?"

Let's hear it for midazolam, Hugh thought with excitement. Maxine had yielded very nicely to the drug.

"Grand National was Clegg's liability insurance carrier. When he called them that morning after Julie became paralyzed, he confessed all about the high CSF protein result that he deliberately ignored. They understood pretty clearly that he was the one who had messed up. To save themselves millions of dollars, they made a deal with me. They gave me all the information about Julie's medical care, and in return, I promised to target you, and not him."

"My God!" Hugh said breathlessly. "So you knew about the CSF protein from the beginning!"

"Yes, I suppose I did."

"You deliberately betrayed the Winters."

"Betray? That's a harsh word. Let's just say they were the unfortunate victims of an ingenious business plan. They could easily sue me for legal malpractice, and if the Oregon State Bar Association ever found out about it, I would certainly be disbarred." Maxine laughed away that possibility as if she couldn't care less.

"Did Clegg ever know what was going on with Grand National?"

"No. He couldn't figure out why he wasn't being sued either, just like you couldn't."

Hugh looked into Maxine's swimming eyes and knew she was completely at his mercy. He wanted to spend some time telling her what he thought of her, but there wasn't enough to spare. If there was ever a moment to ask his final and most important question, it was now.

"Why did Richard Forrester kill himself?"

Maxine suddenly stiffened and her eyes came into focus. A few moments passed before she could muster enough strength to speak. "I'm sorry . . . I'm so sorry about that!"

"What happened?"

"I only found out today. Billy told me all about it before he attacked me."

"*What happened?*" Hugh persisted, his voice strained.

"My informants told me everything about Defendant Forrester and the prostitute in the OR. I made a terrible mistake, though: I passed the information to Billy. He should have gone home and left the matter in my hands, but he didn't. The kid thought he'd take on Defendant Forrester and SOD'M on his own. He printed up a false Summons, *Diamond vs. Forrester,* and served him with it."

"A false Summons?"

"It was only meant to scare him, not kill him."

So that why Richard took his own life! That little jerk, Billy Funk, had played a cruel practical joke on him. Richard had totally believed him and couldn't bare the prospect of living through another lawsuit. He was so emotionally unstable; the slightest provocation was enough to tip him over the edge.

Hugh closed his eyes, bowed his head, and felt completely empty inside.

"If I'd known what Billy was going to do," continued Maxine, "I would have stopped him. You've got to believe me!"

There was a knock and the door opened. Obviously unable to stay outside any longer, Ed Cleveland blustered into the room, closely followed by Pagonis and Carl.

Hugh felt a tremendous sense of relief; his game was over.

When she saw the little Greek, Maxine pointed a finger at him. "I know all about you!" she cried. "Dr. Montrose will do my surgery, thank you very much!"

"Of course he will, Ms. Doggett," said Ed, speaking in a soothing tone. "All of us at Columbia Medical Center want to see you through this terrible ordeal safely." Then, as if a shadow of doubt had just crossed his mind, he shot a threatening glance at Hugh and asked, "You *are* going to operate on her, aren't you?"

"Please!" Maxine begged. *"Please!"*

Despite his earlier promise to Carl and his own Hippocratic oath, Hugh's basic impulse was to drive the knife further in, not take it out. Maxine, however, wasn't the only person in the world capable of making devious plans; he had formulated one of his own—one that would destroy her more thoroughly and effectively than any knife blade might. The first step, already successfully completed, was her confession. The second called for her survival; she *had* to pull through her present predicament in order to suffer immeasurably through the next. The only way he could be relatively sure of *that* happening was if he elbowed Pagonis aside and performed the surgery himself.

"All right, then," he said. "I'll operate on you—"

"Thank you!" cried Maxine. *"Thank—"*

"But first, I want to go over *all* the risks of surgery with you."

"Oh, come now," said Ed. "Surely there's no need to put somebody of Ms. Doggett's stature through any bureaucratic hurdles?"

"Exactly," drawled Maxine. "Besides, I already know the risks. I *am* a fully qualified registered nurse, you know."

Hugh knew that obtaining informed consent from Maxine was a waste of time; loaded with midazolam, she would never remember a word he said. However, Carl was watching and could easily testify against him if something went wrong.

"Sorry," said Hugh, "but I'm afraid it's absolutely necessary. In fact, there's no harm in having a little *extra* protection." He went to the door, culled a couple of nurses into the room, and wrote their names down onto a scrap of paper. They blinked with disbelief at Maxine's shocking wound and backed into corners as far away from her as possible.

"That's better," said Hugh, stuffing the paper into one of his pockets and resuming his position at the bedside. "Now, in front of all these witnesses, I want to go over *all* the risks of surgery with you, *very* slowly, and *very* carefully."

CHAPTER 36

The OR at Columbia Medical Center was large and cavernous. In its heyday, its gleaming hallways had been filled with scurrying surgeons and nurses. The medical liability crisis had turned those days into fading memories. Over the last few years, many of the surgeons had moved on to safer states and the nurses had followed. On this night, row upon row of individual operating rooms stood dark and empty, bearing silent testimony to the struggles between life and death that once had been fought within their walls.

Only one operating room was open: Room 7, tucked away in a remote corner. Inside, Maxine Doggett lay anesthetized on an operating table, a plastic tube inserted between her dried-out crinkly lips. Her head was completely bald, lying on a pillow, and turned to the right. The kitchen knife was buried to the hilt into her skin just above and in front of her left ear. A small pool of fresh blood was accumulating around its entry point and some overflow trickled down her cheek in a crooked line that resembled a fork of lightning. The pale scar from her old aneurysm surgery started from the same point but extended in the opposite direction, shaped like a question mark, facing forward. Her thighs were separated and her genitals were exposed. The circulating nurse, Kelly, was spreading her labia with the fingers of one hand, while threading a Foley catheter up her urethra with the other. Judy, the scrub tech, was standing in front of a table covered with instruments, busily preparing for the operation. The anesthesiologist, Curtis Phillips, had just finished inserting an arterial line into Maxine's wrist so he could accurately monitor her blood pressure throughout the case.

Hugh was watching the preparations from a corner, trying hard to focus on the problem at hand: a knife, a brain, and how best to separate the two. He hadn't realized how badly he had been affected by the lawsuit. The sights, sounds, and smells around him seemed strangely unfamiliar. Even his fingers felt out of condition, preparing for a hundred-meter dash when they seemed hardly capable of tying a knot. Worst of all, the grit and determination required of a neurosurgeon to make it through the most challenging cases was gone. It was as if he no longer cared whether his patient lived or died.

He had hit bottom.

Curtis finished securing the arterial line. Kelly compressed Maxine's bladder with her hand and watched the catheter fill with amber urine. When their tasks were completed, they backed away.

Hugh slowly uncoiled and moved forward. The patient now belonged to him.

"I need somebody to help hold the head, please."

Kelly stepped forward, cradled the back of the head in her hand, and lifted. Hugh removed the detachable portion of the operating table underneath and set it aside. Then he reached for the Mayfield clamp with its three sharp pins and carefully positioned them around the head, avoiding the area of her previous craniotomy. He suddenly ratcheted the arms of the clamp together and felt his biceps strain as he squeezed as hard as he could. The pins pierced through her scalp and bit into bone. When he couldn't close it any further with his arms, he twisted a large screw that dug the pins even deeper. When he was satisfied that her skull wasn't going to move during the case, he relaxed his muscles and attached the device to the table.

After the scrubbing, prepping, and draping were completed, Hugh flexed and loosened his fingers, then made his incision along the line of the old scar. The tissue was as tough as shoe leather, but his scalpel blade was sharp and cut easily. He included the kitchen knife's point of entry within his incision and reflected a curved flap of skin out of the way, taking care not to bump his hands against the handle of the knife. Underneath, the muscle was blanched and scarred and he could feel dimples where the old holes were located. He brought up a yellow cauterizing pen and vaporized the scar tissue until the outline of the bony trapdoor was identified. Years ago, he had discarded some of the bone from this area. It was through this small window of vulnerability that the knife blade had passed. He slipped his wedge-shaped instrument through one of the holes and pressed down hard. The bone flap wrenched itself from surrounding new bone formation and came free with a loud crack.

The knife stayed firmly in place.

Hugh inspected the dura with his sucker in his left hand and his bipolar coagulator in his right. Both instruments hovered around, drying the field. He recognized the fine black interlocking pattern of the suture that he had used to close the dura seven years before. The material was non-absorbable and would still be there on that glorious day when Maxine had sued her last doctor and was lowered into her grave. The knife blade had pierced the dura and clear colorless CSF was welling up. He extended the rent in the dura, exposing the brain underneath. Myriad glistening veins and arteries crossed its surface.

The time had arrived to remove the knife.

"You've got blood on standby, don't you, Curtis?" he asked. "This could get messy."

"Sure thing. I've got four units of packed cells hanging on my IV pole, ready to go."

"Good." Hugh took hold of the handle and pulled gently. The knife came free and its tip was immediately pursued by a torrent of bright red blood.

"Just what I was afraid of," said Hugh with a sinking feeling. He tossed the knife aside and it clattered into a metal pan. Then he dove into the substance of the brain with his sucker and the bipolar, prying the creamy-colored tissue apart as he searched for the source of the bleeding. This was an area that could be explored with relative safety; the highly sensitive areas of speech and understanding were more than an inch or two away, a vast distance in the world of neurosurgery. He found the offending vessel and saw a fine jet of blood pumping out of a small hole in its side. The point of the knife had punctured the artery and, as long as the steel had remained in place, the blood was prevented from escaping. Now that the knife was lying on the scrub tech's table, the plug was gone and the patient was briskly hemorrhaging. He places the tips of his bipolar across the small hole and pressed the pedal with his foot.

Hugh heard the door behind him swing open and Judy draw in a short, sharp breath. He followed her gaze and felt a shock wave surge through his body. Billy was standing in the doorway, dressed in a dark suit that was a jarring sight in the sterile environment of the operating room. He held a double-barreled shotgun cradled in his arm and was pointing it at Maxine's body under the drapes.

"I knew I'd find the bitch in here," snarled Billy. "Now it's time for her to die."

In an instant, Hugh remembered the tension at the plaintiffs' table and was able to make some quick sense out of the situation. "Billy—don't do it!" he cried. "Put the gun down!"

"She made my life hell for two years," Billy said. His hands were shaking and the gun's aim was uncertain.

"I know how you feel! She made my life hell too. We can talk about it!"

"The time for talking is over. She tried to kill me. Now she's going to pay."

"For God's sake—"

"Bye-bye, Maxine."

A tongue of orange blasted from one of the two barrels with a deafening roar. If his intended target had been Maxine, Billy missed by a mile. The buckshot slammed into the anesthesia machine and the inhalant canisters exploded, spraying glass and metal fragments across the room. Clear, colorless liquid poured out the wreckage and splattered across the floor. Curtis dove for cover behind what was left of his machine. Judy screamed and dropped to the floor. Kelly crouched in a corner, her eyes bulging with terror. The air in the OR quickly filled with a pungent odor.

"Shit!" Billy swore. "I won't miss again."

"Billy!" shouted Hugh. "Listen to me! Put the gun *down!*"

Billy stepped forward and raised his shotgun once again. Now he was so close, he couldn't miss. But the anesthetic gases that were rapidly building up in the room were highly potent and his hands were shaking even more than before. He pulled the trigger and a blast roared from the other barrel. This time, the four bags of blood exploded, showering everything in the room with millions of red spots and making the place look as if it had instantaneously broken out with a bad case of the measles. Then Billy succumbed to the gases. His eyes fluttered and he collapsed onto the back table, sending dozens of steel instruments crashing to the ground.

Hugh tried to return his attention to the operation, but the volatile inhalation agent that had incapacitated Billy was quickly rising around him and was beginning to strangle his own mind.

He looked at Maxine's open head. The knife had been removed, but he wasn't sure whether the bleeding was under control. However much he tried, he was unable to concentrate on the operative field. The world was spinning and a ball of nausea was rising in the pit of his stomach. Out of the corner of his eyes he saw Judy, Kelly, and Curtis clutching their throats, fighting feebly for air. Moments later it was his own turn to succumb. He dropped to his knees, choking, gasping, then keeled over onto his back. For a few moments, he stared with unblinking eyes at the ceiling of the OR with its large kettle drum lights.

Soon, nothing remained but swirling clouds of blackness.

"For Christ's sake . . . somebody get me out of this thing!"

Hugh's eyes flickered open. He was lying on the floor of the operating room between the table and the anesthesia machine, looking up at Maxine's smooth, round head above him, still firmly clamped in the Mayfield. Through the fog that gripped his mind he sensed that the OR table was shaking and he could hear her crying and moaning. When he looked around, he dimly saw the clutter of an operating room from an unusual perspective, six inches above the floor. Blood was dripping from everything—the ceiling, the walls, the wreckage of the anesthesia machine . . . *everything*. When he saw bodies lying around him, Billy and the surgical team, memories of what had happened washed through him with frightening clarity.

Maxine's voice pierced the silence. "I can't move! Somebody help me!"

Hugh slowly climbed to his feet and leaned against the suction machine to steady himself. The OR was spinning around and his head was pounding from a terrible headache. Maxine was still lying supine on the operating table, her head firmly locked in place. Her terrified eyes were rapidly looking around, taking in the four bodies lying on the floor and all the blood. In her agitation, she had ripped off all the drapes with her hands, kicked over the instrument-laden Mayo stands with her feet, and had pulled out her endotracheal tube. She was completely naked, her legs and arms flailing helplessly around, attempting to free herself. A Foley catheter disappeared into her thick bush of pubic hair, an arterial line was still threaded into one of her wrists, and EKG pads were stuck to her exposed chest. Most shocking of all, her head was still open. Her brain was in full view, pulsating rapidly as she struggled.

When Hugh saw it, his legs suddenly felt like rubber and he gripped the suction machine so he wouldn't fall. He breathed deeply, but the air was fouled by anesthetic gas and irritated his trachea, making him cough violently. After the spasm subsided, Hugh pieced together what must have happened. When the canister was smashed open by Billy's first shot, the anesthetic inhalant poured out and evaporated into the air, sending everybody in the room to sleep. At the same time, the same gas was no longer passing through the breathing circuit, and without any anesthesiologist keeping an eye on things, there was nothing to keep Maxine in her anesthetized state. Out of all the people in the room, she had been the first to wake up, most likely as a result of the painful stimulation from the Mayfield clamp.

Hugh dropped to his knees and checked Curtis, Judy and Kelly. They weren't dead—just asleep, as he suspected. Billy was peacefully snoring, his shotgun lying on the floor next to him and a finger still curled around the trigger. The blood didn't belong to any of them. Evidently it had come from the four bags that had been prepared for transfusion.

"Please—somebody help me!"

Hugh accidentally knocked over some instruments that were teetering precariously at the edge of a table. They landed on the floor with a deafening clatter.

"Who's there?" Maxine cried.

"It's me."

"Who?"

"*Me.* Dr. Montrose."

"Thank God! What happened? Who are all these dead people?"

"They're not—"

"Is that Billy over there?"

"Yes—"

"What's he doing with a shotgun? Oh, my God—he went *postal*, didn't he?"

"You could say that."

Maxine wailed even louder. "I'm so scared! You've got to help me! And my head . . . it's stuck!" Her left hand wandered up towards her head and, as Hugh watched in horror, she groped around her craniotomy opening and poked a finger into her brain where the knife had once been.

"*No!*" shouted Hugh.

"What's the matter?"

"Your operation . . . It's not over yet!"

"What do you mean?"

"Your head . . . It's still open."

Puzzled, Maxine poked around some more with her finger. When it dawned on her what the squishiness was, she screamed as loud as she could and clawed the air wildly with her arms and legs. Hugh lurched towards the wall phone. He called the operator and within seconds he was speaking with the nursing supervisor.

"Get the on-call back-up operating team to the hospital right away!" he shouted above Maxine's shrieks. "I need an anesthesiologist, a circulator, and a scrub tech as fast as you can to Room 7."

At first, the nurse didn't say anything and Hugh could visualize her calmly checking the clipboard she always carried around with her. Then, in a voice that sounded annoyed, she said, "But you've already got a team, Dr. Montrose."

"I know *that*. They're all asleep! I need another one right away!"

"*Asleep?*"

"Look, I don't have time to explain. Just do as I tell you!"

After another spell of violent coughing, Hugh called 911. He told the dispatcher that there had been a shooting in the OR at Columbia Medical Center. When he had finished summoning help, he slid to the floor and wondered if there was anything he could do to improve Maxine's situation. She was still hollering and flailing around, naked and locked to the table. If he released her from the Mayfield clamp, she would probably escape from the table and stampede out of the room in a panic. For a moment, he visualized the ludicrous image of a medical malpractice attorney running nude through the hospital, screaming blue murder, her skull unhinged and her brain hanging out. No—releasing her didn't seem the wisest option. Neither could he send her back to merciful sleep. The anesthesia machine had been totally destroyed. He supposed he could use one from another room if he had the strength to drag it over, but something could go wrong. If anybody ever got the notion to sue him for practicing anesthesia without the proper credentials, there would be no defense.

No—the best course of action was to do nothing until help arrived.

Maxine's screaming subsided. Both her hands gripped the Mayfield and she shook it in another desperate attempt to free herself.

Hugh crawled towards the door.

"Where are you going?" Maxine sobbed.

"I can't breathe in here," he gasped.

"Don't leave me alone!"

"I need some air. Then I'll get Pagonis."

"Pagonis? What do you want *him* for?"

"To close your wound."

Maxine started to scream again, even louder than before. "I don't want him touching me!"

"You don't have a choice. There's no way I can operate right now."

"But he'll kill me!"

"Don't exaggerate, Maxine. The hard part of the operation is over now; the knife is out. All he has to do is put the bone back in and sew up your scalp."

"You can't leave me in here alone . . . with all these dead bodies!"

Hugh was about to tell her the truth, that the four people lying on the floor were merely asleep and would soon wake up, when Maxine shouted, "Doctor! Doctor Montrose! *Hugh*! I beg you! I need you! Don't go! *You can't leave me like this!*"

Hugh paused and considered her pleas. She was right. He couldn't simply leave her. There was something that needed to be said—something vitally important. He slowly turned around and crawled towards her. When he reached the table he pulled himself up its side with his arms and drew close to her until his face was inches from her own. He saw the fine trembling of her lips, her bare chest heaving up and down, her cherry nipples erect in the cold air of the operating room. Her brain was pulsating rapidly as if trying to climb out of her skull, and this close, he could detect the faint lipid smell he knew so well.

She met his glassy gaze by swiveling her eyes far to the left.

Hugh spoke softly into her ear. "Just one more thing before I go, Maxine: I want you to know that it's—"

"Yes? What? *What?*"

"It's . . . *nothing personal.*"

Then, he gave her a sick grin and staggered away.

CHAPTER 37

Augustus—you'll have *to forgive me now!* thought Maxine with a hopeful heart as she sat at the large breakfast table in her kitchen, dressed in a pink frilly nightgown and drenched with brilliant sunshine. Legal documents gushed forth from the mouth of a yawning elephant bag at her feet and sprawled across the floor. Legal reference books and thick files were stacked along the counters. Interspersed among them were dirty dishes and half-eaten slices of pizza. It was not how she normally liked to keep her house. Recently, however, she had been consumed by the biggest and most important project she'd ever tackled and she didn't have the time to supervise housemaids. At long last, on this beautiful day, she was finished with all the groundwork and was ready to deliver the opening broadside in the biggest battle of her career.

Three months had passed since Billy had stabbed her and it had taken at least two of them to recover from the complications that resulted from her craniotomy, or, to be more precise, the *closure* of her craniotomy. On that terrible night, Pagonis was found and reluctantly agreed to close her head. The little Greek was scared witless about operating on a medical malpractice attorney who obviously didn't like him and, in his agitation, he accidentally dropped her bone flap. It bounced off the floor and spun into a corner with an ignominious clatter. Rather than washing it with antibiotics, cooking it in the autoclave, or even leaving it out, he pretended nothing had happened and screwed it back into her skull. The infection that resulted was horrendous. On the sixth postoperative day, Maxine spiked a high fever. The wound turned red, broke down, and oozed pus. She was given antibiotics, but they were ineffective as long as the infected piece of bone remained in place. Only when she showed signs of sepsis and delirium did Pagonis finally do the right thing and take it out, angrily blaming it, and not himself, for causing so much trouble. With the source of the infection thus eliminated, Maxine rounded a corner and quickly improved.

While her body healed, Maxine remained mired in depression. Without her bone flap, she was left with a big ugly sunken area on the side of her forehead. She couldn't have the defect repaired, at least not until few months had passed and every lingering bug had been wiped out with antibiotics. For now, she had to live with the eyesore, finding that it was difficult to hide under her hair and drew attention wherever she went. The overlying skin pulsated with her heartbeat and a close observer could easily judge the state of her emotions by how rapidly it did so. She resolved to get something done about it as soon as possible, but knew she would have trouble finding a neurosurgeon with the courage to operate on her.

As shocking as it was, Maxine's new appearance was not the principle cause of her depression. Ever since the night she was stabbed, she hadn't seen Augustus and knew he was deliberately staying away from her because of the outrageous things she had shouted from her veranda. Even in her drunkenness, she should have remembered to control herself when addressing the great eagle and not say anything disrespectful or rude. Who could blame him for his disappearance? Now this excommunication from her life's guiding force was becoming unbearable and she was trying hard to think of a way to make amends.

Maxine's immediate solution to the problem was to hurl herself back into her medical malpractice work. The legal papers haphazardly scattered around her kitchen on this sunny day formed the foundations for three—*three* dramatic new lawsuits she had prepared: *Peabody vs. Montrose, Cartwright vs. Montrose,* and *Doggett vs. Montrose.* Hugh Montrose—the defendant in all of them! Obviously, Pagonis had been the moron who had failed to diagnose a recurrent subdural hematoma in one person, had ripped up vital lumbar nerves with a high-speed drill in another, and had dropped her own bone flap onto the floor. However, fortunately for him, he was insured by Grand National and Maxine still didn't want to jeopardize a potentially long and prosperous relationship with that company by suing one of their clients. So, she was going after Montrose instead—over, and over, and over again—accusing him of negligence because he had turned a blind eye to the flagrant incompetence within his department. She relished the idea of facing him and John Denmark in a courtroom again and this time she would work alone; that fruitcake, Billy Funk, had been committed to a lunatic asylum and it would be a long time before anybody would hear from him again.

The Peabody and Cartwright cases were just like the hundreds of other medical malpractice suits she had handled throughout her life and presented little challenge. But the third was a new and exciting experience. Never before had she sued a physician for negligence in her own medical care. She had no doubt, however, that she had been terribly wronged and figured a two million dollar settlement would help her to forget the pain and emotional distress of her pus-exuding wound, not to mention the ongoing embarrassment at having a cave on the left side of her head big enough inside for bats to breed.

Maxine smelled garlic and swung around to see Manfred Horman. He was standing in the open back doorway and was staring at her with jaundiced eyes. In his hand, he gripped a brown paper bag.

"What are you doing here?" demanded Maxine. "You're not due for another week."

"I came for a raise."

"You're wasting your time," said Maxine. "We have a very specific agreement and I don't intend to make any exceptions. Besides, I've got lots of work to do."

Horman advanced into the kitchen. "What have you done to your parrot?" he asked.

Maxine glanced at Toby who was perched on his wooden stand nearby. A thick rubber band was wrapped tightly around his beak, prohibiting him from opening it and making any parrot noises. Ever since he had missed his dinner that one time on account of his owner being stabbed in the head, he had never stopped squawking 'Maxine is a loser' over and over again. One day, after Toby had repeated the same words at least a hundred times, Maxine had lost control of herself and threatened him with a visit to the local taxidermist. Carl had intervened at the last moment and had come up with the idea of a rubber band. It was a satisfactory compromise and Toby had been silenced ever since.

"What have I done to my parrot?" repeated Maxine. "That's none of your business."

Horman shifted his attention to the piles of papers scattered around. "Are these the new lawsuits you discussed with me last week?"

"Yes. Three of them, all to be served today! Montrose will never know what hit him. I can't wait to see the expression on his face!"

"Especially after he remembers how he saved your life . . . twice."

"You disapprove?"

"You know I don't harbor any opinions, except the ones you tell me to express in court."

Maxine smiled her approval, then stood up and gathered together the papers on the table. "I always used to think that *Winter vs. Montrose* was the ultimate case," she said. "Now I know I was greatly mistaken; I wasn't thinking nearly big enough. Just imagine this!" She brandished a fistful of papers in the air. "Three simultaneous lawsuits against the neurosurgeon who saved my life twice! Nothing will stop me from being a superstar now!" She eyed Horman with sudden concern. "You *are* planning to be my testifier, aren't you?"

"That's what I came to talk to you about."

"Is something the matter?" said Maxine with sudden alarm. "You're not still suspended from CANS, are you?"

"No," said Horman, helping himself to a mouthful of cold pepperoni pizza. "They reinstated me, although I'll have to be more careful what I say under oath from now on."

"So, what's left to discuss?"

"Like I said: I came for a raise. Three simultaneous lawsuits will mean a lot of extra work for me."

Maxine couldn't deny that things around the office were about to become much busier. "What do you want?" she asked, her eyes now narrowing with suspicion.

Horman wandered into the nearby guest bathroom, leaving the door open behind him. "Something quite simple," he called from inside. "You might not be enthralled at first, but I'm sure you'll soon grow used to the idea."

"Let me guess. You want—"

Maxine was interrupted by tinkling urine, accompanied by staccato toots of flatus. When the concert ended, without the customary final flush, Horman reappeared, zipping his fly. "What were you saying?" he asked.

"You want to have sex with me more often?"

"Not exactly."

"Then what?"

"This."

Horman handed Maxine the paper bag he had brought with him. She reached inside and, one by one, she produced a bra, panties, garter belt, suspenders, stockings, a vicious-looking whip, and a leather mask that looked like the face of a cat. All the items were black.

"You have *got* to be kidding!" she cried, holding the articles at arm's length, a look of utter horror across her face. "You want me to wear *these*?"

"Actually . . ." said Horman, blushing slightly, "they're for me."

"*You're* going to put this stuff on?"

"I thought I might . . . yes."

"You're such a disgusting, perverted pig, Manfred."

"I've been called far worse."

"Go to hell," said Maxine. She stuffed the paraphernalia back into the paper bag and threw it at him. Then she wiped her hands against her nightgown as if they had been contaminated by filth. "I'm not that kind of woman. I'll use Charles Mortimer as my expert instead. I seriously doubt he goes in for this sort of thing . . . although anything's possible, I suppose."

"Mortimer's not available anymore."

"Why not? I thought he was quite good, except for his mold problem."

"He died last month."

"*Died*? Really?"

"He was so invigorated by his experience testifying against Montrose, he signed up for another case. It happened as he was sitting on the witness chair. The attorneys, and everybody else in the courtroom, were so engrossed in a heated discussion with the judge that nobody noticed he was dead; not breathing or moving, staring out into space with the same lifeless eyes as he's had for years. To tell you the truth, all professional testifiers like me are delighted his Divine Maker finally put a cork in him. The old man was giving us a worse reputation than we already have."

"*You* may have a reason to be pleased," said Maxine. "Unfortunately, his death puts *me* in a rather awkward position."

"So, give me what I'm asking," said Horman, nodding towards the paper bag, "and you can have all the expert testimony you want."

"What *are* you asking . . . exactly?"

"First, we have a few drinks to loosen up our old-fashioned inhibitions; you know how they can often get in the way of good times. When we're ready, I'll slip those . . . *things* on and punish you for being naughty."

"You want to *whip* me?"

Horman fished the whip out of the bag once again and inspected its braided leather thongs with a gleam in his eye. "Just a few well-placed strokes across your buttocks. Nothing too painful. What do you say, my dear?"

Maxine sighed and realized that she was negotiating from a position of weakness. Although the internet was crawling with websites touting expert witnesses from every specialty, the amount of work available for them was huge and the market was currently working in their favor. She didn't have to be part of the rat-race, though; as long as she allowed Horman to dip his quill in her inkwell once in a while, he was willing to sign any declaration she wanted. In fact, he had once told her that she would be *nothing* without him and she had been secretly forced to agree. "I'll think about it," she eventually answered.

"Submit to me now," croaked Horman throatily. "I can punish you right here, with your parrot as a witness. What better way to inaugurate your triple lawsuit?"

Maxine's eyes flooded with fear as if she was actually considering the idea, then the soft spot on her head began to pulsate faster. "Not an inauguration," she said, her voice trembling now. "An atonement! I must offer Augustus a sacrifice and beg for forgiveness. I must offer him . . . *myself*!"

"Who's Augustus?"

Maxine didn't take the trouble to explain. With the air of a sacrificial virgin who had bravely accepted her fate, she slowly reached for her elephant bag, tipped it upside down, and emptied its contents across the floor. Then she put it aside and pushed the papers around with her hands until she had created something that resembled an altar. When she was ready, she turned to face Horman, her eyes resolute and unseeing.

"I've been very naughty, Manfred," she murmured as she loosened her nightgown. "Go and prepare yourself. I'll be right here, awaiting my punishment . . ."

CHAPTER 38

Hugh sat in his office with his feet propped on his desk and rotated his Maxine Doggett voodoo doll slowly in his hands. The figure was about eighteen inches tall and bore a strong resemblance to the woman he had come to despise, right down to the curly red hair and flashy designer outfit. Denmark had found it on some fishing trip to the Caribbean and had sent it to him, together with a shish-kebab skewer and a witty note explaining how to use the gifts for the greatest effect. During moments of boredom, Hugh would play with the doll, sticking the skewer into her from every angle and muttering make-believe curses under his breath. The silly, regressive behavior made him chuckle and relieved his tension.

Certainly, there was plenty of tension in his life that begged to be relieved. Ever since the end of his trial, some of his worst fears were coming true. For the second time in his career, he received a certified letter from SPI. This one informed him that his defense had cost a grand total of $650,000, a huge sum of money by anybody's reckoning, and that he could no longer be kept on as a client. Any appeals would be a waste of time. He was given a deadline to buy a tail policy in case a patient sued him in the future for what he had done in the past. The asking price: $300,000. The letter meant only one thing: he would be forced to enter the high risk insurance pool if he wanted to continue in private practice. The first year's premium for an immature claims-made policy that barely covered him was going to be $140,000, with promises of numbers two or three times higher as the years passed. When he asked once what a mature policy would cost, his broker was unable to tell him; no neurosurgeon had ever survived that long. They were either lucky enough to revert back to the regular insurance market or they were forced to go out of business. Hugh calculated that, in order to keep seeing patients for the first year after being ditched by SPI, he would have to pay over twelve hundred dollars *a day* for medical malpractice insurance alone. Given the relatively low reimbursement rates in this part of the country, this was clearly a price he couldn't afford.

So what was he going to do?

One option would be to ask Ed Cleveland to hire him as an employee of Columbia Medical Center and let *him* pay for the tail. The choice Ed would face was simple: either assume all the liability risks and costs of a neurosurgical practice, or do without any neurosurgery coverage at all and put patients at risk of dying from lack of care, especially in their ER's. Hospitals all across the country were being faced with the same dilemma. As a rule, most of them wanted to do the right thing for their patients and were trying to recruit, but neurosurgeons were becoming increasingly difficult to find. If Ed said no, Hugh supposed he could move out of the state and make a fresh start somewhere else, as Robert Bull had done. Such a move would be highly disruptive to his family, especially to his children who were socked into their schools and would likely balk at leaving their friends. Better doing that, though, than telling the neurosurgical world to go to hell and getting out of the business altogether.

Of all his options, dumping all his liability problems into Ed Cleveland's lap seemed to be the best one and he only hoped that, when the time came, he caught the old blowhard on a good day. Maybe if he brought along a box of Cuban cigars, it would help mollify him . . .

While he mulled over his future, Hugh's interest in neuro-surgery plummeted. He took call and performed a few opera-tions, but his heart wasn't into it and he sent anything remotely challenging to the university. His attitude towards his patients had also soured. He smiled all the time and was polite, but he secretly viewed them as the enemy and was constantly on his guard. He practised defensive medicine as never before, remem-bering how Richard had controlled the demons within himself by trying to bankrupt the system. Hugh, however, gained no solace from it and resisted joining SOD'M's teaming ranks. He also avoided drinking alcohol, wary that the smallest sip might nudge him down the same slippery slope Robert Bull had trav-eled.

He knew about the traditional traps that burned-out sur-geons fell into: drink, mistresses, gambling. . . . What worried him more, though, was some ghastly fate that he could never anticipate, custom-designed especially for him.

As depressing as neurosurgery had become, his relationship with Michelle was much worse. While nobody mentioned sepa-ration or divorce, it was clear that his apathy had opened a great chasm which threatened their future together. He never doubted that her love for him was still alive. Whenever he returned home at the end of the day, she anxiously searched his eyes, looking for the light that had once burned within them. Over the last three months, however, nothing changed. A long face, once so rare, greeted her every day and she would turn away, disappointed and bitter. Hugh knew Michelle was suffering, yet was powerless do anything about it.

Hugh took carefully aim and thrust his skewer through the head of the doll. "Take that, Maxine," he growled.

The telephone rang on his desk.

He picked up the receiver. "Yes?"

"Dr. Graham is on line one, sir," said Trish.

"*Chuck* Graham? The president of CANS?"

"Yes, sir."

"Put him through!" Hugh took his feet off the desk and the Doggett doll tumbled from his lap. "Hello? Chuck? Hugh here."

"Hi, Hugh," said the leader of the neurosurgical world. "Nice to talk to you again. How are you doing?"

"Fine," Hugh lied.

"Congratulations on winning your trial. I know how hard it must have been for you."

And still is, thought Hugh.

"Remember that day you called me a few months ago?" continued Graham. "You talked to me about your idea of CANS having a certified expert witness program."

"I remember."

"Well, you're probably thinking I've forgotten about it, but I haven't. In fact, quite the opposite. The CANS Board met this morning and we unanimously decided to pursue this idea without delay."

"*What?*"

"You heard me correctly, Hugh. We've got to do something about the liability crisis before the whole system of medical care collapses. The political process is important too, but you know as well as I do what kind of problems we've been having with caps on non-economic damages. Medical courts face an uphill climb too. The trial lawyers simply outgun us. It may be years before anything meaningful happens nationwide. No—desperate times require desperate measures. CANS is finally going to strike a blow against those whacko experts everybody knows about."

Hugh leapt to his feet, barely able to keep the receiver to his ear in his excitement. "I can't believe it!"

"I'll tell you something else you won't believe," said Graham. "We want you to run the show—be the first chairman of the committee that will be responsible for setting up the program. It'll mean a lot of work, traveling around the country recruiting neurosurgeons to volunteer as certified experts, and so on. But it'll be good fun, especially since you'll be injecting some fairness and rationality to the system. Are you interested?"

"By God, yes! But do you think anybody else will be willing to donate their time?"

"Are you kidding?" laughed Graham. "As soon as word got out that the Board was considering this proposal, we received a flood of phone calls from neurosurgeons all over the country anxious to help."

"That's fantastic!"

"Let me give you a word of advice before you get started," continued Graham, sounding more serious now. "CATL isn't going to take this sitting down. You can bet your bottom dollar that as soon as those guys get a wind of things, they'll amass a war chest of money, grease the palms of their favorite politicians, and fight us to the death."

"But won't they realize that a program like this would benefit lawyers too," Hugh reasoned. "We want the plaintiff's experts to have credibility too."

"Believe me: change will be resisted until the last trial lawyer is no longer standing."

"What can they do to stop us? This is an internal matter within CANS."

"They'll think of something. What you *really* need is somebody on your committee to give advice on the tactics they're likely to use. Not a neurosurgeon, but . . . one of *them*."

"A trial lawyer?"

"Yes. Preferably one who's experienced in medical malpractice. Somebody who knows and understands how these so-called expert witnesses operate; how they are recruited, how they are paid, and what makes them tick. We want a person who can anticipate every move CATL will make against us and advise us how to respond. Their participation on the committee is going to be critical to our success. Do you know such a person?"

A face immediately loomed in Hugh's mind like a rising phantom: grey eyes, jutting chin, sneering cheek, flamboyant red hair. He shook the unwelcome image from his head and sank back into his chair. "No, I don't," he said firmly.

"In that case, we'll have no choice but to begin a search. It'll be time-consuming and expensive, but I don't see any other way. CANS has decided to make this its highest priority. The future of neurosurgery in this country depends on it. And there's one more thing . . ."

"Yes?"

"Your idea of the coat-of-arms . . . You know: the Crusader's shield with the crossed scalpel and gavel on its front."

"Yes?"

"Nice touch. The Board wants to use it as our emblem for the new program—the banner under which all decent neurosurgeons will rally."

When he hung up, Hugh's mind was a jumble of thoughts. Expert witness certification! His idea actually had a chance of becoming a reality. Suddenly, there were a million important things he had to do and very little time in which to do them. First, he had to form a panel of respected colleagues who would define the type of neurosurgeons they were looking for. They would only be interested in people who were 1) in active practice, 2) able to support their testimony with the scientific literature, 3) willing to work on behalf of both defendants and plaintiffs, and 4) not interested in payment for their services. Some of his ideas might be controversial, others not. As they avalanched through his mind, he scrambled for a pen.

Chuck had strongly recommended that a trial lawyer serve on the committee, but where in the world would he find one? The haunting face of Maxine Doggett had gate-crashed his mind, but the idea of working with that woman was utterly preposterous. She was Ms. Nothing Personal, the Fully Qualified Registered Nurse. . . . She was *The Dog!* Even if she did the unthinkable and abandoned her life's work to take up the cause against professional testifiers, it would only be a matter of time before she transformed Hugh and every other neurosurgeon on the committee into homicidal maniacs, as had happened to that twerp, Billy. She could ruin their plans for putting together a certified expert witness program. Hell—if she tried hard enough, she could even destroy the whole of CANS and reduce it to smoldering ruins. Hugh laughed as he imagined Maxine sitting at a conference table, giving everybody her trademark withering looks and gassing them to death with her perfume.

Perfume?

Hugh sniffed . . . and detected a whiff of perfume—*Maxine's* perfume. He snapped his head up just in time to see The Dog herself sweep into his office in all her hideous glory. She was wearing a dark green designer pantsuit, so heavily laden with gold tassels and frills that Hugh was reminded of a Christmas tree. Shock and awe was a technique that Maxine often used to subdue her opponents, and Hugh felt a pang of fear grip his insides. He spotted an impossibly deep and ugly crater where the left side of her forehead was supposed to be. Even from his chair, Hugh could see the pulsations of her brain underneath.

She approached Hugh's desk, her elephant bag faithfully squeaking along behind her. She was closely followed by Carl, looking unhappy with his chin tucked low and his hands thrust into his pockets.

Trish trailed behind them. "I'm sorry, Dr. Montrose. They just barged right past me!"

"That's okay, Trish," said Hugh. "You can go back to your work."

"Defendant Montrose," said Maxine when the door was closed. "So sorry for interrupting your busy day, but there's something important I am obliged to inform you about."

"I've been expecting you" said Hugh, swallowing deeply.

"Mr. Zeiger is here to keep the peace so don't get any funny ideas," said Maxine.

Remembering their private conversation in the ER three months ago, Hugh looked at Carl but was unable to make eye contact. Evidently, nothing had changed between him and Maxine. Today, like every other day for the last couple of decades, he was still her security chief and nothing more.

Maxine reached into her elephant bag and extracted some papers. "I'm here to serve you with *three* new lawsuits!" she announced with great excitement. She paused to savor the shock she must have been expecting, but when Hugh didn't flinch, bewilderment crept into her voice and she batted her eyelashes double-time. "One—one of them is on behalf of Mrs. Peabody's family. The second is on behalf of Mr. Cartwright, who has lost use of his bowels and bladder, not to mention his ability to participate in marital consortium. The third is my very own. Defendant Montrose, are you listening to me?"

Hugh had plucked up the courage to walk around his desk and draw nearer to Maxine. With his hands clasped behind his back, he was leaning forward slightly and was closely inspecting the defect in the side of her skull. "My goodness," said Hugh, trying to sound studious, "that looks really bad. You simply *must* get it fixed."

"I didn't ask for your opinion!" said Maxine, backing away.

"Let me guess: you haven't found a neurosurgeon that's willing to sacrifice his career to help you. Am I right?"

"That's none of your business."

"I know one in Botswana who might see you."

"Very funny. Now pay attention to me. As I was saying, I am the plaintiff in the third case and I can assure you, my case is absolutely water-tight . . . Good grief! What's *that*?"

"It's you," said Hugh, picking up the Maxine Doggett voodoo doll from the floor.

"Me?"

"John Denmark found it on a fishing trip in the Caribbean and sent it to me. Whenever I think of you, I stick a shish kebab skewer right through its middle. The victim is supposed to suffer excruciating pain. Hey—I have an idea! Let's see if it works." Seeking to gain control of his gnawing fear with some humor, Hugh picked up the skewer and thrust it into the doll's abdomen, all the while keeping one eye and a cocked eyebrow trained on Maxine. "Feel anything?"

"You may think getting served these lawsuits is a joke," said Maxine, "but I can assure you that this is very serious business. You might even win one or two of them in the end, but having three more black marks on your claim history will put an end to your career . . . and undoubtedly boost my own."

Hugh withdrew the needle and tossed the doll aside. "Darn! And to think all this time I thought you were writhing in agony! Something can't be right. I'll have a chat with John about this."

"Here are the Summons and Complaints," said Maxine, casting them onto Hugh's desk with a flourish. "Read them at you leisure." She turned and walked haughtily towards the door, the wheels of her elephant bag once again squeaking across the floor behind her. Carl nodded solemnly at Hugh and obediently followed his boss.

"Just one other thing before you leave . . ." said Hugh, holding up a finger.

Maxine turned and looked at him. "Make it quick. I don't have much time."

Hugh returned to his desk and sat in his chair again. He picked up the legal documents on his desk, crumpled them in his hands, and tossed them into the wastepaper basket.

"Being childish and immature might make you feel better," sneered Maxine, "but it won't make those lawsuits go away."

"I've got something here that might interest you," he said, now opening a drawer in his desk. "I wanted to give you enough time to convalesce from your operation before I let you know about it. No need to cause an unnecessary strokes, you know. Since you were well enough to visit me today, this seems as good a time as any."

"What on earth are you talking about?"

As if he was having second thoughts about what he was about to do, Hugh hesitated for a moment. Then he rallied his courage and produced a micro-cassette tape, slipping it into a tape recorder. He flipped a switch, gently laid the machine on his desk, and leant back, his eyes filled with a small measure of satisfaction as they locked onto Maxine.

The first voice on the tape was his own, a little crackly, but easily understood:

"What were you doing at the Sheraton?"

Maxine's voice was unmistakable: *"Oh, hell—what's the big deal anyhow? Defendant Dickey was attending the CANS meeting—"*

"What the hell is this?" demanded Maxine, creeping closer.

"Shut up and listen," said Hugh.

"Frank Dickey, the neurosurgeon from Astoria?"

"Yes. I had named him in a lawsuit, but he was being pigheaded and was refusing to settle. I was getting desperate, so I . . . made a video so I could blackmail him—a video of him and me having sex. That's when my aneurysm ruptured."

The color in Maxine's face suddenly drained away.

"I know Frank Dickey. Whatever else he might be, he's a good neurosurgeon."

"Since then, I've used the same trick on many other doctors over the years. Not just neurosurgeons either. Gynecologists, pathologists, urologists . . . so many of them, I lost count. Carl would know; he keeps all the videos in my office. It never fails to amaze me how weak and vulnerable doctors are when it comes to carnal pleasures."

"Why didn't you sue Bonehead . . . Dr. Clegg? You must have known—"

"Bonehead? You call him Bonehead?"

"It's just a nickname—"

Peals of laughter, and then the same voice continued. *"Bonehead! What a great name for him! I wanted to sue the bastard, but they wouldn't let me."*

"Who *wouldn't?"*

"Grand National."

"I don't understand."

"I suppose it doesn't matter any more, does it? Why do we have to keep these silly little secrets? Grand National was Clegg's liability insurance carrier. When he called them that morning after Julie became paralyzed, he confessed all about the high CSF protein result that he deliberately ignored. They understood pretty clearly that he was the one who had screwed up. To save themselves millions of dollars, the greedy pigs made a deal with me; they gave me all the information about Julie's medical care, and in return, I promised to target you, and not him."

"My God! So you knew about the CSF protein from the beginning!"

"Yes, I suppose I did."

"You deliberately betrayed the Winters."

"Betray? That's a harsh word. Let's just say they were the unfortunate victims of an ingenious business plan. They could easily sue me for legal malpractice, and if the Oregon State Bar Association ever found out about it, I would certainly be disbarred."

Hugh reached forward and turned off the recorder. "Quite a confession, wouldn't you say?" he said. "You should hear the rest of it—"

"I made no such confession!" said Maxine in a hoarse whisper, her face ashen.

"It sounds to me like you did."

"I remember nothing!"

"Scientific analysis will prove the tape to be authentic. It's all quite shocking, you know: running a network of spies at the hospital, having sexual escapades with physicians and then blackmailing them, making dirty little deals with Grand National . . . I find the truth behind Richard's tragic suicide particularly upsetting. I'm sure there are a lot of people who would like to get their hands on this tape—the Oregon Bar Association, the Portland District Attorney's office . . . especially Gary and Julie; they'd be fascinated to hear why you didn't include Clegg in their lawsuit. I wonder what it would be like getting disbarred, sued for legal malpractice, and sent to jail, all simultaneously—"

With a loud screech, Maxine launched herself at the recorder. She wrenched it open, hooked a perfect red fingernail around the tape inside, and yanked hard. Shiny brown tape exploded through the air and fell to the floor. She gathered it into her hands, bundled it up into a ball, and threw it into the wastepaper basket. She glared at Hugh, the soft spot on her skull hammering like crazy. "I don't know what kind of dirty, low-down trick you played on me," she snarled, "but your puny little scheme is over now. I'll next see you in court!"

"Not so fast, Maxine," said Hugh. He opened a drawer, fished out another micro-cassette tape, and held it out for Maxine. "Here's your own copy. Take it home and listen to it at your leisure. I want to be sure you understand the full extent of your confessions. Go ahead and take it."

Maxine's skin quickly turned from white to a deep crimson. Carl reached out and took the tape for her.

"Before you waste a lot of energy having another tantrum and destroying that one too," continued Hugh, "there are many copies, all in very safe places where you can't reach them. Since I have enough evidence to blast your career out of the water, I think you should consider making a deal with me. "

"A deal?"

Hugh ploughed on, despite the thumping heart in his chest. "I won't make the tape public if you meet two conditions."

"Which are?"

"First, you compensate the Winters for the damage you did to them."

"Never!"

"Five million five hundred and seventy thousand dollars, all the economic damages they originally asked for, plus two hundred and fifty thousand dollars in non-economic damages, and one hundred and twenty thousand for a wheelchair accessible RV. Let's make it six million—a nice, round figure, don't you think? Of course, six million is the amount of spending money I want the Winters to get. Since this isn't a court award, they'll be paying taxes. . . . Or rather, *you'll* be paying their taxes. Better write the check out for a nice, round ten million, Maxine. It's the least you can do for that poor, unfortunate family."

Maxine's deep crimson now changed to purple. She took a threatening step towards Hugh.

Hugh hastily continued, "I have no doubt you've got that kind of money lying around somewhere, waiting to be put to good use. It'll transform Gary and Julie's lives, even if it can't reverse the quadriplegia."

"The second condition?" asked Carl, laying a restraining hand on Maxine's shoulder.

"You must never again represent another plaintiff in a medical malpractice lawsuit. You will send an e-mail to all your other clients, telling them that you're no longer their lawyer and that they'll have to take their cases elsewhere. Move into some other field; divorce law would suit you nicely. It's brimming with confrontation, especially when children are involved. You're sure to thrive in an environment like that, rutting and locking horns with other members of your species for years to come. Just think of all the lives you could ruin!"

"A divorce attorney?" Maxine said breathlessly, as if she believed they were the lowest form of human existence.

"Ten million dollars and a career change," said Hugh, waving around a third micro-cassette tape that had somehow materialized in his hand. "That's what it'll take to keep the tapes secret."

"A *divorce* attorney?" Maxine repeated, shaking now.

"If you don't agree to my terms, I'll send a copy of the tape to a newspaper friend of mine. When the story comes out in print, you won't be practicing *any* kind of law, in or out of a courtroom. At least I'm offering you a chance to—"

Carl cleared his throat. "If I may interrupt, ma'am . . ." He drew close to her and murmured into her ear. "I think you should calm yourself and listen closely to what Dr. Montrose has to say. In my humble opinion, he's got you by the ovaries."

Carl's indelicate choice of words was as effective as a detonator for placating Maxine. With a howl of rage, she lunged at Montrose and was only prevented from locking her hands around his neck by Carl's quick reflexes. He flung his big, strong arms around her and held her back with all his might.

"Nobody gets Maxine Doggett by the ovaries!" she screamed, struggling wildly. "And I'll never—*never* be a divorce attorney! You're making a big mistake, Defendant Montrose! I'll kill you for this! I swear I'll kill you!"

"Trish!" called Hugh, pressing himself deeper into his seat. "*Trish*! Call security! *Now*!"

"You're dead meat, Defendant Montrose!" Maxine clawed and scratched the air with her fingernails, and thrashed around in an attempt to free herself. "If you think you can blackmail me, you don't know half of what I can do to you!"

"Trish!"

"I've got her, Dr. Montrose!" cried Carl, clasping his hands together around her waist for a better grip. "There's no need to call for security."

"He's *Defendant* Montrose to you!" screeched Maxine directly into Carl's ear.

Carl winced from pain. "Please let me take you home, Ms. Doggett," he implored. "Please!"

"I'll kill him! I'll kill him!"

With a hasty apologetic look directed towards Hugh, Carl half carried and half dragged Maxine, kicking and screaming, out of the office.

When his two visitors had gone and all was quiet again, Hugh unpeeled himself from the back of his seat, shaking like a leaf. As if he didn't already have enough on his plate, now he suddenly had one more thing to worry about—the most serious problem of all. Potentially deadly. This whole business of recording Maxine's confession in the ER had been an attempt to silence her forever. However, he hadn't given much thought to how she might react when she heard the tape and realized her medical malpractice career could be over. Now he knew, and given the intensity of her threats, he wished he had handled things very differently from the start.

"My God! You're as white as a sheet!"

Hugh looked up and saw Trish. She was staring at him wide-eyed from the doorway, her hand covering an open mouth.

"Close up the office and go home," said Hugh. "Don't come back until I say you can."

"What? Shut the place down?"

"Yes!" shouted Hugh angrily.

"What about your patients?"

"To hell with my patients. I'm trying to save our own lives now! Shut the office down and lock the door. That crazy bitch could be back here within the hour with a gun and blow us both away."

"You think she really would?"

"In a heartbeat. Didn't you see her as she left? She has blown a fuse. Do as I tell you! Go!"

Trish needed no encouragement. She left in a hurry.

The time for idle jokes was over and the voodoo doll sitting on the desk wasn't funny anymore. Hugh felt an overwhelming need to protect himself—and quickly. With a bitter curse at the scary turn of events, he threw the doll into the wastepaper basket and wondered where he could get his hands on a gun.

CHAPTER 39

That night, the commotion at the Doggett mansion might have attracted considerable attention if anybody had lived close enough, but its owner had surrounded herself with enough acreage to ensure total privacy and none of the distant neighbors were ever the wiser. Two voices inside the house, those of Maxine and Carl, were shouting, pleading, crying, and shrieking at each other for hours. The pitch of the argument followed an undulating pattern, rising and falling as passions flared and cooled, with an unmistakable trend towards hotter temperatures and potential violence. Sure enough, the uproar was eventually embellished by the crashing of dishes, shattering of glass, splintering of wood, and the loud squawking of a macaw. A black elephant bag flew out of an upstairs and disintegrated on the patio below, scattering papers in all directions. Then, for a while, things calmed down. Just as an observer might have hoped the fight was over, a black Bentley Arnage smashed through the back wall of the garage, its engine screaming, and careened into the swimming pool. Carl ran from a side door of the house and rescued a sopping, bedraggled Maxine. Clinging onto each other, they staggered back inside.

After that, a tenuous peace held. A single light burned downstairs, casting its yellowish beam through a window, across the lawn, and as far as the water's edge. Maxine's sobs could be heard above the gentle lapping of waves. Then they gradually faded away, the waters stilled, and silence reigned amongst the old growth sentinels that towered towards the stars. When dawn broke in the east, Mount Hood coalesced from the gloom and its pristine glaciers gradually turned pink from the rays of the rising sun.

The back door to the mansion swung open and Maxine shuffled outside. Her hair was disheveled and her skin was blotchy and sallow in the early morning light. She was wearing the same pink nightgown that Horman had pawed the day before, only now it was torn and splattered with spaghetti sauce. She ambled to the end of her dock and sat down, her feet dangling above the water. The surface of the lake was a perfect mirror and reflected the volcano in the east so clearly that the two images were identical. She remained deep in thought for a long time, gazing into the distance and wrestling with the decisions that had been forced upon her.

Shortly, she was joined by Carl. He was unshaven, limping, and grim-faced. His shirt was torn and covered with the same spaghetti sauce that decorated Maxine. "God, I'm exhausted," he said as he settled next to her on the dock. "I haven't argued so much since I was married. Did you get any sleep?"

"No."

"Me neither."

Maxine listened to the sound of water slapping lazily against the dock's wooden pilings. When she breathed in, she detected the faint smell of creosote hanging in the crisp air. Her eyes followed the shoreline to the south; she had to look more than two hundred yards before she saw any sign of neighbors. A small sailboat was moored at the next dock down, its rigging gently knocking against the mast and sending a mournful clinking sound in her direction. The house above had once belonged to a doctor, but the man had quickly moved out four years ago as soon as he learned who was building the big mansion next door. Now another trial lawyer lived there, but Maxine had never spoken to him.

Carl broke the silence. "What do you want to do about the Bentley?" he asked.

Maxine shrugged and said nothing.

"We'll have to hire a big crane to hoist it out of the pool, you know."

"Don't bother," said Maxine. "Just leave it there."

"Leave it there?"

"Why not? We could throw some fish in the water and turn it into an underwater sanctuary. They'd love it."

Maxine was clearly in no mood for making sense, but Carl was persistent. "About Montrose . . . Did I change your mind about killing him?"

"No."

"And you still want me to do it?"

"Yes."

Carl cleared his throat and said, "I swear I would do anything for you, Maxine, except murder."

Maxine fixed her gaze on Carl. Her eyes were dark and brooding. "Is that your final word?"

"It is."

She sighed and looked away again. "Then I suppose I'll have to do it myself."

"You don't know anything about killing."

"I can learn fast. I'm sure it doesn't take much skill to pull a trigger."

"Killing him will be messier than you think and won't solve anything," said Carl, gently swinging a leg back and forth and skimming the surface of the water with the sole of his shoe. "You'll get caught and end up in prison for the rest of your life, if they don't send you to Death Row."

"So you told me a thousand times last night. But what will I do if I can't sue doctors any longer? It's the only thing I know.

I'll be a nothing, a nobody, irrelevant to the world and quickly forgotten. I might as well be dead."

"There are other things you can do."

"Like divorce law? You've *got* to be kidding."

"Listen to me, Ms. Doggett—"

"You want me to capitulate?"

"Don't think of it in those terms. Life is full of twists and turns, unexpected developments, interesting possibilities . . ."

"I'll be . . . *a loser!*" Maxine's thin lips started quivering as if she was about to burst into tears.

"Come on, Ms. Doggett—what do you say we go inside and give Montrose a call? It won't be so difficult to do and you'll feel much better afterwards. You'll see."

"The time for talking is *over.*"

Wringing his hands, Carl searched for the right words to comfort her, but they wouldn't come.

Maxine managed to compose herself, then felt the need to explain herself more fully. "I've had to scramble and fight all my life for the things I have, Carl: my education, my money, my reputation," she said. "Don't ask me to allow some two-bit blackmailer like Montrose to take it all away without paying a heavy price."

"So you're going to save him the trouble and throw it all away yourself, huh? Is that what you're saying?"

Maxine eyes looked down at Carl's writhing hands. "I can see you are very troubled with my decision," she observed.

"I am!"

"You shouldn't be. If something bad happens to me, you'll be well taken care of. It's all in my will. And if, by any chance, I end up in prison for the rest of my life instead, I'll continue to employ you to look after my interests on the outside. So, for you, there's nothing to worry about."

"I'm not concerned about my own future," said Carl. "I just don't want to see you throwing away yours. I don't think I could bear it if you . . . went away for a long time."

Maxine took pause and regarded Carl closely. Did she hear him correctly? Was he expressing *feelings* for her? If so, he was the first person to do so in her entire life and she was curious to know why.

"I have an idea that will make you feel better, Carl," she said, taking his hand in her own and squeezing it playfully. "I'll pray to Augustus and let *him* decide."

"Oh, no," groaned Carl. "Not your bird thing again."

"Why not?" said Maxine. "I know he feels my pain. He'll tell me what to do."

"But this is an *important* decision!"

"Augustus will give me a sign and I'll interpret it."

"But you haven't seen him in months. You told me yourself."

"He won't let me down—not now, when I need him the most. The sign will be crystal clear. You'll see."

Maxine nestled her bottom against the dock to make herself more comfortable, clasped her hands together in front of her chest, elbows out, and closed her eyes. Then her lips began to move as if in prayer. Some incense might have completed the picture.

Carl surveyed the empty sky. "We could be waiting here all day," he sighed.

"No, we won't," murmured Maxine. "I feel something building in the air already."

Sure enough, a few minutes later, Augustus suddenly made his appearance in the distance and glided effortlessly across the lake towards them.

"There he is!" whispered Maxine, electrified. "He heard my prayer! I *knew* he would come!" Her eyes locked onto him and her face became tense and expectant. As he came closer, she rose to her feet and unfurled her arms into the air as if some extraordinary revelation was about to bestowed upon her. The great bird of prey swooped low, and just as he passed over her head, he released a salvo of dark liquid that was perfectly aimed and splattered across her upturned face—a direct bull's-eye that jolted her as if she'd been zapped by a lightning bolt. Then the eagle slowly, majestically flapped his wings, gained altitude, and melted into the awakening sky. Maxine was left staring through dripping eagle excrement with unblinking eyes, her mind reeling from the impact of the message.

"Man!" cried Carl, howling with laughter. "Even *I* can interpret *that* sign!"

After a long time, Maxine slowly wiped some of the brown slime off her face with her fingers. Then, reeking of dead fish, she pushed her way past Carl and marched back to the house.

Maxine sat in front of the dresser in her bedroom and studied herself in the mirror. She had just spent over an hour in the shower trying to clean the clumpy, foul-smelling eagle poop from her hair and she was still unsure whether she had been entirely successful. She had been to her personal hairdresser only the day before and now the whole work of art was completely ruined. She would have to call back and ask the woman to make an emergency house call—one that would cost three times the usual price, provoke lots of nosy questions, and if the truth ever came out, lead to an embarrassing scandal.

Maxine sighed. How had things come to this? All she ever wanted out of life was to be respected in the world of medical malpractice. Now she was left with nothing—no family, no friends . . . even Augustus had shown her in a most pungent way what he thought of her. She didn't even care for her clients—not the way Hugh Montrose cared about his patients—and the greedy, money-grubbing bastards probably cared even less for her. Her loneliness was made even more acute when she thought of Gary and Julie; those two really loved each other and their relationship gave new meaning to the phrase 'for better or for worse'. *Everybody* around her seemed to be leading normal, happy, productive lives. Where had she gone wrong? Where?

Where?

She honked her nose into a fragrant handkerchief.

Carl was the only person in the world who paid any attention to her. He had served her loyally for years, literally saving her life when he had taken her to the ER at Columbia a couple of times. He had always treated her respectfully, even after editing all those video tapes of her having sex with doctors. She remembered how he had shown concern for her future on the dock earlier that morning and how pleasant his strong hand had felt in her own. It was a lovely memory—a bright moment in the endless, bone dry desert of her life. As her mind replayed it, it seemed to take on a life of its own and gather momentum.

Carl?

Had the missing piece of her life been under her nose all along?

Afraid to answer her own question, Maxine reached for the telephone. No matter how rudely Augustus had delivered his message, she was obliged to obey it without delay and she had already wasted enough time. She dialed a number, and, within moments, she was ordering her astounded banker to transfer ten million dollars from her own account to that of Julie and Gary Winter.

CHAPTER 40

The Shady Rest Cemetery, Richard Forrester's final resting place, was an island of tranquility in the suburbs of Portland. The small plot of land was positioned on a gentle hillside facing east. A small pond lay at its center and several mallard ducks paddled aimlessly around, sending gentle V-shaped ripples across its glassy surface. Their occasional quacks were all that disturbed the utter peace of this place. In the hazy distance, the Cascade Range rose up like a cresting wave, its higher elevations dusted white by the retreating snows of early summer. Headstones ran in neat rows across a closely-cropped lawn. Clustered around each of them, an abundance of colorful flowers showed that those buried here were still cherished by their family and friends.

Hugh was an exhausted, unshaven, rumpled wreck lying on the grass near Richard's grave and trying unsuccessfully to catch up on some sleep. Nobody had ever threatened his life before and his mind hadn't stopped churning like a concrete mixer ever since Maxine had done so the day before. It was partly because he knew the cemetery was so peaceful that he had thought of coming here that morning, hoping that the ambience would settle his frayed nerves. He was also certain that Maxine would never think of looking for him in a place like this. Sleep still evaded him though, and the bulky Beretta 9mm he was keeping in a holster under his jacket dug into his side hardly helped matters either. He was very familiar with the kind of carnage guns caused and hated them. The one he had hurriedly bought from one of his shadier patients felt alien and he wished he could throw the damned weapon away. But things were different now. His first priority was to defend himself and his family and his sensitivities with respect to firearms were no longer relevant.

Hugh's clumsy, amateurish attempt to blackmail Maxine had backfired on him. Now his office was locked up, his practice was suspended indefinitely, and he was a fugitive from a deranged woman. Worst of all, he was shamelessly keeping the whole thing a secret from Michelle. Perhaps he did not want to worry his wife unnecessarily, or, more likely, was too embarrassed to confess his reckless stupidity. Whatever the reason, he prayed that somehow this nightmare would end quickly and painlessly so his life could return to—

"It's very quiet here, isn't it?"

Hugh's eyes flew open and he saw Maxine, complete with flashy clothes, layers of make-up, and billion-dollar hair-do. Her left hand was clutching a black handbag that looked large and bulky enough to carry a handgun. Diamonds flashed angrily from her fingers. The hole in her head was in plain view and her brain underneath pulsated with an ominous rhythm.

Hugh froze.

Oh, God! he thought. *She found me!*

Maxine was slowly closing in.

With his heart pounding inside his chest, Hugh glanced around the cemetery, looking for help. There was nobody else about. Just the two of them, the dead . . .

. . . and no witnesses.

Maxine paid little attention where she was stepping and walked right over several burial plots. "For once," she said grimly, "we're facing each other in a place that isn't a hospital or a courthouse."

"H-how did you know I was here?" Hugh stammered.

"I followed you."

"What . . . what do you want?"

"To settle matters between us."

Hugh heard a gentle gust of wind sighing through the leaves of a nearby oak tree, as if, even in death, Richard was once again rallying to his side. The thought of his old friend gave Hugh inspiration: as difficult as it might be, he *had* to give the impression that he was unafraid and in control. Maybe that was the only thing this crazy woman would understand. "Dr. Forrester was the best surgeon I ever knew," he said, slowly rising to his feet. "Did you know that two hundred of his patients attended the funeral?"

"No, I didn't."

"As you can see," said Hugh, nodding towards some fresh flowers near his feet, "they keep coming back."

"I never intended for anybody to get harmed," said Maxine, moving slowly and smoothly like a cat stalking its prey. "But sometimes, even the best laid plans can take unexpected turns."

Hugh's trembling fingers edged towards the opening of his jacket . . . and his Beretta. *If she reaches into her handbag*, he thought, *I'll blow her head off.*

Maxine slowed her advance as she grew near. "A lot has happened since we first met in the ER at Columbia, don't you think?" she said, her grey eyes never wavering from Hugh, not even for a second.

"Yes. . . . A lot."

"Operations, lawsuits, threats, counter-threats . . ." Maxine carefully shifted her weight from one foot to the other as if she was balancing herself before pouncing. "When are they ever going to end?"

"Not soon enough."

"I couldn't agree more. That's why I've made a decision to say goodbye . . . right here, in the middle of this cemetery. I can't think of a more appropriate place."

She's actually going to do it!

At that moment, Maxine opened her handbag with her right hand. Without stopping to think, Hugh wrenched the Beretta out of its holster, leveled the barrel at her head, and squeezed the trigger.

The gun clicked.

Feeling a sudden burst of panic, Hugh squeezed the trigger again.

Another click.

The safety catch! There must be a safety catch!

Cursing under his breath, Hugh fumbled with the unfamiliar gun.

For a second, total shock filled Maxine's face. Then, suddenly gathering her wits, she dove for cover behind a gravestone. "Don't shoot me!" she screamed. "I'm not ready to die!"

Hugh found the safety catch and flipped it into the 'off' position with his trembling fingers. Then he swung the Beretta up and pointed it in Maxine's direction again, only now she was out of sight.

"You came here to kill me!" he shouted, holding his gun with both hands. He was ready to fire in an instant, should a target present itself.

"That's not true!"

"What were you reaching for in your handbag, then?"

"Just a handkerchief to wipe my nose. This cemetery is full of mold. Didn't you know I have a bad allergy problem?"

Hugh heard only the sound of his own heavy breathing and pounding heart as he desperately tried to think. He didn't remember anything about Maxine having allergies; Denmark had certainly never mentioned it to him. "Why did you follow me here?" he demanded.

"I only came here to tell you that I've accepted your terms," cried Maxine.

"You're lying!"

"No, I'm not! I transferred ten million dollars of my own money to the Winters' bank account this morning. Later on, I sent an e-mail to the Peabody and Cartwright families, and to all the other plaintiffs in my practice, notifying them that I've suddenly and unexpectedly retired from medical malpractice law. I've done everything you told me to do and this is the way you react? Put that horrible thing away!"

Hugh wiped away some sweat that had run into his eyes.

"It's the truth!" continued Maxine, speaking quickly as if she feared her time was running out. "Gary and Julie called me this morning, out of their minds with gratitude for the money. They told me the first thing they're going to do is to buy themselves a brand new wheelchair-accessible camper and call it . . . Oh, hell—what was the name of the silly thing?" Hugh heard flicking fingers behind the gravestone as if Maxine was desperately searching her memory. "Harvey 2! That's it! Then they're going for a trip to the east coast with their children and will be gone the whole summer. After that, they're going to fix up their house and hire nurses to look after Julie around the clock."

"The Winters are *happy*?" asked Hugh incredulously.

"Yes, they are!" answered Maxine. "I've never seen them so happy! They carried on and on about how there really *is* a God who answers prayers. Then it dawned on me that I, Maxine Doggett, had played a part in bringing about a beautiful conclusion to a tragic story, one in which a quadriplegic woman thanks God for her good fortune. Whoever heard of such a thing? I was so taken up by the moment I confessed my secret dealings with

Grand National. Do you understand what I'm telling you? I told them I had known about the high CSF protein right from the beginning. I told them *everything!* They said they had suspected something along those lines but it no longer mattered. They forgave me and insisted on putting everything in the past." Maxine stopped talking, took a deep sucking breath, then said slowly and clearly, "*Please* believe me! I'm telling you the *truth!*"

"Throw your handbag over here," Hugh ordered, staying on high alert for *classic Doggett.*

Maxine's handbag sailed into sight and landed at Hugh's feet with a solid thud, kicking some dust into the air. He picked it up and turned it upside down. A ton of make-up and lipstick tumbled out, a couple of hair brushes, a can of hair spray, a compact mirror, a collection of perfumes, a bottle of allergy medicine, and a flowery handkerchief, but no gun.

"Do you believe me now?" asked Maxine in a tiny voice.

"Stand up!" snapped Hugh. "Put your hands where I can see them!"

Holding her hands high in the air, Maxine slowly appeared from behind the gravestone, pale and wide-eyed as if she were a ghost herself, arising from her coffin.

"Step forward and turn around!"

Maxine did as she was told. Keeping his Beretta trained on her, Hugh carefully looked over her body for a concealed weapon. Her clothes were tight-fitting, however, and it was obvious she wasn't carrying anything. With a feeling of dread growing in his stomach, he carefully circled around her and peered behind the gravestone where she had been taking cover.

Nothing there either.

"*Now* do you believe me?" asked Maxine.

The full horror of what he had nearly done suddenly dawned on Hugh and he threw the Beretta away with a loud yell.

The gun arched across the blue sky and landed in the nearby pond with a loud splash, startling the mallards and triggering an outburst of quacking. "Oh, my God!" he shouted. "I could have *killed* you!"

"Don't you think I already know that?" said Maxine, slowly lowering her hands.

"What the hell happened to me? I'm supposed to be a god-damned neurosurgeon and I came within a hair of blowing your brains out! You've turned me into a monster!"

"It's not your fault," said Maxine. "You had good reason to be concerned about your safety after the way I threatened you yesterday."

"I'm sorry, Maxine!" cried Hugh, running his fingers through his hair. "I don't know what came over me!"

"And I'm sorry for the way I behaved in your office. I lost control and didn't mean what I was saying."

"It's my fault! I've been so tired and nervous, I can't even think straight anymore!"

"No, it's *my* fault!" insisted Maxine. "And I'm . . . sorry for the way I've treated you in the past, especially after you saved my life . . . twice."

The thudding in Hugh's chest eased and, for the first time, he realized what was going on: he and Maxine were actually apologizing to each other! After so much hatred between them, and his own madness with the gun, he welcomed the bizarre development. After a long pause, Hugh finally asked, "Why are you saying these things? It's not like you to apologize for any-thing."

"Augustus sent me a message," explained Maxine.

Hugh frowned. "Augustus?"

"The bald eagle who lives on my lake."

"An eagle?"

"Yes," said Maxine, nodding vigorously. "Early this morning, he ordered me to agree to your terms and make amends. It was the clearest message I've ever received."

"Eagles . . . *communicate* with you?"

"My biggest decisions are always left to birds. I even became a medical malpractice lawyer because of the way a parrot squawked at me once." Maxine moved on quickly before she was asked to elaborate: "Anyhow, I offer you my congratulations, Defendant—I mean, *Doctor* Montrose. From now on, I'm going to leave you alone."

"If that's really true, what will you do with all the extra time you'll have on your hands?"

"I've no idea," said Maxine. "Medical malpractice is the only thing I know. To be perfectly honest, whatever I do, I wish I could be more like *him*." She jerked a thumb towards the grave.

"Richard? Why?"

"You told me two hundred patients came to *his* funeral. If you had killed me just then, not a living soul would have come to mine. Everybody in this world wants to be remembered for something, Dr. Montrose. Why should I be any different? I used to think that if I won the ultimate case, then I would become a superstar lawyer and earn everybody's eternal respect. What a silly dream that was! I've failed miserably and now I'm more irrelevant than ever. Even Julie is better off than I am."

"How can you say that? She'll be quadriplegic for the rest of her life!"

"Maybe she's paralyzed, but *her* prayers were answered," said Maxine with a hint of jealousy in her eyes. "God isn't going to waste His time doing the same for somebody like me. I think I'll stick to my faith in birds. At least they don't seem to care what kind of person I am."

Maxine crouched down and gathered together the clutter Hugh had dumped out of her handbag, handling each item with care as if it was precious to her. As he watched, Hugh felt sorry for the poor woman. Everybody had a piece of goodness inside them. In some, it was more deeply buried than others, but it was always there. If somebody like Carl could see what hers looked like, Hugh was curious enough to have a glimpse too. Disregarding the shrill alarm bells that were ringing furiously inside his mind, he said, "I have a suggestion what you can do with your life."

Maxine's hand stilled.

"Something that people will remember you for."

She looked up, arching her penciled eyebrows.

"CANS is going to start certifying neurosurgeons as expert witnesses," Hugh continued, unable to apply the brakes. "It's an effort to inject some credibility into what people say on the stand. The Board asked me to put together a committee to get things started. We need an experienced medical malpractice trial lawyer to help us. There's nobody more qualified than yourself."

As soon as he had finished speaking, Hugh regretted opening his big mouth. He expected Maxine to explode with indignation at the idea of certifying expert witnesses and cringed with anticipation.

Instead, her jaw dropped.

"Are you asking me to work with you?" she asked in disbelief, straightening up slowly with a variety of lipstick tubes clutched in her fingers.

"It's only an idea," said Hugh with a sheepish grin. "We would have to keep plenty of distance between us, of course—at least, at first . . . until some of my wounds have healed. Call yourself a provisional member of the committee, if you like.

Maybe later, if all goes well, you could be made a permanent member and I could work more closely with you."

"With *me*?"

"Yes. . . . With you."

"After all I've done: my lawsuits against you, the trial, the threats I made against your life yesterday?"

"I know it's hard to believe . . ."

The lipstick tumbled to the grass and Maxine reached for a granite headstone to steady herself. "I—I don't know what to say."

Hugh ploughed on. "You could use your expertise in medical malpractice law to help CANS make it harder for the professional testifiers to do business. You know better than anybody else how experts can be bought and sold on a whim. You could share your own experiences and shock every medical organization in the country into action. The number of frivolous medical malpractice lawsuits will plummet. Physicians will stop practicing so much defensive medicine and health care costs wouldn't go up so fast. Millions of American families will be able to afford health insurance and will be spared financial ruin. You could really make a difference in the world."

"But . . . you've strictly prohibited me from practicing medical malpractice law any longer."

"I said you couldn't represent any plaintiffs in a medical malpractice lawsuit. You can still help CANS, if you want."

Maxine's breathing grew labored and the drumbeat of her skull defect accelerated. Now she gripped the headstone with both hands as if she no longer had the strength to stand. "Why—why are you doing this for me?"

"So CANS is successful," replied Hugh matter-of-factly. "They need a good medical malpractice trial lawyer and you happen to be available right now."

Maxine touched her chest with the fingers of her right hand and, at first, mouthed mere empty words. With the second attempt, she found her voice and said, "There are plenty of trial lawyers around who would do it if you threw enough money at them. Why me?"

"Nothing would be more devastating to our opponents if somebody of your reputation switched sides and threw your support behind physicians for a change," Hugh reasoned. "With you sitting on our committee, we'll be invincible. Whatever I might think of you personally, you're clearly the best there is."

Maxine's eyes fluttered. "You—you think I'm . . . *the best*?"

"The record speaks for itself," said Hugh. "Everybody knows you're the queen of medical malpractice trial lawyers. All others don't compare."

Maxine's face shone with an eerie glow. "Respect and recognition from my fellow trial lawyers is something I've always wanted in life," she murmured, "but hearing it come from you means so much more! I've been so . . . so . . ." Maxine's voice trailed away as if she couldn't find the right word.

"Vile," suggested Hugh, trying to be helpful.

Maxine blinked at him, showing some offense at the ease with which he had spoken. "Thank you," she said woodenly. "I suppose 'vile' will do quite nicely."

"You can still change."

"Me?" Maxine chuckled as if the idea was patently absurd. "Just how am I going to do that?"

Hugh thought of the time when Michelle had made a huge change in her own life, leaving everything she cherished in France to live in America. "Do you have any idea what it's like to be in love?" he asked.

"Don't be ridiculous," scoffed Maxine. "Where's somebody like me ever going to find love?"

"You could start with Carl."

Although Hugh's words were spoken casually, they could not have had a more forceful impact on Maxine, as if the truth had been percolating in the back of her mind all along and had now burst into her awareness with the power of a steam locomotive. Staring at Hugh with shock, she gripped the gravestone tighter in order to weather the rush of emotions that must have been swirling inside her and croaked, "What do you know about Carl?"

"Quite a lot, actually," said Hugh, happy to elaborate. "For instance, that night when you were stabbed in the head, he stood vigil outside your room in the ER and I had a chance to talk with him. He was very worried about you and asked . . . no, *begged* me not to let you die."

"He did?"

"It was obvious that he really cares about you," continued Hugh. "I have to admit I was completely confused. For the life of me, I couldn't understand how it was possible for anybody to—"

Maxine quickly interrupted. "All these years I've known him," she blurted, "he's *never* shown any interest in me!"

"He's afraid to," explained Hugh. "He thinks you might react in the wrong way and fire him . . . never talk to him again, or something like that. He doesn't want to risk losing the woman he loves."

"You really think Carl *loves* me?"

"Don't you think it's possible?"

Maxine suddenly fell silent and looked as if she was seriously considering what Hugh had told her. Then her eyes fell upon the inscription that was carved into the headstone she was holding and widened in terror as if she had read her own name there. She recoiled as if, for a terrifying moment, she had seen a brief vision of her own future: a forgotten grave and nothing more. No family, no friends, no love. Only emptiness and loneliness . . . a wasted life turned to dust. Her brain began to hammer against her sunken scalp and she looked wildly around herself.

"What are you doing?" asked Hugh.

"I need a bird," she declared, desperately scanning the sky and the trees as if she was addicted to her feathered friends and was looking for a fix. "There's got to be one around here somewhere . . ."

At first, Hugh thought she was joking. Then he remembered her telling him that her best advice came from birds, so, instead of laughing, he managed a straight face and said, "There was a bunch of ducks on the pond a few minutes ago."

"Oh, yes!" cried Maxine. "A duck would be perfect right now!"

Hugh watched as Maxine hurriedly threaded her way through the graves to the pond, then stood at the water's edge, studying the mallards intently. Moments later, a pair right in front of her—a male with a handsome green head and a speckled brown female—took flight, circled overhead a couple of times, then headed towards the west. When she returned, Maxine's eyes were alive with inspiration.

"You were right!" she said. "Carl *does* love me! I'll negotiate a relationship with him right away—"

"Don't negotiate," suggested Hugh, wondering what Maxine had seen in the ducks that he hadn't. "Ask him out."

"Ask him out?" said Maxine as if she had never been on a date in her life. "All right . . . if you think so."

"Pick somewhere romantic," he told her.

"*Romantic?*"

"Sure. You know—low lights, a candle on the table, soft music in the background to put both of you in the mood. . . ."

"I see what you mean . . ." said Maxine, thoughtfully rubbing her oversized chin with her fingers.

By now, Hugh realized that Maxine had to be more inexperienced in such matters than he had imagined. If she were to have any chance of success, she would need some more help. "Take him to Luigi's on First Avenue," he suggested. "That's the best place for this sort of thing."

"Okay—"

"Have a good time; talk to him and listen to what he has to say. Try to be nice to him. You can do it if you simply follow your feelings."

"Maybe that's possible. . . ." Then, Maxine's eyes brightened. "Yes, I think I can!"

"That's better, Maxine. You're half way there already."

"I am? Yes, I am!"

"And how do you feel about working for CANS?" Hugh asked, returning to a subject that mattered more to him.

Maxine hesitated as if her mind had been so filled with thoughts of Carl that she had forgotten all about CANS. Then her face broke into a smile as her brain slipped into gear and, with her most decisive courtroom voice, she said, "Yes! That's another good idea. I accept!"

"Damn!" responded Hugh with a wry smile. "I was afraid of that."

"I'll do everything I can to make the certified expert witness program a resounding success!" cried Maxine.

"May God save CANS," Hugh muttered to himself.

"Those trial lawyers in CATL won't know what hit them!" she added, thumping a nearby gravestone with her fist.

"CATL is dead meat."

Now, Maxine stepped closer to Hugh, her hands clasped together in supplication. "May I tell you something . . . of a *personal* nature?" she asked.

"I'm not sure whether that's a good—"

"Long ago," began Maxine without bothering to wait for permission, "I believed that money was the key to my happiness. So I worked hard, sued a bunch of suckers, and became a rich woman. After a few years, however, I realized that I had been sorely mistaken; money meant nothing to me. Are you listening?"

"Of course—"

"Then I came to believe that celebrity and power were what I was looking for. *Winter vs. Montrose* was my brilliant attempt to achieve those things." She rolled her eyes at her own sarcasm. "What a miserable failure *that* was! And yet . . ."

"Yes?"

"And yet, things seemed to have turned out in a most unexpected way," said Maxine dreamily. "I may have lost the battle, but, in the end, I've won the war. Gary and Julie, Carl, Augustus, those two wonderful ducks . . . and even you . . . have shown me what really matters in life."

Hugh noticed that Maxine's eyes were misting over now and he wondered whether he was witnessing an amazing transformation. Could it be possible? Was The Dog morphing into something that resembled a human being?

When Maxine spoke again, her voice was strained and cracked with emotion. "What I want to tell you, Dr. Montrose, is this: thank you for helping me understand things more clearly. *Thank you!*"

Just as an awkward hug seemed to be in the offing, Hugh's

cell phone rang and he snatched it eagerly from his belt. "Hello?"

"Hugh? This is Dave Holz in the ER. Are you nearby?"

"About ten minutes away."

"Thank goodness! We've got a real emergency here: a four year-old girl leaned against a screen window on the second floor of her home and fell through. She landed on a concrete patio, head first. The CT scan shows a giant epidural hematoma compressing her brain. She just blew a pupil!"

"Give her some Mannitol," said Hugh, recognizing that the large pupil meant that the little girl's life was teetering on the edge. "That'll buy us some time. Notify the OR and get them geared up. I'm on my way in."

"Thanks. I'll see you in a few minutes."

Hugh hung up and looked at Maxine who was gazing dreamily into the distance. "Sorry," he said, "I have to go; there's not much time." He gave Richard's gravesite a little wave as if he was saying goodbye and took off. Before he went very far, however, he skidded to a halt and turned.

"Just one last thing, Maxine . . ."

"Yes?"

"You really should do something about that ugly crater in your head. A simple cranioplasty would fix things nicely."

"I've tried, but no neurosurgeon will come near me!"

"Call my office tomorrow and we'll schedule surgery for you," he said, smiling. "CANS can't have its superstar lawyer scaring off the world media!"

Then, without further delay, he ran to his car.

The operation on the little girl was exhilarating.

When Hugh arrived at the hospital, she was already in the OR, intubated and anesthetized. By coincidence, she had curly red hair, and with a stretch of his imagination, Hugh envisioned how a young, innocent Maxine might have looked forty years ago. With blinding speed, he shaved the hair off and fixed her head in the Mayfield. Then after she was prepped and draped, he cut open her scalp, drilled a hole in her skull, and removed the clot. As his hands worked, he felt none of the gloom that had dogged him since the darkest days of his lawsuit. The conversation in the room was refreshingly pleasant, a few jokes were exchanged, and the nurses even ventured to wonder aloud where Hugh's mind had been for the last few years. He kept the truth to himself. Nobody could ever understand what *Winter vs. Montrose* had been like for him unless they had once been a defendant in a medical malpractice lawsuit themselves. So, instead of wallowing in the past, he absorbed the sights and sounds of the operating room like a parched plant that had been sprinkled with life-saving water. Energy flowed into his fingers and he operated as never before. While his mind focused on the task before him, his soul ascended a little closer to heaven and he felt the powerful presence of two people: Sir John Worthington, the Edinburgh neurosurgeon who had once encouraged him to follow his dreams, and Matilda, the patient whose skull Sir John had used to teach medical students. Now Hugh's career was spread before them like a testimonial and he prayed that it did not disappoint. To be sure, he'd had many shortcomings, the greatest of which was his loss of faith in his profession during the darkest days of his trial. He wanted to make amends, and as he saved the little girl's life before him, he solemnly vowed that he would never allow judges, juries, lawyers, and expert witnesses to stand between him and his patients again.

Yes, the operation was exhilarating. Nothing, however, could compare with Hugh's arrival home that evening. Michelle greeted her husband with a dutiful kiss and, as usual, studied his face. This time, however, her beautiful French eyes must have seen something very different for they suddenly lit up with incredible joy.

"Oh, Hugh!" she cried, gripping his shoulders. "You're back!"

"Yes, I am. The nightmare is finally over."

"How—how did it happen?"

"It's a long story. Let's save it for another time. Right now, I just want to look at you." Hugh held Michelle's delicate, smiling face between his hands and drew close. "I'm sorry about the way I've been. I promise I won't let you suffer like that again."

Suddenly tears filled Michelle's eyes and ran down her cheeks. "Je t'aime!" she whispered. I love you!

Hugh wrapped his arms around his wife and hugged her tightly. He wanted to tell her that he loved her too, but was too choked up to say a word.

EPILOGUE

Friday, November 5th, 1965

In early November, 1605, Guy Fawkes, an Englishman and a Roman Catholic, attempted to blow up the protestant King James I and his government by setting off thirty-six barrels of gunpowder secretly stored in the basement of the Houses of Parliament. He knew that if he was caught, he would likely be hung until he was . . . not quite dead. That is, he would be taken down from the scaffold and the contents of his abdomen would be removed and burned while he watched with dying eyes. The potential for such a grim fate, however, didn't stop him from carrying out the Gunpowder Plot, and the rest, as they say, is history. However, he might have had second thoughts about committing his crime had he known that every year following his death for hundreds of years, generations of British school children would celebrate the event on November 5th by making an effigy of him, carting it around the neighborhood in a wheelbarrow, and collecting money to buy fireworks. Then, after dark, they would tie their 'Guy' to a stake atop of a pile of brush, set it ablaze, and run around and around while the fireworks in his pockets exploded in the heat.

The tradition of Guy Fawkes was alive and well at Helmsdale Manor. Hugh Montrose and sixty-two other boys had spent a month enthusiastically gathering branches and sticks that had been blown down by powerful Scottish gales and, by the beginning of November, their bonfire had reached dizzying heights.

The Guy himself was made of a potato sack stuffed with straw. An old soccer ball served as a head and he was dressed in blue overalls. He was sufficiently realistic for the few sheep farmers who lived in the moors to be generous with their money. This year, there would be plenty of fireworks for the festivities and when the great day arrived, the excitement in the school was at a feverish pitch.

Hugh Montrose, however, had lost all interest in the festivities. His bear, Edward, was lying on his bed in the dormitory, critically ill. The great gash in his head was oozing stuffing and it was only a matter of time before the poor animal would die. Grief-stricken, Hugh had spent the day kneeling beside the bed, holding Edward's paw, and offering words of comfort. Beyond that, there was nothing he could do. Although he was a world-famous neurosurgeon, his traumatic experience on the Hall Chair the night before had drained him of his healing powers and made him feel completely helpless.

When the last class was dismissed, the entire school stampeded to the locker rooms, changed into outdoor shoes, and hurried outside, while Hugh slowly followed. At this time of year, darkness fell by five o'clock in the afternoon, and as they ran across the playing fields towards the far corner of the school grounds where the bonfire had been built, the boys were no more than fleeting shapes and shadows. When they drew close, they gathered into groups, pointing, laughing, and trying to discern the Guy in the night. A match flared in the blackness ahead, illuminating the grizzled face of the Master. The wood was dry; flames crackled hungrily into life, spreading quickly through the branches and sending glowing cinders spiraling into the sky.

Hugh looked at the stake and saw the Guy. Only . . . he wasn't alone up there. He was sitting on a chair. A very familiar chair.

The Hall Chair!

The chatter amongst the boys died. They watched wide-eyed as the Guy and the Hall Chair were quickly engulfed by fire. The fireworks inside the Guy's pockets exploded in the searing heat and his body crumpled forward, looking frightfully realistic in the midst of the conflagration. But nobody was interested in him; they were all watching that most hated and feared chair underneath him being incinerated as if it had been sent to hell.

Hugh grew aware of the smell of pipe tobacco. He turned around and saw the Master looming over him.

"Please, sir . . . why is the Hall Chair up there?" he asked timidly, gesturing towards the flames. His friends sidled closer so they might hear the answer.

"I put it there," said the Master.

"But *why*, sir?"

"McKenzie and Sutherland came to see me today," he explained. "They told me the truth about what happened in your dormitory last night. I decided that it was time for a change."

The extraordinary circumstances caused Hugh to momentarily forget his position. "But, the Hall Chair . . ." he gasped. "It's been there for *centuries!* How can Sir destroy it . . . *just like that?*"

The Master wasn't angry. He pondered for a moment, then said, "It was the right thing to do. There *has* to be a better way."

Hugh was stunned. The instrument of his shame was being turned into ashes before his very eyes. His heavy heart was uplifted as if an angel had descended from heaven and had revived the neurosurgeon within him.

Hugh felt an urgent tugging at his sleeve and looked around to see McKenzie and Sutherland.

"Come on, Montrose!" said McKenzie. "The bonfire's burning! Let's go and run around it!"

"*You* go," said Hugh, slowly backing away. "I've got something more important to do."

"More *important*?" cried Sutherland. "What could be more important than running around the bonfire—especially *this* one?" He jabbed his finger towards the Hall Chair, which, by now, was little more than a fading shadow deep in the midst of a roaring inferno.

"I have a life to save," said Hugh with a gleam in his eyes, "and there's not much time left. I'll tell you about it later!"

Then, without another word, he ran back to his dormitory, and Edward.

ABOUT THE AUTHOR

CHRISTOPHER SMYTHIES was born and raised in Great Britain and immigrated to the United States in 1974. He is certified by the American Board of Neurological Surgery and practises at Overlake Hospital Medical Center in Bellevue, Washington.